THE
TOP SECRET
Murders

THE TOP SECRET MURDERS

A Morgan Crew Murder Mystery

Arthur A. Lee

Leeward Publishers, LLC
Orlando, Florida

THE TOP SECRET MURDERS

A Morgan Crew Murder Mystery

By

Arthur A. Lee

This is a work of fiction. Names, characters, places and incidents are either the product of the author's imagination or are used fictionally, and resemblance to actual persons living or dead, business establishments, events or locales is entirely coincidental.

ISBN: 978-0-989-5073-7-0

Silver Cat Press
An Imprint of Leeward Publishers, LLC

THIS BOOK IS DEDECATED TO

All those people I've met
over the years, who do
really bad things so that
good will prevail.

Other Books by the Author

The Morgan Crew Murder Mystery Series

A Storm In From The Sea
The Las Vegas Murders
A Deadly London Fog
The Four Seasons Murders
The Hawaiian Sunset Murders
The Spy Who Would Not Speak
The West Texas Murders
The Hawaiian Island Murders

The Mystery and Adventure Series

Three Families
Wait Until The Dark Of Night

www.leewardpublishers.com

THE TOP SECRET MURDERS

By

Arthur A. Lee

TABLE OF CONTENTS

ONE - Hillsdale Technologies, Inc.

Danny O'Keefe wanted to be a cop. Nothing else in life ever interested him. As a child of five years he would sit on the steps of the Brooklyn brownstone his mother and father called home as he waited for Officer Patrick O'Brian to walk by. Danny would look up and down the street waiting for Officer O'Brian to come walking slowly down the street. O'Brian would stop now and then and speak with a store owner or a woman pushing a baby carriage. Danny would wait his turn.

The Police Officer was tall and burly. He would smile at the children and look with a stern eye at a few of the adults who he knew to be trouble now and then. He would swing his night stick rhythmically and whistle old Irish folk tunes as he walked the sidewalks of Danny's Brooklyn neighborhood.

O'Brian would always stop and say hello to little Danny; he would pat Danny on the head, rumple his curly red hair, and ask him if he was being a good boy. Danny would always smile grandly, sit up very straight, and say he was being good, even if he wasn't being very good that day. The best part of every day for Danny was seeing Officer O'Brian; he wanted to be like Officer O'Brian when he grew up.

As a young boy in school in Brooklyn he raised his hand and almost jumped out of his chair when the Principal asked for volunteers to be school crossing guards. He wanted to wear the bright yellow vest crossing guards wore and stand at the corner telling kids, younger and older than he, when they could cross the street. He would be in control, and he wanted that. And being a cop when he grew up would make him in control over a lot of people, he imagined. That was what he wanted, that was his future, to be in control over other people. He knew it had to be because he wanted it so badly.

In High School he struggled with math; science was a problem; reading the books for his English Literature class was a problem. His undiagnosed dyslexia made reading anything difficult. Danny was small for his age, pimply faced, and thin. His thick red hair was impossible to comb. Boys bigger than Danny would pick on him. They would knock his books out of his arms in the hallways. They would laugh at him as he tried to answer questions in class. They would push him and pull him away when he stood at the urinals in the boy's room. He wanted to fight back, but the boys were all bigger than he, and he was frightened of them.

Girls would laugh at him as they walked away when he asked them to go to a dance with him. The girls were all taller than Danny, and his pimply face was not something the girls wanted to kiss.

He gave up on sports at an early age because he could never be as good as the other boys. But Danny knew all that would change once he wore a policeman's badge and uniform. Then they would all respect him and be afraid of him. Then the girls would line up to be with him. Then the boys would call him 'sir' and respect him.

The day after graduation from High School he put his application in for the N.Y.P.D. He had waited on the steps to the City building an hour before the doors to the office opened, anxious to get his badge and uniform. He stayed up late the night before the written test. He tried to read some of the books the librarian had given him, but it was hard to make sense of the often jumbled words. He did not pass the test with a high enough grade, precluding him from moving on into the Academy. Again, because of his dyslexia the words on the papers of the test were all jumbled and made little sense to him.

But Danny would not give up. Every year he retook the test for four straight years. Every year he could not get a passing grade. He was not dissuaded; he knew that one day he would be a cop and tell people what to do. One day, he was sure, his dream would come true.

In the years of taking the tests over and over again, Danny worked for one private security firm after another. A few of the companies wanted him to wear a dark blue sports jacket and gray slacks. That wasn't good enough for Danny. He felt he looked like everyone else in that drab non-uniform. He wanted a uniform like real police wear. And he wanted a badge, that shield of honor that would make people recognize him as being in charge and better than everyone else on the street.

He was certain that wearing a uniform with a silver badge on his chest naturally gave him the authority to perform his job as a security guard like a real policeman would and be tough on everyone he came in contact with. But there was no badge.

Rules were rules even without the badge, and his job was to enforce the rules. He seldom lasted more than six or seven months with any one security company. Complaints against him piled up until each company let him go.

But that was their fault, he kept telling himself. He knew what a real cop was supposed to do. He would enforce the law regardless of what his bosses said. *'Force,'* that was the important part of the word 'enforce.' Danny was sure of that. No one could tell him differently. They were all wrong, and he was right, he was certain of that. Maybe as a security guard he didn't have a gun, and he didn't have a badge. But he would do his job, telling people in no uncertain terms to do what he told them to do. And if the stupid bosses didn't recognize him as their most valuable employee it was their loss. When he finally became a Police Officer they would regret not listening to him.

That night he was in the guard house at the gated entrance to Hillsdale Technologies, Inc. That was not his permanent post; he had been assigned inside, patrolling the hallway at the cafeteria and restroom areas even though there were no employees working at half past two in the morning. But one thing was good about that post. The cafeteria workers left food on the steam tables for anyone working at night. Danny stuffed himself there and saved his money to buy books that would help him pass the next Police Academy exam. Sooner or later he would get a book he could understand and then he would be a cop.

His first post when he started with the security company had been the day shift at the entrance gate, checking credentials of employees arriving for work each morning. It was a busy post that demanded the guard be on his feet for hours at a time. Therefore it was not the favorite post of experienced guards who preferred a post where they could sit and do nothing.

Danny loved the entrance gate post and looked forward to going to work every morning. But he was too good for the job, he told himself. He knew that merely seeing the company ID card wasn't enough. After all, anybody could walk in with a stolen ID card, he argued. He demanded a second photo ID from everyone, backing the line of employees up and making them angry and late for work.

On his third day at the post he demanded a driver's license from Jeremy Hillsdale, the owner and CEO of Hillsdale Technologies, Inc. and the driver's license of the chauffeur driving Jeremy's limo through the gates to the executive parking area inside the secured technology campus. Danny was immediately put on the late night shift while his boss decided how he would be fired very quietly. The company had to avoid being sued by a disgruntled ex-employee after all.

It was a dark night when he had been told to go to the main gate to relieve the guard there for a dinner break. There was only a finger nail moon that night, and clouds blocked most of the stars. The autumn air was brisk but still. The smell of the fall season was all around.

The gate was locked; a big pad lock and chain ensured that the gate would remain closed that night. Danny hadn't been given the key to the padlock – the guard he had relieved had been told not to give Danny the key – and no employees were expected in that evening. Danny took the opportunity to sit on the stool inside the small guard shack and try to read the latest book he had gotten from the library on how to pass the police exam. His dyslexia made it hard to understand the words, but he was intent on struggling through it. In just two weeks he would take the NYPD Academy exam once again. He was excited because this time he was certain he would pass with flying colors.

****

The Hillsdale Technology campus is located outside of Buffalo, New York. Because of the very sensitive nature of its research for the Federal Government, it is intentionally in a remote, deep valley, in a forested and mountainous area that had been previously undeveloped. The work done inside the high security areas of the campus is in cutting edge electronics: satellite systems, guidance systems, and advanced computer systems. Much of the work is financed by various U.S. Intelligence Agencies; some is sub-contracted to Hillsdale by other companies that hold Government contracts of their own. Some work is done for corporations who don't have Government contracts but pay extremely well for the work the Hillsdale staff can do. All the work done is highly classified.

A two lane road out of Buffalo had been cut through forest and hills to serve the campus as Hillsdale was being built. The road dead-ends at the employee parking lot outside of the campus' fence, in front of the entrance gate so that no unintentional traffic can pass by. If you are on that road you are either going to Hillsdale or coming from Hillsdale. The State Police know that and patrol the road regularly for strangers who have no business there.

Thick forests and rolling hills surround the campus. A small valley of sorts had been found in the forest. The land had been leveled enough to build eight gray concrete buildings, seven of them without windows, which is the Hillsdale Technologies campus. The Administration Building, the tallest building at five stories tall, sits in front of the other seven research buildings. It alone has windows on the front and both sides of the building. The rear of that building has no windows, technically to keep the office workers from seeing the high security buildings.

Office workers are assumed to need some daylight and a view of the trees outside to keep them happy while they type and file and complete their daily routines. Therefore the Admin Building has windows that the research buildings do not have. It is the closest building to the Entrance Gate – misnamed because it is the only entrance into and exit out of the surrounding twelve foot tall, chain link fence that is topped with razor wire.

While Danny O'Keefe was struggling with his text book that night, Tamara Jackson lay on the damp ground next to a tall red cedar tree seventy-five yards from Danny. She was slowly moving her night vision binoculars across the fence surrounding Hillsdale Technology. She counted the tall lights and noted where they were placed. All but the four lights in the parking lot faced inward, lighting the grounds inside the fence. The parking lot was brightly lit but all but empty, the only cars belonging to the nighttime security staff. She shook her head at the stupidity of not lighting the ground outside the fence.

She chuckled at the razor wire running along the top of the chain link fence. "Easy," she murmured to herself. She saw the electric wire running along the fence and a second wire running up from the ground at each fence post. "Difficult," she whispered. "But I can do it."

On each fence post a CCTV camera swung slowly back and forth inside the fenced grounds, each pointed at the gray buildings. She shook her head at the stupidity and thought, 'Outside, you idiots. Watch for people coming from the outside.'

She moved the night vision binoculars across the black asphalt parking lot outside the fence. There were only five cars there, all older models, belonging to the security guards. Well paid employees of Hillsdale Technologies would have better, newer cars. No employees were working that night; that was good, she told herself.

She studied the fence and lights and the cameras for a few minutes, and then she heard a sound. Footsteps cracking twigs and dried leaves. . . And a dog. She knew ahead of time that the woods were patrolled, and she knew also that the security at Hillsdale wasn't the best. Security Contractors were hired by Hillsdale Technologies because theirs was the low bid, not because they could or would do the best job. The dogs wouldn't be any better than the rest of the security system. Like the guards, they were given little training. They could be easily fooled, she knew.

She slid to the far side of the little hill, lying among the tree's fallen pine needles. She took an aerosol spray can from her backpack. She emptied it, spraying cedar scented gas all around her to mask any human odor the dog might pick up. She lay still in the deep shadows until the dog and its handler had passed, ten yards from her. The stupid guard handling the dog was smoking a cigarette. That would aid in masking any smell the dog might pick up. 'Stupid,' she thought again. If the dog had been better trained, she might have been caught, she knew.

When the dog had passed and was far enough away, she moved back to the crest of the hill and peered down to the fence once again. The guard at the gate was reading. Tamara laughed at the man's ignorance. "Stupid rent-a-cops," she mumbled again, out loud this time, in a whisper.

The corner of the fence, a hundred yards to the right of the gate; that was the place, she told herself. There was a triangle of dark in the corner inside the fence left by the lights on either side of the corner. The corner post was the only post without a light on it. The parking lot had lights on tall poles, but they illuminated only the lot. Outside the fence, at the corner, was pitch-black in the moonless night. And there were trees within twenty-five feet of the fence at the corner. Flower beds had been planted artistically underneath the trees by gardeners. 'Stupid,' she told herself again. That was the place, she determined. That is where she would climb the fence.

She checked inside her backpack. There were tools

in it, everything she would need. Everything was there. Without rising from the ground she put her arms through the straps and moved the jet-black pack to her back. She began to crawl down the slope, slowly, head first, without making any noise. Even the dried leaves and twigs that lay everywhere made no sound as she silently crawled down the hill.

She moved slowly, carefully, as she had been taught. The guard with the dog had gone in the opposite direction and would encircle the entire fenced campus before returning to where she had been. She had plenty of time.

She was dressed completely in black, from head to foot. Her head and face were covered with a light weight black mesh hood. Her hands were covered in black vinyl gloves. Her soft rubber soled shoes were black, but she knew she didn't need them to move without sound revealing her presence. She had been taught well.

Tamara kept on her stomach, crawling slowly, making not the slightest sound, as she reached the edge of the employee parking lot. She circled the concrete paved lot, staying far away from the flood lights that illuminated it. She moved through the trees and flower beds to the fence's corner. She stood to a bent-over crouch and ran across the short open space. At the fence corner she knelt in the dark and pulled the backpack from her shoulders. From it she took aramid fiber lined thick rubber gloves and slipped them over her black vinyl gloves.

She had to know if the wire running along the top of the fence meant the fence was carrying enough electricity to stop her or even kill her. She took a small flashlight from the breast pocket of her jacket. She touched the metal case to the fence. Nothing. She touched it again. Nothing again. Maybe a motion sensor, she thought. Maybe the stupid guards had simply not turned on whatever the wire was supposed to do. She would have to take the chance; she had to get inside.

She tightened the black backpack on her shoulders and stood. Slowly, a few inches at a time, Tamara started to climb the fence. Not a sound, she told herself. Don't slip . . . Go slow. At the top, she took out a Kevlar blanket that she had carried in a pouch hung from her belt. She threw it over the razor wire and quickly slid over it.

She almost laughed. 'Stupid,' she thought. They actually thought simple razor wire would keep someone out. Pulling the blanket from the wire she climbed down and put her feet on the ground. The Kevlar blanket was returned to the pouch on her belt, and she slipped the heavy gloves off, returning them carefully to her backpack.

Crouching low in the shadow between the flood lights, she studied the areas they lit and where they didn't. There were great areas lit brightly inside the fence, but there were areas of dark, also. She would stay within those areas.

And then there were the CCTV cameras. There was one at the top of each light pole, and they moved slowly, back and forth, taking in the entire area. She was in the dark at the corner of the fence; a light pole with a camera was twenty feet to her left and one twenty feet to her right. The camera to her right swung away from her to view the side of the tall building. The camera to her left swept the front of the building. But there were a few seconds, probably less than a full minute, when the two cameras were pointing away from each other. That was when she would make her run for the building and the darkness there that would hide her. She waited and then ran.

Danny was bent over his book; his finger slowly traced the words he was trying to understand. A shadow outside the guard house moved. Danny ignored it as he tried to decipher a strange looking word in the book. The book was too important, and after all, there weren't any employees there at that time of the night. Probably just a cat or some other animal looking for garbage to eat, he assured himself.

The shadow moved slowly past the guardhouse. Danny had his head lowered over the book; his eyes squinted almost closed as he strained to read the words, his back to the shadow. The desk lamp lit up the inside of the glass walled room. Tamara knew that it would also hinder the guard seeing anything in the dark outside the guardhouse.

TWO – Agent Of Terror

Tamara was an African-American woman born in South Chicago twenty-one years ago. At twelve years of age she had been attracted to Cool Mathews, a member of the 'Southside Killers' gang. She was introduced to sex and a variety of drugs. At thirteen she had become pregnant and hoped that Cool would marry her. He didn't, and she had the unborn child aborted.

Over the next four years there were a series of boyfriends from several other gangs and a series of abortions. There were no jobs for a young black woman who had no education. There was a series of arrests – six months in juvenile hall for her third shoplifting offense and a year in a woman's prison for heroin possession – that convinced Tamara that white America with its white laws wasn't the best place to live.

Nothing seemed to go right for her. She was filled with hatred for the white America that tormented her. The damn white police wouldn't leave her alone. Everywhere she went she saw the damn white police watching her, making it hard for her to steal in order to stay alive. She knew that hookers walking the streets at night weren't bothered by the cops. They gave their services away to cops to stay in business. Tamara didn't want to sink to that level but she could see no other way to live. She had reached a level of hopelessness that had brought her close to that life of selling her body cheaply.

Then she met Jesse Wilson, a Black man like none other she had ever met. Jesse was older than Tamara's seventeen years when they met. Jesse wasn't in a gang; he dressed well in expensive suits and silk ties; he drove a new Buick; and he was educated. Jesse took her from the slums of South Chicago and showed her what life could be.

They talked for hours over coffee at Starbucks, away from her South Chicago neighborhood, in an area of the city she never knew existed. Tall glass and steel buildings surrounded them. The noise of the city was so different from the rough noises of her neighborhood that were filled with loud, harsh voices and fighting. And it was clean and new and amazing.

He encouraged her to bathe every day, and he took her to a salon where her hair was straightened, cut, and styled, and where she was taught to use makeup that accentuated her beauty. Jesse bought her clothes, and she wore them to the restaurants he took her to. He taught her how to use a knife and fork, and how to be a "lady," as he called it. He took her to the zoo and parks and the shore along Lake Michigan on warm summer days. They laughed, ate popcorn and hotdogs, and had fun together. Tamara would often look at Jesse and wonder if all this was just some dream she would eventually wake from.

He took her to an apartment in a nice area of Chicago, on the fifteenth floor of a new, gleaming hi-rise building, and said she could live there . . . But without him, although he would pay all the expenses. She asked suspiciously if he were a pimp and told him she had no intention of being his high priced hooker. He laughed and assured her he was not a pimp; he just wanted to see if what he thought might be inside her was really there, a smart young woman who should not live in the slums.

And Jesse never made the move she waited for: the

move to get her into bed. That was OK with Tamara; she had had enough of meaningless sex, drugs, and abortions. Jesse was handsome and intelligent and funny, but all Tamara wanted from him was exposure to a new world.

The building had a gymnasium on the ground floor, and Jesse took her to it every day. The workouts made her feel good; she liked the feeling of tired muscles and the energy it gave her. She lost the pounds of the indolent life she had known before Jesse.

Little by little Jesse started talking about politics and economics as they spent day after day together. She was interested because he was telling her of a better way of life, a life where everyone was equal, where the rich didn't dominate the poor, where the sick were taken care of, where everyone was free, where one's skin color didn't matter, where white police didn't have cruel authority over poor blacks.

And she asked questions whose answers from Jesse intrigued her as much as her questions intrigued Jesse. She was excited at what he told her, and she told him she wanted that life. She wanted that freedom. She wanted to get out of the slums she had grown up in.

"Who are you?" she asked one sunny, spring day, two months after they had met, as they lay on a blanket under a tall willow tree in Lincoln Park. They were eating a picnic lunch of delicious little sandwiches of cucumber and watercress; the bread had the crusts cut off. There were creamy cheeses and sharp, white cheddar to be spread on thin crackers. There were little pastries filled with herbs and spinach – Tamara had never tasted spinach before and had never dreamed there could be such foods. They sat in the shade of the tall willow tree drinking fine, light, white wine from delicately thin wine glasses, watching the ducks swim in a nearby pond.

He laughed and answered, "I told you. I'm Jesse Wilson."

"I don't mean that," she said. "I wanna' know *who* d'hell you are. How you know so much? You been t' college, right? I mean, you know stuff I ain't never heard of."

"Well that's easy, Tamara," Jesse said casually as if telling the girl the time of day. "I'm a Communist."

"Communist?" she asked pushing herself up on one elbow. She once again did not understand what Jesse was telling her. "You mean that Russian stuff? I thought that stopped a long time ago. I mean, ain't Russia not Communist no more?"

Jesse laughed once again. "No, Tamara. I'm not Russian . . . And the Government there isn't Communist anymore. But there are a few of us . . . Not many unfortunately . . . Who still believe that Capitalism is destroying the world. We've come together . . . From all over the world. We work together. We are like brothers and sisters no matter what part of the world we live in. We do work for World Communism . . . Sometimes we do very small things, things that might seem meaningless at first, but we work to eventually overthrow Capitalism."

"I don't get it," she said, confused once again.

"I'll tell you what, Tamara. I want to take you somewhere. I want to take you to a place where you can learn and understand."

She frowned again, thinking, and then asked, "There be gangbangers there? I ain't goin' nowhere that there's gangbangers. I done had 'nuff a'them. I likes it here. It's nice, ya'know?"

Jesse laughed again and said, "Oh, Tamara. There aren't any gangbangers where I want to take you. There will be school . . . Education . . . Good food and friends. You'll be safe, and you'll like it. I promise you, it will open a new world to you."

She looked deeply into Jesse's dark eyes. He was a handsome man, tall and slim, muscular, with a handsome, sculptured face. His nose was thin, and his lips were thin, so unlike what she was used to with the boys of her neighborhood. And he always smelled good, so unlike the dirty clothes, perspiration, and unwashed bodies of the boys she knew. His clothes were always clean, and he always wore a suit and tie.

She asked, "How come you ain't never tried t'screw me? You gay or sumpthin'?"

Jesse leaned back and laughed. He said, "No Tamara, I'm not gay. Not that I haven't wanted take you to bed. I've thought about it . . . Oh yes I have," Jesse answered. He took her hand in his, gently and not forcefully. "You're a very lovely young girl, and you can be an even better lady. Maybe someday we will be lovers. I hope so. But first I want to see if what I think is inside of you really is there."

"What's you mean . . . *Inside a'me*?"

"Not what you think, Tamara. I think there might be the making of someone who can do the cause some good."

"What cause?" she asked suspiciously.

"The cause of World Communism, Tamara. The cause of bringing peace to this crazy, warped world. The cause of ending Capitalism. The cause of making everyone equal in this world."

"What can I do? I ain't got no ed'cation and stuff. I don't know nothin'."

"I'm not sure yet," Jesse answered. "Let me take you

away from here, and we'll see what you can do."

Tamara leaned back on the blanket and inched away from Jesse. All she had at home was a drug addicted mother who sold herself to anyone on the streets who would pay her a few dollars. She had no idea who her father was; he could have been any one of the hundreds of men her mother had sex with. She watched two green ducks chasing one brown duck. 'God dam boy ducks afta' one little girl,' she thought. 'Just like out on d'streets.' She turned and looked at Jesse. "Where?" she asked.

"Cuba," he answered simply.

****

Tamara spent 24 months at the Cuban Instituto de Inteligencia Militar – the Institute of Military Intelligence. She was taught Communist ideology and drank it up like a thirsty person offered water in a desert. She went to daily classes in mathematics and socialist economics. She had difficulty reading the writings of Marx and Lenin, but Jesse helped with that. As reading became easier she studied the Russian Revolution and its downfall caused by the crimes of western Capitalism.

She took classes in English and left her South Chicago slang and accent behind her. She learned to speak fluent Spanish and could manage, if she had to, some French and German. She learned how to break into a building without smashing a window or breaking down a door. Overcoming keyed locks came easy to her. The lock-pick set she was given became like another set of fingers. Electronic locks were a bit more difficult, but she practiced, and she learned.

Tamara enjoyed all the physical training. Early every morning she would join a group of eight other young people, black and white and Asian, from all over the world, for calisthenics and long distance running. In a short time she could run full out for two miles and not breathe hard as a result.

A few of these young people could speak accented English; others only spoke languages that were incomprehensible to Tamara. Those she could speak with she enjoyed talking with. Even the white people. They were different from the whites she had known back in Chicago. They were not filled with hate; they were happy, and they all wanted a better world.

And she took a particular enjoyment from the combat training, the unarmed combat, and the tricks of killing silently. In the back of her mind and in her thoughts was how useful killing skills would be against the white people she hated. She wished she had known these things before meeting Jesse.

Her body had still been soft when she arrived at the school in Cuba. When she graduated two years later she was slim and strong. Her hair had been groomed, and she was taught how to dress conservatively and apply makeup. After a while, when she looked at herself in a mirror, she could not remember what she had looked like as a child in South Chicago. The woman she now was would be able to fit in anywhere in the world. She had acquired sophistication and would be a welcomed member of any group she wanted to be with.

Jesse did take Tamara to bed, often, as a reward for having done well in her classes. He taught her all the details of sex, the soft touches, the seductions, the tender words, things she never imagined existed. And he had taught her how to avoid pregnancies. Before Jesse, sex had been rough and quick and seldom satisfying.

They took weekends in Havana where they stayed at the best tourist hotels and took weekend days to travel to the coast, places where Europeans spent money to enjoy the Caribbean beaches and sun. Jesse refined his teachings of what he called 'table manners,' what wine to drink with what food, how an upper class European woman presented herself in the finest of company.

Twenty-four months passed quickly, almost too quickly, and Tamara graduated. She was so proud at all she had accomplished she could hardly hold in the screams of joy. But Tamara was not the guttural girl she had been in Chicago; she was a lady now, a lady with refined manners and social graces. She politely thanked all her instructors, shook their hands, and hugged the woman who had taught her how to dress and speak.

Old Colonel Manuel Jose Barahoma, a strange man with a fierce scar across his right cheek from his boyhood days in the hills with Castro, presided at the graduation. There was no diploma, but the Colonel shook Tamara's hand, congratulated her, and introduced her to Mohamed Al-Rashid.

Over the next eight months, back in the United States, Tamara started stealing things for Mohamed. At first they were simple things, easily opening safes and locks that were meant to protect secrets. The first few assignments were quick and easy. She stole papers she didn't take the time to read. She photographed each page of thick files. She placed miniscule listening devices in telephones. She had no idea what any of this was for or if they were even important. But each assignment was a little bit more difficult than the last. Each lock was a little more difficult to open. But she never failed, and she was never caught.

She travelled to Europe and the Middle East, luxuriating in the First Class sections of airplanes. She stayed at the best hotels and quickly became known as a young, beautiful, desirable, wealthy world traveler. But she was a thief for Islamic radical organizations and stole what she was told to steal all over the world.

Mohamed had Jesse Wilson on his payroll using unlimited cash from Al Qaeda and Iran. Jesse was to find and recruit young men and women who might be trained to be thieves and spies. They cooperated because each, in their own way, wanted Western Capitalism to fall.

Radical groups all over the world cooperated in their war against America and the West. Mohamed had paid a huge sum to the Instituto de Inteligencia Militar for Tamara's training in Cuba, and that investment was paying off. Tamara was proving to be one of the best. Although she had no idea what she was stealing, she never asked, assuming it was meant to further Jesse's cause of World Communism. She didn't know that Al-Rashid had in mind a World Islamic Caliphate in which there was no place for anyone, even a Communist, who was not a follower of Islam.

****

At Hillsdale Technologies that night, Tamara moved slowly, carefully, through the shadows inside the tall fence and found the door at the side of the building she was looking for. There was a keyed pad lock on the door. She grinned knowing how easy it would be to open the lock. The glass in the door, double paned with wire encased inside, revealed darkness inside the Administration Building. No one would be there to see her.

She quickly unscrewed the four screws holding the cover of the lock in place and examined the inside. From her backpack, she removed the small black box, six inches long, three inches wide, and two inches thick. Two wires protruded from it, alligator clips at the ends of each wire. At the front of the device was a screen of red plastic. Under the screen, numbers would flash when she pressed the button next to the screen to turn it on.

It fit easily in one of her hands as she attached the two wires to the proper contacts of the lock, as she had been taught. It would begin to read the codes that would unlock the door as soon as she turned the device on. She pressed the single red button on the box and watched the red numbers on the small screen jump to life and flash by. The flashing stopped and the lock opened, a soft but audible click signaling the unlocking of the door. She removed the device, screwed the cover back onto the lock, and pulled the door open. She stepped inside and quietly closed the door behind her.

She had fifteen seconds before the alarm on the door sounded. The alarm keypad was to her left. It was easy for her to override the alarm; she had stolen the codes the day before from the alarm company that had installed the system. That theft was too easy as the codes were kept in a twenty year old safe that she opened without any problems at all. She touched the six numbers on the keypad, and a green light came on. She quietly laughed again at the stupidity of the people she hated so much.

Tamara stood with her back to a wall near the door. She closed her eyes and slowed her breathing from the excitement of breaking in. This was not her first assignment in the United States, but the preparation for it told her it was the most important thing she had done so far.

Jesse and Al-Rashid had sat at a table in the big

room at the Instituto in Cuba. There were maps and building plans laid out on the big table. There was a photo of Hillsdale Technology taken via a satellite. And there were tools and small electronic devices laid out neatly in line. Every step she would take while breaking into Hillsdale Technology had been planned out. And every step was repeated, over and over again, until Tamara could repeat every detail without hesitation.

When she opened her eyes she was calm, and her eyes had become accustomed to the dark. She walked through the office, found the stairs, and went up slowly.

She was headed for the fourth floor. What she had to find was there. She didn't fully understand what it was she was to steal. She had been told over and over again how important it was but never what it was. That didn't matter to her. If it meant another step towards her freedom and the World Communism Jesse had told her about, it had to be important. Tamara had no idea she was working for Islamic terrorists whose aim was a world dominated by Islam.

At the landing a glass door stood at the office's entrance. It was locked but almost too easy to unlock with her lock-pick set. She stepped inside. The room was dark. There was a clicking sound reverberating in the long room; a ticking sound. A clock she assured herself. She counted the ticking. Yes, sixty seconds, it was nothing but a clock somewhere. Probably put there, she thought, by some overbearing boss who overworked his subservient proletariat every minute of every day. 'Capitalism,' she spit out the word like a disgusting piece of rotten food.

It had to be a big clock, a very large clock intended to intimidate the workers; she was sure. In the new world that was coming, there would be no clocks over workers' heads. *'From each according to his ability, to each according to his need.'* She had been taught the words of the Frenchman,

Louis Blanc that had been adopted by Karl Marx to define Communism.

Desk after desk were lined up in the long office. 'Stupid drones,' she scoffed. They would work their little lives away in drab, dull offices while the bosses pocketed the money and lived like royalty. And at the back of the room she saw in the shadows of the unlit office the black metal cage she was looking for, right where she had been told it would be. It was where the locked filing cabinets would be.

A big, heavy, electronic keypad lock held the cage's door closed. It was bigger than the keypad lock at the building's side door. Her first instinct was to simply break the lock as she had done so many times with the stupid padlocks in those years in the slums of Chicago. A hammer and two or three well directed hits would break it. But she had been told that no one could know she had been there. Again, she removed the cover of the keypad and hooked up the two wires from the little device that would open the lock. She counted the seconds and then the minutes.

It was taking a long time. The little red lights flashed seemingly without end. Maybe it wasn't working? Maybe she would have to just break the damn lock and the hell with it. She looked behind her; no one was there. It would make a loud sound if she were to break the lock, she knew, but she had no choice. She had to get what they sent her to get. Suddenly the flashing red lights stopped and the lock opened; the cage door swung open. She roughly pulled the two alligator clips from the lock's terminals and quickly replaced the cover. Pulling a chair from a nearby desk, she moved it against the door so that it would not close. She had been told that there was no way to unlock the cage from inside.

Inside she went from filing cabinet to filing cabinet. Each cabinet was locked with a padlock that was opened with a key. Once again she laughed at the stupidity of these people.   'Childish padlocks to protect something very important,' she thought and laughed again. She took the lock-pick set from her pack, and in seconds each of the locks popped open. She unlocked each slowly insuring not even a scratch was left to reveal she had been there. She opened each of the five drawers. Nothing but paper files; useless to her. She carefully replaced each padlock and then relocked each.

The fifth one held what she was looking for. Inside the top of the five drawers, alone in that drawer, was the small metal box, gray and dented, with a broken handle on top. It was what she had been sent to find. She took it outside the cage to the nearest desk, a place that held a coffee pot and some cups. The small box also had a keyed lock, small and fragile. But it wasn't locked. She shook her head and wondered how such stupid people could have such power over the world.

Inside the open box were dozens of small flash drives, each a different color.   That was not what she expected. She had been told to find 'the flash drive,' not that there would be several of them. She took the box and hurried back to the line of desks in the office, to the first desk with a computer on it.

She had been quick in learning how to operate a computer. She had never seen one before school in Cuba, except to steal a few for quick resale back in Chicago. She waited for the computer screen to come to life. She put the first of the flash drives in the USB port. She keyed the two words she had been told to find in the search box that appeared on the screen and sat back watching the screen flash in front of her.

When it stopped she looked at the words on the screen. Nothing; not what they had sent her after. She removed the flash drive and took another one going through seven until the screen came alive with the plans she was looking for. She was sure of what it was. She had seen drawings, speculation of what was on the screen. And the words were what she was told to look for. "FIREBIRD GUIDANCE." Yes, that was it.

She took another flash drive, this one from her jacket pocket, and slid it into a secondary USB port as they had shown her. She keyed in what was needed. She downloaded onto her own flash drive what she was told she had to get. She had no idea what it was; only that Jesse and Mohamed Al-Rashid had told her it was important.

It was done. Tamara switched off the computer and returned the box of flash drives to the filing cabinet. She locked the padlock on the filing cabinet, looked around to see if all was as she had found it, and stepped from the cage. She slid the chair back to the desk it had come from and closed the cage door, quietly locking it. She took another look around the room carefully to make sure that she had disturbed nothing. No one would know she had been there. She started for the door.

Outside she relocked the office door and turned for the stairs. In the hallway, at the landing, before going to the stairs, she went to an office, a big corner office with a big glass door that was not locked. Curiosity made her step inside and look around. A long series of windows were on two sides of the room. 'Some tyrannical boss has this big, grand office while the poor subjugated workers sit outside,' she thought.

At the other side of the landing was a window. She went to it and looked down. She saw two guards at the main gate. They were standing outside, talking, and then one of them started to walk away. He was walking towards the building she was in.

He stopped halfway there, turned and started back to the main-gate guard house. There he talked briefly with the other man. He was handed a cigarette by the man inside the gate house. They both lit cigarettes and stood talking. Tamara had to hurry. She had to get down the four flights of stairs and outside before the guard returned. She ran, taking three stairs at a time. At the door she peered through the wired glass. The guard was walking towards her again. She hugged the wall at the side of the door and thought. There was no other way out. It was this door or the big main entrance near the gate house. She could hide, but that would risk being found.

Danny O'Keefe needed a restroom. He had to get back to his post patrolling the cafeteria hallway, and he would use the men's restroom there. He walked fast, holding his bladder in. He had his library book under his arm, and as he walked quickly it slipped out and fell to the ground. He bent to pick it up and walked even faster, hoping he could get to the restroom in time.

Tamara stood against the wall, but she knew the man would see her as soon as he opened the door and stepped inside. She backed away from the door a few steps to her left. She would wait in the dark; maybe he wouldn't see her.

Danny punched in his code to open the door. The door wouldn't open; he had punched in the wrong code. He tried again, hoping he could hold his bladder in. The lock finally moved, and he opened the door.

He stepped inside and turned to his right to make sure the door closed and locked. He saw the shadow out of the corner of his eye. The shadow moved. He turned to face the shadow and froze for a second; looking directly at the head to foot black clad Tamara. "Who are . . ." he started but did not finish. Tamara struck out with her stiffly extend fingers striking at Danny's throat, breaking his wind pipe and cutting off his words. Quickly, quietly, she twisted Danny's head to the right and broke his neck. She lowered his dead body slowly, quietly to the floor and left him lying in the dark. His bladder had opened and his pants were soaked.

She ran from the building along the wall, the door closing loudly behind her. She kept to the shadows, running but avoiding the cameras and the flood lights. She ran to the fence and swung herself over it using the Kevlar blanket. Without stopping, she ran through the trees and over the hills. She didn't care if she made any sounds as she ran through dried leaves and over fallen tree branches. She needed to get to the road a mile away to the east where she had left her car, hidden behind tall bushes.

Mohamed would not be happy, but those things happen. She had been taught to kill quickly and easily, and she had been taught that killing was to be avoided, but sometimes killing was necessary. So she killed Danny O'Keefe.

THREE – To Save The Family Again

It was one of those sultry summer afternoons when all you want to do is sit in the shade and enjoy a very cold beer . . . Or maybe two. Autumn had been nice, and Christmas had been busy but fun. Spring had seen me on the golf course probably too often. July's hot days had given way to August and still more hot days, filled with even more and higher humidity rising up the hillside from the San Marcos harbor below. The air was still and heavy as Sandy and I waited and hoped for a breeze that did not arrive.

I was sitting on the upper level of our teak deck, having moved the thickly cushioned chaise into the shade of a tall cedar tree. Our house in the hills of San Marcos, California, overlooking the harbor below, sported three levels of decks that meandered down the hillside amongst the trees. I had built the house – actually I had it built as I can barely hit a nail with a hammer – nine years ago.

I was raised in the old San Marcos twenty-eight room Crew Family Mansion, with all the servants, across town where all the old mansions still stand, some still occupied by the "New Money" people who have moved to San Marcos. An ever increasing number of the old places stand vacant and unkempt, age having its unstoppable effects on the buildings and grounds.

When my mother and father had passed away I could no longer live in that big stone mansion from another era and be happy. One of my relatives lives there now. He is a

28

distant relative by marriage or something like that. He is a banker in one of the family banks and sits on the Board of Directors of three of the family's banks. He and his stupid, fat wife enjoy what they think is a royal lifestyle in the drafty old mansion. They make a show of being waited on by a butler, four house maids, and a cooking staff of four.

I am Morgan Crew, and the Crew Family own nearly uncounted wealth and businesses and properties all over the world. My lawyers and accountants tell me the combined fortune of the entire family is the second largest family fortune in the world, only a few dollars behind some Saudi family whose name I cannot pronounce. Since I am the only son of the head of the family, I am looked to as his heir and the successor to his position in the family and the businesses.

But I do not enjoy living the lifestyle of the wealthy with servants at my heels every minute of the day. Spending a day on the golf course at the San Marcos Country Club or out on a smelly old fishing barge catching whatever fish might be there is the life I prefer.

There had been a bar, a fisherman's tavern, down at the harbor, along the docks in Harborside. Cap'n Nick's it had been called. I used to spend many an afternoon there, drinking beer and eating the Cap'n's chowders of every variety, some wonderful and some . . . Well, better not demean the cooking skills of the dead. I met my wife, Sandy, there and I buried old Cap'n Nick when he was killed by the police as he tried to save Sandy's sister from a drug running gang. But that was a long time ago. I own the building now, and one day I will re-open Cap'n Nick's. But I know inside of me that it can never be the same place, without the old peg-legged Cap'n there.

San Marcos hasn't changed much since I was a child. Once, a long time ago, San Marcos had been a Northern

California, isolated, summer and sometimes winter retreat for the very, very wealthy. It was a place where the privileged few could imitate a bygone life reminiscent of 19th Century European royalty.

Throughout the 1970's and into the 1980's the new, not inherited wealthy of the U.S. moved to San Marcos. They brought their banks and tall, cold-glass office buildings to Downtown. San Marcos began to change from a quiet little town to a colder, distant place where people do business but are not friends. But I am not a part of that; I leave that to the lawyers and accountants. Sandy and I have a small circle of close friends, and we enjoy life.

As I dozed in the heat that day, I was watching my daughter, Caroline, play with her cars and trucks on the deck. Sandy walked from the house with a cold bottle of beer for me and a tall, icy vodka and tonic with a wedge of lime for herself. She sat on the foot of the chaise and smiled, watching her daughter play in the sun.

"I need to put more sun block on her," she said.

"Yeah . . . Sure," I mumbled and drank some of the ice cold beer. I closed my eyes against the sun filtering through the trees.

"It's hot," she said.

I answered, "Yeah . . . Sure," once again.

"Are you going to Bar-B-Q tonight?" she asked.

"Yeah . . . Sure."

"I think we should go to the club," Sandy suggested. "The baby can splash around in the pool, and we can eat inside where it's cool."

"Yeah . . . Sure," I answered again. My eyes were closed, and I was very close to welcomed sleep.

Sandy turned and looked at me. She poked me in my side and said, "You're not listening to me."

I opened my eyes a little, sat up and said, "I am listening . . . And she's not a baby. Caroline is four years old, and she will be starting pre-kindergarten this year."

"Well, she's my baby, Morgan," Sandy said, grinning. Sandy is without a doubt the most beautiful woman I have ever seen in all my forty something years. Her hair is long and thick and golden brown. It has never seen any other color. She is tall, and in spite of her appetite she has stayed slim and gorgeous. And she bears the scar of a bullet that almost killed her in Las Vegas. That scar is a testimony to her willingness to follow me in the life I lead, doing for others what they cannot or will not do for themselves.

I leaned back on the chaise and heard the phone ringing inside the house. "Get that will you," I mumbled.

Sandy didn't move. She said, "I've told you to put a phone out here."

"Get that will you?" I repeated.

"Betsy's inside. She'll answer it."

And sure enough Betsy, our 'nanny,' came outside with a phone in her hand. "You should have a phone out here with you," she said.

"See," Sandy said snidely. "That's two to one. We should have a phone out here."

Betsy handed the phone to me and said, "It's for you. I think it's long distance. Sounds like a secretary."

I took the phone, put it to my ear and grumbled, "What! It's too damn hot for anything."

"Please hold for Mr. Jascro," a woman's very officious voice said. I held, and another woman came on the phone.

This voice I recognized. Maureen is Peter Jascro's private secretary.

"Hello, Morgan," she said. "Peter wants to talk to you. Hold the line . . . I'll get him."

Peter Jascro is the managing partner of Harper, Harper, Jascro and Nettles, the law firm that has handled Crew family business for many, many years. Peter, a few years younger than my father, had quickly become his close friend. My father sought him out in the huge law firm and recognized his abilities at the law. That relationship took Peter to the top of the firm where he now sits as Managing Partner. Since my father's death he has acted as a kind and close uncle, taking care of me as best as he can.

Peter came on the line, "Morgan, I hope I'm not interrupting anything important, like a golf game or something."

"It's too damn hot, Peter. But you are interrupting my second beer, and you'll probably delay my third. What is it?"

"I'm afraid I am going to have to impose upon you once again Morgan," he said. His voice sounded like he was enjoying this. I could hear a little chuckle, and the words sounded like he was smiling as he spoke.

"Yeah, right," I said. "Just get to the point, Peter. I need a nap, and Sandy wants to go to dinner at the club."

"I suggest you do just that, Morgan. Have a good time this evening. I need you here in my office tomorrow morning."

"Look, Peter. Just messenger the papers out here for me to sign. Or fax them if you want. I don't care what they are. It's too damn hot."

There was silence on the line for a moment, and then Peter said, his voice a bit more serious, "No Morgan. I don't need your signature. There is a bit of a problem, and I need to speak with you here . . . Tomorrow morning. You'll probably need to leave this evening I suppose. Nine in the morning here, alright?"

Peter hung up, and a dial tone told me that I was on the phone alone. I had been given instructions, and I knew exactly what it was all about. I was expected to save the family, or maybe some family member, or maybe some family money, from some disaster. It had to do with someone else, but it was all going to be on me once again.

That is my lot in life, you see. It is always *me* who has to put my life on hold . . . Often at risk . . . To save someone else. As I said, I am expected to do for others what they cannot . . . Or will not . . . Do for themselves.

I laid the phone on the chaise, drained the bottle of beer, and tossed it angrily over the deck's railing onto the tree covered hillside.

"What the hell, Morgan," Sandy said. She was surprised that I would toss trash down onto our property. "What's wrong? Who was on the phone?"

"Peter Jascro," I said.

Sandy's face went pale all of a sudden, reflecting her deep worry that I was about to walk into trouble once again. She knows what my life is, and she had been with me often when danger and death came close to engulfing me. She herself had faced death by being with me when we saved her sister from vicious drug dealers here in San Marcos. She had been shot and almost died in Las Vegas. We had faced down a vicious killer in London. In Texas she put herself in the line of fire to save me. It was Sandy's intelligence that allowed us to capture and kill a very strange, very dangerous, and very huge spy. Her hand touched my knee. She asked, "What does he want you to do now?"

"I don't know," I answered. "He wants me in his office tomorrow morning."

"Well," she began speaking slowly, maybe hoping it wasn't anything too serious. "Maybe there's just something about one of the businesses. Maybe it's just business."

I, of course, knew I wouldn't be called in on short notice if it were just business. There were family members, cousins and nephews and nieces and in-laws all over the world who ran each business. Sure, I am my father's only son, and I am considered the head of the family, but business decisions have been made without me for a couple of decades. Everyone, including Peter Jascro, knows that I just don't give a damn about the money and the business.

But I had been given my travelling orders, and I would comply. Peter was too close of a favorite and respected uncle to say 'no' to.

I sat up and swung my legs off the chaise onto the teak deck. "OK," I said. "Let's go to the Club. Caroline can splash in the pool, and you can watch while I cool off in the bar."

"And dinner, too?" Sandy asked.

"And dinner too," I said. "But first I have to get plane tickets to New York. I'll do a redeye so we can relax for a few hours."

****

I took a two-thirty AM flight out of San Francisco, non-stop to New York's Newark airport. The First Class cabin had those seats that doubled as semi-private beds, reclining fully and sort of walled in. I was given a double bourbon and a thin blanket, and I was asleep before the jet reached its cruising altitude.

Some rough weather woke me momentarily, but didn't keep me awake. An hour before landing a guy was gently touching my shoulder, waking me. I was about to mumble something about not being interested until I realized he was a flight attendant.

"We're about to start our landing pattern, Mr. Crew," he said softly. "Would you like some coffee? Maybe some breakfast?"

"Yeah . . . Sure," I said as I rubbed the sleep from my eyes. "Coffee would be good."

I grabbed my electric razor from my bag in the overhead and quickly shaved in the restroom, throwing some cold water on my face when I was done. The coffee was just OK, not as strong as I really like, but it was better than not having coffee. While I was shaving the other front cabin passengers were given a breakfast of eggs and sausage and fruit and juice. I was too late leaving the restroom, so as I sat I was offered a bagel, but I turned it down. Breakfast would have to wait.

It was nearly ten AM EST by the time I got off the plane in Newark. 'What the hell,' I thought. So I would be late. I took a commercial helicopter to JFK and a cab from there to Peter Jascro's office. I walked in the front door at half past eleven, dragging my small overnight roll-aboard behind me.

As I walked out of the elevator I was met by Maureen Maxwell, Peter Jascro's private secretary. "Good morning, Morgan," she said brightly. "You're late." Of course she knew me well enough to call me by my first name and to know I would always be late for everything. I am always late because I really get a kick out of telling people, anyone, that they aren't all that important. "Please come with me," she said, and I followed.

I smiled and said nothing by way of apologizing for being late in favor of not pissing her off. That would gain nothing. So I followed her down the hallway, pulling my small roll-aboard behind me, around two corners and down another hallway. Now, I had been in Peter Jascro's office many, many times over the years. Wherever we were going, it wasn't to Peter Jascro's office. So I asked as we walked, "Where are we going? Did Peter get a new office?"

Maureen said nothing. She was holding a steady smile as she always did with me. She glanced over her shoulder at me without stopping or slowing her quick pace. Maureen had been working for Peter for nearly thirty years. Truth be told, Maureen ran the office. She did scheduling and handled personnel. When a question came up, that question went first to Maureen. She is what many would describe as a 'handsome' woman who once was young and very pretty. Her hair had grayed over the years, but she maintained a slim and attractive body.

We stopped in a lonely, thin hallway I had never been in before. There was only one door in the entire hallway. Peter couldn't be here, I thought. Unless he was demoted somehow to mail boy.

Maureen opened the single pale oak door and stepped aside. She held her smile but said nothing. So I took the hint and walked into the room. Maureen took my roll-aboard from me as I passed, and she closed the door with her on the outside.

The room was a dusty and musty storage room that must have been used to store boxes of very old paper records that couldn't be thrown out but would have very little use currently. I imagined that eventually, each piece of paper would be scanned and placed into a computer file. But that would take a very long time.

The long wall across the room from me was lined from corner to corner, floor to ceiling, with cardboard boxes filled with file folders. The wall to my right was similarly hidden with more boxes. A heavy odor of old cardboard and musty paper filled the room.

In the center of the room was a ten foot long conference table, dusty and scratched and dented from years of past use, obviously having been replaced years before by one much newer and in better shape. 'Not unlike many people in business,' I mused.

To my left, sitting at the head of the table, were a man and a woman. They were close to the table, their hands folded and their arms resting on the table top. They were looking directly at me, unblinking and not smiling.

The man was young but not too young, maybe early 40's. He was in good shape, very athletic looking, and he was dressed well in a dark suit, starched white shirt, and dark tie. His hair was cropped short and combed back. I immediately thought, 'FBI.' I had seen his type many times before.

The woman was older, fiftyish and not in very good athletic condition. Her hair was dull brown, with more than a few grey hairs showing, and needed brushing badly. Her face was puffy, probably from stress as much as age, I thought. She was dressed in a not-too-expensive blue dress, belted with a thin black belt that had to be imitation leather. Over it she wore a not new tan cotton jacket. I didn't see a wedding ring, but if she were married and a mommy she would be described as a frumpy housewife and grandmother.

Their stares were uncomfortable and made me think

that maybe they were just some statues rather than real people.

"Please sit down, Mr. Crew," the man said.

I didn't. "Where the hell is Peter Jascro?" I asked, trying to sound angry to hide the anxiety I was feeling. "I'm supposed to meet him this morning."

"Mr. Jascro will see you at a later time, Mr. Crew. Please sit down," the man repeated.

One of the great joys of my life, other than a day of golf or fishing, is challenging authority. So I said, "No."

The man moved for the first time, his right hand going inside his jacket. I was ready to duck under the table in case he drew a gun from a shoulder holster and started shooting. But it wasn't a gun he took out; it was his black leather ID case. He opened it and held it out in front of him. I recognized the small gold badge and ID card of FBI Agents.

I looked at it and said, "Yeah, that's just great. Now, I'm going to leave and find Peter Jascro."

I tried the door but found it locked. So I turned back and looked at the two. "OK, so I'm under arrest for something, right? I want a lawyer, got it?"

"You're not under arrest, Mr. Crew. We simply want to speak with you. It's very important."

"So who the hell are you?" I asked. I leaned back against the locked door, crossed my legs and folded my arms across my chest. I tried to look tough; I hoped they thought I really was tough. But I knew my paunch and lack of real muscles gave the lie to me being a tough guy.

"I am Special Agent in Charge, Adam Carter, Federal Bureau of Investigation. This is Ms. Donna Evans, Homeland Security. Now please sit down, Mr. Crew." He wasn't trying to sound demanding or threatening, in fact he was smiling. The woman had a stone-faced non-smile plastered on her face.

In an attempt to keep an upper hand I asked, "Just what the hell are you in charge of, Agent Carter?"

"I am Agent in Charge of Counter Intelligence for the District of New York," he answered.

I turned to Ms. Evans and said, "And I suppose you have a similar job, except you get a whole lot more of my tax dollars than he does to do your job?"

She said nothing, she didn't move, and the hard expression on her face didn't change. I had to do a double take; I realized she had one blue eye and one green eye. 'Very strange,' I thought.

"Please sit down, Mr. Crew, so we can talk," Agent Carter said once again.

"Am I gonna' be shipped off to Gitmo or something?" I asked as snidely as I could manage.

Finally Ms. Evans said something. Her voice was raspy and deep, the voice of a heavy, long time smoker. But she didn't move or change her expression as she spoke. "Mr. Crew, all we want to do is talk with you. Something very serious has happened, and you may be able to help us. All we want is to ask a few questions."

That seemed about as reasonable as I could expect. So I walked to them, pulled the only other chair in the room, a dirty, metal folding chair with a torn vinyl seat, from the table and slid it back against the wall as far from the two of them as I could manage. I sat and leaned the chair back against the wall. I folded my arms in front of me and hoped I had put an angry enough look on my face.

Agent Carter started the conversation, such as it was.

He asked, "Do you own a company called Hillsdale Technology, Incorporated?"

I knew enough of the law to hopefully keep me out of trouble. I knew that lying to a Federal Agent was a crime in itself. So I decided to be truthful but not to volunteer anything. I said, "I . . . Myself . . . Don't own Hillsdale Technologies. It is a company owned by the Crew family. One of many, I might add."

"But you do own it, correct?" Carter insisted.

"You weren't listening to me, were you?" I said. "My family owns a holding company named Crew Enterprises. It was started by my Great Grandfather. I am the majority shareholder of that corporation. That company owns a lot of stuff. Hillsdale is one of the things that Crew Enterprises owns."

"But you are Morgan Crew, and we are told you control everything your family owns," Carter said. He was trying as hard as he could to get me to admit to something I wasn't going to admit to.

Evans looked sideways at him and then back at me. She said, for the first time cracking a small smile, "Please excuse Agent Carter. He's really a good man, but he needs to be extremely specific and detailed. I understand your affiliation with Hillsdale Technology, Mr. Crew. We only wish to ascertain if you are knowledgeable of the company and how it operates."

"I know *of* the company, Ms. Evans. If you will be specific, I might be able to tell you more. You see, like Agent Carter, I don't like to deal in non-specifics either."

"Alright, then let's start with the Chief Operating Officer of Hillsdale. Do you know who that is?" she asked.

"Yes," I answered simply.

They waited, but I wasn't about to say anything more. Answering their questions was something I had to do. But I wanted them to understand that they had to be very specific in their questions. They needed to know very quickly that I was not going to volunteer anything.

I felt I was at least a little bit in control, and I wasn't about to let them have the ball back in their court. I had the feeling I was in some sort of pseudo-secret court with people who held my life in their hands, and I wasn't about to help them in any way.

"So who is it?" Carter asked. He was getting a little frustrated. That was good. I wanted both of them to be frustrated. When they were frustrated, and I wasn't, I could be in control.

"Who is what?" I asked. Yes, I wanted to be a wiseass, and I wanted these people to get angry, because when you get angry you say things you wouldn't ordinarily say.

Ms. Evans gently touched Agent Carter's arm to tell him she would take over. She cracked a thin smile once again; it seemed that was something she wasn't used to doing, as it appeared to be almost painful to her. She said, "Mr. Crew. Something happened a few months ago at Hillsdale Technologies. A security guard was murdered. We need to find out what happened."

It was getting late, I was tired from the flight, and I was hungry. Breakfast would have to be in the past, but lunch had to be in the very near future. So I thought it best to bring an end to this farce.

I pulled the chair to the table, and I sat forward. I rested my arms on the table top and said, "I know very little about Hillsdale. I know it is a medium size corporation that does electronic research and development. I know it has several contracts with the Federal Government and a few other corporations that have Government contracts. I have a cousin-in-law, Mr. Jeremy Hillsdale, who is the CEO and COO. It is well funded in the research it does but seldom makes a very large profit. I've never been there. I've never examined the books, but I hear reports at the annual corporate meetings. I don't understand the reports to look at them, so I rely on the people . . . Accountants and lawyers . . . Who give the reports orally. I see Mr. Hillsdale maybe once a year when the extended family gathers for Christmas. I know little about him."

The two of them sat stone faced, hardly blinking an eye. I guessed they were waiting for me to say something more. So I asked, "You said a murder had been committed . . . Several months ago. Why did it take you so long to talk to me?"

Carter started, "That's irrelevant . . ."

Evans touched his arm once again, looking sideways at him like a kindly but disapproving mother. She looked back at me and said, "The local police have been investigating, but they have come up with nothing."

"So who was killed?" I asked. "Someone I'm supposed to know?"

"A security guard, Mr. Crew. Probably someone you didn't know."

"Is that meant as an insult, Ms. Evans?" I asked, again as snidely as I could manage. "Do you mean I'm too good to associate with the common folk?"

"Not at all," she answered without a change in her stone-stiff expression.

"Then what the hell does this have to do with me?" I demanded. "Have the police found the killer? Do you somehow suspect me?"

"Not at all, Mr. Crew," she said. "All we want is information. We are asking for your help, that is all."

"OK, then tell me why Homeland Security and the F.B.I. are interested in the murder of a security guard."

Ms. Evans cleared her throat, and I wondered if she was longing for another cigarette. She said, "You are aware that Hillsdale has several Federal Government contracts?"

"I already told you I know what Hillsdale does. I know Hillsdale does some work for the Government. I told you that already. So what?"

"We have concerns that the theft of some classified information may have been the cause of the guard's death."

Now it was getting serious. If the Feds had some information about secret stuff leaving Hillsdale, the whole family could be at risk, not only Hillsdale. I had to find out what was going on, and the best way I could do that was to cooperate to some extent and keep the two of them talking.

"OK," I said. "If I can help you with that I will. What do you want to know?"

"That's fine, Mr. Crew," Ms. Evans said, trying to smile again. It looked almost painful for her as she struggled to crack a smile. "Now, can you tell us what you do know about Mr. Hillsdale, please?"

I felt like saying, 'I *can*, but I *will* not,' but I didn't. My Yale education taught me the difference. And besides, my stomach was starting to growl. So I said, "I understand he is a graduate of Harvard . . . I am not aware of his major. I think he has some graduate studies somewhere, but I don't know where. He married some relative of mine, a cousin two or three times removed or something like that. As I recall, she's not very attractive . . . I have a hunch Jeremy married her to get into some of the Crew money and businesses. I think Hillsdale Technologies was started by his father, but I'm not certain of that. After Jeremy's wedding, the Crew Family acquired Hillsdale through a merger instituted by Jeremy. But let me ask you, Ms. Evans. Why the hell are you asking me and not him?"

"That is being done, Mr. Crew," she answered. "I will need you to sign a release for us to examine the records at Hillsdale."

"What records?" I asked.

"All the damn records," FBI Agent Carter said suddenly and angrily. "Look, I need to know if anything was taken the night that damn guard was killed. Now I need you to sign the release."

"Sorry about that, Agent Carter," I said. "I told you I would help if I can. I just don't like your attitude. Get a court order or get your IRS to subpoena what you want. In the meantime, if you can't talk civilly to me, go talk to Mr. Peter Jascro, my attorney. And if you've got Jeremy locked up somewhere . . . Gitmo or someplace . . . Ask *him* to sign a release. I imagine he might if he's not being water boarded down in Gitmo."

Ms. Evans touched the Agent's arm once again trying to calm him. He sat back, his face was red, and his breathing was too short and too quick. I said, "Hey, you gonna' have a stroke or somethin'? I'd dial 911 for you . . . if I knew the number."

I got up, pushing the chair back against the wall behind me. It hit the wall, folded upon itself, and crashed to the floor. At the door, I tried the doorknob, but it was still locked. I pounded my fist on the door and yelled, "OPEN THE DAMN DOOR!"

The door swung open. Maureen stood there, looking embarrassed but still with that very businesslike forced smile all over her face and my little roll-aboard's handle in her hand.

"Show me the way to Peter's office," I demanded.

FOUR - To Rescue Jeremy Hillsdale

Peter Jascro is, to me, of an indeterminate age. He was a good friend of my father for many years before my father passed away, although he was some years younger than my father. When my grandfather passed away, my father took over as CEO of Crew Enterprises. He was just a young man at the time, barely into his 30's. My father told me that on his first day at the head of the corporate table he became surrounded by a flock of attorneys. They were all talking at once, all telling him things he probably needed to know, but none of them were able to get through to him for the cacophony all around him.

After ten minutes of that my father stormed out of the office in San Francisco and caught a plane to New York. He spent, he told me, three full weeks going from law office to law office looking for new lawyers. He merely walked into the offices of the biggest law firms on Wall Street without appointments. Once they knew who he was there wasn't any problem spending hours with him, selling what they could offer.

It was on a Thursday afternoon; he was exhausted and gave some thought to selling his shares in the family business and buying a chicken farm somewhere in an isolated corner of Iowa. He was walking out of the offices of one of the law firms - Harper and Harper, LLP - that did some minor work for the Crew family. It had been a frustrating two hours of what he called 'bull turds,' listening to lawyers try to sell themselves into more work for, and more money from, the Crew family. My father was at the elevators when a young man stopped him. "Excuse me, Mr. Crew. May I have a minute or two?"

That was when the lifelong relationship and friendship between my father and Peter Jascro began. Peter was a recent member of the Bar and a low level associate of the firm. Peter was doing grunt work as any new associate attorney would do. But he had the guts to just walk up to my father and talk to him. And my father liked the honesty he heard from young Peter Jascro.

In short, my father hired Peter, and as a result his rise in the world of international law was rapid. At my father's insistence Peter was assigned to nothing but Crew Enterprises' work. Five years later, Peter was offered a partnership. Ten years after that he became a full, named partner, of Harper, Harper, Jascro and Nettles. He became the managing partner soon after.

My father passed away at a fairly early age, as had his father. I think it was from too much work, and that thought has kept me at arm's length from the family business. Since my father's death, Peter, as I have said, has been an uncle to me, advising me as a father would. Today Peter has aged gracefully. His hair is no less thick than it was thirty years ago even though it has turned silver grey. Excess weight has evaded Peter all his life. He wears glasses elegantly. He speaks slowly, carefully, but never in anger. When he enters a room, at work, in a courtroom, or anyplace else, his presence tends to dominate.

But what I admire most about Peter Jascro is his handwriting. In an age of computers, iPads, iPhones, texting and tweeting, and all that other stuff, Peter can handwrite a letter on fine stationary with elegant penmanship the like of which hasn't been seen since the 19th Century.

He was in his grand office on the twentieth floor when I stormed in. His office was big – you could play tennis in it. And it had floor to ceiling windows on two walls. His desk was always clear on top with only the work at hand in front of him.

Maureen opened both of the ten foot tall double oak doors and quickly stepped aside, perhaps fearing I would knock her down as I raced past. I let the roll-aboard drop from my hand and crash to the floor. Peter put the screw top on his ink pen and put it down slowly and grandly on the desk. He leaned back in his tall red leather chair and greeted me with a broad smile.

"Oh, Morgan, my boy," he said, his voice echoing splendidly through the big room. "It's so good to see you again. It's been too long. And how are Sandy and Caroline?"

I didn't stop walking as fast as I could until I had crossed the polished wood floor, my heels clicking loudly, and I was standing in front of Peter's desk. I stood there, breathing hard, and said, "What the hell's going on, Peter? I thought I came all the way out here to see you."

"And here you are, aren't you, Morgan? You are in fact seeing me. Isn't that wonderful?" His smile was electric, and as was usual, it tended to calm me.

I moved in front of one of the two tall, red leather wing chairs in front of Peter's desk and fell into it. I was exhausted and very hungry. And I was angry at Peter for the first time in my life. I asked, trying to calm my voice, "Why the hell was I locked in that damn room with those two cops?"

Peter saw what I was feeling; I have a very hard time hiding my emotions. He leaned forward and said in a low, calm, measured voice, "I'm sorry, Morgan. I will explain . . .

But first I'm a little hungry for lunch. I assume you are, also," he said, anticipating my need for some food.

He pushed a small red button at his right hand, and almost immediately his office's double doors opened. Maureen walked in carrying a silver tray. On it was a large, silver, coffee pot, two delicate china cups, thin and white, rimmed in gold, with sailing ships emblazoned on them as with the saucers, and a plate of sandwiches. There were ham and cheese, duck liver pate, and delicate cucumber and crab, all with the crusts carefully trimmed from the bread. Peter and I ate everything on the plate and drank all the excellent coffee without saying a word.

When the plate was empty I felt better, but I wasn't any less angry. I wiped my mouth with a soft, pale green, linen napkin, laid it on the desk, sat back and said, "So tell me what this is all about."

Peter cleared his throat and began. He told me that the previous October a security guard at Hillsdale Technologies had been killed, murdered in fact. I interrupted, "So what? I mean, I'm sorry he's dead . . . But what does that have to do with me?"

"Let me go on, please Morgan," he said.

He told me the death was murder rather than an accident because of the way the guard had been killed. His wind pipe had been broken, Peter said, and then his neck was snapped. Peter said the police, actually the County Sheriff, had described it as very professional. They doubt that another guard would have done it. The dead guard was the youngest man on duty that night. The other four were all older or retired men, all over fifty-five years of age. None were retired cops who might have known how to kill like that. Plus the Sheriff's office could not come up with a motive or a suspect.

Then, Peter said, as the police were meandering on after six months of getting nowhere, they contacted the FBI for assistance.

"The FBI?" I asked. "You mean that Carter jerk?"

"No, Morgan. Not him. Other Agents. You see, as you know Hillsdale has numerous Government contracts. A murder occurred at a place where very sensitive and secretive work was being done. So the FBI was interested, although they don't investigate a murder unless it has some bearing on the Government, or if they are called in to assist the local authorities. They, at first, did a complete audit of the facility. That took over a month of intense work. But nothing was missing. Everything was checked and nothing was missing. So they called in their science people. A minute examination . . . Under microscopes . . . Found that a few screws had recently been tampered with."

"Screws? What the hell, Peter?"

"They seem to think that someone may have removed the screws from the cases of a couple of door locks. Old paint on the screws had microscopic chips of paint scratched off."

"So what the hell are they bothering me about?" I asked.

Peter ran a hand through his hair and looked up at the ceiling. I think he was looking for the right words. He said, "They speculate that someone got onto the Hillsdale campus and killed the guard. They think that maybe . . . Just maybe, that someone was after something very classified."

"But you said nothing was missing."

"Yes, but now," Peter started. He sat forward, leaned his elbows on his desk and said, "Please don't be offended, Morgan. They seem to think that security at Hillsdale was so lax that it was easy for someone to get in. They want to know why security was so slipshod. They suspect that someone intentionally made the security easy to break through."

"That's ridiculous," I said, astonished that the Feds could think such a thing. But then it occurred to me that they wanted to talk about Jeremy and not me. They didn't ask me anything about myself. They suspect Jeremy. They suspect that Jeremy intentionally let someone in to steal something.

After a few brief moments of thought I asked Peter, "What was stolen? They said nothing."

"They don't know exactly what was stolen . . . If anything was in fact stolen . . . But they think something was. They won't tell me why they believe that. Hillsdale has so many top secret projects going. I'm thinking they just have to cover all the bases. But they could know something else. It's very possible that some intelligence came in indicating something was stolen. I really don't know."

"But suppose . . ." I suggested. "What if someone did break in and the guard caught them. What if, after killing the guard whoever broke in just wanted to get the hell outta' there. You know . . . They were scared of being caught."

Peter grinned and said, "That's a reasonable speculation. But it's not what the FBI and Homeland Security want to believe. They have to assume the worst, and they seem to know something they aren't telling us. Morgan, you need to represent the family in this. Go speak with Jeremy; see what he says. Go to Hillsdale and take a look around. Look at the books, and look at any records of the security operation there."

"Why?" I asked. "Why me? Why not someone else? Why not one of your people? You've got detectives working for you."

"Because it's your family, and your family depends on you. We need to keep this as quiet as possible, in house so to speak. If it gets out to Wall Street, Hillsdale stock will plummet. We can't have that, now can we?"

So that was it. Once again I was being thrown into a damn den of lions to save someone else. Sure, if the Feds got angry they could cancel all the contracts with Hillsdale, and the family would lose a few million dollars. Peanuts when it comes to all the damn billions the family has already.

Then there was Jeremy, a distant family member by marriage to some distant relative. I was expected to save him, too. How many family members have I saved over the years? And for what? How many have thanked me rather than asking for more from me?

But that is my life, doing for others what they cannot . . . Or will not . . . Do for themselves. Saving others when they cannot save themselves. I resigned myself to the fact that I had to do something for Jeremy Hillsdale and the family money, so I asked for legal advice from Peter.

"You said the FBI did an audit. Yet those two back there, they wanted me to sign some papers giving them access to the entire business and all the records. Why?"

"The Federal Government wants access to their contracts without a warrant or court order, that's all. Their audit involved only routine day to day records and bookkeeping. They want to examine everything."

"Should I sign the papers?"

"Certainly not, Morgan," Peter said. "Limit anyone's access to giving them the very minimum of what they need to know. Give them only what they ask for and nothing more. It will take some time for them to get warrants. Even the FISA courts run slow in a non-emergency. The Federal Government isn't going to cancel contracts that quickly. In the long run, they need the work that Hillsdale does. It would take a year or more to find a replacement company."

"OK," I relented. "I'll refuse to sign the paper, and I'll go speak with Jeremy, but there is a limit to what I will do this time."

"Fine," Peter said, smiling a satisfied smile. He had talked me into it once again. "Jeremy is in custody. They have him here in the City . . . At the Federal Building. You can talk to him there."

"They arrested him! For what?"

"He's not under arrest . . . Yet. They are merely questioning him. I have an attorney assigned to him. He'll talk to you if no one else is there with the two of you."

****

The Jacob K. Javits Federal Office Building is located at 26 Federal Plaza on Foley Square in the Civic Center district of Manhattan. At over 41 stories tall it houses many Federal government agencies. Homeland Security and Donna Evans have offices there. The FBI and Adam Carter have offices there. And in the fifth basement, five stories below ground, there are holding cells where people can be placed 'away from the light of day' for questioning.

One might expect to find suspected terrorists, foreign spies, big time drug smugglers, syndicate crime bosses, and assassins locked up down there. Just about anybody who is suspected of something bad can be found down there. The afternoon I walked into the building, Jeremy Hillsdale was also down there.

I stopped at a line of people waiting to pass through a metal detector. Photo IDs were examined closely. Briefcases and handbags were opened and the contents examined. Laptops were turned on and examined. Cameras were examined. A few people were pulled to the side and given a thorough pat down search of very private parts of their bodies. Men in uniform patted down men, and one woman, a good looking red head with a nice shape filling out her uniform, was patting down the women. I was going to request the woman if I was to be patted down, but they just waived me through the metal detector. Oh well.

I passed through the exam point fairly easily and walked to the front desk and the young woman sitting there. In front of her was a bank of four big computer screens. The desk had manila folders lined up vertically in a black plastic holder, and a small teddy bear sat off to the side. 'Cute,' I thought; probably meant to give the visitor the feeling everyone in the building was soft, cuddly, and gentle. How many people were surprised when they found out who were really in the offices upstairs?

"Hi!" I said, smiling brightly to the young lady. "I'd like to see Mr. Jeremy Hillsdale, please."

She looked questioningly at me, as if I were speaking a foreign language. She said nothing.

"Mr. Hillsdale," I repeated. "I'd like to see him."

"I'm sorry," she finally spoke. "Where does Mr. Hillsdale work?"

"Not here," I said. "Unless you have him working on the rock pile, breaking big rocks into small rocks."

The questioning look only got more questioning. "I'm sorry," she said. "I don't understand."

"Look, you have a Mr. Jeremy Hillsdale here . . . Somewhere . . . In custody I guess . . . For questioning . . . Or something. I'd like to talk to him, please."

She changed her face from questioning to totally baffled. Her eyes dropped from me to her work station. She hesitated for a moment, her hand floating above a telephone. Then she picked it up, touched a few buttons and waited. She spoke into the phone, "There is a man here . . . A gentleman . . . Who wants to speak with someone named Jeremy Hillsdale."

She paused and waited while she listened. She looked up at me and raised her index finger to tell me it would be just a moment. She said into the phone, "Yes, sir . . . That's right . . . Just a minute, please."

She looked up at me again and asked, "Who are you?"

"I am Morgan Crew. Tell whoever it is you're talking to that I own Hillsdale Technologies."

She repeated what I had said, and then she hung up her phone and said to me, "Just a moment, please. Someone will be with you very soon."

I paced around the lobby as I waited . . . And then I paced some more. The floor was polished gray marble, and a lot of windows made up the front wall of the lobby. A coffee cart stood at the end of, and to the side of, the front desk. I went there and bought a paper cup of not-too-good black coffee and a stale powdered donut. I sometimes take the opportunity to eat stuff like donuts Sandy wouldn't let me eat when she is with me. As I ate I looked out the big windows at the throngs of people walking by, all unaware of what was going on five floors below their feet.

Five minutes went by . . . And then another five

minutes. I finished the donut and drank what I could of the coffee, tossing the half empty cup into a trash can. There was no sense going back to the young lady at the reception desk. She looked really uncomfortable and maybe ready to cry.

I turned to start another walk to the opposite wall. Out of the corner of my eye I saw three men in police uniforms step off an elevator. They were walking right at me, so I stopped and waited for them. The crowd of people in the lobby must have sensed what was happening. They stood aside and watched . . . Quietly . . . Anticipating some excitement.

When they got to me, the guy on my left stepped to my left side, and the guy on my right stepped to my right side. They stood facing me, fencing me in sort of. They intended to make me feel surrounded, and they did a damn good job at it, too. The guy in the middle said, "Please come with us."

"Where to?" I asked.

Apparently that was the wrong question because the two guys at my side grabbed me by my arms, and we all 'walked,' very quickly, back to the elevator they had gotten off of; the doors were standing open waiting for us. The doors closed us inside, and we zipped up to the twenty-eighth floor. When the doors slid open, FBI Special Agent Adam Carter was standing there, and he wasn't very happy. His face was crimson, he was breathing hard, his arms were crossed tightly in front of him, and he wasn't wearing his suit jacket, which allowed me to see the very big gun holstered at his waist.

"What the hell are you doing here?" he demanded.

"First," I said. "I'd like these two gorillas to let go of my arms. I promise not to run away . . . Or to beat everybody to a pulp."

Agent Carter nodded, and they let go of my arms.

"Now that that's done," I said. "I'd like to see Jeremy Hillsdale."

"That's not possible," Carter said.

"Excuse me," I said. "But there are only two reasons why that is not possible. One, he's not here. Two, he's dead. So which one is it?"

"You can't see him," Carter repeated without explaining why I couldn't see him.

There are four elevators in that part of the building. One that we had not come up in opened, and Peter Jascro stepped out. He walked slowly to us. He was dressed in an elegant muted pinstriped suit with a bright red handkerchief in the breast pocket, and he was carrying a polished leather attaché. He was walking so slowly that all Carter could do was stare at him and wait. I stepped aside and watched, smiling and holding back laughter.

When he reached us he said, "I am Mr. Hillsdale's attorney. I want to see him . . . Right now, please."

Agent Carter stammered and shifted from one foot to another. He said, "You can't. He's being held . . ."

"That being the case," Peter said interrupting the Agent. "Please accompany me down to Judge Brenda Michelson's court and explain to her why you won't let Mr. Hillsdale's attorney see him."

Carter's forehead wrinkled in a frown as he thought about what was happening. Judge Michelson, he knew, was appointed to the Federal Appeals Court by a Democrat President, and she had the reputation of being very liberal, left-wing, and pro-accused. She had been an attorney working for the ACLU when she was nominated for the bench.

Not having any obvious options, not wanting the break-in at Hillsdale to become public yet, not wanting a liberal judge to put her foot into the whole operation, he relented. "Alright," he said. "I'll take you to an interrogation room, and you can talk to him. But only you, Mr. Jascro. Mr. Crew cannot see him."

"Two points, Agent Carter," Peter said calmly. "One, I will speak with my client in a conference room without cameras or recording devices, not an interrogation room. Have you ever heard of Attorney / Client privilege? Two, Mr. Crew will accompany me."

Carter knew he had no good choice here. He relented once again and said, "I'll take you to a conference room."

At either end of the hallway where we stood were doors of pale, solid wood without windows or glass of any kind. There were no signs to indicate what offices were inside the doors. Only a white sign with black letters indicating 'No unauthorized entry' was pasted to the wall at the side of each of the doors. Electronic locks with little red and green lights secured each door, I imagined operated by FBI ID cards. Carter led us to the door to our right; he slid his card through the lock, the green light lit up, and the door buzzed open. I looked up, and at each corner above the door there were cameras pointed down at anyone passing through the door.

We walked through the doorway and into a large office where a couple dozen people spent their work days. Peter and I followed Carter through the office of gray, five foot tall cubicles that seemed to go on forever. In each, people were busy, almost mesmerized by their computer screens. We finally reached a conference room that was walled in glass. Inside was a long table surrounded by tall, blue leather chairs. A flat screen TV hung from one side wall, and a table carrying strange looking electronics was along the other side wall.

Carter opened the door and stepped inside but didn't hold the door open for us. I grabbed it before it could close and held it open for Peter. Carter went to a phone on the table, punched in a number and waited. A moment later we heard him say, "Send Hillsdale up to Conference Room C . . . That's right . . . You heard me . . . I'll take responsibility for this."

He hung up the phone and turned to us. "He'll be here in a minute. I have to stay here, of course."

"Of course . . . Not," Peter said. He laid his attaché case on the table. "As I said, I will have an Attorney / Client privileged conversation with Mr. Hillsdale. Since you have a law degree and you graduated from . . . What was that school? Western Something School of Agriculture and Law or something like that? As a person who has a law degree, you must know what Attorney / Client privilege is."

Carter's face flushed, his fists clenched; he had to force himself to hold in his anger. All he did was walk out of the room without saying anything.

Peter pulled a chair away from the table and sat. He told me, "Sit with your back to the glass. We don't want any lip reading going on."

Before I sat I went to the table holding all the electronic devices and unplugged each from their power outlets. Each black box went dead. I went to the big TV and unplugged the power cord. I looked around the room for cameras. There was a clock, big and brass, hanging from a wall. I went to it, reached up and took it from the wall. There was a power cord behind it; I unplugged it. I laid it face down on the table.

Peter was smiling broadly as I returned to the desk and sat next to him. He said, "That's good, Morgan. The FBI sees this as a possible terrorist or espionage matter. They'll stop at little to do their job."

"And I agree that the world today needs what they do," I said. "But I guess I have to see evidence that Jeremy is a spy or a terrorist or something. I can't bring myself to believe he did anything wrong."

"I've read the preliminary reports, Morgan," Peter said. "Even I have a hard time believing the lax security up there. A child could break in there. With all the top secret work they do, you'd think security would be better."

We waited, not speaking. Ten minutes went by. I stood and started pacing back and forth from one side of the room to the other. If Sandy had been there she would have recognized that I was beginning to lose my temper. She would have calmed me down and taken the lead. But she wasn't there. All I could do was think of what she would do and try to calm myself. I stopped pacing and took several deep, slow breaths. It didn't help.

The glass door opened suddenly, and Jeremy Hillsdale was brought in. He looked . . . Terrible is the only word I can use to describe him. He was in the same clothes he had been in for a couple of days. They were wrinkled, and his expensive suit had to have been ruined; it was torn at his right shoulder and frayed where the shackles had been fastened around his waist. The fly on his pants was open exposing his tidy whitey underwear.

His arms were chained at the wrist with heavy shackles, and the chains were fastened to a thick leather belt at his waist, keeping his arms held straight down at his sides. His hair was an uncombed mess; he had a growth of beard starting. His eyes had heavy dark circles under them, and they were red, probably from overnight tears and deprived sleep.

Peter and I stood as he entered the room. Two men, big and as mean looking as the FBI could manage to find, held Jeremy by his arms.

Peter ordered, "Take the chains off."

"Sorry, but . . ."

"Take the damn chains off while I speak with my client!" he spoke with a fierce voice, that of a threatening lion. I was impressed, and even I was just a little frightened by his voice. I could only imagine what that voice would do in a courtroom, in front of a jury.

The two men looked at each other and then started unlocking the chains and unfastening the thick belt. When they were off of Jeremy, Peter pulled a chair at his right from the table and told him to sit. He turned back to the two men and told them they could leave.

When we were alone in the conference room with the door closed Peter and I sat. We all had our backs to the glass wall. Jeremy put his hands to his face and started to cry.

I'm not good at saying the right thing to people who are sick or who are crying. I have a really hard time visiting people in the hospital. I always seem to say the wrong things. But I started to say something anyway. Peter stopped me and shook his head. He whispered, "Let him get it out."

When the tears ended, Jeremy lowered his hands and turned sideways to look at us. He started to say something, but Peter stopped him. He said, "When you speak, don't turn to look at us. Look at the wall in front of you. Speak softly, no loud words. They are watching outside."

Jeremy looked at the blank wall and whispered, "What the hell's going on? Why am I here?"

Peter elbowed me and nodded without turning to me. I took it to mean that I was to take the lead. So I said, speaking as softly as I could, and looking straight ahead, "There was a death at the campus, Jeremy. They want to know why the security was so soft."

"But . . . But . . ." He turned his head toward me but was stopped by Peter's hand on his arm. He faced the wall again and said, "I had nothing to do with that, Morgan. I had nothing to do with that."

"Jeremy," I said, trying to be consoling. "You are the boss out there. You owned the company before merging with Crew Enterprises. You are in charge."

"But I had nothing to do with security," Jeremy pleaded. He started to raise his voice in frustration, but Peter laid his hand on Jeremy's arm, gently this time. Jeremy whispered again, "Damn it, Morgan. I have people who work there who do the day to day stuff. I didn't set up the security."

"You had to approve the plan at some point along the way," I said. "Whoever did the plan had to have you OK it."

Now, if I had been in Jeremy's place at Hillsdale I would have done things differently than Jeremy would. I would have people do stuff while I played golf or went fishing. But that is me. Jeremy is nothing like me. I was told he had inherited the company from his father, and people told me he felt a familial responsibility to keep the company in good shape. I knew he had a Harvard education, and I found out years after first meeting him that he had an impressive MBA, I think from Wharton School of Business. His knowledge of business was prodigious. I remember those annual meetings that I was forced to attend, and I tried to stay awake while businessmen and accountants and lawyers droned on. Jeremy spoke for hours, and I understood very little of what he said, but it all sounded good, even if it was putting me to sleep.

"Morgan, I work seven days a week from morning to late into the night. I have so much on my plate that . . . Christ, my marriage is failing. You have no idea what it's like to run a company that big. I live on an airplane . . . I sleep maybe four or five hours a night . . . The Federal Government is always on my back . . . There's always auditors and inspectors, and the damn military is always sending Colonels and Generals out to bug me. I haven't been to a birthday party for any of my kids in years. If I can lay something less important off on someone else, then I will."

I understood all of that; what he said is the reason I stay as uninvolved in Crew Enterprises as I can. But Jeremy, I always thought anyway, was a better man than me. He was smart and knew things I would never know.

It seemed logical that I ask another question. "What have the Feds asked you? What have you told them?"

"Jesus, Morgan. I told them over and over again what I told you. I had nothing to do with the security."

"What did they ask you?" I repeated.

"They were tough, Morgan. They kept me awake all night, one person after another. They kept asking over and over again why I intentionally made the security so easy to breach. They accused me of wanting that security guard killed. They tried to make me say I had some personal relationship with the dead guy. They wouldn't let me sleep;

they didn't give me any water, nothing."

It was senseless to go on talking about Jeremy's failures. The Government was close to cancelling hundreds of millions of dollars of contracts. Hillsdale Technologies would fail. Jeremy would be a failure. His family would leave him, certainly. And the Crew family would lose. Hillsdale was not the only Crew Company with Government contracts. The Government would certainly examine those companies closely. Over a billion dollars was potentially at stake.

But, the thought occurred to me, all that had happened was a murder. There was no evidence of anything else happening. At least no one would tell me something else happened. No one could find anything missing. I took a deep breath and sighed loudly in desperation. It was up to me as it always is.

I turned to Peter, ignoring the fact that someone outside could see me speaking and said, "I need to go to the Hillsdale campus. What will happen to Jeremy?"

Peter stood and went to the door. He opened it and found that the two men who had brought Jeremy to us were still there. Peter told them, "I want to see someone with some authority."

He closed the door before either of the men could reply. Through the glass we saw one of them nod to the other, and that man walked away leaving the bigger of the two alone and staring back at us. We turned and waited without speaking, our backs to the glass wall, until Agent Carter walked into the room.

"What is it?" he asked heatedly. "Are you done with him?"

Peter stood once again, turned slowly, very

dramatically, and stepped very close to Carter, less than a foot away. He said, "Is my client under arrest?"

"No," Carter answered. "But he's going to stay here for further questioning."

"No, he isn't," Peter said. He picked up his attaché and said, "I have instructed my client to not talk to you or anyone else. If there are no charges against him, he's coming with me. I'll examine the possibility of torture charges and false arrest later."

We three walked out of the glass walled conference room past a fuming Agent Carter who grudgingly stepped aside for us. Without anyone's help, we found the elevators. Carter and the two guards followed us at a discreet distance. At the ground floor I expected a half dozen armed Federal Agents to be waiting, guns and rifles raised, who would shoot three escaping prisoners. But all we were greeted with was a fairly busy lobby. Uniformed guards looked at Jeremy closely and suspiciously because of his wrinkled clothes and general ragged condition.

As we walked I told Jeremy, "Close your fly."

Federal Plaza was crowded with lawyers and bureaucrats and people on their way to fill out reams of paper to comply with all the Federal laws and regulations that burden businesses and people alike. Some would argue with the Federal Government; a few others would try bribes. Most would just do what was required.

We weaved our way through the crowd to the curb, hoping to find a taxi. At the curb we saw a very long and very black stretch limo, its windows blackened, the motor running, parked at a red curb in front of a fire hydrant. We started to walk past it when the back door opened. The Homeland Security official I had met earlier, Ms. Donna Evans, was sitting there. "Get in Mr. Crew, please. We have places to go and things to talk about."

I looked at Peter, wondering what the hell I should do. He told me, "Go on, Morgan. You need to clear all this up. I'll take care of Jeremy."

FIVE - Instituto de Inteligencia Militar

Jesse Wilson, Mohamed Al-Rashid, and Tamara Jackson were in the conference room, sitting at the round table. The table was big and made of a beautifully ornate and polished wood. There were eight tall backed, brown leather chairs surrounding the table. The room was cool in the Caribbean summer heat, and a glass pitcher of a sweet, fruity drink was nearby. None of the three touched it; they had too much on their minds and too much to talk about.

Mohamed was speaking. His voice was low, making the heavily accented words even harder to understand, but Jesse and Tamara had listened to him often over the past years, and they knew what he was saying.

"It was a bad thing that the guard had to die," he said.

"It had to be . . ." Tamara started in her own defense.

Jesse took her hand in his and smiled kindly at the young woman. "It wasn't your fault, Tamara," he said. He turned to look at Mohamed and said, "It was just chance, bad luck, Mohamed. Tamara could not have known the guard would be there."

"That is all very true," Mohamed said, a sadness in his voice now. "But now they know we were there, and the police have called in the F.B.I. That is bad."

"We have what we wanted," Jesse argued. "Tamara

got the plans we wanted."

Mohamed looked towards the ceiling and said, "By the grace of Allah, all praise be to him, we have the plans. Many lives of our warriors will be saved. This Firebird Guidance will now work for us. We will misdirect the drones and bombs of the hated United States."

"Then what's the problem?" Jesse asked. "Why are we here?"

"The F.B.I. has begun an investigation. It is but logic that the operating system will be changed now so that the operation plans we have will soon be . . . What is the word? . . . Obsolete? Is that the word?"

"Then we get the new plans," Tamara said. "I got in once; I can get in again."

"Yes, Tamara," Mohamed began, and he smiled kindly at the girl. "There is much work for you to do. But there is something that must be done first."

The three sat silently, Jesse and Tamara waiting for Mohamed to say something. Finally Jesse could not hold his patience any longer. He asked roughly, "OK, damn it! What the hell needs to be done first!"

"Allah . . . All praise be to him . . . Will forgive your speech because of the good work you do."

"OK . . . Good! . . . Now tell us what you want done."

Before Mohamed could say anything, the door to the conference room opened, and a man walked in. He was young, handsome, tall and well-built with strong arms. His skin was that of the Middle East and dark. He stood in front of the closed door and smiled, looking from one person to the next.

"Welcome Omar," Mohamed said.   "As-salaam

'alaykum."

"Peace be upon you, Mohamed my friend," Omar answered. He sat next to Mohamed and folded his arms across the table top, still smiling and looking back and forth from Jesse to Tamara.

Mohamed made the introductions. He did not know that Jesse and Omar had met a long time ago. They had worked together several times, Omar doing the killing that needed to be done. "This is Omar Maalouf. Omar will do what needs to be done."

Omar nodded to Jesse. The simple nod did not escape Mohamed's notice. 'No need for an explanation,' he thought. He had to maintain his authority, and asking questions would reveal he did not know a detail. He had to make them think he knew of their past work together.

Jesse and Tamara were silent, not knowing what was happening. Finally Jesse asked, "Tell us . . . What needs to be done . . . As you say."

"We must insure that the trail the F.B.I. will follow does not lead to us . . . And of course, to our friends here in Cuba. Omar will silence the people who have been of assistance to us."

"You mean kill someone?" Tamara asked. "I can do that."

"Yes you can . . . Of course you can, my dear girl," Mohamed said, smiling kindly at her once again. "But your task will be to bring to us the new operations once they are made. I cannot risk someone as talented as you are at thefts. Omar is a skilled killer, but he is not a thief. All praise be to Allah for bringing such people to us."

****

Omar drove the nondescript Ford through the streets of Buffalo, not too fast and not too slow, so as not to draw attention to himself. He turned on the street he was looking for and slowed as the sign at the corner said the speed limit in the neighborhood was 25 MPH.

It was a nice neighborhood, a very nice one in fact, Omar thought. So different from the rough brown stone of his own crumbling home in the dry desert of Syria. There was green all around, thick grass and trees and flowers. And the streets were clean and lined with tall street lights. He shook his head in disgust at the obscene wealth Americans enjoyed while his own people suffered.

He found the house he was looking for. It was big and well kept. He rolled down the window of the car and took a deep breath. The air smelled clean and fresh; so unlike what he had left behind when he joined the ranks of Al Qaeda so many years ago.

He drove past the house without slowing and drove as anyone would in that neighborhood until he found a McDonalds. He would wait there, drinking the pitiful coffee – so unlike the strong bitter brew he had grown up on. He would wait for the sun to go down and for people to be relaxed in front of their televisions.

It was time finally. Omar drove the car and parked in the block behind the house. No one was in the street, and street lights were far enough apart to allow some darkness where he stood when he got out of the car. He slipped on the thin, black lambskin gloves that he always used when killing people close-up. Quickly, he ran between two houses, deftly jumped a white picket fence, and slowed as he approached the house. Keeping to the shadows, he saw through a wide window the woman in the kitchen at her sink.

There was a darkened window next to the kitchen, a room with no light on inside. He went to it, and using the thin bladed knife he carried, he opened it. Inside he found a small bathroom, its door open and light from the hallway passing by the open door. He could hear voices; a man and a woman. And there was the voice of a boy arguing about doing homework. But the woman was alone in the kitchen. He stepped into the hallway and moved as silently as a cat to the woman whose back was to him.

Omar's hand went over her mouth as he dragged her backwards. With a quick snap her neck was broken. He slowly and quietly lowered her to the floor. He stepped to the side of the doorway from the kitchen and waited.

"Hey, Hon. Would you come here and help Stevie with this damn French?" a man called. There was no answer, and he repeated, "Hon, did you hear? Can you come help Stevie?"

Omar pressed himself against the kitchen wall. The man came into the room. "Hon, where are . . ." The words were cut off when Omar's arm went around the man's throat. He pulled the man back, out of the doorway. The man gasped before his neck was snapped.

The boy called out, "What the heck, Mom. I'm gonna' be up all night if you don't help me with this."

Omar waited. The boy started for the kitchen. "What the heck's goin' on?" He stopped short as Omar stepped away from the wall.

"Boy." Omar said. "Boy you come here to me."

The boy looked down at the bodies of his parents. He wanted to scream, but his throat and his fear wouldn't let the sounds out. Omar grabbed the boy's shirt collar and pulled the teenager to him.

"Tell me who else is in the house, boy . . . Tell me and I will not hurt you."

"My . . . My sister . . . My brother . . . Who are you . . ."

"Where?"

"My mom and dad . . . Who are you?"

"Where?" Omar repeated.

"Upstairs . . . Let go of me, damn you!" the boy cried, trying to pull away from Omar's grip, as Omar snapped the boy's thin neck. He let the boy slip to the floor.

Omar turned away and without making a sound climbed the stairs. Lights shown from a room with an open door and from another room, under a closed door. He clung to the hallway's wall as he inched toward the room with the open door. Inside a young boy lay stretched out on his bed, playing with a game-boy toy. The boy looked up as Omar pulled him from the bed and slashed across the boy's throat with is hand, breaking the boy's wind pipe. Omar covered the boy's mouth to stifle any sound the dying boy might make.

He then left the room and stood outside the room with the closed door. He whispered, "Little girl . . . Little girl . . . Come out, little girl."

"Who are you?" a child's voice stammered. "Billy, is that you? You're scaring me."

"Come out little girl," Omar said again.

The door opened, and Omar's hand closed like a vice around the child's thin neck. He squeezed until he heard the child's bones crack. He laid the dead girl on her bed and left the house.

****

Three days later Omar was back in the conference room with Mohamed and Jesse. Tamara was not with them.

"They are dead?" Mohamed asked.

"Of course. Why do you ask?" Omar answered, feeling insulted that Mohamed, someone, anyone would question him.

"And of the other?"

"I could not find him. I think he may be in hiding. But there is another problem," Omar said. He straightened himself up in his chair, cleared his throat, and said, "There is a man . . . Someone I have read about . . . This man could be dangerous to us."

Jesse asked, "Who is he? What's his name?"

"He is Morgan Crew," Omar answered. "He owns Hillsdale Technologies. He is now involved in what Tamara did."

"Can he be eliminated?" Mohamed asked.

"Many others have tried, my brother. They have all failed. It will not be impossible . . . Just very difficult."

Mohamed and Jesse looked at each other. Jesse had read about Morgan in newspapers. He told Mohamed, "He's very dangerous."

Mohamed nodded, thought for a moment, and then asked Omar, "What of the girl?"

"I will have her soon, my brother."

"Good."

SIX - I'm In Charge Now

I stood on the sidewalk in front of the Jacob K. Javits Federal Office Building and watched Peter and Jeremy walk away. Donna Evans was waiting inside the limo, its door open for me. All I really wanted to do was to go home and pick up where I had left off, sitting in the sun on the deck, drinking cold beer. But I knew I didn't have a choice. So I climbed into the back seat of Donna Evans' limo as Peter and Jeremy walked away. Jeremy turned once to look over his shoulder at us, obviously worried about what would happen to him.

Inside the limo was dark as night with only two small lamps in the roof casting just enough light to make everything grey but visible. Ms. Evans looked even older in the dim light, the shadows emphasizing her face's wrinkles, puffiness, and age. And her unblinking stare was even creepier.

The rear of the limo was big, very big. I had been raised on stretch limos, so I knew there was a fold-down jump seat at the back of the front seat. Rather than sit next to Ms. Evans, I pulled the jump-seat down and sat. The driver turned his head ever so slightly and said, "Please buckle up sir."

I buckled the seat belt around me and looked for the bottles of booze that had been in every limo I had ever been in. Usually, there is a small bar between the jump-seats. There wasn't any booze in that limo. There was a long console on my right, stretching from me towards Ms. Evans. It held two computer screens pointed at her, a couple of keyboards, four telephones – each a different color – and two cellphones resting in chargers.

I flicked my thumb at the array of electronics and asked Ms. Evans, "You afraid of being out of touch with someone?"

She forced a little, very short laugh. Her frown and downturned eyes told me she wasn't used to laughing, and it hurt when she did laugh.

"We need to go up to Hillsdale, Mr. Crew."

"Why?" I asked. "Why are you so interested? I mean, I don't want to talk bad about the dead, but he was just a low level security guard. What could that possibly have to do with Homeland Security?"

"We've picked up some chatter," she said. She looked to her left and pushed a button on the edge of the console. Behind me a thick black metal screen rose and cut us off from the limo driver. I guessed limo drivers, even if they were Federal employees and probably carried a gun or two, weren't supposed to hear everything.

"Chatter?" I asked. "What the hell is chatter?"

She pushed another button and heavy black curtains rose up at the windows all around us and behind Ms. Evans. Two more small lights in the ceiling came on, working with the first two to wash away some, but not all, of the blackness. I heard a very faint buzzing coming from everywhere around me. Evans saw that I had heard it and said, almost as if explaining something everyone should know, "It's called 'Black Noise.' It and the curtains keep sound in and eavesdroppers out."

OK, so I was impressed. I decided I needed a car like

that. I made a mental note to go shopping when I got back to San Marcos. Arriving at the Country Club in a limo like that would make for a lot of gossip that I would enjoy to the fullest.

"We can talk now," she said. "There is some information that the guard was killed during a break-in at Hillsdale."

"Information," I asked. "Like what? I mean, what makes you think the guard was killed during a break-in? Other than the paint chipped off of a couple of screws, you don't have any evidence of a break-in. By the way, that's not much of a clue. That could have happened during routine maintenance. And how about the other guards? Any of them have crappy backgrounds?"

"All that has been investigated, Mr. Crew," she said; her eerie stare with different colored eyes remained unblinking.

"So then what the hell is it? If not a simple murder . . . Then what? What information do you have?"

"We have something else that may be associated with the murder."

"I hate to repeat myself . . . But I will, until I get an answer. What information? From what source?"

"Sorry, but the source is way above your clearance level, Mr. Crew."

"So you've been spying on everybody all over the world, and you may have finally turned up something of value?" I said sarcastically. "I guess I should be grateful that the billions of tax dollars you spend finally did something good?"

She tried to smile once again but did not tear her unblinking eyes away from mine. Ms. Evans, apparently, was able to stare for long periods of time without blinking. Those blue and green eyes were creepy. I began wondering if Homeland Security had finally invented a human-like robot.

She chose to ignore my snide comment and said, "We think that something may have been compromised."

"Like what?"

"I can't tell you that."

"So why am I here?"

"I need your help, Mr. Crew."

That, of course didn't make sense to me. What could I do for Homeland Security except pay more taxes this year than I did last year? So I asked, "You can't tell me anything, but you need my help? I assume you're looking for something, and you want me to help you look for it. But if I don't know what we're looking for, how am I going to find it for you? That doesn't make sense."

"We aren't quite ready to pull the Federal contracts from Hillsdale," she said almost as a threat. "If I go to the FISA Court for a warrant to search Hillsdale, others in the Government, especially the military and Congress, will know, and they will be worried. They will want the contracts pulled, at least temporarily. I want you to help me look around at Hillsdale."

I tried an experiment. I pulled my gaze from her and looked around inside the limo. I figured that if I tore my stare away from hers and looked around I might find a bottle of bourbon hidden somewhere. I didn't. But I did wait long enough for Evans to say something.

"I can easily get a warrant at this point. If that's what you prefer, just say so. I really don't care. I really don't care if your company shuts its doors."

"I'm supposed to find evidence of a theft? I have no idea what it is you're looking at having been stolen. I mean was it money? I doubt it. Then it must be some secret stuff that I know nothing about. I'm supposed to help you hunt down some James Bond character? You're kidding, right? Look, I play golf . . . I go fishing . . . I like my bourbon . . . I take care of my wife and daughter . . . That's all I do. Tell me please, just what the hell do you expect me to do."

All Evans did was grin a little and continue to stare at me. The Limo was moving, not very fast yet because, although I couldn't see outside I could sense, due to the stopping and starting and corners turned, that we were still in the City. I could have just jumped out, but without being able to see outside the limo I might have jumped in front of a bus or truck. We were making some more turns, stopping and starting less, and we gradually started going faster. I asked her, "Where are we going? I really want to get out and go home."

"We're going to the airport, Mr. Crew."

"The airport! What the hell! Am I being kidnapped?"

Ms. Evans would play a good game of poker. Her facial expression didn't change. She didn't blink those damned annoying eyes of hers. And she didn't say anything. I got tired of her forced little grin and stare. My hand went to the door handle; I was going to take my chances and jump from the limo before it was too late. I pulled on the handle, but the door was locked. She didn't move or smile. I guess I should have seen that one coming. I'd seen the same thing in the movies and on TV. It seems I was trapped.

So I sat back on the small jump seat, folding my arms across my chest. I figured the best fight I could make at the time was to go into a staring contest with the woman. We'd see, I thought, who would blink first.

As it turned out, I lost after only a minute or less. We drove on while I checked my watch frequently. Fifty minutes went by while Ms. Evans continued her unblinking stare at me. Finally the limo came to a stop. The back door locks clicked loudly, and the two rear doors opened all on their own. I jumped from the limo as fast as I could, but there was nowhere to run. We had arrived at a small airport. There was a highway sign on the road. We were in New Jersey. I stood, looking around as Ms. Evans slowly stepped from the car. She started walking toward a black Huey Helicopter.

The limo driver climbed from the driver's seat, walked around the car, and stood next to me. "Go with her," he said. The driver stood about six foot six inches tall, and he held a really big, mean looking gun in his right hand.

He was meant to be intimidating, and he was doing a very good job at it. But I couldn't let him know that, so I asked, "You gonna' shoot me?"

"Maybe just a painful wound, Mr. Crew. You know . . . Your knee . . . Or maybe your balls. Nothing that'll kill you . . . Just change your life a little, ya' know? Now why don't you just be nice and go with her? Nothing is going to happen to you. She just wants you to help."

With that good advice I started to follow Ms. Evans to the Huey. She was sitting inside by the time I got there. One of the pilots helped me climb into the helicopter, assistance that Ms. Evans didn't seem to need. She was buckled in, so I sat next to her and buckled myself in, too. No sense falling out of an airborne chopper.

The flight to Buffalo was noisy. The earphones I put on did little to help. The helicopter rattled my insides to the point of my tossing my cookies. I didn't, but I was very grateful when we landed in the almost empty parking lot at

Hillsdale Technologies.

The warmth of summer seemed not to have hit Hillsdale yet. The air was cool, and the blue sky had been hidden behind black clouds that day. The thought came to me that the black clouds might have been a warning of what was ahead of me. Black clouds often follow me when I'm getting into something I shouldn't get into. I'm sometimes superstitious like that.

And I often hear a little voice in the back of my head start yelling, "Run away! Run away!" when I am close to trouble. I heard that little voice screaming as I stepped off the chopper, but I had nowhere to go. When both Ms. Evans and I were out, bending low to avoid the spinning blades, and standing on the ground, the blades of the copter came to a slow stop and the engine died. The quiet was what I noticed. Not even a bird in a tree was chirping.

Evans started toward the entrance gate to the Hillsdale campus. I followed her, three or four steps behind. Once or twice I looked behind me to see if someone with a gun was behind me, taking aim at the back of my head. All I saw were the two pilots standing next to the quiet helicopter. But with all the spies and spooks Evans must work with, I couldn't be sure someone wasn't hiding somewhere in the surrounding trees ready to take me out.

The tall chain link entrance gate was closed, chained and padlocked, reinforcing the electronic lock. A uniformed guard was standing inside the closed gate, watching us as we approached. Evans stopped at the gate and showed the guard her Homeland Security ID.

"Sorry," the guard said. "Unless you have a warrant, you'll need prior approval to come in."

The guard was not a young cop wanna'-be. He was older, heavy in muscle, and had the bearing of a retired cop.

Gray hair edged out from the rim of his dark blue baseball type cap. And he wore a gun at his waist. The security company had replaced all their guards with ex-cops and retired law enforcement. He knew what he was doing, and he wasn't going to let anyone intimidate him. Ms. Evans didn't try to throw her political weight around. She turned to me, handed me a cell phone she took from her purse, and said, "Phone someone. We need to get inside."

I took the phone and dialed in the only number I could think of.

"Hi," I said when the phone was answered. "This is Morgan Crew. I need to speak with Peter Jascro, please."

When Peter came to the phone I told him, "I'm at Hillsdale, believe it or not. This Evans lady wants us to get inside. The gates are locked, and we can't get in. There's this big guard who won't open the gate. What can you do about that?"

Peter hung up without a word, and we waited. It surprised me when Ms. Evans pulled a pack of Marlboros from her purse and lit one. She didn't offer me one; I would have turned it down anyway. She surprised me again when she said, "I know you don't smoke. Your wife would give you hell if she knew you were smoking."

I thought, 'What the hell else does she know about me?'

The black clouds thickened, and it started to shower ever so lightly. But neither the guard, still standing at the locked gate, his right hand on his holstered pistol, nor Ms. Evans seemed to notice. By the time she had finished her cigarette, the phone inside the guard shack started ringing. The guard turned slowly and walked even slower to the little wooden building. He went inside and picked up the black phone with the curled wire hanging from it. He listened for a minute or two and then came back to us and asked me, "Are you Morgan Crew?"

I said I was, and he asked for a photo ID. I flipped open my wallet and showed him my California Driver's License. He said, "Please remove it from your wallet, and hand it to me through the gate."

I did as he told me. He took it and looked at it very closely. He examined the front and the sides. He looked for telltale evidence of a recent lamination. He looked at the back and then at the front again. He held the license up and compared the picture to me. He seemed satisfied that I was who I said I was, and I was happy that such good security existed when a Homeland Security Official was there to witness it. I guess I wished the same security had always been there. If it had, I would be home in the sun, playing golf or watching my daughter play, or drinking a cold beer, or doing anything else except dealing with Ms. Evans. I turned and looked at her; that same pasted on smile was there. There was no recognition that security at Hillsdale had been upgraded.

The guard handed my license back to me through the chain link fence. He chose a key on a ring with a dozen more keys on it and unlocked the padlock. He took it and the chain and hung them loosely on the chain link fence. He said nothing as he turned and slowly, almost too deliberately, walked back to the guard shack. Inside he did what he had to do to open the electronic lock, and the gate slid sideways, slowly, on tracks. He was able to control it so that it opened just enough, not more than two feet, for me to walk through if I stepped sideways. When I was through, he quickly closed the gate before Ms. Evans could walk through.

"She's with me!" I told him, calling out loudly so that he could hear me.

He stepped from the guard shack and said, "You'll have to sign for her, Mr. Crew. Come over here please."

I left the woman standing outside in the light rain as I walked to the guard and into his little guard house. I felt good being in charge for a change, making Evans wait in the rain for me rather than her ordering me around. The thought occurred to me that if I refused to sign for her, she might just go away. But I knew that wouldn't happen. She was there for a purpose that was very important to her, and nothing I could do would dissuade her.

The guard searched for a paper in his filing cabinet and finally found it. He filled in some blank spaces and then handed me a well-used plastic ballpoint pen. "Fill in her name and agency here," he said pointing to a line on the form. When I had done that he then pointed to a line at the bottom of the page and said, "Sign your full name here, please." I signed without bothering to read the form. What the hell, I probably wasn't signing over ownership of everything I had. After the guard took the paper and put it inside a drawer, locking the drawer, I thought that maybe I had given them permission to shoot me if they were bored or if they just felt they wanted to.

Looking out the window I saw Evans still standing where we had left her, immobile as a statue. She was wet, but she didn't seem to mind. I waited in the shelter of the guard shack and watched as he pushed some buttons on a control panel to open the gate to let her in. Again, he opened the gate just enough for her to squeeze through and closed it quickly behind her. She walked past the guard shack without looking at me as I stood inside, out of the rain.

Inside the surrounding tall chain link fence, the several buildings were all encircled by concrete walkways through very green lawn. A few trees and some shrubbery had been well placed by landscape designers. A rock waterfall gurgled to the left, falling into a small rock encircled pool; a few park-like benches surrounded it on three sides. Two concrete cylinders filled with sand and cigarette butts stood near the benches telling me that was where smokers went to light one up.   On the opposite side of the guard shack were a few parking spaces with signs on metal poles identifying them for Hillsdale executives.

It was a very attractive place in which, I imagined, some not very nice things were developed for our military.

Twenty or thirty yards away were the glass doors at the front of the Administration Building. A red tiled roof hung over the doors, big enough to protect people from the weather as they stood waiting to get into the administration building.

It was Friday, not quite three in the afternoon, and it was dark inside the building. I hadn't noticed when the helicopter landed, but the big parking lot was empty except for a few old cars, probably belonging to the security staff. No one was working that afternoon. My first thought was that the Feds had shut the place down. I made up my mind to tell Peter as soon as I could get a few minutes alone. I was angry . . . If in fact the Feds had shut Hillsdale down without any evidence of a compromised situation, I would insist on court action to order the place be allowed to reopen.

Ms. Evans stood under the roof at the glass doors, looked right, then left, and then right again. She turned and waived to me to come to her. I didn't want to walk out into the rain, but I did. It wasn't raining terribly hard, but it was raining enough to get me wet as I ran to the doors. I skidded to a stop on the wet concrete, almost falling on my ass, as I reached the front door. Evans stood stoically, drenched, but she didn't seem to notice.

I stood next to her, waiting for her to say something. The dark grey clouds were obscuring any blue the sky might have to offer, and the rain intensified. The darkness of the afternoon rain caused the security lights to come on suddenly. Ms. Evans looked around, and I noticed that same, very annoying little grin was plastered on her face. I thought maybe she might have had some surgery to affix her thin lips in that position.

"Look around," she said. "If you had to get in . . . How would you do it?"

So I looked around, trying to stay under the protecting little roof. I shivered in the damp cold, but it only took me a moment or two to figure it out. The lights, the remoteness, the fact that the guard house was a distance away, the far corner to our right, the cameras that turned away from each other . . . That was the place I would choose. I told her, "Over there . . . That corner."

"That's good, Mr. Crew," she said.

"If that's all you want can we please get out of the damn rain?"

She turned to look at me, nodded, and put her hand on the handle of the glass door. The door was locked, of course. The keypad lock was at the right of the doors.

"Can you open the door?" she asked.

"I've never been here before," I said. A cold wind started to blow rain sideways on us as we stood under the small roof. I pressed myself against the glass for some shelter. Ms. Evans just stood there, getting wet as the wind continued to blow the rain sideways, under the little roof; I guessed she was just ignoring the rain.

She reached into her purse and pulled her iPhone from it. "Phone someone," she commanded.

The only person I could think of, again, was Peter Jascro. I phoned him on his private, direct number and walked away from Ms. Evans, into the rain so she couldn't hear.

"Hello Peter. This is Morgan."

"Where are you?"

"I'm still at Hillsdale," I said. "In the friggin' rain. If I come down with pneumonia I'm gonna' damn well sue somebody. Do you know what's going on?"

"About as much as you do. Look, we're busting our butts trying to calm the Feds. If they pull all the contracts, which they may do any minute now, Hillsdale will file bankruptcy. I know that means very little to you . . . But to the rest of your family, it means a lot. Once the media gets this, the Crew Enterprises stock will plummet."

"So what the hell do I do?"

"Do what they tell you to do for the time being. Be nice and no wise cracks, please. Keep everyone happy. Anything else?"

"Yeah, do you know why Hillsdale is shut down? Have the Feds shut it down? The place is dark, and no one is here."

"I'll look into it. I haven't received any notices from anyone. Anything else?"

"Is Jeremy still with you?"

"Yes, he's sleeping on a couch in a vacant office. Why?"

"Keep him there. Don't let him leave. You probably know he shouldn't be talking to anyone." I said. "Wake him up now and get the code to open the front doors of the Admin Building. I'll wait."

I looked at my watch and paced around in a circle in the rain. I pulled my jacket over my head but that did nothing more than ruin my jacket. Ms. Evans had not moved from the front doors. She seemed frozen as she gazed at the glass and the dark room beyond. I remember thinking at the time that this middle aged woman could very well be mentally unbalanced. I resolved to watch her closely and to be very careful and wary of her, not because she was with Homeland Security but because she might be crazy.

Peter came back on the line and told me the six numbers that would unlock the front doors. They surprised me and gave me an indication of the level of security at Hillsdale. The numbers were 6 5 4 3 2 1! "Jeremy wants to go home," he added.

"No. Keep him there. I need to talk to him, and I don't know how long I'll be here. Keep him overnight if you have to, but don't let him leave your office. Don't let anyone talk to him. And although this may sound crazy . . . I just have a gut feeling, don't let anyone hurt him. Put some armed security on him."

I went back to Ms. Evans who hadn't moved at all. I punched in the numbers without telling her what they were, standing so that she could not see what I punched in and blocking the key pad with my left hand. I pulled one of the doors open and stood aside for her to walk in past me. There was no alarm sounding at the opening of the door. Evans looked at me, silently questioning why. I said, like I knew the answer, "The code to open the door is Jeremy's. It overrides the alarm system." I had no idea of the real reason, but it sounded good.

We were finally able to get in, out of the rain. Standing in the marbled entry, she didn't look at me as she said almost as if talking to herself, "No, they wouldn't have gotten in this way. There must be another door."

She finally turned to look at me and asked, "Is there another door?"

"I don't know. I told you I've never been here before."

She looked to her left and then to her right. She started walking to her right, a hound dog following a scent, I imagined. I had no choice but to follow her. The hallway was dimly lit, and there wasn't a sound coming from anywhere, save for our wet shoes squeaking on the tile floor. Friday afternoon would normally be crowded and noisy with people hurrying to get their work done and go home for the weekend. It was eerie being in the darkened building knowing no one else was there, walking hallways without lights.

We left a trail of water dripping from us on the tiled floor as we turned a corner and came to the end of the hall. There was a door there, steel half way up and glass with wire encased in it on the top half. Ms. Evans pushed the handle, but the door was locked.

"This is it," she said. "Don't you think so, Mr. Crew?"

"Think what? What the hell do you mean?"

"This is where they got in. Don't you agree?"

"And what makes you think that?" I asked her. "You're assuming someone broke in. Is that what your 'chatter' told you?"

She turned to look up at me as she took another Marlboro from her purse and lit it. She inhaled deeply while her eyes locked on mine.

She explained, "I think that someone got in mainly because the dead guard was found inside this door and not outside. Get it? He was killed inside. That means the killer was inside. Add that to the fact that this door is the closest to the corner of the fence where we agree that someone could get onto the property in the shadows, without being seen. Look outside," she said, nodding to the glass at the door. "It's very dark out there at three in the afternoon. Imagine how dark it would be in the middle of the night. The security lights don't reach here. The guard at the gate wouldn't see anything here unless he was looking this way. The guard's wallet was in his pocket with $18.00 in it. His wristwatch was still on his wrist. It wasn't a robbery. The police found a text book with the body. We know he was at the main gate while the guard assigned to the gate ate his dinner. He was reading his book instead of keeping watch."

"Ok, so the guard was found inside and all that other stuff. But then you assume that whoever killed the guard got into the building through a locked door. It doesn't look like anyone broke the lock or smashed the door down. Could be whoever killed the guy was already in the building . . . An employee or something."

"No, it doesn't look like anyone smashed in, does it?" she said. "But . . . If someone had the code to open the door, it would be easy to get in, wouldn't it?"

"So . . . That would point to an employee again. Maybe someone was pissed off at the guy. Maybe the guy was screwing somebody's wife or girlfriend. So you're saying that some employee of Hillsdale climbed over a chain link fence topped with razor wire, used his or her code to open the locked door, and then killed a security guard. Why not just use the front door? Why not just come in as a regular employee?"

"Now *that* is a very good question, Mr. Crew. Why wouldn't a regular employee just come through the front door? The answer to that . . . To me anyway . . . Is twofold. First, there would be a record of an employee coming in through the entrance gate. There is no record. We know that from checking the computer record. Second, whoever came through this door was not a regular employee." She paused for a moment, long enough to take a deep cloud of cigarette smoke into her lungs and blow it out.

Then she said, "These locks are not just electronic. If an employee used their personal code to unlock the door, I'll bet your last million that there is some kind of record of who uses them. Or, on the other hand, as our forensic people found, the electronic keypad outside has been tampered with. Paint had been chipped off of a couple of the screws on the keypad box," she said not even looking at me as she spoke. "Let's eliminate one of those options. Let's go find a computer somewhere and have a look, shall we?"

"What the hell did you say?"

"I said let's go find a computer."

"Not that," I said. "Before that."

"You mean about betting your last million?"

"I've said that a million times," I said. "Where did you pick it up?"

"Mr. Crew . . . There's nothing about you that Homeland Security doesn't know. Now, let's go find a computer."

Now that frightened the hell out of me. I mean, all I've done . . . The people I've killed . . . The laws I've broken . . . It all flashed through my mind. My God! If they know all that, I could wind up in jail.

****

It was useless, of course. I had no choice. If I refused to do what she told me to do, the Sword of

Damocles would certainly fall on me. Donna Evans and I went from desk to desk, from computer to computer, but we could not get into the files we wanted, and most of the computers were password protected so we couldn't even get started on them. She started to chain smoke which told me she was getting nervous. I held back a knowing smile, because if she was getting nervous that meant I was finally getting the upper hand.

She had a job to do, and she couldn't fail. If she felt failure on her shoulder, she would turn to anything, anyone, desperately seeking help. She had started by ordering me to help. I stood aside and let her reach that point of desperation when I knew I could step in and tell her what to do.

It took less than an hour of trying every computer on two floors of the Admin Building. She finally slumped back in the chair she was in, and that look of anxiety and fear raced across her face. I had her.

I sat on the corner of the desk she was at. "Can I have a cigarette?" I asked.

She opened her purse and reached for her pack of Marlboros, stopping as it was halfway out of her purse. "Your wife wouldn't like this," she said.

"She's not here."

Evans looked up at me. That pasted on, robot-like expression she had been carrying had disappeared. She looked wondering at me, trying to reason out just what the hell I was doing. I was smiling, knowing I was now in control.

"You're testing me," the woman said. "The cigarette is a test. You want to know how far I will go to give you what you want. It's a stupid test, Morgan." It was the first time she had called me Morgan. "You know what you really want," she said. "Why not just tell me."

"OK," I began. I stood and took two steps away from the desk. I paced in a circle in front of the desk and Ms. Evans as I said, "You want to be assured that nothing was taken from here . . . Nothing that has any secretive value anyway. I want to be sure that the Government contracts are not pulled. I want Hillsdale to open up and go on with its work as soon as possible. Delays cost money. We can make an agreement here. I give you what you want, and you put a halt to anyone wanting to cancel Hillsdale's contracts. Plus, whatever you did to close this place today . . . I want it open and doing business Monday morning."

"And how do you do that, Morgan? How do you assure me nothing was stolen from here? I won't give you anything until I know you can give me what I want."

"Well, I won't go snooping around aimlessly, wasting time, like you're doing right now."

"That's what I'm doing?" she asked.

"Plain and simple . . . Yes. You may well be a lot of things, but you are certainly not a computer engineer. You've been typing anything that comes to mind into every computer you find and getting nothing back. I've seen computer people do stuff that's just amazing. Hell, my own daughter's nanny could do better than you're doing. You have no idea how to get what you need without a FISA court's warrant and a bunch of people trooping in here with the world's media close behind them. And if you do that and find nothing, and shut down Hillsdale as a result, you will have spent a great deal of time and money, and not made anyone happy. Your job will be in jeopardy. And I will bring legal action against you. You and a lot of other people will be dragged into court over and over again, for years to come. So it's time for the two of us to cooperate."

"And if I agree to cooperate with you, what else do you want?"

"I want freedom of movement," I began. "I want that idiot FBI Agent, Adam Carter, off my back. I want Jeremy Hillsdale free to help me. He stays out of jail and out of any holding facility . . . Including Gitmo. His interrogations are all over with. I want Hillsdale engineers in here with me to do what you can't do. And I don't want you looking over my shoulder limiting what I do and telling me what I can't do. And I want the media in the dark. No press releases, no news conferences. And no leaks, either."

"And how long will all this go on?" she asked.

"As long as it takes," I said. "You think something wrong happened here . . . I think nothing more than a murder happened here. When I find out which one of us is right it will all be over." I stopped pacing and stood in front of her. I looked her directly in her blue and green eyes as I said, "One other thing. If I ask you for anything . . . Classified or not . . . I get it."

"Within limits . . . I can agree to all that. But don't ask for anything that is not directly linked to this problem."

"Fine, let's get back to New York, then. I need a shower, some dry clothes, and some food."

****

The ride in the Huey was much worse going back to New York than it was going to Hillsdale Technologies. The light rain that had soaked Ms. Evans and me had turned into a storm that tossed the helicopter around violently. Once out of the mountains and south towards the city, the weather eased, and my stomach began to settle.

We made it back to the little airfield in Northern New Jersey without me tossing my cookies all over Ms. Evans' nice but soaking wet, motherly blue dress. Neither the rain nor the bumpy ride seemed to affect her, however. She just sat buckled into her seat and gazed into nothingness for the entire flight. Strange woman.

The stretch limo that had taken us from New York was waiting for us when the helicopter touched down. The ride back into Manhattan was without one word being spoken by anyone. I decided to sit once again in the fold-down jump seat rather than sit next to Donna. I don't think she even noticed. Her one green and one blue eye were focused on something that no one else could see.

The driver stopped at Peter's office building. The rear door unlocked and opened once again all without human intervention; I suspected the driver had punched some button up front. I got out as quickly as I could, and before I could shut the door, Ms. Evans said, "Don't screw this up, Morgan. We have a bargain. Get me results, or you won't like what will happen to you."

I ran into the lobby of the building. I shared the elevator with five other people who stood against the walls trying to avoid me. I guess I looked like some homeless street person, soaked from the rain and probably a bit smelly, too.

Peter didn't seem to mind what I looked like, but he did sniff a few times at my odor, I suspected that of a wet dog. He asked Maureen to bring hot coffee as soon as he saw me enter his office.

"My God, Morgan!" he said. "You look like you fell into a sewer."

"I feel like I did, too. Look, I need to speak with Jeremy. And I need to get a hotel room. Can Maureen fix me up with a good one?"

"No need for a hotel. The firm keeps a couple of apartments here, upstairs, for out of town clients. I'll have one stocked with food for you."

Maureen brought the silver coffee set into the room, and I drank three cups of the really good coffee very quickly. It did warm me a little, but it did nothing for my hunger. Steam was coming off of my wet clothes, but gradually they were drying. I was shivering when I first sat down; the coffee stopped that.

When I had finished the last cup Peter stood and said, "Come with me, and I'll show you where Jeremy is hiding. He's really scared you know."

As I followed Peter out of his office I said, "Well, he really should be. The Feds are hot on proving something very classified was stolen out there. I doubt there's anything they won't do to prove it. I think they know what end they want to all this. They're like sharks circling a drowning man."

"You're right, Morgan. They'll keep hounding everyone until they prove what they want proven," Peter said as we walked down a wide hallway.

"No, they won't do that," I said not able to hide my pride. I suppose the smirk on my face gave it all away.

Peter's hand on my shoulder stopped me in my tracks. He turned to look at me. He said, "Why not? What the hell did you do? These are tough people, Morgan. You don't want to mess around with them. They bend the law like a sapling in the wind."

I grinned like a kid knowing a sex secret. "I made a deal with them. They're going to leave us alone and let me find out if anything was stolen."

Peter grabbed both of my shoulders. I thought he might want to shake me like an unruly child. He said, "You did what?"

"I told you. I made a deal with Homeland Security. I check everything and find out if anything was stolen. In return, they are going to leave us alone."

"Morgan! I don't believe you! Are you totally insane?"

"I've been told I am," I said. "As I recall, you've told me that once or twice over the years. But it's the best chance we've got to save the company . . . And all that damn money that my stupid family will lose. I've done worse in the past, you know."

"I know. And you've almost gotten yourself killed in the past, too. You can't do this. Look, I'll tie them up in court for years until they lose interest in this. You don't have to do this."

"And while you're in court with them, Hillsdale Technologies loses all the contracts, shuts its doors, and the family takes a big hit. No, I have to do this. Why the hell did you have me come all the way here? You knew I was going to get involved, or you wouldn't have phoned me, right?"

"I thought you would just represent your family, that's all."

"Yeah," I said. "Represent . . . Like I always do . . . Right?"

"I had no intention of you getting yourself killed, Morgan. If some classified data was stolen, who could have done that but some kind of spy? Those people will kill you if they have to."

"OK," I said. "Leave it at that. Let's go see Jeremy."

****

Harper, Harper, Jascro and Nettles occupied the top seven floors of The Crossley Building in Manhattan, on Madison Avenue. The forty-five story building was tall enough that from any of the top seven floors, Central Park could be clearly seen. The top two floors had been converted to four grand apartments, two on each floor, and they were lavishly furnished for out of town clients of the firm to use.

Apartment #1, the larger of the two apartments on the forty-fifth floor was occupied that day by two executives from England, and they would be there for three more days. Jeremy Hillsdale was in apartment #2 on the forty-fourth floor. Maureen, Peter's secretary, wanted to take us up to the apartment, but I asked her not to. She didn't appear to like being told what to do, not just by me but any anyone. She had been in charge of the entire office for too many years, and she assumed everyone, even the Partners, would do what she told them to do. When she had turned and walked away in a huff, I explained to Peter, "The fewer witnesses the better." He nodded, understanding that some Federal Agency might be able to insist she tell them secrets they shouldn't know. Peter stepped in front of me as we got in the elevator.

The doors opened after the short ride up to the forty-fourth floor. We stepped out into a wide hallway, carpeted in a green and gold Asian pattern. The walls were muted tan with finely finished carpentry of expensive and rare woods from floor to ceiling. Large Asian paintings hung in just the right places, obviously placed there by a very good interior designer.

"I guess you've got a lot of Japanese clients," I said.

Peter simply answered, "Yes," as we walked into the hallway. "One in particular."

At one end of the hallway were elaborately carved, shiny red enameled, double doors that led to the apartment. We turned to the right and walked to the big doors with me a few steps behind Peter. He stopped at the doors, but before he could open it I said, "I want armed guards in the hallway, Peter. Twenty-four–seven. Not rent-a-cops. Get off duty NYPD cops or at least retired cops. And I want another one inside with Jeremy."

"You really think it's that bad?"

"I don't know yet. But it may be. It's cheap insurance anyway."

Inside Apartment #2 it was starkly different from the formal and grand Asian inspired hallway. It was like a New Orleans bordello I had seen in my younger years and I would not tell Sandy about. There were too bright colors everywhere. It was almost too much to take in when I first entered the place. The wall to my left was mirrored from floor to ceiling, with streaks of gold marbling running through the glass. Two very large and very cheap paintings of naked women, unusually extravagant in their physiques and painted on black velvet, hung on the mirrored wall. To the right was flame red wallpaper, flocked with gold embossed images of tall herons against bamboo. The floors were blue marble. Gaudy chandeliers of bright brass and fake crystal hung everywhere.

I turned to Peter and asked, "What the hell is this? Did your decorator come to work stoned or something?"

"Mr. Akane Kaori thinks this is beautiful. He spends a dozen weeks a year here with a half dozen women. We don't have anyone else use this apartment. No need to explain that. Mr. Kaori is worth many millions to the firm."

Jeremy came from one of the three bedrooms in the apartment. He was dressed in a short white silk kimono that didn't reach his knees. It was belted with a gold cord with very big gold tassels on the ends that hung below the length of the robe. His feet were bare. He looked rested, but he hadn't shaved yet. His hair was rumpled, and his eyes were red and puffy. I figured he hadn't yet gotten rid of all the tears.

"Morgan . . . Mr. Jascro," he said as he walked to us. "I want to go home. When can I go home?"

I waited for him to reach us rather than meet him halfway, and I didn't offer to shake his hand when he held his hand out to me. Whatever the cause, whoever was at fault, I was being put to a lot of trouble once again, this time to save Jeremy's sorry ass.

"You can't go home yet, Jeremy," I said. "We have things to do."

The doorbell rang behind us as we stood in the entryway. I stopped both Peter and Jeremy from going to the door. I went to it and looked through the peep-hole. One man was there, dressed in a blue overalls uniform. I called without opening the door, "Who are you? What do you want?"

"Delivery," a man answered. "You ordered groceries."

"Wait there," I said. I went to a telephone in the living room and asked Peter, "How do I get the reception desk?"

"Dial 3-3-3," he answered.

A woman answered; I asked, "I'm calling for Peter Jascro. Did you send a delivery person up just now?"

"Why, yes," she answered. "Is there a problem?"

I hung up and asked Peter again, "Who ordered the

groceries?"

"I told Maureen to take care of it."

I phoned her and asked, "What company was to deliver the groceries?"

"Mathew's Market," she answered.   "Is there a problem?"

I once again hung up without answering. At the door I looked through the peep-hole again. The man had a name patch under his left shoulder.   It read: 'MATHEW'S MARKET.'

I called through the door, "Thank you. Just leave the groceries there. I'll get them later."

"Yeah," the man said, a little aggravation in his voice, "I usually get a tip."

"Go down to reception six floors down at Harper, Harper, Jascro and Nettles. Ask for Maureen. Tell her Morgan Crew sent you. She'll give you your tip."

He left, and I watched as he entered the elevator and the doors closed. I counted to thirty and then opened the apartment doors to get the two bags of groceries. I emptied each bag onto the hallway floor, examining each box and bag, and each piece of vegetable and package of meat carefully. I didn't want any bombs hidden in the packages. Poisons would be a problem, but I thought without speaking it that I would let Jeremy eat first, and if he lived I would then eat.

When all that was done I carried the two bags into the apartment. As I walked past Peter and Jeremy, Jeremy asked, "What the hell, Morgan. What the hell are you doing?"

Peter asked, "Is it that bad, Morgan?"

"One person is dead," I said as I placed the groceries on a table in what I imagined, except for the unexplained and outlandishly cheap and garish furniture and decorations, was a dining room. "I don't want a second person to be dead. I have no idea what's going on here, Peter. Until I do, I'm not going to take any chances. If you want me to be responsible and represent the family, it has to be my way."

It took some stern and to the point words, but Jeremy finally understood that he was not going anywhere. Peter left the apartment to make arrangements for the armed guards. As he was walking away I stopped him and said, "I want you to personally check each one, Peter. Don't take any chances, OK?" Jeremy took the bags of groceries to the kitchen while I phoned Sandy.

"I guess I'm going to be here for a while," I told her. "There's a really wild apartment that one of Peter's Japanese clients uses. You wouldn't believe this place. Anyway, I'm staying here."

I gave her the direct phone number to the apartment. "Don't use my cell phone or the home phone. They're too easy to trace and track. Go to the club and use a phone there if you need to phone me."

She asked, "How long will you be there? Caroline is missing you already. And I'm missing you, too."

"Maybe a couple of days. I just have to find out what's going on out here. I'll make it as fast as I can."

"Just what is going on out there, Morgan?" Sandy asked. She and I have been together for a long time. She knows what my life is and the danger I place myself in every time someone asks.

There was no sense trying to lie to her or hold back on the truth. Sandy knows when I'm lying, so I said, "There's been a murder at one of the businesses. The Feds are involved. I just need to get a few answers, that's all."

"God, Morgan . . . Not again."

"Don't worry, babe. This won't take long, and I'll be careful. I managed to put myself in charge of a bunch of Federal cops who seem to want to do what I tell them to do. I'm in a good position, and they'll be there to protect me if that's necessary."

"Yeah, right," she said sarcastically. "Like always?"

SEVEN – Because I Said So

Now, I consider myself to be a good cook. I was raised in a house with servants who provided everything to me and my parents, including cooking and serving meals. I did spend a lot of time in the kitchen watching and talking to the staff. I learned a lot, but I got out of that environment as soon as I could.

On my own, at Yale, my best friend Bob Sommers and I ate a lot of pizza and burgers, along with a whole lot of beer. After I graduated, I spent a long year in Los Angeles working at one of the family's banks where I ate out almost all the time. Now, except for the meals I eat at the Country Club, I love to spend time in the kitchen at home cooking for Sandy and Caroline and Betsy. I can do a mean B-B-Q in the summer. And I can do some good stews and Italian pastas, and a lot of fancy French foods. So that night I found a couple of big, thick, T-bone steaks in the groceries that had been delivered, thank you to Maureen for that one.

The kitchen in the apartment had a big, eight burner gas stove with a grill on it, so on went the steaks. The smell of cooking prime beef quickly filled the room and caused my stomach to growl since it hadn't seen much food since the day before.

"I'm not very hungry," Jeremy said. He was sitting on a weird looking industrial metal chair at a glass top table watching me. His face was pale and drawn. If ever there was a sadder looking person, I had not seen him. And it was all too apparent that he had nothing at all on under the robe. The family jewels were exposed.

"That's OK," I said. "I'll eat yours if you can't. But you need to get something in your stomach. So I want you to eat something." I needed a food tester, but I wasn't going to tell him that. "You and I have a busy day tomorrow."

I had found a bottle of fairly good bourbon in a liquor cabinet, not my Wild Turkey 101 but good stuff anyway, and filled two glasses over ice. I finished mine and poured a second. Jeremy choked on his; I guess he wasn't a drinker. He laid the glass on the table in front of him and looked away from it. His hands were shaking. There were dark rings under his eyes from lack of sleep. I put the plate with the big steak on it in front of him and said, "Take a bite . . . Let me know if it's . . . Tough or tender," I said instead of 'poisoned.'

He cut a small piece and chewed on it. "What's tomorrow? What do you want me to do?" he asked while chewing. He was twirling his glass of bourbon and ice so fast that some of it spilled out. He seemed not to notice.

"We're going to go to the campus. And we're going to take a few computer experts of yours along. We're going to spend a pleasant day gazing hopefully at computer screens."

"Why?" Jeremy asked. I had opened a bottle of red wine, a label I didn't recognize, but I figure after two tall bourbons, how bad could it be?

"Take another bite of the steak, Jeremy," I said. My steak was sitting in front of me, waiting to see if Jeremy lived through enough of his. When he finished chewing on another piece of meat and seemed to have no ill effects, I cut into my steak, and red juices ran. I like my beef rare.

"Please, Morgan. Tell me why we have to go to the

office."

"Mainly because I said so, Jeremy," I said with a big chunk of meat in my mouth as I sat across the table from him. "I've made arrangements for you to stay out of jail until this whole mess is cleared up. So long as you do what I tell you to do, you won't be eating prison food or be some gorilla's wife. Look, I didn't get you into this fix, but I'm going to do my best to get you out. So, for the next day or two, you'll do what I tell you to do."

"Ok, Morgan. OK. Anything you say." He stared down at the charred meat but only reached for the wine. I cut into mine and relished it, nicely burnt on the outside and pink and juicy on the inside. My empty stomach said, 'thank you.'

After I had finished my steak and Jeremy had taken a few more bites of his own, I asked, "I need the names and phone numbers of two or three of your best computer guys. I figure you have to have top of the line people. I'm going to need them with us tomorrow."

I found some pale pink writing paper and a silver Monte Blanc pen at a small pale blue plastic writing desk in the living room. Jeremy gave me three names of managers who were also computer engineers, and I wrote them down, figuring Jeremy's hands were shaking so much I wouldn't be able to read what he wrote.

"I guess they'll know just about everything about the systems we run. But I don't know their contact information," he said.

It was in the late evening already that Friday. Too late to make phone calls or do much of anything else. It would have to wait until the next day. While we sat quietly at the table, without speaking, I finished the bottle of red wine and forced myself to stay away from the bourbon for the night. I knew I would need a clear head the next day.

Jeremy had taken only four bites of his steak, and I wasn't about to toss out prime meat that I didn't often get to enjoy at home. So I wrapped it in plastic and put it in the fridge, intending to enjoy it the next day.

Jeremy wandered off to the bedroom he was using. I didn't check, but I assumed he was either sleeping or crying some more. My trying to be comforting to him wouldn't help him, so I just left him alone.

I flopped down on a too soft bright blue leather couch in front of a sixty inch TV. I discovered that Mr. Akane Kaori liked his porn channels. Rather than waste time with that I decided on a west coast baseball game that put me to sleep quickly.

The phone rang, waking me. It was Maureen. "What the hell time is it?" I growled.

"Thirty-five minutes past eight, Mr. Crew," she said, adding, "Please don't use foul language with me."

"AM or PM?"

"It's the morning, of course, Mr. Crew," she said. "Are you alright?" I had slept the night away on the uncomfortable couch. My back and neck were sore, but some stretching would work that out.

"Yeah . . . I just woke up."

"I'm sorry," she said without sounding like she was sorry at all. She said, "I'm sending some clothes up for you and Mr. Hillsdale. I think the sizes are correct. They may be off here and there, but I think they'll do. Now, are you going to open the door for the two men who will be delivering them?"

"It's Saturday, right?" I asked, rubbing the sleep from

my eyes. "Who else is in the office with you?"

She paused for a moment; I assumed she was looking around. "Only a janitor," she said.

"Do you know him?" I asked. "Is he a regular employee?"

She paused for a moment and then said, "Why, yes. I've seen him before . . . Many times."

"Give the clothes to him and send him up. Send the delivery guys home. And stay by this phone for a few minutes."

"Alright, Mr. Crew. If you say so."

It took only ten or fifteen minutes for the doorbell to ring. I used the peep-hole and saw a short, older man with a protruding belly standing there with a cart full of boxes and bags from clothing stores. He was wearing a gray janitor's uniform. His hair was thick, greying, and roughly combed. And he was looking around the hallway like he had never seen anything like that place before.

I had taken the phone with me to the door, so I punched in Maureen's phone number.

"Tell me what your janitor looks like," I said.

"He is Carlos Arciba. He is about fifty years old, short, fat. His hair is greying but thick. He's been with us for . . . God, a long time."

I thanked her, told her to go home, and opened the door. Carlos smiled nervously and pushed the cart of boxes towards me. I took a twenty dollar bill from my money clip and handed it to him.

"Gracias," he stammered smiling broadly. "Gracias, Meester."

****

I found a second bedroom in the apartment that I hadn't known existed, next door to where Jeremy had spent the night. I intended to shower and change into clean clothes. I immediately knew why Jeremy had taken the other. The room was painted red and purple, the ceiling was one big mirror, and the bed was round and covered in bright pink satin. There were huge color photos of naked men and women plastered on every wall. On a small black table next to the bed was an assortment of prophylactics each wrapped in brightly colored cellophane. Lined up alongside of the condoms were several bottles of little purple pills whose purpose told me Mr. Akane Kaori had a difficult time getting it up.

I found the bathroom which was indescribably gaudy and obscene. But I showered in a bright, iridescent, blue tiled shower big enough for four or five people. I found a gold, jewel studded razor near one of the four sinks in the bathroom. I shaved and dressed and started to go find Jeremy to wake him. The phone rang. It was Maureen. "Good morning, Mr. Crew. I have a car waiting downstairs for you. The driver knows his way around. Have you had breakfast yet?"

"No to the breakfast and another no to the driver. Get a very ordinary car for me. Nothing flashy, gray or tan. I'll drive. And so long as you don't blab to my wife, bring up a plate of Danish and donuts. Bring it up yourself please." I figured I might as well live it up while I had the chance.

I made my way to the kitchen and found Jeremy sitting there, still in the kimono, hair still rumpled and still unshaven, and smelling really bad, too, gazing off into space. I don't know how long he had been awake or if he had slept at all, and I doubt he knew either. There was something wrong there; it was easy to recognize.

Oh, I could understand how upset and scared he would be if he were locked up in the cellar of the Justice Building, but he wasn't there. He was free . . . Sort of anyway. Something was hanging over his head. If Donna Evans was right, and he had insured lax security so someone could get in, and I could prove that, I would throw him to the wolves and to hell with the family's money. Maybe, I thought, that's what was worrying him. Maybe he was afraid of being caught.

I let him sit there while I made a pot of coffee. I made it extra strong because I had a feeling it would be a long day. When it was done brewing, I put a tall mug of it in front of him, but he just kept up his mesmerized stare.

"Jeremy . . . Jeremy! Can you hear me?" I asked, reaching across the table to shake him on his shoulder, trying to wake him from wherever he was. I considered slapping him across his face.

He looked up at me and said faintly, "Huh? What? Huh?"

"Are you OK, Jeremy?" I asked.

"Huh? What? Yeah."

"I need to talk to you, Jeremy. Can you hear me?"

"Yeah . . . Of course," he stammered. "What?"

"Drink some of the coffee, Jeremy. I need you awake."

He looked down at the big mug, grasped it in both hands and put it to his lips. It was hot, and he felt that. It seemed to shock him into some semblance of being awake. He took a small sip and then another. He looked up at me and tried to smile.

I told him, "I need you to phone your secretary or somebody. Someone who can go to your office and get the addresses for the computer people you named last night."

"Yeah . . . Sure . . . Anything you say, Morgan."

I brought the phone to Jeremy thinking he might not be able to walk to the phone. After three tries he did manage to dial his private secretary's home phone number. He told her who I am and that I wanted to speak with her. He handed the phone to me. I told her what I needed, and she said she would go to the office right away.

"What's going on, Mr. Crew?" she asked. "Everyone wants to know if Hillsdale Tech is going out of business."

"Nothing like that," I said trying to sound positive when I wasn't. "If anybody asks, there's just a small problem that Jeremy and I are taking care of. Nothing to worry about. Everybody will be back at work in a day or two. And tell everybody they are all still on payroll, too. Look, there will be a rough neck guard at the entrance gate to the campus. I'm going to have someone phone ahead to let him know you are coming. If you have any problems getting in, phone me here right away, but stay at the gate, OK?"

I gave her the direct line to the apartment and hung the phone up. As I hung up the phone the doorbell rang; I ran for it knowing there were donuts on the other side and that Maureen had brought them up. But when I threw the door open this huge man stood there. He stood taller than me, and I'm 6'2". He was wearing a cheap, brown, tweed sport coat in the middle of summer and cheaper gray slacks; both needed the attention of an iron. His black shoes were thick soled and scuffed. His hair was close cropped and greying at the temples. He was a cop. There was no doubt about that. I'd seen so many cops in my life that I'd bet my last million there was a regulation that cops in plain clothes had to look scruffy.

"I'm Roger Schwartz," he said. When I said nothing he said, "You're supposed to be expecting me . . . I'm supposed to be protection for someone."

I couldn't look over his shoulder because of his height and his too broad shoulders, but looking around the side of him I saw two more men, equally inexpensively dressed, standing at either side of the elevator. They were cops, also.

"Look," Schwartz said. "Either I come in, or I go home. Either way, I get paid, got it? So you gonna' let me in or what?"

"You're a cop . . . Off duty I imagine . . . Can I see a badge?" I said.

He reached into his jacket's inside pocket. He pulled out an old brown leather case. He flipped it open and held it, obnoxiously like cops like to do, too close to my face. I saw the silver badge and ID card. He was a cop. Not a detective whose badge would be gold, but a cop anyway.

I figured he wasn't very happy being there, that he would rather be home on his day off. But like most cops, he needed the extra money.

Holding the case in front of me, he said, "So, do I get in or not?"

"Yeah . . . Of course . . . Sorry."

I stood aside, and he came into the apartment. He looked around at the garishness of the place and asked, "What the hell you got goin' here? This some kind'a cat house or somethin'?"

The other two men remained in the hallway, one smoking a cigar, letting the ash drop onto the expensive carpet. I closed the door and led him through the apartment. I said as we walked, "It would take too much time to explain all this. Just try your best to ignore it."

In the kitchen I shook Jeremy from his reverie and told him he would have guards to keep him safe while I was gone. I turned to Schwartz and said, "He doesn't leave here unless he's with me . . . And you. I'm going to be gone for a day or two. Food and anything else you guys need will be sent up. Call Peter Jascro for anything you need. No one gets in here to talk to him, and that includes any Feds. Send them down to see Peter Jascro. Make sure you know the men who will replace you. If you don't know them personally, send them away. I don't want anyone in here except me and you guys, OK?"

"No problem," Schwartz said. "I'm gonna' need your cell phone number if you're gonna' be gone."

I gave him the number, and he said somewhat derisively, "That's a California number, ain't it?"

"Yes. I'm just one of them long haired beach bum surfer dude drug addicts you hear about. On welfare, you know? That OK with you?"

He didn't say anything, and he didn't seem to find what I said funny at all.

"But please don't use the number except in extreme emergencies. I don't have to tell you how easy it is to track cell phones."

I heard a loud knocking on the front door. 'Donuts,' I thought. I started to run to the door to get them. I had made a mistake opening the door without checking when Schwartz was there. This time I looked through the peephole. One of the two guards was standing there holding Maureen by her arm. She was about to faint or at least burst out in tears.

She had a plastic tray full of really good looking pastries.

I opened the door and the cop asked, "This yours?"

"Yes, thank you." I took the tray and added, "You can let her go now. I don't think she's a danger to anyone."

Maureen was either shaken or angry; I settled on angry. I told her, "Look, I'm sorry, Maureen. I just need to know Mr. Hillsdale is safe."

"Yes," she said in a huff. "I can assure I will not hurt him." She turned and stepped lively as she walked down the hall.

I sat at the glass kitchen table eating a few too many pastries. Schwartz went to the coffee pot, filled a large mug, took two cheese filled Danish, and walked out of the room. Jeremy didn't move.

As I started on the third pastry the phone rang. It was Jeremy's secretary. "I have the names you wanted, Mr. Crew."

"You didn't have a problem at the gate?" I asked.

"The man was frightening, but he let me in. Thank you for the warning."

I wrote down the names and contact information, asking for spellings of the names. "Thank you," I said. "I assume I need not tell you that nothing is said to the press?"

"Of course not, Mr. Crew. Several have phoned, but I've told them nothing."

"Good, now stay handy," I told her. "I may need something else."

When I was satisfied that I had eaten enough to have Sandy furious with me if she ever found out, I went to the telephone. The first of the three computer experts was

Susan Strellman.

"Yes, of course," she said when I told her to meet me at the Hillsdale campus. "I'll leave right away."

"Give me time to get there," I said. "I'm in the City. It's a long drive."

"Can I ask what this is all about?" she asked. "I mean, everyone was told to stay home . . . Since the murder, I mean."

"Who told you that?"

"The police. And I think the FBI, too."

Jeremy's secretary didn't say anything about that. If others knew, she had to know.

"OK, thanks for that. Look, it's going to take me a while to get there," I said. "Meet me there about 5 PM, OK? It'll take me six or seven hours to get there."

I then phoned Bill Trangent. The phone rang a dozen times with no answer.

George Bosnian was home and agreed to meet me at Hillsdale at 5 PM. There were no questions, no conversation. It was as if he had been expecting my call. I thought that strange, but I didn't think about it very long.

****

As I started out of the apartment Schwartz stopped me. "I'm gonna' send one'a the guys with you." I didn't argue with him. That was probably a good idea.

We stepped into the hallway, and Schwartz introduced me to one of the cops there. "This here is Vinnie

DeFazio," he said. "Vinnie, you go take Mr. Crew to his car, then come back, OK?"

At the street doors of the building DeFazio told me to wait inside while he looked up and down the street. It was Saturday, and the normally busy street was nearly deserted. DeFazio waived me out when he thought it was safe.

Maureen had rented a nice, beige Chevy Malibu for me. It was what I wanted; one of thousands and sure to blend in well with everything else on the road. DeFazio took one more look around and then opened the car door for me.

****

On the fifth floor of a building across the street, in an office that was empty that Saturday, at a window open only a few inches, Omar Maalouf waited with a Russian Dragunov SVD Sniper Rifle. Through the high-power scope, he waited and watched the doors of the office building for Morgan Crew to appear. He had several photos of Morgan, clipped from magazines and newspapers. It was a quiet Saturday, he thought. It would be an easy shot. No one on the street below who might get between Omar and Morgan Crew.

The big glass doors of the office opened, and a man stepped out onto the sidewalk. He was a man a little taller than Morgan Crew and darker, heavier set. The man looked left and then right and then left again. 'A guard,' Omar said to himself and eased his finger on the rifle's trigger.

The guard waived, and another man stepped out onto the broad sidewalk. Omar put his eye to the rifle's scope. Yes, that was Morgan Crew. His finger went to the trigger. But Morgan stepped too quickly to the guard's side. Omar could not get a clean head shot. And it would do no good to shoot the guard first. Morgan would use the car at the curb as cover. Omar had only one shot.

His finger tightened on the trigger. The guard bent to open the car's door. But Morgan was too quick jumping into the car. That was it, Omar told himself. It would have to wait for the next opportunity. And it would be impossible for Omar to get to his car in time to follow Morgan. It would happen, he assured himself. But not then.

****

The drive up I-80 to Buffalo took almost seven hours. Along the way I tried Bill Trangent's number eight times. No answer. I hesitated using my cell phone because I didn't want anyone to know where I was, but I had to speak with Bill Trangent.

It was nearly five when I hit Buffalo. I had Trangent's home address. I phoned both Strellman and Bosnian and told them I would be a little late, to wait for me at the parking lot of the campus. I didn't want them going inside without me, although without me they weren't likely to get in anyway. At that point I trusted no one.

As Jeremy's personal secretary had told me, all of the three computer experts lived in the same neighborhood. I found it, and she was right; it was a very, very upscale neighborhood. The homes were all custom, really big, and all built with a lot of stone. The homes and the lots were huge. The landscaping on each must have cost a pretty penny as they say. I found Trangent's home and pulled into the circular drive.

I rang the doorbell, knocked on the door, and rang the doorbell again. No answer. Maybe they had taken advantage of the time off and gone out of town, I thought. I was about to walk back to the car when out of the corner of my eye I noticed that there was a table lamp on in a window. Strange, I thought. It was the middle of summer which meant the sun set late and it wasn't dark yet; too early to have lights on in the house.

I tried the front door; it was locked. So I walked around the side of the house to the backyard. I found a swimming pool and a manicured garden of flowers, not doing well from the hot weather, and a lot of trees. A wide sliding glass door led from the house to a slate stone patio. I tried it, but it too was locked.

I glanced down the rear of the house and saw a small window half way down to the end. It was open a little, not much, not more than a half an inch, but it was open. In spite of that damn little voice in the back of my head that was screaming, "Run away! Run away!" I opened it and climbed inside. Yes, I knew something wasn't right, but I had to know anyway.

I was in a small bathroom, a powder room. Lights inside the house were on everywhere. I hesitated, but finally I stepped from the bathroom. I was in a hallway; to the left was the kitchen. On the travertine tile floor of the kitchen was a woman's body, a man's body laid across it. There was no blood, but the total lack of color on either's face and hands told me they were dead. Nearby, next to a refrigerator, a teenage boy lay face down, his mouth open in a frozen, silent scream. The three were dead, without wounds.

I walked out of the kitchen into a large family room. On a coffee table school books were spread out, and a laptop computer lay open, its battery drained.

I wanted to run; that damn little voice was screaming

in my head. But I didn't. There was a staircase across the room. I forced myself to go to it, and I took the stairs slowly. I didn't think a killer was in the house; the three bodies were cold and grey. They had been murdered some days before.

Upstairs I found two more children, a girl and a boy, neither yet in their teens and both dead. The boy was on his back, on his bed in what was a very boy's bedroom, full of sports equipment and posters. The girl was in her bedroom, all pink and white with a white lace canopy bed. She was lying face down on her bed, school books open all around her. None of the dead were bleeding.

The entire Trangent family had all been killed quietly . . . By hand. An expert at murder had to have done this. I made a quick walkthrough of the big house. Silver picture frames, silver candle sticks, laptop computers, drawers of expensive silverware; nothing had been touched or stolen. This was not a burglary gone bad. It was too neat, too clean, and nothing had been stolen. The killings were done to cover something up. To protect someone. Perhaps, I thought, Donna Evans and that F.B.I. guy knew what they were talking about.

I had to report this, of course. But I knew that if I did, my report would bring in the FBI, and a decision would be made to shut down Hillsdale Technologies. And I would be held for questioning, keeping me from finding out what the hell this was all about. I needed answers first. Answers like, why these people? Why the children? And did Bill Trangent have anything to do with the murder at Hillsdale?

To the last question, I could come up with only one possible answer. If this were a professional murder, then Bill Trangent did have something to do with the security guard's murder, and that knowledge meant he had to be killed. But why the wife and kids? It didn't make sense, but as has always happened when I am confronted with cold blooded murder, I cannot think like a killer. The person who did murder the entire Trangent family could not be fully sane, and I cannot think like an insane person.

I decided to look through the house more closely before calling the police. If there was something there, the police wouldn't let me have it, and it might be something I would need. It took less than an hour for me to go through every drawer and every closet, look under every bed, dig through the kitchen cabinets, and open boxes on garage shelves. The only thing I found of any value was some personal information on Bill Trangent. I found some paper and a pencil and wrote down his Social Security number, his date of birth, the family checking account number and the bank branch.

Having done this sort of thing several times in the past, I was very careful about not leaving finger prints anywhere and not destroying evidence. I wiped everything I touched with my handkerchief right after touching it. And I made sure everything was put back where I had found it. I left nothing disturbed, not even a pair of socks in a drawer.

Before leaving the house by the same bathroom window I had entered through, I took one last look around. I left the window open less than an inch, as I had found it.

I carefully stepped on the flagstone path at the side of the house and stopped at the rental car. Somebody in the neighborhood might have seen me drive up and might have noticed how long I was inside the house. That couldn't be helped. It was Saturday and although still light out it was late in the afternoon. Lawns had been cut; kid's baseball games were over; dinners were being prepared. I felt I had a good chance that no one would write down the license plate number of my car. To cover my bases, I would phone Peter after leaving the neighborhood.

As I opened the door of the car I looked down the street to my left. About fifty yards away a black car was parked on the wrong side of the street, its engine running. The driver's door opened, and a man climbed out. He was tall and dark and muscled. He took two steps toward me and then stopped. He got back in the car and pulled away from the curb, driving very slowly. I looked to my right, and a white and blue community security patrol car drove towards me, moving slowly. The black car passed me and crossed by the security car. The windows of the black car were blackened, so I could not see inside. The driver of the security car passed by slowly, looked at me, waved and smiled at me. I smiled and casually waved back like I was supposed to be there. It happened so quickly, and all I could think of was what story I would tell if caught there, that I didn't even look at the license plate of the black car.

Alone, standing in the driveway at the side of my car, I turned back and forth to watch each car drive slowly away in the distance. My heart was pounding, but I knew I had slid safely out of whatever danger had driven past me. In my car, as I drove out of the neighborhood, I used my cell phone to call Peter.

"Hi, Peter," I said. "Look, wait a half an hour. Phone the Buffalo Police and report five dead bodies."

"Oh, for God's sake, Morgan. Not again."

I gave him the Trangents' home address. "Bill Trangent worked at Hillsdale Technologies. The whole damn family was killed. Make up something legal, but don't tell the police how you found out about the murders. I'm on my way to the Hillsdale campus now. Talk to you later."

I hung up before Peter could say anything else. I took my time leaving the neighborhood; no sense attracting attention by speeding through the quiet streets.

****

I managed to find the road that would take me through the hills to Hillsdale Technologies. Both George Bosnian and Susan Strellman would be waiting there, sitting in their cars because the new guards at the gate would not have let them in.

When I arrived at the parking lot I found it strange that their cars were parked next to each other, yet they were sitting in their own cars, the windows rolled up, not in one car together, and not speaking to each other. They had parked in the third row of parking spaces; I parked in the first, as close to the gate as I could. The rest of the lot was empty except for the few cars of the security guards that occupied the very last row at the back of the lot.

Although it was six PM, it was summer, and it was still bright with sunlight. The rain clouds and unseasonably cold weather had long passed. I was an hour late. They had waited there for me anyway. I guessed they might be a little upset at my interfering with their Saturday at home. I really didn't care.

I got out of my car and walked the few paces to the gate without approaching George or Susan. They got out of their cars, I guess assuming it was me, and walked to the gate, still not speaking to one another. The guard left his little gate house and strolled slowly towards the gate, his right hand on the pistol holstered at his side. He was eyeing me and the other two closely. I didn't mind; that is what I wanted the guards to do.

"Are you Mr. Crew?" he asked.

"Yes. You're supposed to be expecting me."

"Someone called our office. Can I see some photo

ID?"

I handed my driver's license through the chain link fence. He went through the same process as the previous guard had done the other day and handed the license back to me.

"Are these people with you?" he asked.

"Yes," I answered and turned to them. "I assume you are George Bosnian and Susan Strellman? If so, give the man your driver's licenses and your employee IDs."

They did, and the guard walked back to his gate house. I saw him through the glass of the small shack writing what I assume was our names in a log book. I was happy to see that; the security here had been improved, only too late to keep me away from a day of golf back home.

The guard walked slowly back to the gate, unlocked the pad lock and hung it and the chain through the fence. He walked slowly once again, back to the guard shack, and inside he opened the gate as he stood inside his little guard shack looking at us, and locked up after we were inside. We walked to the guard and stood at the door. The guard returned our identifications to us, and I asked the guard, "Don't I have to sign for these two? I did that the last time I was here."

"Only if the people with you are not employees," he said.

At the front door I punched in the code number that would unlock the door. I held it open and stood aside for the two to enter.

Bosnian asked, before either walked into the Admin Building, "Why are we here?"

"I guess because I asked you to be here," I answered with a broad and I hoped obnoxious grin. "You know who I am . . . I own this place, and you work for me."

"I know that," he said, trying to sound polite, but I could hear an edge of irritation in his voice. "But why? What are we supposed to do? Look, I know what happened out here. Somebody was killed, and we were all told to go home and not leave town."

"Who told you that? Sounds like something out of an old cops and robbers movie."

"An FBI Agent," Bosnian said.

"Let me guess . . . Adam Carter, right?"

"Yes, that's right. You're not FBI. Can you override what he says? I don't want to get in trouble."

"You won't be in trouble as long as you help me out here. I made a deal with the Feds. Remember, I own this place."

Susan Strellman spoke up, "I know who you are, Mr. Crew. I'm willing to help . . . I think we both are. We're just worried. We don't want to get into trouble."

"Don't worry," I said. "I've got a lot of pull around here. Now, let's get inside and get done what needs to be done."

Inside we took the elevator to the fourth floor where all the computer stations were. There were no lights on; Susan went right to a wall switch, and the place lit up. It was eerily quiet inside; the room was filled with unmanned desks and computers, but none were turned on. The only sound was a faint buzzing of the air-conditioning system blowing cool air and a clock ticking away in the silence.

We stood gazing around for a moment or two, maybe waiting for a ghost or the killer to jump out at us. I broke the silence by saying, "OK. I need two things to begin with.

One, the doors to this building have electronic locks. I need to see a record of who opened the doors and when they were opened the night the guard was killed. I assume you can do that?"

George said, "I work in the electronics lab. I have no idea about systems out here."

Susan said, "I think I can find that if you'll let me sit at a computer for a while."

I nodded, and she went immediately to the nearest desk, sat and switched on the computer there. The computer lit up, and she smiled a little satisfied smile. She started typing, and very soon she said, "I've got it."

"Good . . . Great," I said.

"Before I start, I need to tell you that I'm not going to get into anything that is classified. I know who you are, but I don't know you. I'm guessing you don't have any kind of security clearance. So, if I say 'no,' just accept that, OK?"

"Fine. All I want to know right now is who opened the side door of this building the night of the murder. Can you do that?"

"Yes . . . I think so."

She started typing, pausing now and then to think. It took a minute or two . . . Very long minutes as I paced around trying not to peer over her shoulder. George Bosnian stood off to the side, his arms folded, watching everything that was happening.

We both waited . . . We waited for Susan to say, "OK, I have the access records." She pressed a few keys and then said, "The night the guard was killed . . . I see . . . Yes . . . The side door was opened at 2:16 AM."

"And does the record show who opened it?"

"Not 'who'," she said. "The code used is a general code used mainly by maintenance people. One code assigned to all the maintenance staff."

"So there isn't a name of who opened the door?"

"No, sorry . . . But it's strange . . . Unusual, you know?"

"What?"

"It took nearly a full minute for the code to be entered. It shouldn't take that long to enter a six digit code, you know?"

I thought for a minute and then asked, "Can you print out a copy of that?"

"Sure," she said. "I have to find a printer first . . . Ahh, there it is. George can you switch on the printer . . . It's across the room . . . Over there."

George found the printer and turned it on, and it spit out a single sheet of paper. He brought it to me.

"Now," I said. "I need a record of how the security here was set up: who did the planning, when it was talked about, who attended any meetings about the security, who supervised the work. Anything you can find for me."

Susan started typing, but she was obviously having a hard time. She stopped, looked up at me and said, "I think I can get this, but it's going to take some time. I don't work in Admin. I'm in Technical Systems Design."

I nodded and walked away from Susan. Motioning for George Bosnian to follow we walked to the back of the room. At a work station that backed up to a black metal cage full of file cabinets, I asked George, "Use this computer. I need to know if anyone accessed anything in here that night. Can you do that?"

"I can try," he said.   "I'm not familiar with these systems . . . But I'll try."

I started walking aimlessly around the big office. Walled cubicle work stations were lined up along two walls, left and right. These were for the managers and supervisors I guessed.   Special places, slightly larger than others, to make low paid managers feel special.

In the middle of the room was desk after desk with low work station cubicle walls, exposed to everything and everybody. The people who sat there were, I imagined, the young ladies fresh from High School with the ability to type administrative garbage day after day.   They would do payrolls or time sheets or just type meaningless letters for some manager.   The same routine over and over again. They would work a year or two and either be promoted to something more interesting or find a guy to marry and leave Hillsdale Technologies to pump out babies.

I found a small alcove with a soft drink machine and two snack machines.   Once again I took advantage of the fact that Sandy wasn't with me. I slid a couple of dollar bills in and bought a can of full sugar Coke and a big chocolate candy bar. I thought it would taste good after all those years without having tasted such sinful stuff, but the taste, surprisingly enough, was not so great.   My taste buds had been changed to enjoy the good, healthy food Sandy insisted on. I tossed most of the candy bar into a nearby trash can and left the half empty can of Coke on a desk.

I went on pacing, looking at bulletin boards hanging on the walls and personal things on every desk. There were a lot of green plants that needed water and cards pinned to the fabric walls of managers' work stations. And there were a whole lot of teddy bears everywhere.

I was holding one of them, a particularly stupid one

that was holding an artificial rose in its teeth. I was about to rip its head off when George called out, "Mr. Crew! I think I found something here!"

I raced back to him. He was leaning back in his chair, rocking back and forth while gazing at the computer screen in front of him.

"What is it?" I asked, out of breath from the short distance run across the room.

"I'm not sure. But I think someone used this computer that night. There's an audit trail for everything that's not administrative . . . You know, payroll and that kind of thing. Anything that is even of the lowest classification is recorded. There is a record of every entry and what was accessed. It shows who accessed it and when."

"OK," I said, anxious to get some solid answers. "So what do you see?"

"This computer that I'm at was accessed the night the guard was killed; at about the same time that side door lock was opened, about ten minutes later. This office is all administrative. No one would be here at that time of night. I've got a user log here. It's on the main Administrative Network. I think they use it to make sure everybody spends their eight hours working and not looking at porn. I pulled up what was done that night. It looks like someone turned it on and used it to read a file of some kind. It looks like they may have copied something, too."

"What was it?"

"Here it is," he said, pointing at the screen.

I looked, but all I saw were jumbled masses of numbers and letters.

"What the hell is that?" I asked him. "Looks like someone threw up on the computer."

"It's encrypted. Highly encrypted."

"So unencrypt it," I said. Now understand here that I can push the right button to turn on a computer. I can use Word to type fairly well. I can search the web if I have to, but I seldom want to. But my computer expertise ends there. If Betsy, our nanny, had been with me she might have been able to get past the encryption.

George answered, "Not possible without the encryption key. At least not quickly. I mean, I can do it but it will take hours or longer. I've never seen anything like this. We use similar encryption when designing electronics, you know, wiring and things for the military . . . But nothing like this."

"Who was it? Who did the copying?"

"The record doesn't show who did it, only that it was done. As I said, this is an administrative work station. You're not supposed to access anything classified here. They only want to know what was done and when it was done. But it recorded the fact that someone accessed this file from some outside source. I don't know what. Maybe a disk . . . Or maybe a flash drive . . . I don't know."

"But what you're seeing is something classified?" I asked.

"Has to be," George answered. He leaned back in the chair, staring at the screen and said, "I've never seen anything like this. It has to be big. I'll try to get through it." He leaned forward and started typing.

Susan Strellman spoke up from the front of the office, "Wait a minute, George. He's not privy to classified information. We'll need to get permission from somewhere higher up before he sees that."

I didn't have days or weeks to wait for some

bureaucratic ritual of passing this from person to person, agency to agency. So I said, "Forget it. Can you tell me the file name that was copied?"

George keyed in a few letters and then said, "Something called FIREBIRD GUIDANCE."

I walked around the office some more, finishing the Coke I had left on the desk and considered buying another candy bar. Susan called to me before I could make it to the candy machine, "Mr. Crew. I've got some records here. There are hundreds of files and emails. I could be here for days going through everything."

I ran back to her, out of breath again when I got there, and said, "Forget the details. Who was in charge of the project?"

She looked back at the computer screen and said, "Well, Hillsdale Technologies was started back in 1968. It was a small firm back then; a warehouse and office in New Jersey. In the early nineties Mr. Hillsdale, Sr. had built it into a sizeable company and moved it here, to where we are today. A security firm, Rathmore Security, built the fences and whatever security we had back then. Nothing much was done since, until the Federal Government demanded more onsite security. That was in 2010 and once again last year. Another upgrade they demanded. The latest project was led by Bill Trangent."

I dropped the can of Coke to the floor, spilling it all over my shoes as well as the floor.

"What's the matter?" she asked. "What's wrong?"

Neither she nor George needed to know about Trangent's death. It wasn't their business . . . Unless one of them killed that whole family. That seemed unlikely looking at both of them. Susan Strellman was middle aged but still fairly good looking. She wore nice clothes and good jewelry. Her hair was colored blond from a bottle but not brassy; she was thin, and the skin at her triceps hung loose. She wouldn't have the strength to kill five people with only her hands.

George Bosnian was older than Susan, in his late fifties. His hair was grey, his stomach was as big as mine, his shoulders were thin, his face was soft and puffy, and he wore thick eyeglasses rimmed in cheap black plastic.

No, neither one would have killed the security guard and the Trangent family. But that didn't mean they needed to know everything.

I told Susan, "Print out a few pages, enough to show Trangent was in charge of the project. And see if you can find any record of Jeremy Hillsdale being involved in the projects."

She did, quickly, and found Jeremy had signed off on approval of every step of the projects. When I had the papers I needed, I told them, "OK, thanks to both of you. Go home now, and don't talk about this to anyone . . . Especially not that Carter guy with the FBI. If he asks you anything, direct him to me."

"When can we come back to work?" Susan asked.

"I don't know. But I assure you everyone will stay on the payroll. You can tell everyone that but nothing else, understand? Now, go home and thanks again."

As they started to walk away I stopped them and asked, "Out of curiosity, did the police or FBI ask you or anyone else to do what you did tonight?"

They looked at each other, and Susan answered, "Not that we know of. Why?"

"Just curious," I answered.

****

I was alone in the building. The air conditioner was running; the lights were on; the clock was ticking away. The silence was creepy. It was past eight PM, and it was dark outside. Too late to drive all the way back to New York City. I had to think about what I would do next. I sat at one of the desks as I thought and wished I had finished the can of coke rather than drop it to the floor.

Bill Trangent had twice led the remake of the security system, and now he was dead. I remembered something from too many years ago, at Yale. 'Occam's Razor' it was called in one of my psychology classes. Occam's Razor states: "When more than one solution exists for a problem, the most logical is often the correct solution."

The most logical solution at hand was that Bill Trangent had been in charge of the latest security changes. He might have been paid to weaken the security. But if he did, could it have passed a Federal inspection? The Fed's had to have some standards, some demands. The system in place was a little less than a year old. Maybe the Fed's hadn't inspected yet? Anything was possible.

And what the hell was Firebird Guidance? It could be anything, and I wouldn't know without a security clearance. It was time to call Donna Evans in.

I drove into Buffalo and found a nice looking motel in the downtown area, what I figured would be a quiet part of the city on a Saturday night. I checked in and had a fairly good steak and a mediocre bottle of red wine in the restaurant a short walk from the hotel. In my room I sat on the bed and phoned Ms. Evans.

"Hello, Morgan. I'm surprised to hear from you

already."

"I found something . . . Something that's not too good, I'm afraid. I almost don't want to tell you, but I know I have to."

"What is it?"

"Not over the phone," I said. "I'm staying in Buffalo tonight.   I want you to come up to Hillsdale tomorrow morning. Stop at Peter Jascro's office and bring Jeremy with you.   And I have some guards with Jeremy, NYPD cops. Bring one of them, too. Not your own people; I want my own guards.   In fact, don't drive; take your helicopter.   And be careful."

"I have my own people for security, Morgan."

"Not good enough," I said. "I want people I hired, who answer to me, and who get paid by me."

"Why all the caution?" she asked.

"I'll tell you tomorrow. Have a good night."

I hung up and phoned Peter. I didn't think about the time of day, I just phoned his direct line at his office thinking Maureen would answer. It was late, Peter was still at his desk and Maureen had gone home. He answered the phone himself.

"Sorry, Peter," I said. "I forgot what time it is."

"Not a problem, Morgan. What do you need?"

"Did you call the cops?"

"Yes. They wanted to know how I knew about the murders."

"And what did you tell them?"

He laughed and said, "A confidential informant, a

client whose name I can't reveal."

"That's good. Thanks. Look, I have that Homeland Security lady coming up here tomorrow. I told her to bring Jeremy. Let the guards know. I want one of them to come with Jeremy . . . With a gun."

"That sounds bad, Morgan," Peter said a little more seriously. "What have you found out?"

"Not over the phone, Peter. I don't trust any of these spy types. Remember all that Sandy and I went through with that foreign spy who wouldn't speak?"

"OK, Morgan. But please be careful."

I phoned Sandy and told her I was staying in Buffalo. I said I would be a day or two more. I didn't tell her what I had found or that there had been more murders. No sense worrying her. I assured her I would be careful. I spoke with Caroline, and I assured her I would be careful. She sounded worried; she was learning at an early age what my life is all about. And then I assured Betsy I would be careful. It's nice to have the ladies worry about you. But it would be even nicer if they didn't have to worry at all. Maybe someday that would happen.

EIGHT – Someone Wants Me Dead

The room's mini-bar didn't have any Wild Turkey; few mini-bars do. I guess not everyone knows of the enticing pleasure of Wild Turkey 101. But there were two bottles of Jack Daniels, so I finished both, drinking them straight from the airline size bottles. Those, along with the good steak I had for dinner, and I was asleep quickly.

The buzzing of the A/C unit in the room woke me twice during the night, but I managed to get back to sleep quickly the first time. The second time, the sound at the door of the room kept me awake, and I didn't go back to sleep. Someone was at the room's keycard-locked door, trying to get in.

I threw the blanket off of me and sat up, swinging my legs to sit up. The clock with the red numbers on the night stand table read 3:46. At first I thought I was just dreaming. I rubbed my eyes and shook my head. I was awake, and someone was trying to get into my room.

At home I would have opened the nightstand drawer and grabbed my .38. I looked around the hotel room for a weapon. There was nothing there, not even a big ashtray to hit someone with. I quickly did a trick I had seen too many times on T.V. I pulled the bed's two pillows under the blanket hoping it would look like someone sleeping there. I ran to the bathroom and closed the door, leaving it open just enough to see out.

The room's door opened slowly, and a man stepped in very quietly. It was dark in the room, so all I could make out was a figure, tall, dark, and muscular, and the weirdest thing about him were his black hands. Later, after my adrenaline had settled down, I realized his black hands had to be gloves. He walked without making any sound to the bed, threw down the cover and then turned quickly realizing I wasn't there.

I locked the bathroom door and stepped away from it. If it was the same man who had killed the Trangent family, I knew I was in trouble. And I had nothing with me to use as a weapon. I looked down and saw a small thin metal trash can. That was the best thing I had.

I picked it up as the man outside put his shoulder to the door. On the second try the lock gave way, and the door slammed open. I swung the trash can as the man rushed into the room, hitting the side of his head. It didn't stop him, but he did stumble sideways. I did a High School high-body football tackle, and we fell into the tub, tearing the shower curtain off its rail. The man hit his head on the tiled wall. That gave me a chance to run from the room.

In the hallway I started yelling, "HELP! HELP!" as loud as I could. Doors started opening, and people started looking out of their rooms. The man who had broken in pushed me to the side and ran past me, down the hall. It was all too quick for me to get a good look at his face, but I was sure he was Arabic.

Hotel security finally arrived, and I filed a report with them. The man could not be found, and it was assumed he had left the property. The police were called, and I filed a report with them. I knew what operations like that were like. My reports would be filed, everybody would go back to work, and the guests would go back to bed.

****

I didn't sleep much the rest of the night. I awoke early and had a breakfast of hotcakes and fat sausages, with lots of black coffee. I hope Sandy never finds out what I'd been eating while she wasn't around. At the breakfast table while I was finishing my third cup of coffee, the hotel's manager came by to tell me my stay would not be charged. She sounded truly sincere and sorry for what had happened, so I didn't make a big deal out of it. That would have gained me nothing. I smiled and simply said thank you. But I did leave a big tip on the table for the waitress.

The sky was clear and blue as I drove back to Hillsdale Technologies. The road was dry and free of traffic as it twisted and turned through the hills and forests. Mine was the only car on the road built specifically to go to Hillsdale and no place else, so I had some fun by flooring the gas pedal. I watched the speedometer go up to 90. The tires screeched on several bends of the road, and I almost lost it once, so I slowed a little. No sense getting killed without anyone trying to kill me.

It was Sunday morning, and again the parking lot at Hillsdale was empty except for the cars of the security guards. It was a nice sunny morning so I decided not to wait inside the Administration Building for Ms. Evans to arrive. The area was so remote and so mountainous that I couldn't get a clear radio station on the rental car. It was equipped with satellite radio, but even that was spotty in the high surrounding mountains. So I rolled down the car's windows to let the clean mountain air in, reclined the seat back, and closed my eyes. It had been a long night without much sleep.

I don't know if I dozed off or not, but a knocking on the

car's door and someone shaking me on my shoulder stirred me. It was a security guard.

"You can't sleep here," he said in a rather threatening voice, his right hand on his holstered pistol.

I pulled the seat back up and told him, "Sorry. I'm waiting for some people to meet me here."

"Why?"

"I'm Morgan Crew," I explained. "Have you been told I might be here today?"

"I need to see some ID, please."

I went through the same process with my California driver's license as I had the day before. I didn't complain; if security had been that tight before the murder of the security guard, maybe the murder wouldn't have happened. After looking very carefully at the license, the guard handed it back to me and walked away.

Twenty minutes later the roar of the helicopter signaled that Donna Evans and Jeremy Hillsdale had arrived. A man, the off-duty cop who had accompanied them, followed them off the helicopter, all ducking low to avoid the chopper's blades. Jeremy and Evans walked away from the helicopter; the cop/bodyguard stayed behind. As the spinning blades slowed to a stop, the pilots climbed down and joined the man at the side of the copter. They waited there, watching Evans and Hillsdale walk away and talking between each other.

I got out of my car and walked ahead of Jeremy and Donna, meeting them at the locked gate, the guard waiting on the other side for us. The same process repeated itself, including giving the guard inside the fence my driver's license once again.

While we waited at the locked gate in the bright

sunlight, we said nothing to each other. Donna Evans stood stoically with that damn little forced smile on her face. Jeremy's shoulders were slumped as he looked down at the ground, shifting from foot to foot nervously. I would have preferred he not do that because it meant besides being nervous, he could have a secret to be nervous about. And I knew Evans saw this even though she didn't look directly at him.

It looked like Maureen had been sure Jeremy wore new, clean clothes. But his white shirt's collar was unbuttoned revealing the fact that he had forgotten to shave the beard from his neck.

The guard unlocked the pad lock and inside his little shack he pushed the right buttons to open the gate. We walked in, side by side. The gate slammed closed quickly behind us. We went directly to the guard shack. The guard had Jeremy sign for Donna this time. The guard looked Donna and me up and down very carefully while Jeremy was signing the log. Jeremy's hands were shaking visibly; his signature was more of a scrawl.

At the big glass doors of the Administration Building I motioned to Jeremy to key in his personal code that would open the door. I watched, and that code turned out to be the same stupid series of numbers I had used. Inside, after the doors closed and locked us in, the first thing I noticed was the artificially cold air and the absolute silence, save for the faint buzz of the A/C. The entire building was without lights still. It was as creepy as it had been the last time I was there.

I led my little group to the elevator and stepped inside with them following. I pushed the button for the fourth floor and watched the doors slide close.

"Why the fourth floor?" Ms. Evans asked.

"Because that's where it happened."

"Where what happened?" she asked, turning to face me.

The doors opened to the fourth floor. I stepped out and waited for the doors to close, leaving the three of us standing there in the still and creepy office.

I turned to face both of them. "Firebird Guidance." I said simply.

"Where the hell did you hear about that!" she said, startled. For the first time Donna Evans showed some semblance of emotion.

"Why?"

"Because that's highly classified! I should cuff you and take you to . . . To someplace where I can learn the truth!"

The smirk on my face, I hoped, would tell Donna Evans that I was right in talking her into our deal. I reminded her that we had agreed on me finding out what happened. And I told her that I thought I had found out what happened. I walked to the workstation at the rear of the long room, to the computer that George Bosnian used to find Firebird Guidance.

I turned to face Evans and explained, "The night the guard was killed, someone used this computer to copy a file called Firebird Guidance. Apparently, it had been stored on some kind of external storage thing. I don't know what. But the computer stored the record of what was opened and copied. I saw the file, but it was encrypted. I have no idea what Firebird Guidance is . . . But someone made a copy of that file. That is why the guard was killed."

"So who did this?" she asked.

"I know it happened and how whoever it was got in, but I don't know who did it. The side door to this building was accessed using a code generally used by maintenance crews. The same code used by anyone doing cleaning and maintenance. I suggest you do backgrounds on all the maintenance staff . . . But I doubt anyone like that did this."

"Why do you doubt that?"

"This was too professional."

"How about a sleeper?"

"You'll find that out when you do the backgrounds. I'd be very surprised if you find anything there. But there is another problem."

"What?" she demanded.

"Someone tried to kill me last night."

Donna's jaw dropped in surprise. "Someone tried to kill you? Who? Why?"

"I'm not sure yet. But I have a hunch I'm getting too close to something."

Donna glared at me. I could see the anger rising in her. Was she jealous that I was finding things she hadn't? Was she frightened that her record would be blemished? Or was there something I wasn't yet aware of? I didn't know . . . But I would find out. Nothing could stop me now . . . Except maybe the guy who wanted to kill me.

I turned to look at Jeremy. He stood, slope shouldered, looking down at the floor, drawn and pale. He had the appearance of someone who had given up, surrendered to what he saw as the inevitable. Jeremy must have felt that he had lost everything. He must have felt the business he had inherited was gone. He would be destroyed; his family would leave him. There was nothing left for him.

"Jeremy," I asked him. "Last year the security systems here were gone over and changed. You had a team working on that. Bill Trangent was in charge of that team, wasn't he?"

"Yes . . . I guess so . . . I don't know . . . Why?"

"Bill Trangent and his whole family were found murdered yesterday."

"What! Bill is dead!" Jeremy said, his head shooting up. I watched his face closely. It was flame red; his eyes were as wide as they could get. He wasn't acting. He was truly surprised. He looked like he might pass out or toss his cookies.

But Donna Evans wasn't surprised at all to hear that. She stood stone faced, staring ahead at nothing. I asked Donna, "I guess you've heard about the Trangent family. What have you learned about the murders?"

"The local police have the case," she said.

"That's fine," I said. "But what have you learned about the murders? I assume the locals are telling you everything."

"You know I can't discuss that with you."

"We have an agreement, Donna."

She stared at me for a moment and then said, "Give me to the end of the day. If there's something I can share, I will."

"OK, I can accept that," I said. "Now, what is Firebird Guidance, and who would be interested in getting the details of whatever that is?"

Evans turned away from me, her forehead creased. I

looked at Jeremy, questioning without words. His face had turned pale with fear, and there was a throbbing of an artery on his neck. He said, "It's a new remote guidance system for drones. That's all I think I should tell you."

I looked back at Evans and said, "So, I can assume that the drones are being used in the Middle East . . . So . . . The people who the drones are being used on might be very interested in how the drones are controlled. Right?"

She said nothing, but I could read the answer on her face. I knew then that she was tossing around the idea of shutting the place down. Whatever Firebird Guidance was, it was important. Too important to let Hillsdale continue if someone who worked at Hillsdale helped the file be stolen. If I knew about Firebird Guidance then a lot of others knew, also.

I was right, of course; I knew that. But if I was right, what was I to do? The Crew family was about to lose millions of dollars. Crew Enterprises stock would take a hit. Jeremy would lose everything. So I took a gamble.

"Ms. Evans, I want to have security here upgraded to the extreme. There will be no limit to the budget. Within two weeks this place will be as secure as Fort Knox. I want those two weeks. Once that is done I will see to it that whatever Firebird Guidance is, changes will be made to make whatever was stolen obsolete. I will take full responsibility for everything. I guarantee that after what I want is done, one of your SEAL Teams will have a hard time breaking into this place."

"Morgan," Donna said, "There's little harm telling you a few things. We've suspected what you know for a long time. Our drones have been mysteriously going off course. They're crashing in the desert. They've been dropping bombs where they shouldn't be dropped. They've been inspected for mechanical problems. We've only had suspicions before today. Now I know what's been happening. People have been overriding the guidance system. You've proven that someone broke in here and stole some top secret files regarding that guidance system. Why shouldn't I just close this place up? Why should I let you revamp the system?"

"Because Hillsdale Technologies does good work for you. You know that. The best people available work here. If you close this place and ship the contracts to some other company, that company will hire the same people who work here. There is no one else out there. These people know the system. You'll have the same operations and the same people in a different location. If you don't and you can find new people, they'll have to start from scratch, and it will be years before a new system can be designed. And if you hire Hillsdale people and someone here is responsible, that same person will be at a new location, and that same person may be responsible for a new theft. Let me make this place so secure it will be virtually impossible for this to be repeated. Let Hillsdale continue to do the good work for you. And I will also find out who it was who did this."

"Morgan . . . You know that no security is perfect. No matter what you do, you cannot guarantee no one will break in again."

"And you can't guarantee that a similar theft will not occur no matter where the contracts are sent to. Give me two weeks, Donna."

She was thinking about what I asked. I imagined she was trying to figure out how she could explain to her bosses what she was doing. How could she defend what I asked for? But for whatever reason she did finally agree.

"Alright, Morgan. You have your two weeks. But I

need to know what is done to better the security here before Government work is started again. Once you are satisfied with the security you can have your people make changes to Firebird Guidance that will make it secure again, but I want my people to see those changes before they go operational. In the meantime, I will recommend that drones not use Firebird at all. And I'm going to have military security here. You can keep your own people, your own security guards, but the military security will oversee everything."

"Agreed. Thank you. Now, I'm going to stay here for a while with Jeremy. He and I will drive back to the City. You can leave in the chopper. Tell the police guard to stay here with us. Tell him to wait by my car. Tell him no one gets in here . . . No matter who. He has my cell number if anyone wants in."

Her glare was almost painful, but I managed to win the Mexican Standoff. She said, "Two weeks, Morgan. Two weeks . . . No more. You won't like it in Gitmo . . . Or someplace worse. We do have worse places, you know."

She turned and walked away. Jeremy fell into a chair and covered his face with his hands. He was about to start crying again. I never had a good image of the man; he was always too businesslike, cold, and self-centered. All he could ever talk about at family gatherings was himself and what he was doing with his company. The cost of money and the world's economy was seemingly Jeremy's favorite subject. His family, his wife and children, seemed never to enter his mind. But he was revealing himself to be weak in front of me. What little respect I had for the man was rapidly going away. I felt my anger rising quickly.

I grabbed him by his shoulders and lifted him from the chair. "Stop it! Stop the friggin' crying you son of a bitch!" I slapped him across his face, and then I slapped him again.

His tears stopped. He looked shocked that I would hit him. "It's all gone, Morgan," he sobbed. "It's all gone."

"No it isn't, Jeremy. Unless you go on crying like some child. Man up! You've got work to do. Now stop the damn crying."

He did manage to regain control finally. He wiped his eyes on his suit jacket sleeve. I sat at a desk and pulled a chair from the next desk for Jeremy.

"Sit down and tell me all you know about Bill Trangent. I want everything. And I want you to pull up his personnel file, too. Use this computer," I said, pushing a keyboard toward him. "Now talk and start typing."

As Jeremy slowly punched some keys, not really knowing why he was doing what I told him to do, he told me that Bill Trangent had been with the company for eleven years. He had come from InterAir in Washington State, a manufacturer of primarily corporate jets, but also a sub-contractor to manufacturers of military fighter jets. He had been hired by Hillsdale as an engineer and was soon a manager and then a division manager. He was the best in his field, according to Jeremy, and also a friend.

Over the years Bill and his wife had become close friends with Jeremy and his wife. Their families often got together for bar-b-ques and dinners. Their children went to the same schools.

It was obvious that Jeremy couldn't talk about Bill Trangent and pull up the man's personnel record at the same time. He was in no mental state to do two things at the same time. I was losing my patience with the man. I spun his chair away from the desktop computer and keyboard and said, "Tell me about the man. Tell me more than the work he did. What were his likes and dislikes? What were his politics? What were his problems? Who didn't like him?"

"He's a good guy . . . I mean he was a good guy," Jeremy said as he wiped a tear from the corner of his bloodshot eyes. "He played tennis, and he was good at it. He tried to get me to play, but I'm not good at sports . . . And it took too much time away from business. I don't know who he voted for; we never talked politics. In fact I can't remember him ever saying anything bad about anybody or anything. He always seemed to see the good side of everything. He wasn't a church goer or anything like that, but he seemed like he was. He was always fun to be with . . . Outside of work, I mean."

"Come on, Jeremy," I said. "The guy and his whole family were murdered. He had to have someone who didn't like him."

"I don't know. Nobody I ever talked to said anything bad about him. Everybody liked him."

Tears were filling Jeremy's bloodshot eyes. He couldn't look at me; his face was drained of color. It hadn't escaped me that when I mentioned the murder of the Trangent family, Jeremy had reacted as I would have expected him to react. The news was new to him. That meant something on the good side for Jeremy. He hadn't known of the killing. That much at least he wasn't involved in.

It was still mid-morning, twenty minutes to noon, but I wished I had a bourbon right about then. I was feeling confused and at a roadblock. I don't like feeling like that, not when I have a responsibility, not when people are depending on me. There had to be something about Trangent to get him and his whole family murdered. All that had happened, the security guard, the entire Trangent family, the Hillsdale break-in, Trangent being in charge of lax security; it was all connected somehow, I knew that. All I had to do was find the connection to prove it.

I have never seen a coincidence; I don't believe in them; they just don't happen. When a leaf falls from a tree it doesn't just happen; there is always something that causes it to fall. A breeze, a squirrel on a branch, something. What happened at Hillsdale Technologies and with the Trangent family was all connected; I just had to find that connection.

Jeremy wiped his nose on his sleeve again and said, "His whole family wasn't murdered were they Morgan? They just couldn't have been. I can't believe that."

"Of course they were. I saw them. The wife and the three kids and Bill."

"There's another daughter," he said, looking down at his folded hands. "She wasn't there. She didn't live with them. She was in a home . . . You know . . . Mental problems of some kind. She ran away when she was thirteen. Bill spent months trying to find her. When he did, he got her to voluntarily go to a treatment center, a sort of care home for people with mental problems. He said she wouldn't come home, but she would go to the live-in place so long as it wasn't a hospital. It was a very expensive place, Morgan. I helped him pay the bill. Bill never talked about her . . . Except to me. No one, other than he and I, knew where she was."

"That's past tense, Jeremy," I said. "You mean she's not in the home anymore?"

"She left some time ago. We never found out where she went. She just disappeared."

I found a pad of paper in one of the desk drawers, and I wrote down whatever Jeremy had on the Trangent daughter, especially where she was living. She was the only lead I had. She might know something of her father that no one else knew. If nothing else, she had to be told that her family was dead. I would try somehow to tell her, anyway. It was a task I wasn't looking forward to. I have a difficult time talking to people who are ill. I never know the right things to say.

"OK, Jeremy," I said when I had filled a page and a half of paper. "Now let's go to your office. Where is it?"

"Fifth floor," he answered and struggled to get out of the chair he was in. He led the way to the hallway and to the elevators. I stopped him there.

"Let's take the stairs. We both could use the exercise."

"Come on, Morgan. I'm beat. Can't we just use the elevator?"

"No, the stairs."

I didn't want to tell him, but I didn't want to get boxed in anywhere. When I feel myself getting into trouble, I make it a habit to trust no one . . . Except Sandy, of course. If I needed to run, I wanted somewhere to run. It was a big building, and in the back of my mind was the possibility that we weren't alone.

We made it up the stairs with me breathing harder than Jeremy. I tried not to make that obvious to him. Jeremy's office was a big corner room, glass walled on two sides so that the green thickly forested hillside outside could be seen.

His office was furnished grandly in a modern, very masculine fashion. Paintings of sailing ships in rough waters hung on a side wall of dark cherry paneling. Jeremy's desk was very big and very modern dark glass on black metal legs. A red leather couch and two matching arm chairs sat against one of the glass walls. A row of flat screened TVs lined a long desk behind Jeremy's tall black leather chair. I was disappointed to see Jeremy did not keep a selection of booze in his office. It wasn't noon yet, but I would have taken a drink right then, to try to calm my nerves.

Jeremy walked into his office without holding the door for me. He stood inside, head bent, looking like he could collapse at any moment. "What do you want me to do, Morgan?" he asked.

"I want you to print out Bill Trangent's entire personnel file."

"I could have done that downstairs, Morgan."

"I don't think it's a good idea for us to use those computers anymore, Jeremy. The Feds are eventually going to start an investigation. Whoever broke in used a computer there. I don't want to answer their useless questions about having used the same computer. Just do what I ask, OK, Jeremy?"

He sat in front of a big monitor and pulled a wireless keyboard onto his lap. It took only a few seconds to power up the computer. I stood behind him so I could see what he was doing. I didn't trust Jeremy yet, and I didn't know if I ever would trust him again.

He started typing, and shortly a printer on the table behind his desk started spitting out paper. At page fourteen the printer stopped. I grabbed up the papers, folded them in three and slid them into my inside jacket pocket. I would read them later.

"OK, Jeremy. Turn that thing off." I said. "We're going to drive back to Manhattan now. When we get there, you're going to work with whoever Peter Jascro says you should work with. No questions asked, understand? I want the best damn security operation ever seen on this whole damn planet set up here, and you have two weeks to do that."

"The money, Morgan. That'll cost a fortune. It's not in my budget."

"To hell with your damn budget. Spend whatever it takes. I'll cover the costs. In the long term, Hillsdale Technologies has to continue. Money means nothing if your employees can continue doing the important work they do. Just do what I tell you to do."

Outside the gate, in the parking lot, the off-duty cop we had as a bodyguard was waiting by my car. The helicopter was gone and so was Donna Evans. The guard took a couple of steps towards us as we approached.

"Something strange, Mr. Crew. While you were inside this here black car drove up. It stopped down the road, just before the parking lot. I started towards it, and it turned fast and took off. Do you know what that was all about?"

"I'm really not sure yet," I said. "But I want you guys to stay close, OK?" There was no use telling him about the black car at Trangent's house. But having it here did confirm what I had hoped was not true, that someone was following me.

NINE – Morgan Crew Must Be Stopped

Jesse Wilson and Mohamed Al-Rashid were drinking strong Cuban coffee in the conference room of the Instituto de Inteligencia Militar outside of Havana. They spoke little while they waited for Omar Maalouf to arrive.

"Something has to be done," Mohamed said, breaking the silence. "We cannot continue to take this risk."

"Omar is a good man," Jesse replied. "He knows what he's doing."

Jesse was worried, but he couldn't let Mohamed know that. He looked out the big floor-to-ceiling window. The palm trees were swaying slowly in the light Caribbean breeze. The lawn outside was thick and green, the air soft and filled with the sweet smells of flowers and fruits.

Mohamed saw him looking out the window and he, too, looked out. How different he thought from the desert of his home in Saudi Arabia. He longed for the day when the royal family would be overthrown and an Islamic Republic established. Then he could go home once again. Going home any sooner meant certain, very painful, and very long to come death.

The door opened behind them, and Omar walked in. He looked tired and pale. His shoulders were slumped, and there were dark rings under his eyes. He sat on the opposite side of the big table.

"You look terrible," Jesse said.

"I haven't slept in a couple of days," he answered. Except for a couple of hours on the flight from Mexico City."

"You must leave again tomorrow," Mohamed demanded roughly. "This Morgan Crew must be eliminated. He is learning too much."

"Wait a minute," Jesse interrupted. "Omar has been doing a good job. It's not his fault . . ."

Mohamed glared at Jesse. He wasn't pleased with what had not been done. He said, his voice low and with obvious threats behind the words, "I know you and Omar are friends. I know you have worked together before. But friendship means nothing. Only results matter." Mohamed paused and turned to look at Omar. "Your results are not acceptable."

Omar leaned back in the chair and said, his voice reflecting his exhaustion, "I could have gotten him in New York. I had good line of site from across the street. But he had a man with him who got in the way. I had only one shot. At the hotel I should have done better. I admit that. This Morgan Crew is not as weak as I thought. And I was able to find him once again at Hillsdale Technologies by following his cell phone signals. But again there was a guard and several armed security guards. But he can't be perfect. I will get him. I will find a way."

Jesse leaned his elbows on the table, cleared his throat, and said, "Omar, you know I respect you. I know what you can do." That did not surprise Mohamed; it did cause his anger to rise. But he said nothing. Expressing his anger would have taken away some of his authority. He had to act as if he knew their work history already. Jesse continued, "But this man is different. I'd like the chance to get him myself."

"You've never killed anyone, Jesse," Omar said. He almost laughed, but Jesse was a friend.

"I don't mean to kill him. I want the opportunity to . . . To convert him so to speak."

"You mean use some of those famous 50's Communist brainwashing techniques?"

"Those things work more than they fail," Jesse argued.

Mohamed was silent, listening carefully, listening not so much for the words but the frame of mind that formed the words. Omar was desperate. Jesse sounded confident. Omar was defending himself. Jesse had hopeful ideas and thoughts. He spoke finally, "Jesse, I will give you one week. Omar will rest, and if you fail, he will take control of the operation."

Jesse smiled, satisfied, and said, "When I get him it will take more than a week."

"When you get him . . . If you get him . . . I will give you more time. If you don't have him within one week . . . Omar will resume. Now, Omar, what of the girl?"

"I have her," he answered. "She is safe, and I will keep her."

"Why is she still alive?" Jesse asked. Mohamed nodded and looked with hard eyes at Omar.

"As I said . . . I have her, and she is safe. She may be useful to us. If not . . . Then I will kill her."

Mohamed glared at Omar. He said, his voice threateningly deep and dark, "Do you have feelings for this girl?"

"Feelings? Do you mean do I love her? That's ludicrous. She is someone we may be able to use."

"Do you sleep with her?" Jesse asked.

"Of course," Omar answered with a laugh. "She is nothing. She is merely an infidel, after all."

TEN – The Seaside Home

I drove back to New York City from the Hillsdale complex with the guard in the passenger seat. Jeremy slept most of the way home, stretched out in the small backseat. In over seven hours, not a word was spoken. I switched on the radio and found the satellite jazz station. I felt a little better knowing I had a cop with a gun sitting next to me, but he made it obvious he wasn't a fan of American jazz.

I parked the car in front of The Cromwell Building, ignoring the red curb there. Maureen would have the car moved before it could be towed away. We stood as far from each other as we could as we rode the elevator up. When we got to Harper, Harper, Jascro and Nettles' floor the guard said, "I gotta' go now. I got a shift in the morning."

"You're a fulltime cop?" I asked.

"Yeah, all the guys are. There'll be someone here waiting to take over." He stepped back into the elevator, and the doors closed. Jeremy and I went to find Peter.

****

Peter was in his office reading briefs written by some junior associates. He seemed tired. His eyes were puffy and ringed in dark circles, and he was slouching in his chair. I had never thought of Peter Jascro as an old man, but he

155

looked like an old man when I walked into his office that day.

"Are you OK?" I asked.

He looked up at me and forced a drowsy smile. "Yes, Morgan," he answered as he put the briefs aside. "It's been a long couple of days, that's all."

"You've been dealing with the Feds, I'll bet."

"Department of Justice attorneys. A dozen of them are trying for promotions. But I can handle them. Most of them are young enough to be my grandchildren."

It was early evening, so Peter suggested we retreat to the upstairs apartments. Maureen volunteered to cook a dinner for us. She did a good job with a nice green salad and a roasted chicken. She even found a bottle of half way decent chardonnay. After setting three places – Peter decided to stay and have dinner with us – at the kitchen's table, Maureen left without a word to go home.

I did what I could to force Jeremy to eat something, and I limited his wine to one glass, in spite of his wanting more. I cleared the dishes and filled the sink with them. They would be washed and put away in the morning by someone Maureen would send up. The apartment was cleaned daily by people Maureen would have cleared as safe to be there.

We went to the gaudy, bright living room and sat on some very uncomfortable chairs that Peter's Japanese client liked. I had found some cheap bourbon in a bar cabinet and drank a glass or two of it. I told Jeremy he couldn't have any of it, and Peter declined when I offered him some.

"So anyway, Peter," I said. "I want Jeremy to install the best security available, physical, electronic, and manpower, everything, up at Hillsdale. Please assign a couple of your lawyers to help with the contracts and all that stuff. Find out who's the best in that business. And keep Jeremy here. Don't let him leave for any reason. Keep the guards, also."

"No problem, Morgan. Dare I ask what you're going to be doing while we're busy here?"

"Well, first I'm going to try to find Bill Trangent's missing daughter."

"What the hell?" Peter said.

I told Peter about the Trangent family and that there was another daughter still out there.

"What does that have to do with anything? How is that going to get my business going again?" Jeremy asked.

"It probably means nothing, Jeremy. But right now she's the only lead I have. And besides she needs to know her family is dead. It's the right thing to do . . . Even though it won't bring a profit in." I said that intentionally, a slight jab at the man who thought of nothing but profit.

Jeremy lowered his head and slouched down in the chair. He took a deep sigh and said, "I've talked with Bill and his wife about that. They've had detectives on it for a couple of months. Every time a hint of her shows up they send people out. It all leads to nothing."

"Yeah, well, I'm going to try anyway, Jeremy."

"And after that?" Peter asked.

"I've got questions for Donna Evans. Something stinks to high heaven here."

Peter frowned, and a suspicious look clouded his face. "Like what?" he asked.

"Do you wonder why the hell Homeland Security and the FBI are letting me into this? They can't be that magnanimous or good-hearted. And do they really think I'm better at solving crimes than they are? So what if Hillsdale closes up? What's it to them? They won't lose anything. Why do they care? It just doesn't make any sense."

"Good question, Morgan. I've thought about the same thing. Maybe they're trying to hang responsibility on you. That would be great publicity for them. Can you imagine the headlines? *'Billionaire Morgan Crew accused of treason.'* Just be careful. Those people can be dangerous, and remember, whatever they say is probably a lie. Truth is all too often too highly classified to be talked about."

We talked until past one in the morning. Jeremy was able to remember the group home the Trangent daughter had been in. It was in New Jersey in a very upscale neighborhood near Cape May, a restored Victorian resort town. After five hours of fretful sleep, I got my suitcase with all the new clothes Maureen had purchased for me and started driving south.

****

Cape May is at the very southern tip of New Jersey. It is a quaint little seaside town of restored, very Victorian homes and hotels. The main drag in town is Beach Avenue which runs along the shore. There is a wide, white sand beach and a boardwalk for the tourists. I found a nice, small hotel – The Captain's Rest – and checked in under a phony name. I paid in cash so as not to leave a trail. And I turned off my cell phone and left it off all the way down to Cape May. I kept the black car that had been following me in mind. Better to be careful no matter where I was, I reasoned.

The group home where Ashley Trangent had resided was in a part of town known as West Cape May. 'Seaside Home' was a misnomer because it was nowhere near the sea. But it seemed like a nice place, more like a small apartment building. It was painted white with an ocean blue trim. It was fenced in white pickets with colorful flowers and tall shade trees all over the front yard. There were no locks on the gate, or at the double glass front door that had some kind of big birds with long necks etched on the glass. So I just walked in.

Inside was very cheerful with lots of pale ocean blues and greens and mauves. Pleasant paintings in soft colors of the ocean and beaches and seaside birds hung on the walls. None of the paintings were of storms and high seas; it was all very calming. The furniture in the lobby was all pale oak with brightly colored cushions. Potted plants were everywhere. Long, sliding glass doors opened onto a large patio surrounding a good sized swimming pool with a dozen patio chairs, umbrellas, and tables nicely placed around it. I could imagine that the people living there might be very happy with the Seaside Home.

A reception desk was to the left as I walked in. A woman, fortyish and dressed very nicely in a colorfully flowered, high neck dress, smiled at me in welcome. "Can I help you? Are you here to visit someone?"

"Actually I'd like to speak with the manager."

The smile didn't diminish as she asked, "And may I ask what this concerns?"

"It concerns my wanting to speak with the manager," I said, smiling broadly and being the wise ass I usually am.

The lady lost her smile quickly, picked up the phone and dialed a four digit number. She didn't whisper, intending that I hear everything she said. "There is someone here to see you . . . He wouldn't give me his name . . . I think we should call security . . . Alright."

She hung up and glared at me. "Ms. Anderson will be here in a minute. Please have a seat."

"Just to be clear, I didn't give you my name because you didn't ask."

Rather than sit, and to keep being obnoxious, I remained on my feet and walked to the big glass doors to the patio and garden. It was a bright, sunny day. A half dozen people, some young and some older, were sitting around the pool, a few in loudly colored swim suits, others in shorts and shirts. None of them looked much like maniac serial killers, but maybe the Seaside Home wasn't the kind of group home that took maniac serial killers.

I saw a woman's reflection in the glass as she approached. She was dressed in a light blue gingham suit and white blouse. Her greying brunette hair was cut short and nicely styled. She looked very 'executive.' I turned and asked, "Mrs. Anderson?"

"Actually it's Ms. Anderson," she said in a suspicious voice being very specific with the 'Ms.' "May I help you with something?"

"Hello," I said and held my hand out to her. She took it lightly and quickly pulled her hand away. "I'd like to speak with you about a former resident here."

"I'm very sorry but our records are very confidential."

Out of the corner of my eye I saw two very big men in white hospital uniforms walking towards us. They stood behind me, about six feet away.

"Look, I'm sorry. I didn't mean to come across as a jerk. My name is Morgan Crew. I own Hillsdale Technologies. Bill Trangent worked there. His daughter,

Ashley, once stayed here. Can we go to your office, please?"

"Are you a relative of Ms. Trangent?"

"No. I told you, her father used to work for me."

"And he doesn't work for you anymore?"

"Ms. Anderson . . . Bill Trangent, his wife, and his three kids were all murdered the other day. I need to find Ashley. If she's not in danger, she at least should know her family is dead."

"Murdered! But . . ." Her hand went to her lips, and she took a step backward.

"Please, Ms. Anderson," I said. Five of the residents of Seaside Home were gathering nearby, hoping to be in on anything out of the routine of the place. "Can we go to someplace less public? Take the two guys standing behind me if you wish."

She weighed what I said, glanced around at the small crowd gathering, and quickly turned, waiving to the two men to follow. We walked into her small office, and she closed the door behind us. She and I sat; the two aides stood with their backs to the door.

Ms. Anderson's face was pale; her breathing was short. She was either very upset at hearing about the murders, or she had something else to worry about. I played the second option.

"What are you worried about, Ms. Anderson?" I asked, getting right to the point.

She didn't answer. She kept an unblinking gaze on me.

"Ms. Anderson, what's wrong?"

"You say Ashley's entire family was . . . Murdered?"

"That's right. Her mother, father, sister and brothers. Everyone I think . . . I hope . . . But for Ashley. Now, tell me about Ashley. I think you can help me find her. She needs to know about her mother and father. And . . . You have to understand that she, too, may be in trouble."

"I . . . I . . . I just don't know. Should I be talking to our lawyer?"

"Now that surprises me, Ms. Anderson," I said and leaned back in the chair. "Do you know something that needs a lawyer to protect you?"

"I . . ." She took a deep breath and straightened in her chair. "Tell me again who you are."

"I'm Morgan Crew. I own the place where Ashley's father worked."

"And all you want is to tell Ashley . . . About her family?"

"Ms. Anderson, Ashley may be in danger, also. I keep saying that. Her entire family has been murdered. Don't you understand?"

"What makes you think Ashley is in danger?" she asked.

I took a minute to think about that. I couldn't tell her about the security breach at Hillsdale. If that got out, the media would eat it up like a hungry shark. But I had to tell her something.

"There is a very personal family problem involved here. Please don't ask what that family problem is. I can't tell you, but believe me it is something that would destroy the memories of the family if made public."

"Why you and not the police?"

"If the police haven't been here yet, they will be. And they will not be as talkative and nice as I am. If you don't answer their questions they will arrest you. You will be forced to answer questions in court. The news media will eat that up, and you will probably be out of business in a short time. If I can find Ashley quickly, they will have no need to question you."

She first rubbed her chin and then ran a hand through her hair as she thought about what I said. A thermos and a single glass sat on a small wooden tray at the side of her desk. She poured water into the glass, drank a small mouthful of it, and then said, "I can't tell you anything in Ashley's medical file. HIPPA laws forbid that. Other than that, what do you want to know?"

"Let's start with how long she was here."

"Ashley came to us when she was thirteen years old. She was here almost six years."

"Without giving me details," I asked carefully. "She had some kind of mental issue?"

"We don't refer to *mental issues*. Ashley had problems that were a combination of physical and social issues."

"Problems at home?"

"You could say that," she answered and looked away from me, tilting her head downward and to the left. That body language, looking down and to the left, told me she was either lying or hiding something.

"Were the problems at home physical abuse or sexual abuse? And I don't think that is medical. It's more a legal and social issue."

"It borders on the psychological and psychiatric records. So that is certainly medical. But I can say there were problems inside the home and outside."

"I'm going to guess, and all you have to tell me is if I am right or wrong, or maybe close. Ashley, as a young girl, was sexually promiscuous. She was being punished at home for this, probably punishment that went too far. And she may have been involved with drugs. How close am I?"

She didn't say anything, but a thin smile crossed her lips, she closed her eyes, and she nodded her head ever so slightly. I was right. It was just a wild guess, but I was right.

"So," I went on. "Ashley was finally sent here. How did she do here?"

"At first she was very . . . Disruptive. But she settled in once she began to understand that we do not allow physical punishment here. This is a home, not a prison."

"So she was used to physical punishment at home?" I asked.

"She did tell us that. I have no evidence to corroborate that, however. She had no signs of bodily injury . . . Bruising, scars and the like."

"Was she sexually active here?"

"At first, she was. But with the proper care she understood that kind of activity was not correct."

"She had medical as well as psychiatric care?"

Ms. Anderson paused for a moment. She said, "Ashley was on a program of care. That's all I can say."

"And she was being treated for drug abuse, also?"

"She was on a program of care, as I said."

"Alright," I changed the subject. "Did she have any visitors?"

"Yes," she answered, sitting forward and a little more comfortable with the question. "Her mother was here on a regular basis."

"Not her father?"

"Once or twice when Ashley first came here."

"So she didn't like her father? And I assume her father didn't like her?"

"There seemed to be an element of . . . I want to say mutual anger. But my training tells me it is disrespect . . . One for the other."

"So her mother was her only visitor?"

Ms. Anderson paused once again. There was something she had to be very careful of. Some issue that might come back to bite her on the ass. She shifted uncomfortably in her chair.

She looked over my shoulder and told the two aides to leave her and me alone. When the door had been closed and we sat looking at each other without the two aides, she said, "There was a physical therapist here . . . He was hired a year after Ashley first arrived. He and Ashley . . . Were involved for . . . We believe . . . Several months . . . Perhaps longer. He was fired. She was just a child at the time. We had no choice."

"He was fired because of the affair, I assume?"

"No . . . We stopped that soon after it started . . . At least I think we did. Freedom is very important here. He was fired because we found out he was not who he said he was."

"I don't understand."

She took a deep breath and then said, "He was hired under the name James Bifford. We received an anonymous report that his name really was Omar Maalouf. I questioned him, and he denied the report. The next day he didn't show up for work. He never returned to collect his last paycheck."

"Did you ever find out who made the report?" I asked.

"No . . . But I have a suspicion it may have been Ashley's mother."

"Why do you suspect that?"

"Her mother seemed to be the only person who cared about Ashley. It's just a suspicion, as I said."

"Was that close to the time Ashley walked away?"

"She left shortly after he was terminated. Ashley was nearly twenty years old," Anderson sighed deeply. "She was not here on a court order. We don't lock residents up here. As far as we are concerned she was free to leave whenever she wanted to leave."

"Did she leave to be with this Omar?" I asked.

"I don't know, but they were corresponding . . . By mail and by phone for quite some time after Omar left. I can't help but think she went to him."

"Did you read any of the letters?"

She stood slowly, paused and then walked to a small, two drawer filing cabinet that sat on the floor in a corner. She opened the bottom drawer and pulled out a two inch thick stack of envelopes that were tied with a thin string.

"Towards the end of Ashley's stay here, she reverted to extreme anger. She was breaking things and . . . And confronting other residents. She had to be restrained several times to keep her from hurting herself and others. She refused her medications. She was becoming disruptive to the other residents here. We were ready to tell her parents that she could not stay here any longer.

"I . . . I don't know if I should have done this," she went on, obviously uncomfortable, "but I instructed the staff to let me see mail from her before it was sent out and to retrieve letters to her from her desk and trash. I felt I had to find out what was causing her anger. These are photocopies of the letters she wrote and the originals of most of the letters she received." She handed the bundle to me.

I untied the bow of the string that held the bundle together and took the photocopy of the letter from the bottom of the pile. It was from Ashley and addressed to Omar. It read:

> Oh Omar,
>
> I miss you so much. I miss fucking you and I miss kissing you. My damn mother came today. God how I hate her and my god damn father, too. I wish they were dead.
>
> I wish you and I could be together always. Please write to me, please phone me. I want to hear your voice.
>
> I want to feel your cock inside of me even more.
>
> Please,
>
> Ashley

I read three more of the letters. They were all the same. I counted ten letters from Ashley before there was one from Omar. The words were printed and childlike. Many words were misspelled.

Ashely my little hen,

I do mis you very much. I to want to be with you. Maybe we can.   Maybe I can talk with you father.

Where is he? At what addres house he is?

  Omar

I took the time to read the next several letters. Ashley told Omar her family's address and where her father worked. At the time he was at Hillsdale Technologies, having left Seattle many years before. Two months after the last letter from Omar, Ashley left The Seaside Home.

"I assume I can't take these letters with me?" I asked Ms. Anderson.

"I wish I didn't have them, Mr. Crew. If the police come . . . Will they want them?"

"I'd be very surprised if they didn't take them."

"If Ashley is in trouble, what will you do?" she asked. Her face was flushed, and she was frowning deeply.

"If I can find her . . . And if she is in trouble . . . I will protect her from whoever killed her family. I will also protect her from the other trouble I think she may be in."

"You mean Omar?" she asked.

"Yes . . . Omar. One more thing, Ms. Anderson," I asked. "Who was paying Ashley's bill here?"

"That's the strange thing, Mr. Crew," she said.

"Families of our residents pay the bills. All except for Ashley's. Once a month we received a bank check from a small bank in Texas. I frankly forget the name of the bank . . . Lone Star or something like that. I can find that out if it's important. And each check was for a little more than was due. We put the excess in Ashley's personal account here. She used it to buy little things, you know, makeup and the like."

That struck me as strange because Jeremy had told me he was helping Bill Trangent pay Ashley's bill. Either Jeremy had lied to me or Bill Trangent had lied to Jeremy. But why?

"Did you ever ask her parents about that?"

"I did, but they were very evasive. Mr. Trangent told me twice that I wasn't to be worried about where the money came from as long as it came regularly and on time. He was quite short with me the second time I asked."

She let me take the letters with me. I think in some way she was relieved to be rid of them. With them I had an address for Omar. Someplace called San Pedro Escobar in Texas. And Texas is where the checks came from. And as I said, I don't believe in coincidences.

That is where I would go to find her. But I have this little voice that lives in the back of my head. When that little voice has a hunch that I am headed for trouble it starts shouting, "RUN AWAY! RUN AWAY!" It was shouting as loud as I had ever heard it as I left The Seaside Home.

ELEVEN - San Pedro Escobar

I spent the night at the Captain's Rest and got a restless night's sleep. The next morning I found a small, rundown diner and ate a marginal breakfast of greasy eggs, sausage, wet toast, and coffee that been on the burner way too long.

I drove back to Manhattan, parked in front of Peter's office building, and took the elevator up to the obscenely gaudy apartment above Peter's offices. Jeremy was deeply depressed and said very little to me. Peter did tell me he had assigned two of his attorneys to handle the security upgrade at Hillsdale Technologies. They would interview security companies and make whatever changes were necessary to upgrade Hillsdale Technologies to beyond the point that would make the Feds happy. Jeremy, Peter told me, was of very little help, but he would, I was assured, sign all the necessary contracts whether he wanted to or not. I told Peter that neither Jeremy nor anyone else was to approve or oversee the security changes.

I phoned Sandy and spoke with her for over an hour. She wanted me to come home as much as I wanted to go home. Caroline was asking where I was and wanting to play trucks with me. But my responsibility to the family kept me away from Sandy and our daughter. I didn't mention all the food I had been eating. After all, I'm not stupid.

I stayed that night in the apartment with Jeremy. He said little; his depression seemed to be deepening. But his saying little was alright with me. I didn't like Jeremy, and not talking with him seemed like a good idea. I watched some TV and went to bed early.

The next morning I took a taxi to JFK and flew to Houston. I had Maureen rent a car there through an account the law office had. Once again my own credit card would have left a trail. I asked her to avoid all the small imported cars and pay an outrageous price for a big Lincoln SUV. After getting lost a couple of times, I was able to point the car south, and by early evening I drove into a decrepit little place called San Pedro Escobar.

San Pedro was a collection of mud adobe buildings that had seen better days. The entire town sat on one side of an unnamed, cracked and pot hole filled, two lane road miles off of anything that could be called a highway. It was perhaps a hundred yards from the Rio Grande, Mexico being within sight a short distance away.

The town consisted of a ratty looking tavern – a weather faded sign that was barely readable hung over an open door saying 'TABERNA.' Next to it was another faded and weather beaten sign, this time advertising Coca Cola. It said 'BODEGA' but could have fooled me. And a couple of what might loosely be called homes with broken windows finished the town.

A few children were playing in the dusty street, and a bone thin, old, yellow dog sat in what little shade was cast under a withered and skinny tree watching them. In front of the taberna two old men sat on a bench smoking and drinking something from a green glass bottle they passed back and forth between them.

Based on their leathery, sun burnt, wrinkled skin and thick gray hair, they looked like they could be a hundred years old. They watched me as I climbed from the big SUV.

I went to them and greeted them, "Hola, señor." My Spanish isn't as good as Sandy's, but I know a few words. I guessed my Spanish wasn't as good as I thought it was, because the two men just sat and stared at me without saying anything.

"Do you speak English? Habla English?"

One of them spit to the side and said, "Sí, I speak English."

"Great. I'm looking for a man. Omar Maalouf. Do you know him? Where can I find him?"

"Omar?" the old man asked. A suspicious frown crossed his face.

"Yes . . . Sí . . . Omar. I have an address."

I gave him the address Ashley had been writing to. The old man spat again, took a swig of whatever they were drinking, handed the bottle to his friend, took a long drag on his thick, hand rolled cigarette, and finally said, "Omar, he is gone. Long time now."

"How about the address? How do I get there?"

He pointed to his left and said, "Two, three miles maybe."

I thanked them both and got back in the car. As I started the engine it occurred to me that I was hungry. I pulled the car a few feet away to the bodega. Inside was dark and dusty, but it smelled of luscious Mexican food and hot chilies. An enormously fat woman sat inside the front door on an old pickup truck's bench seat, its brown vinyl cracked and split enough to let stuffing protrude from it. Communication was tough, but I managed to walk out with two big pork burritos which were really spicy and really good and two bottles of ice cold beer.

I wolfed down the burritos and drank both bottles of

beer quickly. The road out of town led to a shallow point in the Rio Grande, and I crossed it, driving into Mexico. For the next three miles I saw no one and nothing but scrub bush, cactus, and sand, and one really big nasty looking lizard sunning itself on top of a rock. I slowed to turn a corner, and there, behind a low rocky hill, sat an ancient looking, single wide trailer. The desert hadn't been kind to it, beating it badly with wind-blown sand, but it was still there. The brown and white paint on the aluminum was all but gone, and two of the three windows were broken. Dry bush and some cactus were all there was around the trailer besides rocks and sand.

I parked at the side of the road and started towards it. I stopped suddenly when a fat rattlesnake, sitting in the shade under some scrub, hissed and shook its rattled tail. By the way, I hate snakes.

I gave it about ten feet of room by making a big arc around it and made it to the trailer. The door hung open and loose from one hinge. I stuck my head in, thinking there might be the rattler's friend inside. It was dark, and the only thing visible was filth and sand. The old man was right; Omar was long gone.

Evening was settling in, and it would take me well into the morning to drive back to Houston. I figured I wouldn't find any kind of hotel or motel in San Pedro Escobar, so I decided I would stay where I was for the night. I considered stripping and jumping into the brown water of the Rio Grande, but I figured walking around in the night might cause me to run into another snake. So I didn't.

In the morning I would make a stop at the bodega and get some more terrific food for breakfast. Maybe, I sort of hoped, they would have some stuff Sandy would not have let me eat if she had been there.

I sat on the car's hood enjoying the cooling air as night began to fall. After staring up at a couple million stars in a cloudless sky for a couple of hours, I climbed into the SUV. I lowered the back seats of the SUV and stretched out. The night got cold, and I didn't have anything to cover myself with. But I managed to curl up and finally fell asleep.

It was light outside, and the sun was above the horizon when a knocking on the car's window woke me. My first thought was bandits, and I wished I had a gun with me. I jumped quickly into the front seat and fiddled with the keys, trying to find the ignition. Whoever had done the knocking called out, "Whoa there! Ya'll don't need to go nowhere. I ain't gonna hurt you none."

A man stood by the closed driver's side window smiling at me. He was clearly not Mexican. He wore a tattered old cowboy hat that at one time was tan in color and now was dirty brown with a sweat stained brim. He sported a two or three day growth of beard, and his lower lip was puffed out from the snuff packed behind it.

I looked him up and down. He was wearing a red plaid shirt. The sleeves were rolled up to his elbows. Old, faded blue jeans, wrinkled and not exactly clean, were cuffed high enough to show off scuffed cowboy boots that hadn't been cleaned or polished in a couple of years. His belt was old brown leather, cracked and wrinkled, with a big silvery buckle that needed polishing. His belted jeans were pulled down low under a prodigious beer belly. He needed a haircut badly, but he was smiling broadly. I couldn't see a gun anywhere – I sort of expected to see a 'six shooter' in a cowboy holster – so I felt a little better about having been woken by him.

"Mr. Crew," he said through the window. "You are that there Morgan Crew fella' now ain't ya'll?"

The man's southern drawl was pronounced and almost made me want to smile. I rolled down the window half way and asked, "Who the hell are you?"

"Mah' name is Pierre Gustave Toutant Beauregard. Ah' was named afta' my great-great-great grand-pappy of the same name. Gen'l Beauregard was the best damn ol' Gen'l in the whole damn Confederate Army. But ya'll can call me Bubba. Ever'body does."

"OK," I said, not the least astonished. "So who the hell are you?"

"Well, I guess Ah' am a agent with the O.S.I."

"What the hell is the O.S.I.?"

"Why, that there is the *U*-nited States Air Force Office of Special Investigations."

"You're kidding right? The friggin' Air Force? You're joking."

Bubba reached into his back pocket and pulled out a bent and overused blue leather case. He opened it, grinned like a kid on Christmas morning and showed me the silver badge with wings at the top and an ID card that did in fact identify Bubba as an O.S.I. Agent.

"I've never heard of the O.S.I." I said.

"Ya'll ever watch TV? They got this here show called NCIS. Ever seen that one? Pretty damn good show if'n ya'll ask me. Anyway, that there's the Navy and Ah' am the Air Force."

All I could think of saying was, "You're kidding."

"No, suh. Ah' am the real McCoy as they say. Now, why don't ya'll climb outta' that there purty car, and we kin' talk some."

I still didn't know what to make of Bubba. I mean, he shows up out of nowhere and says he's some kind of Air Force cop. But I did open the door, and I climbed out of the SUV anyway.

Bubba was about as tall as I am, but even though I was twenty-five pounds overweight, he was still heavier than me. Most of that weight was carried in his belly.

He held out his hand, grinned broadly, and said, "Well now, Ah' sure am glad t'meet ya'll Mr. Crew."

I shook his hand gingerly and asked, "How do you know my name?"

"Well now, that there Donna Evans . . . Ya'll met her Ah' think, now didn't ya'll? Anyway, she done put out one a'them there Inter Agency notices that you was working with them there folks."

"And just how the hell did you find me here?"

"Well now, Ah' been afta' that there Omar fella' for some time now. Been wantin' t'talk with him, ya'll know? When ya'll flew down t'Houston Ah' jest figgered ya'll might be lookin' for Omar, too. So, here Ah' am. Ah' was right, wasn't Ah'?"

"Why are you looking for Omar?" I asked. It couldn't be because of Ashley. There had to be some other reason.

"That there Omar fella', he been runnin' 'round like a stuck pig," Bubba laughed. "I been tryin' to get him fer a couple years now."

"But why?" I insisted.

"Well . . . 'cause he been workin' for a couple terrorist gangs back there in that there Middle East."

"What! You mean Omar is a terrorist?"

"Well, not exactly. Ya'll gott'a unner'stan'. They's them that fights over there and them's that helps'em along from back here."

"You mean he sends money to Al-Qaida?"

"Not exactly, Mr. Crew," Bubba smiled and sighed. "Omar, he is more a'one of them there spy folks."

I didn't know what to say. I had absolutely no response. Bubba, realizing I was dumbfounded, said, "Now, Ah' know you been lookin' for that there Ashley Trangent l'il girl. That's why you done come all the ways down here. Ah' unner'stan'. But now ya'll know who this here Omar fell'a is, might be purty smart for ya'll to go on home, don't ya'll think?"

I asked him, "Is Ashley still with Omar?"

"Far as I can tell, she is."

"Where are they?"

"Now, Mr. Crew. Ya'll just gotta' stay away from this whole thing. Ya'll just go on home, and leave ever'thin' t'me."

"OK," I lied. "I'll go home. Just tell me where she is, and I can tell her friends and family she's alright."

"If I got ya'll word on that . . ." he began.

"My word as a gentleman," I said, knowing I am as far from being a gentleman as anyone can be.

"Last I heard they was in a little town outside a' Mexico City. Some place called Tuactualco or some such."

"And Ashely's OK?" I asked. "I mean, she's not in any danger or anything?"

"So long as the child is with that there Omar, well she's in some danger. But she'll be OK. We gonna find her and Omar soon, don't ya'll worry none 'bout that."

"OK, that's all I need to know. Now, if I can go, I'll head back to Houston and catch a plane home."

"Now that there is the right thing t'do, Mr. Crew. Ah certainly am glad t'have met ya'll. Ya'll drive safe now, hear?"

Bubba walked to a dirt covered Ford pickup truck that might have been red under all the dust and dirt and mud, turned to wave goodbye, and drove away.

****

I stopped at San Pedro and bought some kind of pastries that were stuffed with a creamy cheese and lathered in sweet honey. I bought some bitter coffee that the fat old lady was kind enough to give me in a clay mug. I had to pay for the mug, too, but I didn't care. The pastries, even though sticky and sweet, were very good. One more thing I intended to not mention to Sandy.

The drive to Houston was long and lonely. I tried to find some radio stations, but without satellite radio most of what I found was country preachers and static. I found a nice looking hotel, The Martin Inn, at the Houston airport that had a room available for cash. After a long shower I phoned Sandy.

"Hi, babe. Everything OK back there?" I asked as I looked through the room service menu for a dinner that Sandy wouldn't let me have if she were there.

"Yes, but we all miss you. Any idea of when you'll be home?"

"In a day or two . . . If I can find Ashley."

I wasn't going to mention meeting Bubba, and I certainly wasn't going to tell her about Omar.

"So you know where she is?"

"I think so," I said. "Down in Mexico. Look, I need my passport. Can you overnight it to me? I'm at the Martin Inn in Houston at the airport."

We talked for an hour, but sleep was catching up with me, and my stomach was growling for food. The night in the back of the SUV wasn't very comfortable, and I woke up often and with a backache in the morning.

After we hung up I ordered a big steak with a side of onion rings and showered a second time while I waited for it to be delivered. I had to pay cash when the meal was delivered, not wanting to leave a credit card trail. I was able to eat most of it. I wanted to raid the room's honor bar fridge for a drink or two, but I was more tired than I needed booze. Sleep was calling my name, so I crawled into bed. I had just fallen asleep when my cell phone rang and woke me. I had forgotten to turn it off after using the GPS to find my way back to Houston. At first I was going to ignore it, but it wouldn't stop, so I picked it up.

"Hello, Morgan. This is Donna Evans. How are you?"

"Sleepy," I said.

"I understand you met Bubba today."

That should not have surprised me, but it did. I assumed that all the damn spies talk to one another. I answered, "Yes, I sure did. Is he for real?"

"Don't let him fool you. He's the best. He specializes in technology and science. He investigates anything in those fields for the Air Force. Thefts and treason are his specialties."

"And that's why he's here?" I asked. I yawned.

"I'm going to tell you something you probably shouldn't know. Bill Trangent used to work for InterAir in Seattle. Quite a few secrets were stolen from InterAir while he was there. No one knew who was doing the thefts or why at the time. Now secrets have been stolen from Hillsdale where Bill worked. We think there is a connection."

I put two and two together and asked before thinking that I probably shouldn't say anything, "Ashley Trangent ran off with Omar Maalouf. Omar Maalouf is a spy for Al-Qaida type terrorist groups. There's a connection there, too, isn't there."

She said nothing, and then the line went dead. I wasn't supposed to know that, I guessed. Exhaustion had caused me to make a mistake. There was nothing to do that night, so I went back to bed, spending an hour or more thinking about all of this. Sleep had overcome me at ten PM, and I didn't wake until half past ten AM. I stretched and yawned and scratched that part of me where only Sandy and I go.

I rubbed the sleep from my eyes, opened them and saw a man sitting on the chair by the desk.

"Good morning, Mr. Crew." He said.

He was a black man, light skinned, well dressed, slim, but well built. He sat comfortably, his legs crossed, a friendly smile on his handsome face. My eyes caught the light reflected from his highly polished shoes.

I jumped out of bed; my immediate reaction was to back away from him. I wished at the time I had my little .38 with me. Imagine I thought, someone breaking into a hotel room! All I could think of with my sleep fogged brain was how terrible that had to be. I looked at the room's door; it was not broken. The room's windows didn't open as is common in hotels today to prevent jumpers' suicides. So how the hell did he get in?

"Who the hell are you?" I asked, struggling to get the words out.

"Oh, please excuse me," he said. "My name is Jesse Wilson."

"OK, Jesse Wilson. What the hell do you want . . . And how did you get in here?"

"You know, Mr. Crew," Jesse began. He straightened himself in the chair and switched his crossed legs, left to right. "The world is such a sad place. I gave a very nice maid, Mexican I think, ten dollars, and she opened the door for me. Imagine, only ten dollars. I'll bet it was a lot of money to her. You should have seen her face light up. She must have thought it a fortune."

"OK . . . So what?"

"Of course," he said. "You want to know why I'm here. I am so very sorry for not explaining immediately. You would like to find Ashley Trangent. I can help you with that."

I had the big king-sized bed between Jesse and me so I sat on it, took a deep breath, and asked, "What friggin' spy agency are you with? CIA . . . NSA . . . FBI . . . FAH?"

Jesse frowned and asked, "FAH? Is that a spy agency? I've never heard of it."

"FAH stands for Friggin' Ass Hole. I kind of made that one up."

Jesse laughed. "That's a good joke. I'll have to remember that one. Do you mind if I use it now and then?"

"You didn't answer my question," I said. "What

agency are you with?"

"None . . . None that you've ever heard of in any case. I'm with a private NGO, a non-government organization. But all I want to do is help you speak with Ms. Trangent."

"So you know where she is?"

"Of course. But she is not where . . . Bubba? . . . What a humorous man he is, with such a humorous name. Not where Bubba told you she is."

"So I'm asking again. Where is she?" I insisted.

"I can take you to her . . . If you agree, of course. But if I tell you where Ashley is, and you decline my most kind offer to take you to her, you might tell Donna Evans. That would be unfortunate. Both for you and for whomever Ms. Evans sends out to get Ashley."

"That sounds like a threat," I said.

"Oh, please! No! I am only looking out for Ashley's welfare and yours, of course. If Agents try to get to her, the people she is with will certainly harm her. Let me take you to her."

"Tell me where she is first," I said.

"I will . . . But only if you agree to allow me to take you to her."

So I had a 'Hobson's Choice.' Take what Jesse Wilson offered or be no closer to Ashley Trangent than I was yesterday. There was no in-between. I gambled, but in the end I knew I had to take his offer.

"Would you object if I checked you out?"

"Oh, please do," he said jovially. "Please phone whomever you wish."

I circled the bed, walked cautiously in front of Jesse,

and went to the phone at the bedside table. I phoned Peter, my first choice in asking for anything.

"Hello, Peter," I said as I glared at the man who had gotten into my room. "I have two favors. First, have your people run a background on a Jesse Wilson. Then get in touch with Donna Evans. Ask her about the same man. Do it fast and immediate. I need an answer in less than an hour."

I watched Jesse as I spoke to Peter. He was smiling casually and nodding his approval.

"That's fine," Jesse said after I had hung up. "I haven't had any breakfast yet this morning. What say while we wait we order some room service. Shall I do that while you shower and dress?"

I stood in the shower letting steaming water revive me from sleep and surprise. I figured that if this Jesse Wilson wanted to kill me, he would have done it already. He could have killed me in bed as I slept. He seemed friendly enough, but I have met a couple of very friendly blood-thirsty killers over the years. I'm not a doctor or a psychologist, but I've come to understand that some crazy and dangerous people can come across as very nice and friendly folks . . . Until they kill you.

He said he knew where Ashley was, and he would take me to her. There was a reason he wouldn't just tell me where she was. That meant he wanted me where she was. That could be dangerous, like walking into the spider's web. In the end, as I stepped from the shower and shaved, I resolved to take Jesse up on his offer. I had no choice at the time. Life is nothing but risks if one is not to sit on a couch and watch time go by. Learning by taking risks may not be for everyone, but it is the way I lead my life.

Jesse had ordered scrambled eggs, sausage and

bacon. "I didn't know which you would prefer, so I ordered both," he explained. There was toast and yogurt and orange juice and a lot of coffee.

I enjoyed all of it and thanked him. "Please, don't thank me. After all, I paid for it with money from your wallet. I guess you paid cash for the room; they wouldn't let me sign for it." He laughed as he said that and then bit into a piece of toast. I found it strange that I found the humor in that, too. I drank some coffee as we were both laughing.

When breakfast was done I started to pack my single suitcase. Jesse lit a cigarette and watched. I said, "You know this is a non-smoking room."

"Yes, I know that," was all he said as he continued to smoke.

The phone rang, and I jumped for it. It would tell me if Jesse was to be trusted or not. Jesse didn't move, but he smiled as I went for the phone. It was Peter. He told me his investigators could find hundreds of people with the name Jesse Wilson. I looked at Jesse and gave Peter a description. Peter looked at his list and then said, "Could be a couple of people. Four are currently in prison. One died a month ago. Three are preachers. There are others, but older or much younger than your guy. I'm afraid I've nothing for you."

"How about Donna?" I asked.

"I just got off the phone with her. She never heard of a Jesse Wilson in her business. Morgan, I suggest you get out of whatever you're in. Go home. Don't walk into a blind alley."

I hung up the phone without answering Peter. Over the years he has always taken the opportunity to try to protect me and keep me out of trouble. He has called on me many, many times to do things for my family, but he has always advised me to stay away from trouble. I often told him how damn contradictory that was. What I had to do for my family was always trouble, or they wouldn't call on me.

I said to Jesse, "I guess no one has ever heard of you. Why is that?"

"Why should they? My friends and I lead a quiet life. We stay away from the media . . . And the police, of course. Breaking the law is something very serious and something we seldom ever do. We work for the good, and like you, we don't always observe what is legal. But we do it very carefully, very quietly, only bending the law rather than breaking it. I'm not at all surprised no one has ever heard of me."

I had to accept that. If I were to do what I knew I had to do, I had to accept what this Jesse Wilson was telling me. I knew that Omar Maalouf had to be connected somehow with the thefts at Hillsdale, and I knew that Bill Trangent had to be connected with Omar. Bill's daughter had to be the connection between the two. If I were to save Hillsdale and Jeremy and my family, I had to find Ashley. So, I had to go along with this Jesse Wilson.

How many times over the years have I walked into the lion's den and walked out alive? I had to enter that den once again. It was my lot in life. I had to do it.

"When do we leave?" I asked as I folded a shirt and packed it.

"No rush, Mr. Crew. I have a plane waiting."

"A private plane? I'm impressed. I'll stop at the desk and get my passport. My wife is sending it out to me."

"That's fine," Jesse answered. He stood and walked to the room service cart and the remnants of the breakfast dishes. He crushed out his cigarette on a plate that once held eggs. "I find it rather intrusive that they don't allow smoking in these rooms."

I smiled in agreement and turned to get the last of my socks from a drawer in the bureau. I felt the sharp stabbing of the needle in the side of my neck. Whatever Jesse had injected into me worked very fast. A soft black cloud engulfed me as I fell to the floor.

TWELVE – And Then There Was Pain

When I woke up I had a splitting headache, my stomach was painfully twisted, and I could taste bile. I was strapped down to a hospital bed; the mattress was thin, and it covered a solid metal bed. It was lumpy and smelled really bad. It was more than just filth. I had smelled the odor before. It was the smell of dried blood, human excrement, and death.

My arms were spread out to my sides, shackled with heavy, tight leather straps at my wrists, each fastened to a side rail of the bed. My feet were spread out, and similar leather straps held them to the metal frame of the bed on each side. I pulled at the wrist straps, but it only hurt to do that. The same happened when I tried to move my feet. I tried shifting in the bed, but yet another thick and tight leather strap encircled my waist; it cut into my stomach and side when I tried to move. Lifting my head I found was also impossible, because a similar leather strap at my forehead held my head down. Each strap felt like razor blades cutting into my skin when I moved.

My eyes slowly focused, and I looked around as far as my eyes could see without turning my head. Above me was a white ceiling of sound dampening tiles. A big light hung from the ceiling, but it was not turned on. To my right and left, as far as I could see, were blank walls of white; past my feet was another solid wall of white. And I found I was lying there completely naked.

I felt something at my right elbow. Shifting my eyes, being careful not to move my head, I saw a tube hanging from a drip bag. The tube ended at the needle stuck in the inside of my elbow. I could see a clear liquid dripping from the bag, very slowly, down the tube and into my arm.

It was cold in the room; I could feel cold air being blown from somewhere. I began to shiver in the cold. I forced myself not to shake to avoid the extreme pain of the leather holding me down.

My throat was very dry, but I tried to call out as best I could, "HELLO! ANYBODY! HELLO!" My voice was thick and raspy.

I could hear a door opening behind me; the hinges needed oil. A woman in a nurse's uniform came to the side of my bed.

"Where am I?" I managed to whisper.

She checked the needle and tube from the drip bag but said nothing.

"Where am I?" I repeated.

She checked each of the restraints. She put her hand on my forehead and checked my pulse.

"What's going on?"

She put a stethoscope to my chest and listened.

"Where am I? Is this a hospital?"

She ignored me, as if I hadn't said anything.

"Where am I? Who are you?" I asked again, my throat raw from both lack of water and whatever Jesse had injected me with.

The nurse walked away, and I heard the door close.

I closed my eyes against the throbbing in my head. Whatever Jesse had injected into my neck must have been powerful stuff. My eyes started watering but I had no way of wiping them. My nose was running; I sniffled, but even that slight movement caused pain at my forehead under the leather. I was shivering from the icy cold air being blown on me.

Clearing my throat with some coughing, even though the strap at my waist cut into me, I was able to start yelling as loud as I could, which wasn't very loud. "WHERE THE HELL AM I? SOMEBODY! GET ME OUTTA' HERE! HEY! CAN ANYBODY HEAR ME?" My head rebelled against the yelling, so I stopped. Nobody was answering the calls anyway.

My eyes were getting heavy; I could feel drug induced sleep forcing itself on me in spite of the cold. I didn't fight it, because I thought sleep might make the headache go away. And maybe what I was experiencing was just a dream, a nightmare. And when I woke up . . . If I woke up . . . I would be home in California with Sandy and Caroline and Betsy.

It was a dreamless, restless sleep that woke me several times when I tossed and tried to turn, causing the leather straps to bite into my wrists and ankles. But I slept. I don't know for how long.

I woke up slowly, afraid to open my eyes. Was it all just a dream? A nightmare? I soon learned it wasn't because I could still feel the restraints. When I did finally rejoin the waking world the white room hadn't changed. What had changed was that Jesse Wilson was sitting on a stool at the side of the bed, a few feet from me, and the room was warmer.

"Well, good morning, Morgan . . . Or is it afternoon?"

He laughed. "The drug I gave you will have worn off by now. I am sorry it gave you such a headache. It did leave you with a headache I assume? All of the test subjects reported strident headaches, but we know it will have no long lasting negative effects."

"Where the hell am I?" I demanded as strongly as my weak voice could manage.

"We'll get to that later," he said. "We will have several days of conversation first. I've read a report on you, Morgan. Yale grad, aren't you? Quite impressive. And all that money! I've seen photos of your wife. Wow, she is beautiful. And that little child of yours, how cute. Takes after her mother I see, not to insult you at all, of course."

"Who are you?" I asked, interrupting him as I twisted my eyes to the right in order to see him.

"I told you that, Morgan. I am Jesse Wilson."

"These straps, they really hurt. Are they necessary?"

"I'm afraid so . . . At least for the time being. It all depends on how our conversations progress."

"You're black . . . African . . . You sound American . . . African American . . ."

"I am of African heritage . . . And ancestry. I was born and raised in the United States. But to say I am an American is a stretch."

"Then just who the hell are you?" I said.

"For the time being, let's just say I am a man of the world who is working to change the world. Again, we'll get into details later."

"I want to get out of here."

"I'm sorry, but that is not possible. You will eventually

leave . . . Either dead or alive. When and how depends on you and how successful our conversations are. But eventually you will leave. For now, I must leave you. I will be back. Please just relax and try not to fight what will happen the next few days."

"Wait! . . . Don't go! . . . Wait!"

Jesse got to his feet, smiled down at me and patted my arm gently, almost kindly. He turned and left. I heard the squeaky door open, and then the big light hanging from the ceiling directly over my head came on. The light was so strong and sudden it was painful. I closed my eyes immediately but that did little good. The light pierced my closed eyelids. I started to scream. I felt my muscles tense up against the pain, and that only caused more pain as the leather straps cut into me.

I have no idea how long I lay like that, screaming in pain, the piercing light as painful as the straps. Hours may have gone by; days may have gone by. The endless pain was affecting my mind and thought process. I lost track of time. A minute could have been an hour; a second could have been a day.

The light suddenly went off, and I was left in complete darkness. I wondered if I was blind. Would I ever again see Sandy's face or Caroline playing with her trucks?

Someone pulled my right eyelid up and shown a soft light into my eye. The same thing to my left. A hand touched my forehead and took my pulse. Then I heard the door squeaking again, and I was alone.

My bladder was rebelling; I called out but no one came. I couldn't hold it back any longer. I was wet, and the bed was soaked. I closed my eyes and began to cry, God help me, I was crying. I wanted pain to stop the tears. I twisted my head and wrists, I moved my hips. The pain was excruciating, I kept it coming, I needed it, and it did what I wanted it to do. I kept it up, twisting and turning, until I blacked out again and slumped back onto the bed.

****

I don't know how long I was unconscious; once again, time meant nothing. Hours and days meant nothing. The room was lit, but the light above my face was not on. I moved my eyes to the right and saw Jesse sitting there, smiling at me.

"You're back with us," he said. "What you did was meaningless and only wasted your time and mine. The pain was entirely your fault. I didn't want that to happen. I am very sorry that you wet yourself. Had you told me, I would have had someone hold a vessel for you to pee into. But not to mind. While you were unconscious I had the nurse insert a urinary catheter. Just let your bladder do what it will do."

"Please . . . Why?" All I could do was whisper. My throat was raw and dry.

"Your throat is dry," he said as he stood. "Ice chips . . . Ice chips will relieve that."

"Please . . ."

"Yes, of course. For a bit of cooperation I will get you some ice chips. You see, we will have a conversation. For your involvement . . . And for the truth . . . You will be rewarded."

"Please," was all I could manage.

"But first, I have something to show you," Jesse said standing a few feet away from the bed. He walked behind me and returned to the stool as he held a small brown leather case. He opened it and held it out so that I could see it. Inside were six hypodermic needles.

"This first one," he said, touching one on the left. "This one with the clear liquid is a mild calmative, a tranquilizer. It will help you sleep when you need sleep. There are no after affects with this one. You will awaken refreshed. The second one, this one with the pale green liquid, causes extreme pain. Much less than half a cc, just a few drops added to your drip tube, will cause your body to feel as if it were on fire. Your brain will feel like it will explode. Believe me, I've seen this work on test subjects. A few have even died when more than three or four small drops were injected."

Jesse smiled as he spoke. His finger went to the third hypodermic. "This one, pale blue in color, is euphoric. It will give you pleasure; much like sexual pleasure. It is a reward for the truth and your cooperation."

He paused and sighed. I wondered if this guy was sane or some deranged sadist? I saw on his hand a gold ring. It was a school ring; I recognized it. I whispered, "U.C.L.A."

"Oh, very good, Morgan! Very good. Make friends with your captor. S.O.P as they say. Friendship will work on your side. Very good. But let's continue. This next hypodermic, dark brown in color as you can see, causes death. When entered into your body, your death will be long and painful. It may take more than an hour, perhaps even two, of agonizing pain before you die. This is a last resort when all else has failed. When we determine that you will not cooperate and be truthful . . . When we determine that there is nothing left to do . . . This will put an end to everything for you."

Jesse looked down at the hypodermic and the dark brown liquid in it. He ran a finger across the length of it and sighed, sounding almost sad at the thought of it.

He looked up, and a thin smile crossed his lips. He said, "The next, yellow in color, is an alternative last resort. It is what you would call a truth serum. Once entered into a body, the recipient will be unable to speak anything but the truth. Of course, it does . . . What is the phrase? . . . It does fry the brain. You will be a vegetable after two or three injections and hours of telling the truth. And finally, this last needle, clear liquid again, is a path to a peaceful, quiet, and painless death. You will simply go to sleep and never wake. There will be no pain at all. We will withhold this until you have cooperated fully and you do not wish to go on living. Most of my test subjects pleaded for this after experiencing the yellow truth serum."

He closed the case and walked behind me. I heard the squeaky hinges of the door. Jesse returned with the woman, the nurse, who had checked me . . . How long ago?

Jesse sat on the stool and said, "Now, to begin, this is Alexandra. She is a trained nurse. She will be taking care of you. I will be here as she cleans whatever wounds you have. After all, I need your cooperation, and therefore you must be in good condition. Please proceed, Alexandra."

She carefully unfastened the leather strap around my forehead. It hurt as she slowly pulled it away. She used cotton swabs and what smelled like alcohol to clean my forehead. It stung, but I was grateful that the pain of the strap had been taken away. As she tossed away one swab after another, I saw the blood she was cleaning away.

Jesse said, "I assume you wonder why the restraints are so very painful. The leather is lined with fine metal piano wire. The wire cuts into flesh when the restraints are tightened. When you move it cuts even more. The restraints are only minimally tight right now . . . And they hurt dreadfully, am I correct? Can you imagine what it would be like if we tightened them fully? Blood flow from your head, hands and feet would stop, but the pain would continue."

Alexandra turned to Jesse and asked if the head strap was to be replaced. She had an accent; middle European without mistake. She was tall and slim, but her hips were heavy. Her hair was brown and long, hanging to her shoulders. Her face reflected her age, perhaps even making her look older than her years. Dark circles made her eyes deep. Wrinkles and heavy cheeks covered her face, a face that was without makeup.

"No," Jesse answered. "Let's leave it off for the time being. And the waist strap, please leave it undone after you clean that up. Please clean up his wrists and ankles. But replace those straps when you are done. Not too tight now, please. As we had them."

He watched as she cleaned one wrist at a time, replacing each strap but without tightening them as much as they hand been. I said nothing in thanks because perhaps Jesse didn't know this. Maybe she had done this without his knowledge.

As Alexandra started to clean my ankles, Jesse spoke.

"Let's start now, Morgan. Let's start at the beginning. I know quite a lot about you . . . Your extreme wealth, your family, your friends. But you know nothing of me. So I will briefly give you an autobiography. I was born in Louisiana . . . into poverty I'm very sad to say. My father and his father were share croppers. Life was hard . . . Food was scarce and hardly healthy for a growing boy. But my parents were good people. They were church goers, and I can remember many nights when dinner for me was a slice of bread with sorghum molasses, while my parents ate nothing. I studied in school, my mother insisted on that. The school was an old wooden building with a roof that could not stop the rain. It was hardly equipped to teach students. But there was a small library nearby, and my parents insisted I read everything. It was difficult, but I managed to gain a scholarship to U.C.L.A., as you so brightly noticed."

He held up his right hand and extended it out for both him and me to admire the school ring.

"I did very well in school. I say that with utmost pride. It was hard work because my prior education had been so limited. But I managed excellent grades in all subjects. There was no time for sports or girls, just study. I majored in world history and English. Can you possibly imagine that? A poor farm boy from Louisiana with a duel major at U.C.L.A.?

"I was surprised when one afternoon as I sat under a tree on campus reading a work by Chaucer, I was approached by a man." Jesse paused, smiled and shook his head, still unbelieving in what happened. "The Central Intelligence Agency recruited me. Isn't that incredible? The C.I.A actually wanted me. I had never given a thought to such a career. I wanted to be a teacher. To go home and teach the children where I grew up. To teach the children who lacked so much."

I interrupted Jesse, "Throat . . . Water . . . Please."

"Oh, I am so sorry. I completely forgot. Alexandra, please bring some ice chips for Morgan. Thank you."

With the head restraint gone I was able to turn my head slightly, and I watched the woman as she walked away, out of my sight, to the squeaky door behind me.

"While we wait," Jesse said. He sat up straight on the stool and crossed his left leg over his right, hooking his arms around them. "I studied Sociology and Psychology as minors in school besides my majors. They are fascinating subjects. I thought I knew everything about people. But my eyes were opened working inside the C.I.A. As an aside, did you know that after the Second World War, the OSS . . . America's spy organization during the war . . . Was disbanded? The U.S. had no intelligence operations outside the military and State Department. I understand it was thought to be ungentlemanly, can you imagine that? In 1947, by necessity because of The Soviet Union's rise, the National Security Act established the Central Intelligence Agency and put it into operation. But . . . And this is a huge *but* . . . People in Washington were afraid of such an organization. Congress and the powerful elites were afraid such a super-secret organization would become too powerful. So they did not give the Agency the power and authority to make arrests nor to work inside the United States. Without the power to arrest what was left to it? Rather than arrest someone, secret kidnapping, torture, and murder became the norm for the agency."

Jesse paused and took a deep breath, almost a sigh. He went on, "I looked at the world as I travelled for the Agency. Poverty was endemic. Everywhere, a few people had money, and a majority of people barely eked out a day to day living. Children died of hunger. Women sold themselves for a scrap of bread. Men killed other men for food. War became normal because of the inequality worldwide. But in Russia no one starved. Oh, I know. There was and still is an elite class. But the Russian intelligentsia existed to care for the masses. The few are there to make sure the many do not live without the basics of life. So, I knew the answer to the problem. The true philosophy of Communism. Absolute equality amongst the majority."

Alexandra returned with a small, red plastic, covered container filled with ice chips. She used a plastic spoon to bring a few to my mouth. I chewed these hungrily, and she gave me more. The fourth spoonful I held in my mouth and let the cooling ice melt slowly.

"That's enough for now, Alexandra. Thank you," Jesse said, and she stepped away.

She stood next to him, looking down at the floor, not looking at him, and asked, "I stay or go?"

"No, no, no," he answered brightly. "Please stay. Morgan will need more ice shortly." Alexandra stepped backwards and stood against the wall behind Jesse holding the plastic ice filled container, her eyes focused subserviently on the floor at her feet.

Jesse paused long enough to light a cigarette. He blew the smoke towards the ceiling, but the smell of it didn't do me any good. My stomach started to turn. I said nothing.

"So, Morgan," he said. "You've said nothing. Is your mouth still dry? More ice perhaps? No?"

I cleared my throat and licked my lips. My voice was weak and strained. I wanted to complain about the pain and about lying there naked. But I knew that complaining or arguing would get me nowhere. I had to debate with him, to keep him going and maybe have him forget why I was there. I was confident I could talk my way out of any danger. I'd done that so many times in the past. So I said in a whispered voice, "Communism . . . Doesn't work . . . Never has . . ."

My attempt didn't work. Jesse turned to Alexandra and said calmly and softly, "The traxicalpalon I think. Just a mere half cc. Morgan needs to learn."

Alexandra walked away, behind me, and returned with the brown leather case. She opened it and took the hypodermic with the pale green liquid from it. She held it up, squeezed a small bit from it, and started for the drip tube. I watched; her lips mouthed the silent words, "I'm sorry." She inserted the needle into the tube and the small drop of liquid entered.

I waited and smiled when I felt nothing. Then a sudden rush of white hot iron streamed through my body. I arched against the harnesses at my wrists and ankles. My brain felt as if it were bursting from my skull. I pulled at the straps. The pain from the wire lined straps was insignificant compared to what had been injected into me. I screamed and kept screaming against pain I had never imagined existed.

Jesse watched as I writhed in agony for an interminable period. How long had the excruciating pain lasted? I didn't know; it could have been a few seconds or many hours. All I could feel was the fire twisting my guts apart and the black hell that filled my brain. Finally he told Alexandra, "The hexophilrate, please. He's had enough."

Alexandra shot a few cc's from the syringe into the tube, and within seconds the pain was gone. I fell back onto the bed; blood streamed from my wrists and ankles where the wired leather had cut into them. I looked down. Blood had stained the mattress and was flowing from me.

I turned my head to Jesse and managed to asked, "Why?"

He spoke in a soft voice, almost consoling in tone. "Our conversation will entail my speaking the truth to you and you asking what questions you wish in order to learn. It will not descend into an oral argument. You will learn; that is all. Do not tell me I am wrong, in other words."

I heard the last of the words as I drifted off into drug induced dreams of Sandy and Caroline. Again, time meant nothing. I do not know how long I slept. I woke to find myself alone in the white room. My head remained free of the strap; I was able to turn left and right. To my right I saw the small plastic pitcher that contained the ice chips alone on the stool Jesse had been sitting on. How I wished I could reach that, but my arms were tied.

I cleared my throat and tried to moisten my lips. I called out faintly in a raspy voice, "Hello . . . Anybody."

That simple exertion tired me. I let my head fall back onto the bed. I closed my eyes and started counting the seconds. I thought that even the simplest tracking of time might help me to keep my sanity. I was into the five hundreds when I heard the squeaky hinged door open. I turned to the right and saw Jesse and Alexandra walk to the bedside.

Jesse waited while Alexandra took the plastic pitcher and pulled the stool to him. He sat, smiled and asked, "How do you feel, Morgan? Did you sleep comfortably?"

I licked my lips again and strained the words out, "Straps . . . Hurt . . . Please."

"In time, Morgan. In time. For now, let's continue our conversation where we left off. As I was saying before the very unfortunate object lesson, Communism, I came to realize, is the true social equalizer. 'From each according to his ability, to each according to their need.' How more beautiful could society be? Think of it, no want, no hunger, no untreated illness, no desire or avarice. A very few insuring the needs of the many are seen to. What a world we could live in."

I moistened my mouth as best I could and asked for more ice chips. Jesse nodded, and Alexandra spooned a few into my parched mouth. I let them melt, the cold comforting and welcomed. Two more spoons and I was able to ask, "Question?"

Jesse said, "You wish to ask a question? Is that it? Of course you may. We are here for you to learn. Please ask."

"When . . . did . . . Communism . . . work?" The words were a struggle. My voice was dry and harsh.

"Oh, of course, Communism has never worked, Morgan. Excellent question, however," he said, straightening himself up on the stool. "In Soviet Russia you had the very privileged, the Government rulers, riding around in armor plated limousines, being driven to their luxurious dachas and being serviced by beautiful women and little boys. The proletariat, the workers, were left to struggle and live on the meager handouts of what was rationed. The same thing happened in China. Millions died of hunger while the Great Leaders such as Mao got fat. North Korea, Vietnam, Cuba, Venezuela, every Country that has called itself Communist, they are just greedy men who use Communism for their own benefit and let the people suffer. No, real Communism has never been tried and exists today only in books and the minds of a few people such as myself."

My lips burned from dryness, but I managed to ask, "How?"

"Do you mean how will true Communism be attained worldwide? The people I work with are convinced it will be difficult, and it will take a very long time. Perhaps not in our lifetimes. You see, wealth in this world is concentrated amongst the very few; they say the top one percent of people worldwide. You are one of these people. There is no way to take all of your money from you as the world exists today. But if we can just bring about a worldwide conflagration, a war such as the world has never seen, that will topple Governments, we can then install a new society."

"War? . . . World war? . . . People die . . . Crazy."

"Alexandra," Jesse said. "I think one cc of the traxicalpalon will be enough. Wait a full two minutes and then the hexophilrate. I am going to have some lunch. Tell me when he wakes."

I watched Jesse walk out of my sight. The door squeaked closed leaving me alone with Alexandra. She took the green hypodermic needle from the case. She held the needle up and flicked the hypodermic with her finger.

"No! No! Please! No!" I pleaded. The pain was still in my memory. I pleaded and did nothing to stop the tears from pouring from my eyes.

Alexandra stood over me, holding the needle in front of my eyes. She leaned towards me, twisting her back as if trying to hide from something. She mouthed words without a sound. She repeated the same silent word over and over until I understood what she was saying. "Camera . . . Camera . . . Camera." Her finger went to her lips; her eyes moved to her right. I looked over her shoulder, and in the corner across the room, at the ceiling, was a small black CCV camera watching.

Alexandra mouthed, "Pain . . . Pain."

Standing between the bed and the camera, she made a motion towards the drip tube and hid the fact that she feigned injecting the drug. I waited and watched her. She closed her eyes and opened them, very slowly, twice. It was a signal. The drug was supposed to start working. I arched my body and twisted against the restraints, ignoring the pain of the piano wire. It was nothing compared to what I would have felt if Alexandra had injected the drug into me. I screamed and hoped I was doing enough to make anyone watching believe the drug was coursing through my body.

Two minutes passed, and Alexandra once again pretended to inject the hexophilrate. A slight, almost imperceptible nod of her head signaled me to stop twisting in make believe pain. I slumped back onto the bed and closed my eyes. Alexandra left the room. I had a friend.

THIRTEEN – We Are Dangerous People

Sandy got off the elevator at Peter Jascro's office in New York. She pushed the glass doors of the reception area so hard the doors crashed against the walls, but the thick glass took the punishment without breaking. The receptionist stood, fearful of a crazy woman bursting into the office. Her hand went to the phone. Security, she would call for security. It would take several minutes for security guards to get there. She decided the best thing she could do was to run away to save herself. She pushed herself out of her chair and started for the door to the offices.

Sandy stopped her, yelling, "STOP! I want to see Peter Jascro! Get him out here right now!"

The door from the reception area to the offices opened, and three men, attorneys, walked into the reception room. Sandy pointed at them and demanded, "Peter Jascro! Tell him Mrs. Morgan Crew is here, and he better get his ass out here damn fast!"

Peter pushed his way past the men and went to Sandy. He put his arms out to hug her. She stopped him and said, "Where the hell is my husband! What crazy thing have you sent him out on this time?"

"Please, Sandy. Come to my office. Please calm down. Come with me," he said.

He turned, and Sandy followed him into the hallways

of glass walled offices. She stayed three steps behind him until they reached his office. Maureen and the six secretaries who sat outside Peter's office were all on their feet, frightened. He opened the oak door and stood aside. Sandy walked in and sat down hard in a chair at his desk. Her face was red with anger. She dropped her purse onto the floor and glared at Peter as he cautiously stepped past her.

Peter walked slowly around his big desk and sat. "Coffee, Sandy?" he offered.

"Cut the shit, Peter," she growled. "I want to know where Morgan is."

"Calm down, Sandy. He told me he was going to Mexico."

"HE TOLD ME THAT, TOO!" She was screaming the words, her hands curled tightly into fists. "He asked me to overnight his passport to the motel he was at in Houston. He never got the passport. It was returned to me. The motel says he left without signing for the bill and without taking his suitcase. I had the San Marcos police check the airlines. He did not fly to Mexico or anywhere else. His rental car was left at the motel. It's been 19 days . . . almost three weeks since I have talked with him. I kept trying to believe that he was just busy, on one of those stupid missions you send him on. But it's been too damn long. NOW, WHERE THE HELL IS HE?" she shouted. She pounded her fist on Peter's desk and demanded, "Is he alive or dead?"

"Sandy, please calm down. It does no good to shout. Now, if all you say is correct . . . And I'm not accusing you of anything . . . Then I don't know where Morgan is."

"You don't know where he is?" she said, incredulous that Peter could say such a thing. "If he's dead . . . I will not stop until you are ruined, Peter. If he's dead . . . It's your fault for sending him off on some stupid quest to save his stupid family and their stupid money.   Now, tell me everything he did before he disappeared."

Peter told her about FBI Agent Adam Carter and Homeland Security Agent Donna Evans. He told her about the murder at Hillsdale Technologies and the murders of Bill Trangent's family. He told her that Hillsdale Technologies was open again, the people working under new security measures, but that the Federal contracts were in limbo.

"Morgan phoned me from Houston," Peter said. "He asked me to run a name past Donna Evans and for me to do a background check on someone. That's all I know."

"Who? What name did he give you?"

"Jesse Wilson," Peter answered. "But neither Donna Evans nor my people could come up with anything solid."

"There's something else," Sandy said. "What are you not telling me?"

Peter leaned back in his tall backed chair and thought for a moment. He decided that Sandy should know everything. He said, "I have Jeremy Hillsdale upstairs. Morgan wanted armed guards with him twenty-four seven."

"And that didn't frighten you?" she said. "You didn't think that maybe there was some danger out there? You let Morgan go rampaging around when guns and killers are involved? You know you're a real son of a bitch, Peter, you know that right?"

"Sandy, dear. You know Morgan. What could I say? . . . What could you say that would stop him? . . . Would anything stop him?"

Sandy knew, of course, that Peter was right. She knew me as well as Peter knew me. Nothing could stop me from doing what I had to do. It was my life and what I am meant to do. She and I have been through so much in the few years we have been together. Nothing could stop me from saving Sandy and her sister back in San Marcos. She was almost killed in Las Vegas, but I didn't run away with her. In London I took on the defense of a family friend against a maniac. Nothing could stop me in Texas or in Hawaii. Sandy took a deep breath and slumped down in the chair.

"Alright, Peter," she said calm once again. "I'm sorry. I want to speak with this Donna Evans and Adam Carter. Get them here, will you? And I want to speak with Jeremy, too. He's upstairs? Have someone take me to him."

****

There were two off-duty policemen standing outside the door to the apartment Jeremy was staying in. Peter had told them that Sandy was on her way up. They said nothing to her as one of them opened the door and stood aside for her to walk into the apartment.

Sandy took two steps into the crazy apartment that had been decorated for Peter's very weird Japanese client, and she stopped. She stood in the open door, looked around, rubbed her eyes to make sure she was actually seeing what she saw, and shook her head, finding the obscenity of the place hard to believe. She had seen a lot in her years, inhumanity, vicious murderers, drugs, every evil possible, and she had come to realize that human lust when released without tethers met no ends.

Jeremy walked from the kitchen with a sandwich in his hand. He was wearing bright blue, silk boxer underwear and nothing else. They hung low under his soft belly. His hairy legs, arms, and chest were comically ugly, but Sandy didn't laugh. She had met Jeremy several times at family gatherings and at a few business meetings she had attended with me. She knew Jeremy as a smart businessman but a man with a weak character and a poor self-image of himself. And she knew that Jeremy tried to cover up his short comings by being unduly forward and aggressive with women.

"Oh, excuse me, Sandy," he said, his smirking mouth framed in yellow mustard. "I didn't know you were coming."

"Bullshit, Jeremy," Sandy said. "Peter phoned up here. You were told I'd be coming to see you. You dressed like you are because you knew I would be here. If you think you're sexy . . . You're not. You're as obnoxious as I remember, and you have the sex appeal of a hairy ape."

"Why, Sandy. I just don't understand," he said, still hoping that he could get close to Sandy.

"Remember last Christmas, Jeremy? When you made a pass at me? Now drop the sandwich and go get some clothes on. Come any closer to me, and I'll rip your balls off."

The grin dropped suddenly from Jeremy's face. He wiped some mustard away from his chin with the back of his hand. He turned and went to the bedroom where he dressed in wrinkled pants and the white shirt he had worn for the past two days. He hadn't shaved for those same two days, and his hair was uncombed and greasy when he returned to the living room.

He found Sandy sitting in an orange colored, satin upholstered, overstuff chair. It was uncomfortable, and Sandy hoped that nothing too obscene had occurred on the chair recently. She shifted around trying to keep pictures of

Peter's client rambunctiously enjoying the company of several women out of her mind. The chair was in a part of what she imagined must have been a 'living room.' It was carpeted in deep pile, fuzzy white material. There were stains on it, but she refused to think about them.

Jeremy walked to the matching chair next to Sandy, but she stopped him and pointed to the couch on the other side of a glass topped metal framed coffee table that would keep them separated.

"So, Sandy," he said as he sat down hard on the couch. "It's so good to see you again."

"Cut it out, Jeremy. I want to know everything you told Morgan."

"Why? I don't know what you're talking about."

"Jeremy . . . In about ten seconds I'm going to jump across this table and put my spike heeled shoe covered foot in your face. Now, tell me what you told Morgan."

Jeremy thought it would be best to tell Sandy what she wanted to know. He knew his life – his business life which was the only important thing to him – was over. All he could hope for was that the Crew family would not abandon him totally. After all, he was a mere in-law and totally dependent on the family he had married into, the only reason being for the wealth of the Crew family. Cooperation, that was the only hope he had to maintain a place within the Crew family.

Sandy spent an hour listening to Jeremy, but most of what he said was in his own defense. He kept repeating that all that had happened, all that had drawn the FBI and Homeland Security to Hillsdale Technologies was not his fault. She interrupted him several times to ask questions, but she learned little that would help. He was being too defensive and too pleading. She left Jeremy sitting there, feeling deflated, and worrying that his time with the Crew family had come to an end. She walked away without saying goodbye.

Back in Peter's office she found him sitting at a small table next to the tall windows at the side of his office. The view outside, of New York and Central Park, was magnificent. Two chairs were at the table. On the table were sandwiches, a bottle of red wine, and a silver coffee pot.

"Please join me, Sandy," he offered. He stood and pulled the second chair away from the table for Sandy. "We have an hour or so to wait for Ms. Evans. Agent Carter declined my invitation."

Sandy's blood pressure was up, and her temper, usually well under control, was boiling over. Peter did his best to calm Sandy. He kept the conversation on everything except me as he encouraged her to eat something. "You know, it's been too long since I've seen Caroline," he said. "I must make some time to get to the West Coast."

Sandy sipped at the excellent red wine, took a deep breath to calm herself, and said, "She starts school this year. She's very excited, and she can read already. She's very smart." Sandy loved to brag about our daughter, as do I. We share the opinion that there has never been a smarter or lovelier child in the history of mankind. But maybe we are just a little prejudiced.

Peter agreed with what Sandy said, "And she's as pretty as you, Sandy."

The bottle of wine was drained; all the sandwiches were eaten. And all the conversation had been used up. Sandy and Peter sat silently, looking at the walls and out the windows. An hour passed and then another thirty minutes.

Sandy broke the silence, "I thought this Homeland Security person was supposed to be here."

"Give her some time, Sandy. The world might have something else going right at the moment."

"Something else might be important to that woman . . . But Morgan is important to me," Sandy said.

At ten past two Donna Evans walked into Peter's office.

"Oh, I'm sorry I missed lunch. I haven't eaten since dinner last night," she said. She sat in an upholstered chair across the room, next to a matching couch and another chair. She seemed to be waiting, so Sandy and Peter walked across the office and sat with her.

That pasted on, forced smile was stapled onto Donna's pale, puffy face. The officiousness of her demeanor immediately got under Sandy's skin, and she felt her temper rise again.

"So, I assume you asked me here for a reason?" Donna asked.

Peter leaned forward and said, "This is Morgan's wife, Sandy . . ."

"Yes," Donna said. "I am aware of Mrs. Crew." She looked at Sandy and asked, "And how is that lovely daughter of yours . . . Caroline, isn't it? I hear she starts school this year."

"How do you know that?" Sandy started and then added, "Of course. You spy types know everything about everybody, don't you? You think to keep America safe you have to spy on everybody, right? Privacy is a dangerous thing, right?"

Donna's expression didn't change. She stared at

Sandy and then finally said, "Why am I here?"

Peter answered, "It appears Morgan is missing."

She nodded and said, "I thought that might happen."

"You *thought* that might happen?" Sandy said. "Tell me now . . . Everything . . . Or I promise the entire United States Senate will be after your ass."

Donna opened her purse and took a cigarette from it. She lit it with a paper match, looked for an ashtray, but there weren't any. She shook the match out and dropped it on the carpet.

"We had an agreement," she began. "Morgan discovered that something was in fact stolen from Hillsdale Technologies . . ."

"What was it?" Sandy interrupted.

"I'm sorry, but I can't tell you that. In any case, he also found that an employee of Hillsdale had rigged the security so that it could be easily breached. That person and his entire family were murdered. Well, not his whole family. Morgan learned that a daughter is still alive. She has . . . Problems . . . And was at a care home outside of Cape May, New Jersey. He went there and found she had walked away. She was twenty years old, and they couldn't keep her there . . . . He had traced her . . . And the man she ran off with . . . To an off the map place in Texas . . . San Pedro Escobar or something like that. He went there and met an Agent from Air Force Intelligence. That man told Morgan that the girl ran off with a man from the Middle East, and they were in a small town outside of Mexico City. Someplace called Tuactualco. That Air Force Agent, by the way, is now missing, also."

Donna finished speaking but did not move from her very relaxed position on the chair. That damn annoying false grin never left her face. She held the burning cigarette out, her elbow resting on the arm of the chair. Ash fell from the cigarette onto the carpet.

"That's it? That's all you know?" Sandy demanded.

"That's all I can tell you. We have people out looking for both Morgan and the Agent. I suggest you go home and wait. I will phone you when we find them."

"I have a feeling you told Morgan to do the same thing . . . To go home. And I have a feeling Peter here told Morgan to do the same thing. And I have yet another feeling, that Morgan told you both *NO* . . . Very firmly. So, I'm telling you the same damn thing. I will not go home like a good little wife. Since you obviously can't . . . or *won't* . . . find Morgan . . . I will."

Donna asked, "Your daughter, is she alright? You need to keep her safe. This is a dangerous situation, you know." Sandy looked hard at Donna. She wondered if that was good advice or a threat.

Sandy said, "If you're threatening me, you really don't know me as well as you think you do."

"My dear," Donna said softly. "I am merely giving you some good advice that you should listen to. I would be absolutely devastated if anything were to happen to you or Morgan or your sweet little child. If you'd like protection, I can arrange that."

A couple of times before, Betsy Concanon had taken our daughter to a motorcycle gang in San Francisco to keep her safe. As a child, Betsy lived with that gang for a while. Now they protect her when necessary, and in return I send them some cash now and then. But they have told me that they would protect her and Caroline even if I paid them nothing.

"My daughter is with our nanny, Betsy Concanon," Sandy said. "Betsy has protected my daughter before. She has taken Caroline to a safe place where neither you nor anyone else will find her. There are very dangerous people there who will protect her. We don't need your protection."

Donna just stared at Sandy but said nothing. I think she may have been wondering why there was a place she and Homeland Security didn't know about, a place where someone could hide and be protected. She made a mental note to bring that up at the next meeting of all the intelligence and security agencies. If there were such a place, they needed to know about it.

Sandy sat forward and asked directly, "Is that all you're going to tell me? Because I think you're not telling me everything. You're either intentionally withholding something, or you're lying to me. Which is it?"

"I've told you all I can tell you. I cannot release classified information to you. I can tell you that the deal I made with your husband is intended to keep classified Government contracts with Hillsdale Technologies. I assume that is as important to you as it is to your husband? There are people involved who want to pull those contracts immediately. That would ruin one of your family's businesses."

"Frankly, Ms. Evans," Sandy started, speaking slowly, "I couldn't give a shit less about Hillsdale and the money. And I know Morgan doesn't care about the money either. What he does is for other people, not for him and me, nor the money. But . . . it's not the Crew family who will be to blame if he dies doing what he must do. It will be you and all your little spy friends. Then . . . If that happens . . . I will use every penny we have . . . And in case you didn't know, that's billions of dollars . . . To destroy you and everyone else involved in this. Do you understand me?"

Donna said nothing, but she understood. She had a complete record of all that Sandy and I had done over the years, and she knew how dangerous we could be. Sandy stood and started for the door. Peter stopped her by asking, "Do I dare ask where you're going?"

"Texas and then Mexico, of course," she answered as if it were a foregone conclusion. "I've got to find Morgan."

FOURTEEN – My Education

As time passed . . . And I was unable to keep track of the days . . . I had decided that my only chance of surviving Jesse Wilson was to become his friend. It would do no good to argue with him; when I did, the punishment was terrible. Alexandra did what she could, but when Jesse was nearby and watching, she had to inject the one or two drops of the liquid that would bring me close to the edge of a painful death. But Jesse's timing was good, and she would be told to use the drug that would stop the intense pain and bring on euphoric sleep.

I was intent on slowly gaining his trust. I would not rush because I felt Jesse was smart enough to see me lying to him. I would talk with him, conversation as he called it. I would question as if I were interested, but I would not argue with him or insult him. Time, that's what I needed. Time mixed with a healthy dose of patience. In time he would make a mistake. In time I was certain I would find a way out, a way to survive.

The nurse, Alexandra, helped me as much as she could. As I lay in the bed, strapped down, when Jesse was not in the room but the camera was watching, she would blink twice when I was on the wrong course and once when I was doing well. She would fake the injections into the tube in my arm when she could, and I would act out the necessary results. On what I guessed . . . I had no way of being sure . . . Was more than a week since waking up

216

there, I asked for food. Jesse was sitting on his stool, and Alexandra was standing behind him, against the wall, her head lowered in what I felt was pure shame.

"I'm hungry . . . Please . . . I feel dizzy," I pleaded.

"Well, I must say, I am happy with the progress we've made," Jesse said. He stood from his stool and paced around the room, thinking, considering. He went to Alexandra and whispered in her ear. Her face went white, but she nodded and left the room.

I waited, and I worried. I hate not knowing what is happening. I hate not being in control. My mind went to memories of being tied up in that warehouse in West Texas when I was beaten with the rubber hose. But the memory quickly disappeared when I heard the squeaky hinges of the door behind me open, and fear wiped away the memory.

Alexandra pushed a hospital gurney into the room and stopped it a few feet from the side of my bed. A white sheet was draped across the gurney. It didn't take much guessing on my part to know that it had to be a body under the sheet. It was bulky and had the rough outline of a fat human body.

Jesse stood at the foot of my bed, grinned, and slowly, dramatically, pulled the sheet off of the body. Bubba Beauregard, the Air Force investigator, lay there; at least I think it used to be Bubba. He was naked, covered in his own blood from scores of cuts and whippings. His face was bloody mush; his right arm was twisted and broken; the fingers of his left hand were missing.

"This is what the people outside this room do when they want information from someone. It is an old fashioned way of getting at things. It seldom works on professionals. It didn't work on Mr. Beauregard. He died before saying a word. I respect the man, believe it or not. I respect brave men who accept death before dishonor. I think you, Morgan, might be that kind of man." He paused and pulled the sheet over Bubba. He looked down at me and said, "Now, you and I are talking very productively. But, if at any time I feel you are trying to play me . . . If I feel you are lying to me . . . if I feel you aren't listening to what I say . . . If I feel the drugs aren't doing what is intended . . . I will turn you over to the people who did this to Bubba. Do you understand?"

It was difficult for me to look at the body. I was in a weakened condition. I had nothing but ice chips since waking up in the room. That made it harder for me to look at such savagery. My stomach knotted, and my head was spinning. I hoped I could just pass out, but I didn't. I said I did understand, turning away from Bubba's body.

"Good. Now, I believe you are beginning to understand what we have been talking about. I am going to take a risk here, but if I am wrong about you, I promise you will not like the consequences. I am going to have Alexandra undo the restraints on your wrists. For the time being I will leave your legs bound. I am going to allow her to raise the head of your bed. I am going to have her remove your catheter. I am going to have her remove the drip tube from your arm, so you may drink water like a normal person. And then I will have some broth brought here for you. Broth, because we need to progress slowly. Solid food would not sit on your stomach very well right now. And I need you to be healthy."

Alexandra did as she was told; I had hoped my ankle restraints would be opened also, but I would live with that for a while. I guessed that Jesse needed to know I wasn't going to try to make a run for freedom. She carefully removed the catheter and sponged me clean. When the head of the bed was raised I thought my back would snap, but the pain of stretching my muscles actually felt good.

Alexandra cleaned and dressed the wounds on my wrists. I flexed my arms and stretched my shoulders. The stiffness from my prolonged confinement was ebbing away. I was making progress.

I managed to finish most of the clay bowl of broth that Alexandra brought me, with her help. I found, after such a long time of confinement, I could not close my fingers enough to hold the wooden spoon. She smiled and gently wiped the corners of my mouth with a rough cloth as she spooned broth to me.

The brown broth was hot, thin but with some spice to flavor it. When I had finished I felt almost good for the first time in . . . Actually, I had no idea how long I had been there. With no windows in the room and with the room lit by lights in the ceiling and never turned off, time had been standing still for me. It may have been days, but I knew it had been longer than that. Probably a week at least, not unlikely more than that.

Alexandra took the empty bowl and spoon and walked away, nodding to Jesse who had been on the stool watching. I saw her smile a faint smile, but she had diverted her eyes from him. There was something other than compassion there. Alexandra was carrying fear herself. I saw that, and I knew I could use that.

"You did very well, Morgan," Jesse said. "I think we should continue our conversation now."

"I'm tired," I said. "But I want to go on. I'm beginning to enjoy our conversations, even though I still have some doubts." Slow and easy, I thought. Not too fast; he wouldn't believe that. Make him feel good, as if he were succeeding in his efforts to make me into a Communist. Make him feel as if we were friends. Time was beginning to be on my side, and soon I would be able to kill the man.

"That's good, Morgan. That's good. I can ask no more for such a short time. Eventually, I will show you the errors of your life, and I will convert you, because you will come to understand the truth of how wealth is destructive to peace. I believe you are an intelligent person, and if you listen to reason and the truth, you will change."

I can only guess at the passage of time. Jesse sat at my bedside for what had to be hours at a time. I was exhausted and weak, my head hurt terribly, but I made a pretense to be interested in what he had to say. As much as I wanted to tell him he was a friggin' idiot, I listened intently to what he was saying. I didn't argue with him; I did ask what I hoped would be insightful questions aimed at making him believe I was really interested.

Alexandra began to bring me food on what seemed like a regular basis. I tried to keep mental track of the meals . . . Three a day, I thought; that might be right. That could be a clock. And there were more hours when I was allowed to rest and sleep. The meals were small things at first, watery soups, but with each meal there was more solid food in the clay bowls. With the regular meals I would begin to measure the passage of time. I waited two 'days' of meals and then I pressed an issue.

"Jesse," I said after a meal of watery carrots and some kind of beans. "I feel really stupid lying here all naked. Can I get some clothes? A sheet or something to cover myself . . . At least when the woman comes in here?"

Jesse laughed and said, "Of course, Morgan! I should have known that! I am so sorry! Please forgive me!"

In a short time Alexandra brought a pale green hospital gown to me. With her help I struggled into it, trying to accept the pain of the straps at my ankles.

Alexandra once again cleaned my wounded wrists

and the healing wounds on my forehead and stomach, as she did after every third meal. I then lay back on the bed, exhausted from the small effort. The hard steel bed had been raised a little at my first meal and not lowered again. Lying on the raised bed was not better than lying flat. My back and legs cramped often, but there was nothing I could do about that with my ankles tightly restrained.

Jesse patted me kindly on my shoulder and said, "Sleep awhile." I did.

I don't know how long I slept, but I do remember dreaming of Sandy and Caroline. We were on the beach, and a wave crashed over us. I was dragged out to sea and tried to fight the current. The last thing I saw was my wife and child on the beach, playing happily with no knowledge of my drowning slowly. I awoke with a start, and someone shook my shoulder. It was Jesse. He said, "You were dreaming, Morgan."

I rubbed my eyes and relaxed back on the hard bed. My ankles hurt, and I could feel the blood running from them. I must have been kicking while dreaming.

I closed my eyes against the pain and said, "My legs . . . I'm in pain . . . The straps are cutting me badly . . . My legs are cramping . . . I've been cooperating, haven't I? . . . I need to get out of this bed . . . Can I please have the restraints removed . . . Maybe for only a few minutes to let me move my legs?"

"Well, Morgan," he said thoughtfully. "You've made good progress so far. I haven't had to use any drugs on you for a number of days. You've had reasoned questions, and you've listened. I hope you've been trying to learn." He paused, scratched his chin, and then said, "I guess I can try . . . As a reward you understand. But if you attempt anything unwarranted . . . I will turn you over to the people outside.

Remember Bubba. They will do terrible things to you."

Jesse told Alexandra to remove my ankle straps. When she did I looked down at what was under the heavy leather and piano wire. My ankles were swollen, bloody, black, and obviously infected. Alexandra cleaned the wounds professionally. She applied a cooling cream, but I think she knew that would not be enough.

She asked Jesse in a quiet, fearful voice, "There is infection. May I use something?"

"Yes, of course. We want Morgan to be healthy because we have work for him to do."

She disappeared for a short moment and came back with a small bottle and a glass of cool water. I took the two pills she gave me out of the bottle and drank the water thankfully. She then applied a yellowish cream to my wounds and wrapped my ankles in gauze.

I was able to stretch out my legs, for the first time without pain. My cramps and stiff calves and thighs began to ease. With a struggle and with Alexandra's help I sat up in bed and swung my legs over the side. I had to hold onto the edge of the bed to keep from falling, but I sat up and stretched out my sore back. It felt wonderful to finally be off of the thin mattress and steel bed. Alexandra touched my shoulder; she seemed happy and relieved that I was able to sit up after so many days . . . Or was it weeks . . . Of torture.

"That's very good, Morgan," Jesse said. "And if you continue to progress we will not have to put you back in the restraints. Now, shall we continue your education?"

"Yes," I said. "But I'm hungry . . . And not for broth. Can I have something solid? I mean, if we are to continue . . . And I want us to continue, don't get me wrong . . . I'm going to need some food to keep me going."

Jesse nodded, and Alexandra left the room. I watched her walk away, to the squeaky door and out of the room. For the first time I was able to see the entire room. It was small and square and windowless as I had suspected.

The gurney carrying Bubba's body was only a few feet away but out of my vision as I lay on the bed. I could see it now. It was uncovered, the body grey and covered in dried blood. I had no idea how long it had been there, but I figured that soon it would start to smell. Maybe that was just another object lesson made by Jesse.

"Does he have to stay?" I asked. "Shouldn't he be buried? I mean . . . Pretty soon . . ."

"Oh, we'll leave him here for a while. Just a reminder of what can happen to people who don't cooperate. But now, let's talk about the accumulation of money in the hands of a few. Let's talk about how your wealth affects the world."

"I'm not going to argue with you . . . Or call you crazy. I know what will happen if I do. But can I tell you my thoughts on the subject?" I asked.

"I assume you *can* tell me your thoughts . . . And you *may*. There is a difference, you know. I'm surprised a Yale man doesn't know that."

"Yes . . . Well, anyway. My family has acquired a great deal of wealth over the years. I wasn't around to see how they did that. My great-grandfather started it all. But today, we employ thousands of people all over the world. These people receive money from my family to support their families. They spend that money on food, and the people who grow that food earn a living by selling the food. What can be better than that?"

Jesse shook his head; a sad frown creased his forehead. "You have uncounted hundreds of millions . . .

Some reports on your family say billions . . . and employ thousands. What happens to the millions who do not receive your largess? What happens to the hundreds of millions you make in profits from the labor of your employees? You live in grandeur while many millions die of starvation."

"That's all true," I said. "Many in my family live too grandly, too lavishly. They think that's what the money is for. But you must know that I, personally, don't live in the old estate my parents and grandparents lived in. My life is pretty simple. I live like the people who are employed by my family's companies. I freely admit that many people in my family live a grand life. They use the money for personal things . . . Expensive cars and things like that . . . Things that I could care less about. Yes, they have vast bank accounts that the people who work for them don't. If that is truly a problem, will world Communism solve that problem?" I asked. I was taking a risk in the debate. I had to keep Jesse happy until I was able to escape. I needed strength and time. Jesse was frowning still and looking questioningly at me. A chill of fear ran through me, so I added, "It's a real question, Jesse. I really want to know. I want to learn."

He started to say something when Alexandra returned carrying a simple clay bowl, bigger than the bowls of broth she had brought me. This one had a tasty beef broth with a few pieces of meat and several large chunks of overcooked vegetables in it. I took the bowl and smiled my thanks to her. The soup was bland, without any of the seasoning the bowls of broth had, but I didn't care. I had no idea how long it had been since my stomach had enjoyed real solid food; a week or more at least. I relished what I had and drained the bowl quickly using my fingers to pick out the few strands of meat and the soggy vegetables.

Jesse watched me eat; I could sense some impatience on his part. I knew what his anger would bring, so I spread it on thick as I set the bowl aside.

"I'm sorry, Jesse. I really want to learn. But I was hungry. I understand hunger now. I've never been hungry before. I understand now what people must suffer without enough food. I've heard all the stories of people going without food and clean water, but it never really hit me until now. Please forgive me, and tell me how Communism would end world hunger."

"Are you being facetious with me? Are you being the joker? Are you trying to make me the fool?"

"No, of course not. Look, I'm not stupid," I said. "I was suffering terrible hunger. How many days had I been without food? I know there must be millions who suffer hunger every day. I've always been open to new ideas. If you know me, I don't live a royal life. I've told you, I like simple things, a simple life, and I've never taken advantage of the money like others do. If you know of a better way of life, I want to know about it."

"OK, Morgan. I'll take you at your word. But you must understand what will happen to you if you are lying." He took a deep breath, and then a very audible sigh. He straightened himself on the stool and turned his head to look at Bubba's dead body on the gurney. It was a wordless message from him that I could end my days as Bubba had done if I tried to fool him.

He turned back to me and said, "The profit you make from the labor of the poor is what is wrong with the world. You don't need that profit to live, yet you keep that profit from those who earn that profit for you. Under a Communist society, everyone would have what is needed to live comfortably and nothing more. People everywhere would want for nothing. Children would not go to bed hungry at night. No one would dress in dirty rags. All the people would own your companies equally, and all would share in the profits."

"I'm sorry," I said, carefully, trying to sound like a student. "But you said '*under* a Communist society.' Does that mean there is something people live under? Does that mean there is . . . Something . . . A controlling something . . . A government . . . To watch over people and make sure they live according to the Communist ideal?"

"I hope you are simply debating with me in order to learn, Morgan."

"I am," I said as honestly as I could manage. "I want to learn. I hope that by asking questions you will give me the truth in answers. After all, I was raised within a different philosophy."

"Once again, I will accept that, Morgan. But please do not tread too harshly. Yes, I meant *under*. Worldwide Communism would be a protective umbrella under which everyone, not only the wealthy few, would have all the benefits of a good life. That is food, education, work, housing, health care . . . Everything."

"I understand what you're saying, Jesse. I have seen poor people, and I understand what you're saying." I hesitated a moment, feigning deep thought. Then I said, "You see, I have been taught my whole life that *incentive* is why people work. The goal to better themselves and their children is why people labor. If a person works hard and is given the same things that a person who does not work is given . . . Why work?"

Jesse sat upright, and a look of pure joy brightened his face. Was it enlightenment, he thought? Had I cracked the shell of truth? He said, "People, under World Communism, will work at what they enjoy . . . At the labor they love. If one is an artist, they will create willingly and share their art with everyone. If one is a maker of shoes, they will make shoes willingly because they love to make shoes. Doctors will heal . . . Farmers will grow . . . Everyone will do what they enjoy doing, what they have been born to do, for the good of the entire society. They will not labor at what they hate to do just because they are paid for it."

"That sounds logical," I said, and I nodded trying to sound and appear authentic, although I knew the foolishness of this, knowing what human nature is. I paused again and then asked, "But what if a person enjoys lying back on the grass in the sun and not doing anything?"

"The good of the whole takes precedence over the wishes of the individual," he said slowly and very seriously. "When want is done away with, people will have the chance to be happy and will become a member of the entire society, equal to everyone. When people see others happily producing they will join them."

Alexandra stood to the side, leaning against the white wall, her thin arms slack to her sides. Her head was bowed, and sadness was evident on her work and worry worn face. She was not a particularly attractive woman. She was in her late forties; her wrinkled, thin, gray face did nothing to hide her age. Her hair was graying and, other than being combed, was not cared for. But I felt she had a conscience, and I thought at the time that she might be ashamed to be taking a part in what Jesse was doing.

I looked at the big clay bowl sitting next to me on the bed. The wooden spoon was there. Both could be a weapon, I thought. I could use the bowl to hit Jesse and perhaps use the handle of the spoon as a knife of sorts; into his eye or at his throat. Alexandra might help. But I needed to regain some strength. I knew I was not strong enough to overtake Jesse. I needed to wait. I needed to regain some strength. And if I did kill Jesse, what waited for me outside the room, past the squeaky door? I didn't know, and would the clay bowl and wooden spoon be weapons enough?

And more than anything else, where was I? Some inner-city somewhere or some isolated corner of the world? How long had I been unconscious after whatever Jesse had injected me with? The bowls of soup were rough clay, the spoons roughly carved wood; things that third world people might use. I could be anywhere, I thought. Anywhere in the world isolated enough to allow Jesse a free hand in what he was doing.

I took the time it took to recuperate a little, over what I thought might be five or six days, to ask occasional questions I needed to know the answers to. One day, after yet another bowl of soup, this one with more meat among the vegetables, I risked asking, "I've been thinking, Jesse. The Hillsdale thing. Was that you and your friends?"

Jesse stood and circled the room around its walls, his hands clenched behind his back. He stopped, looked down at Bubba's deteriorating body and turned to me. He said, "I suppose there's no real harm in you knowing. After all, you will either leave here a devoted member of our cause, or you will leave here dead. Yes, that was . . . My friends, as you say."

"And the security guard? I hope his death was a pure accident. After all you've told me and your obvious concern for the good of mankind, I can't imagine his death was anything but an unfortunate accident. I hear concern in your voice . . . Compassion for the ordinary man."

Jesse liked that. He smiled. I am really good at flattering people who need to be flattered so I can get what I need from them.

"It was an accident. He simply was in the wrong place at the wrong time. Unfortunate as you say. I am very sorry that he had to die. I understand he had no family, and he was a troubled young man. That does not change the fact that it was a needless death. If he hadn't come across our agent, he would be alive today, and everything would be different today."

"So, you had someone in there that night to get something, right? You stole something, right? I mean, there was no reason to kill that guy, so your friends had to be after something very important."

Jesse couldn't know that I had found out what was stolen that night at Hillsdale. If he did, I might not survive the day. I hoped that the plans for whatever Firebird Guidance was were being changed. I should have thought to tell someone at Hillsdale to do that, but Donna Evans had assured me it would be done. The necessary changes to Firebird Guidance would be made quickly, so that whatever killing the military wanted to do using Firebird would be done successfully, and the stolen plans would be useless to whoever had them.

"Of course," he answered. "But that's not for you to know right now. Maybe later, but not right now."

I waited two more days . . . Two periods of three bowls of food a day which was my only clock . . . during which time I talked with Jesse, making him believe I was really interested in what he was saying. I even made a suggestion of how my own personal wealth could be used to better the condition of the world. Jesse liked the idea and went so far as to write down what I said, telling me he would relay it to his group.

I also found I could stand for short periods at a time. Alexandra kept my infected ankles clean and bandaged, and she kept up the antibiotics. Jesse didn't seem to mind, even when I started taking a few steps before returning to the bed, exhausted after such little effort. I took the risk to ask, "Bill Trangent . . . Do you know why he was killed?"

Again, I had walked on thin ice. I could see that I had come close to the edge with Jesse. Quick flashes of anger crossed his face. But he decided, again, that it would do no harm for me to know.

"Mr. Trangent had worked for us for a number of years."

"When he was with InterAir in Seattle?"

"Yes, of course," Jesse said, perhaps a little exasperated at my questions, but willing to answer anyway. I had figured that Bill had been selling secrets for a number of years. But I had thought some Russians or some other Government had been buying them.

I knew the connection between his death and that night at Hillsdale, but I couldn't let Jesse know that I knew. The break-in that night had been planned with the aid of Bill Trangent's lowered security. The plan must have been that no one was supposed to know that anything had been stolen. Whoever broke in that night was supposed to be in and out quietly and unseen. The death of the security guard blew that plan apart. The murder would be investigated, and the police would question everyone, including Bill Trangent. He had to be silenced to be certain he would not cave to pressure and confess his involvement while he talked to the police. And if his family knew he was being paid to sell secrets, they had to be eliminated, too. No chances could be taken. No assumptions could be made. Death was the only absolute screen that Jesse could hide behind.

I waited another day, listening to Jesse drone on about all the good world Communism would do. He told me of the misery in third world Countries and how people suffer at the hands of Capitalists. I didn't argue; I didn't tell him all I had personally seen: the petty dictators and military socialists such as the Castro brothers. I didn't tell him about the anti-American 'leaders' who lived in luxury while the people of their nations starved and dressed in rags.

I ventured into what was important to me. I said, "Not meaning to change the subject, Jesse. I mean, I see the logic in what you're saying. Just thinking about all the poor and suffering makes me feel terrible. But I can't get Ashley Trangent off my mind. You know I was looking for her. Do you have any idea where she might be? I mean, is she safe somewhere? I really don't want the poor girl to be harmed in anyway."

"Yes . . . Poor Ashley. She is being well cared for," is all Jesse would say in a very condescending tone.

"Where?" I risked. "Can I see her?"

"Soon . . . If our conversations progress as well as they have. She is nearby."

"Where? Where am I?"

"Why, we're in Cuba, of course."

FIFTEEN - I'm Going To Mexico

When Sandy's plane landed in Houston she went directly from the airport to the motel I had stayed at. She went to the front desk to collect my luggage, which I had left there, considering I was unconscious when Jesse took me away. She spoke with the on-duty manager, Teresa Gonzalez, a young woman not too many years out of a two year Community College course in hotel management.

"As I told the police," Teresa said with only a faint Spanish accent. "As far as we are concerned, Mr. Crew left without paying the bill. We may, by law, keep his luggage until the bill is paid."

Sandy took her wallet from her purse, paid the bill in cash, and demanded a receipt and my small suitcase. She received both.

"Now," Sandy said. "I want to speak with the staff who were working the day my husband disappeared."

"I'm afraid that's not possible, Mrs. Crew," the young woman said with an officious sniff of the air, looking away from Sandy as if my wife were some demanding tradesman.

"I will either speak with all the staff, or I will return with an army of lawyers who will sue this establishment and all its owners for wantonly allowing my husband to be kidnapped."

"Kidnapped! I . . . What do you mean kidnapped?"

"I have reason to believe my husband is in some

jeopardy. I can prove that in court prior to you and your employers paying me a grossly large amount of money for your indifference to the safety and security of your paying guests. And of course, I will let the media know of this. It will make a really good story to run on the nightly news. They may follow the story for days, considering who my husband is."

It took only one phone call to the motel's corporate offices. One by one, the entire staff who were working when Jesse jabbed the hypodermic needle into my neck were called into a small conference room off the lobby of the motel. It was into the evening hours when Sandy sat across the table from Rosa Ramirez.

"Rosa, I am Mrs. Morgan Crew. Do you remember my husband staying here? I believe he stayed in one of the rooms you maintained."

Rosa's face turned crimson at first then quickly faded to ash white. She looked down at the floor and started twisting her hands together. "Sí . . . I do remember."

"Tell me what happened, Rosa. You're not in any trouble, and what you tell me will stay between you and me. I promise."

Rosa was a middle aged woman from Mexico whose life had been hard from the day she was born. She crossed the border into the United States late one night hoping to find a better life than she had in Mexico. Years, starting as a child, working the hot Mexican fields during plantings and harvests, and trying to stay alive when she couldn't find work, prematurely aged the woman. Her dark skin was wrinkled, and her black hair was filled with grey. The work she found as a hotel maid, although with low pay, was far better than a day in the sun, bent over a short hoe or picking crops.

She wore her house maid's uniform that day, a white dress with green stripes, which was not new. She wore old Nike running shoes that had a hole in one toe. Rosa wiped a tear from her eye with her sleeve. She said, "The man, he give me money."

"Who gave you money, Rosa?"

"The black man. He was kind, and he smile."

"What did the black man want, Rosa? You can tell me."

"I open the door for him."

"Mr. Crew's door?"

"Sí . . . I know I do wrong, but he give me much money." Rosa pleaded. "I no get fired? You promise."

"Who was this man, Rosa? Did he tell you who he was?" Sandy asked. She reached across the table and gently touched Rosa's hand, comforting her.

"No, he say he want to surprise the man in the room. He no look like a man who is bad. He wears the good clothes, you know?"

"What time was this, Rosa? What time did you open the door for this man?"

"It was early. I just come to work. Maybe siete . . . seven, yes?" Sandy knew that given every opportunity I would sleep the day away if she did not wake me. Seven in the morning would mean I was not yet awake. She knew it was a safe bet to assume the man would walk into the room with me still in bed.

Sandy thanked the woman and promised again not to say anything that would cause her to lose her job. She finished speaking with the last few people who worked that day. There was a new person sitting in the manager's office by the time Sandy had finished. This one was a man, well dressed, who looked more like an attorney than a hotel manager. Sandy quickly learned that in fact, he was an attorney, sent by the corporate offices.

He stood when Sandy walked into the office. He held out his hand to her and introduced himself. "I'm Kenneth Freemont, Mrs. Crew. I'm an attorney who represents the owners of this chain of motels. I'm very glad to meet you. I've heard a lot about you and Mr. Crew."

"You're an attorney," Sandy said.   It wasn't a question; it was more of a surprised statement. "Should I get my army of attorneys here?"

"No need for that," Freemont laughed. He waived Sandy to a chair next to the desk as he sat. "I'm going to help you as much as I can. So, what can we do?"

"Well, to start, I need to see all your security recordings for the day my husband disappeared."

"That's easily done . . . But are you sure your husband disappeared? I mean . . . Are you sure he's not just taking a . . . vacation, shall we say? You know how men are."

"If you are here to insult me, you're doing a very good job. No, my husband is not off with some floozy. I spoke with your employee, the one who illegally opened the door to my husband's room for the person I believe kidnapped my husband. So cut the crap Mr. Freemont. Now, let's see those recordings . . . From inside the building and the ones from the parking lot."

"Who was it opened the door?" he asked.

"Never mind . . . Not important . . . Let's go see the recordings."

"I'm afraid I need to know who it was. We can't have

employees breaking the rules."

"I said forget it. I'm not giving you the person's name. I'm not stupid. When I sue your bosses you won't be able to lay this whole thing off on one of your staff. Now, do I get my lawyers here and march into court and do a press release so the whole world will know my husband was kidnapped from here . . . Or do we see the recordings?"

The attorney gave up. I haven't met the person yet who could win an argument with Sandy. He took her to a small office behind the reception desk. The room was big enough for only one small wooden desk and a well-used secretary's chair whose vinyl seat was cracked. An ancient looking desktop computer sat on the desk. Sandy sat and pushed the button to turn the thing on. It was so old that it took a full minute and a half to come to life. At the right side of the keyboard was an external disk drive plugged into the computer's one and only USB port.

Sandy swung around in the chair and asked the attorney, "So where are the recordings?"

He stepped out of the room without saying anything, leaving the door open. It took a few minutes, but when he returned he had two disks, each in a thin red plastic case. He laid them on the desk and said, "These are the recordings for the night Mr. Crew checked in and the following morning." He was careful not to say, 'The night Mr. Crew was kidnapped.'

Sandy thanked him and said, "You can leave now. I can handle this. And please shut the door when you leave."

Freemont was not happy, but he did leave, very slowly, and he slammed the office door shut after him to let Sandy know he wasn't happy. Sandy had a good laugh at that.

She set the computer to go through the recording very slowly, the hallway outside my room first. It took a long time, but she finally came to the point where Rosa had opened the door. There was a well-dressed man there, as Rosa described, but he kept his back to the camera, and he wore a brimmed hat. Sandy backed the recording up until the man first appeared. He had come from behind the camera so that his face was not recorded. But the elevators were at the opposite end of the hallway, the cameras set to record people getting off the elevators and walking down the hallway, toward the camera.

'How the hell did he get in?' she asked herself. She backed the recording up to the beginning which was ten hours before Rosa opened the door. The man did not appear anywhere in that time. She went through the recording from the time the man entered the room to the end of the disk. There was nothing about anyone leaving the room.

She switched to the disk from the parking lot cameras. People came and went, into and out of the motel, to their cars and from their cars; cars drove into the lot, and cars drove out. But no sign of a well-dressed single man with a hat. She ran through the entire disk again and then stopped it as a delivery truck, small and white, without any business signs on it, entered the lot and drove to the rear of the motel, out of camera range.

She ran through that part of the recording several times. There was no license plate on the front of the truck, and the windshield had been darkened so she couldn't see in. But that had to be it, she thought. Thirty minutes of recording later, the white van left the parking lot. Again, the license plate was missing at the back of the van. And what better way to get a kidnapped victim out of the motel than inside a van?

That was it, she thought. She switched off the old computer, took the two disks with her, and left the room, stopping at the front desk where Attorney Freemont was waiting. He had been leaning against the front counter, but he stood quickly when Sandy stepped out of the room.

"So," he said. "Did you find anything?"

"These are the only recordings for that time period?" she asked holding the two disks out in front of her.

"Yes, that's it. You'll need to leave those with me."

"Something is missing," Sandy said, ignoring what he said. She glared at the man; without words, she accused him of lying to her.

"I don't get it," he said. "It's the time period you asked for. So, tell me what's missing."

"There is video of a man entering my husband's room . . . But no video of anyone ever leaving. I think there's a blank spot in the recording."

Freemont said nothing. Sandy asked, "And you're absolutely sure that you have all the recordings? Nothing is missing?"

"I'm sure," he answered.

"Then someone has tampered with the recordings. Whatever was recorded of my husband leaving his room has been erased. I'm going to have some people check these disks to see if anything was edited out."

At that point Sandy knew that either the man who had entered my room had erased the record . . . Or he had found some other employee who took money to do the erasing. But knowing that part was now gone was all she needed to know. She slipped the two disks into he purse.

"I need to go to the rear of the building," she said as

she walked past Freemont.

"Sure," he said. He followed Sandy and started for the front doors.

"Not that way," she said stopping him. "I need to go out through the rear door."

"I'm not sure there is a rear door," he said. There was a college aged kid working the front desk that evening. Freemont looked at him for an answer.

The young man looked from Freemont to Sandy and back to Freemont and then said, "There's a service door. Where the garbage goes and the linens are delivered. I guess that's what you mean. But it isn't used by guests."

"OK," Sandy said. "I want to go there."

Freemont told the desk clerk to take Sandy and him to that door. "But the desk?" the kid said. His job, he had been told, was to remain at the front desk until 9 that night. He needed the job for rent and food, and he didn't want to go hungry while trying to study.

"Don't worry. It's OK to be gone for a few minutes," Freemont assured him.

The three walked down a hallway, past the two elevators and through a double swinging door that had a sign on it that read 'EMPLOYEES ONLY.' They made their way past a few rows of metal shelves on which everything a motel would need was stored. Cleaning supplies and brooms and mops and buckets and linens filled the shelves. A row of green plastic garbage cans lined a wall. Opposite them were eight rolling carts the housekeeping staff used. And there was an unclean smell permeating the storage room, as if the trash had not been picked up for too many days.

At the rear was a single, gray metal door with a push

bar lock keeping it closed. Sandy pushed it, and the door swung open.

"No alarms on this door?" she asked Freemont.

"I guess not," he answered. "I'll report that." The desk clerk kid kind of backed away, maybe a little ashamed or maybe a little scared.

Sandy looked up and around the ceiling. "And no cameras, either," she said.

On the wall outside, to the right of the door, there was a keypad that operated the electric lock on the door. Sandy looked questioningly at Freemont. He shrugged his shoulders and looked at the clerk.

"There's only one code for the linen delivery and for the garbage guys. I guess anyone else who wants in uses the same code."

Freemont added, "I guess I'll report that, too. I guess someone got the code somewhere. Is that what you think, Mrs. Crew?"

Sandy was looking at the brown painted metal box that held the keypad. She said, "I think someone opened the box to override the lock. Look here. There are four screws that hold the keypad down. The paint has been chipped off of all four of them. Somebody removed the screws and then put them back. Is there a record of this door being opened?"

The college kid answered, "No, not that I'm aware of. I mean, we use the computer for reservations and billings. The damn system is so old, I doubt it could hold anything else. You've seen the old computer behind the front desk. I'm a business major at The University of Houston. The computer system here is a joke. I'd be surprised if someone hasn't stolen credit card numbers."

"Something else to report, Mr. Freemont?" Sandy

asked.

The Attorney glared at the college kid who immediately regretted saying anything.

They went back to the front desk without speaking. Freemont knew what a bad position he and his employer were in. A very wealthy and very prominent man had been taken from the motel with the aid of a motel employee. If that ever hit the media, or if the police ever got their hands on that . . . He didn't want to think about it.

Sandy decided to spend the night at the motel that night. Freemont, in an effort to keep her happy, waived any fee for the room. Sandy wanted the same room I had been in, and she got it quickly.

She had a good idea of what had happened. Whoever was on the video going into my room had opened the rear door and taken the emergency stairs up. The white van had come behind the motel, and Sandy could close her eyes and see her husband being dragged to it and driven away.

She was eating a salad for dinner, sitting at the work station desk in the room, when a knock on the door stopped her, a forkful of lettuce half way to her mouth. She grabbed the knife from the table and went to the door. She looked at the dinner knife in her hand; it was a poor weapon but all she had.

"Who is it?" she called through the door as she checked the double locks.

"Donna Evans, Homeland Security," she said. "May I speak with you, Mrs. Crew?"

Sandy left the chain on the door as she opened it a few inches. She put her shoulder to the door knowing that she couldn't stop anyone from pushing the door open, but she would try anyway. When she saw it was, in fact, Evans, she pulled the chain away and opened the door.

"I'm surprised you're here," Sandy said as Evans walked into the room. "How did you find me?"

"Come on, Mrs. Crew. Homeland Security?"

"Oh, yeah. I forgot. Anyway, why are you here?"

"I made an agreement with your husband. I'm offering the same deal to you. We'll leave you alone. Just keep me up to date on what you find out."

"I can do that up to a point. When I feel letting anyone know something that might hurt Morgan . . . I won't talk to you."

"I can understand that," Donna Evans said. She stepped slowly across the room and sat on the edge of the bed, laying her purse next to her. She was wearing a light gray jacket over another of her very motherly flowered print dresses. "You've learned something here. What is it?"

"How do you know I learned anything?" Sandy asked. She pulled the wheeled chair from the desk where her dinner waited for her. She made a great show of dropping the knife on the plate of salad. She wanted Evans to know she was ready to fight with whatever weapon she had, but fight she would. She sat and looked deeply at the woman.

Evans saw the show with the knife and smiled that exasperating little smile. She answered, "You wouldn't be here right now if you hadn't found something. I can help you, Sandy." It was the first time she had called her Sandy. Her smile, although forced, seemed almost kind and sympathetic, like that of a worried parent.

"OK, if you can help. I looked at the security video for the parking lot, for the night Morgan disappeared. I saw a small white van pull into the parking lot and drive around to the rear of the building. There aren't any security cameras back there, but I think I found evidence that someone may have broken into the electronic keypad lock at the rear service door and overrode the lock. I also looked at the security recording of the hallway outside this room. A man paid a maid to open the door here. That, I believe, is how Morgan went missing."

"And you saw someone take your husband from the room?" she asked.

"No, I believe that part of the recording has been erased."

"That's unfortunate . . . But not surprising," she said. She started to take a pack of cigarettes from her purse, but the stern look of disapproval from Sandy stopped her.

"Did you identify the man?" she asked.

"No. He kept his back to the camera, and there was no license plate on the van, front or back."

"And what can I do to help?"

"I expect you have people who can look at the recordings and computer and see if anything can be recovered. Will you do that?"

"Of course I can. It may take a few days, but I have people who can do that."

Sandy reached for her purse and took the two disks from it. She handed them to Donna.

"And what will you do now?" Evans asked.

"Morgan was going to go to Mexico. That's where I'm going. But I have to ask. What have *you* learned about Morgan's disappearance?"

"Nothing," she answered. "I've checked all our

sources. There's nothing, not even rumors."

"You must be looking into the theft at Hillsdale. What do you know? What have you learned?"

"Only that it was very professional. Nothing much more than you already know. If you wish to go home, we will take over. But it may not be good for your family. I think my superiors will certainly close down Hillsdale Technologies once we step in. Not many people where I work are as generous as I am."

"I guess you'll have to do what you have to do, Ms. Evans," Sandy said. "But it is back open, isn't it? The people are back at their jobs?"

"Yes, of course."

"And what are they doing? Are they working on the Government contracts?"

"I can't discuss that with you, Sandy. You know that."

Evans, without thinking about it, once again pulled a pack of cigarettes from her purse but stopped when she saw that same look on Sandy's face. She put the pack back and asked again, "What will you do now? What can I do to help?"

"As I said, I'm going to Mexico," Sandy said. "Just give me some time."

SIXTEEN – Lover's Revenge

The meals continued, but they didn't improve. Watery soups with some overcooked vegetables and scraps of meat. They were my only clock and calendar. Three meals I took to mean one day. But my rest and sleep came irregularly. Sometimes Jesse left me alone after my first meal, sometimes after my fourth or fifth. I think he was intentionally trying to keep the passage of time from me.

The room was lit by ceiling lights constantly; they were never turned off even when I tried to sleep. The big light over the bed that had been so blinding had not been turned on again. I took that as a sign that my efforts to fake a 'Stockholm Syndrome' were successful. Jesse seemed happy at my feigned interest in his education program. There was no sign of the case of hypodermic needles, and there was no threat of using them again. I was satisfied, even if I wished I could do something to escape. Little by little I was regaining some strength, even though the meager soups did little to add to that strength. Soon, I hoped, I would be able to make that try. But if I could escape . . . How would I get out of Cuba?

Jesse was doing a lot of pacing around the small room every day, his hands held behind his back, as he lectured me on the history of Communism. I think he was having a very good time playing the role of a professor. I knew a little about history; what I knew is left over from my wasted years at Yale. Jesse's teachings were, at best, twisted history. I think he was making up much of what he was saying, trying, obviously, to convert me, or maybe to convince himself. I did my best to show interest and ask questions that would make him believe I was bending to his beliefs. But I knew that Fascists and Communists have in common a desire to get everyone marching in lock step. Freedom of thought under Communist rule, to perhaps think Communism is bad, is not allowed. So I didn't argue the truth with him.

It may have been days or weeks, I had no way of knowing, since I had been tied down to the bed, but gradually I was able to walk around the room. Exercise was important. Alexandra brought my food, bowls of thin soup with a few pieces of tough meat and over cooked vegetables, and when she did, Jesse would leave the room while I ate, alone, sitting on the edge of the bed. Poor Bubba had been wheeled out of the room several meals ago when Jesse could not take the smell anymore. His body had begun to deteriorate and smelled really bad. I hoped he had been given a decent burial at least.

I looked at the far corner of the room, at the ceiling, to see if the little red light on the CCV camera was on. It never went off. Someone, somewhere, was watching. That would be a problem when I tried my escape.

The camera was at the top of the seven or eight foot tall wall. I could try jumping high enough to rip it down. Although it wasn't very high up on the wall, I doubted that I had the strength to do that. And besides, someone was sure to see me reach for it. The bed had been bolted down to the floor; I would not be able to use that to reach the camera. Jesse's stool was there. I might be able to use that, I thought. But something intervened.

Alexandra brought my clay bowl of soup and wooden spoon on an old, scratched and dented metal tray. The tray was something new and so was the clay cup of water. Normally, Alexandra would bring the bowl and spoon and nothing else. Jesse got up and walked out of the room while I ate, as usual, without saying a word.

I sat on the bed; Alexandra, rather than handing me the bowl and spoon and leaving the room, handed me the tray. She whispered that I should lie back on the bed, the head of the bed having been raised. She nodded towards the bowl and silently mouthed the word, "Eat." She stood between me and the camera, her back to the camera. As I spooned the soup from the bowl she feigned checking my pulse and mouthed words, "Will you help me?"

I nodded just enough to answer her as I took a spoonful of the soup into my mouth. I picked the bowl up off the tray to bring it closer to my mouth. There was a piece of rough gray cloth on the tray, a napkin I assumed. Alexandra picked it up just enough for me to see the knife under it. The blade was that of a broad hunting knife, six inches long. The handle had been removed leaving a flat piece of steel before the blade. It was not a new knife; it was not shiny, but I hoped it would be sharp enough.

Alexandra, standing with her back to the camera, took the knife and slid it under the thin mattress I was on. She tried to smile but I could sense the trepidation and fear she was feeling. I mouthed, "The camera?"

Her lips moved slowly, "I will . . ."

Before she could finish, Jesse walked back into the room.

"What's goin' on here?" he demanded.

Alexandra turned to him and said, "I was spooning soup for him."

"He can do that himself. Get out."

Alexandra left the room quickly, her head down, her hands shaking and folded in front of her tightly.

Jesse sat on his stool. The anger he had expressed quickly disappeared. He forced a thin smile and asked, "Is the soup good?"

"No," I answered. "It's little more than water flavored with something along with a couple bits of tough meat, and a few overcooked vegetables sunk into it. I need some food."

"Well, for the time being, that's all you're going to get. You see, this is a system I learned some years ago. First, there is the pain for lies and pleasure for the truth. There is confinement with pain when you protest the confinement. The loss of the passage of time is important. After that there is some little reward for cooperation. We are there now. Your soup is your reward for your cooperation in our lessons. It is enough to keep you alive, but little more than that. Soon we will progress to the next step of your education, Morgan. At that time there will be better food."

"How about a hint?" I asked. "What's the next step?"

"That will come in time, Morgan. But it will entail your agreement to physical cooperation with a project. For now, let's continue with our conversation about the sins of Capitalism and the blessings of Communism."

I finished the soup as I listened to Jesse ramble on. He had reached the point in his vocal dissertation where he was repeating much of what he had already said in days past. I drank the clay cup of water dry and put the tray on the bed. I swung my legs over the edge.

"I think I'll walk around for a minute. You know, stretch my legs. And I need to use the tin can. Is that OK?" I asked.

There was a rusty metal gallon size can in a far

corner that I used as a toilet when needed. Alexandra took the bucket out every day and brought it back clean.

"Certainly, Morgan. You've been very good, and I'd like you to be as comfortable as possible."

I hesitated for a moment, my hands on the edge of the bed, my fingers feeling for the knife under the mattress. I looked to my left, at the camera. The red light was on. Then, suddenly, it was off. Alexandra had switched it off.

I didn't hesitate; I grabbed the knife and threw myself at Jesse. We fell over backwards off his stool and rolled on the floor. I was weak from days of starvation, but I was able to get on top of him and put the knife to his throat.

"You're going to do exactly what I want you to do, Jesse. Understand? Now, slowly, stand up."

We got to our feet; I moved behind Jesse and held the knife tightly at his throat.

"You won't get away with this, Morgan. There'll be a lot of people here soon. They'll kill you. I'm your only friend here. I'm the only one who can keep you alive. You saw what they did to Bubba. They will do worse to you."

I turned Jesse around slowly so he could see the camera. He saw the light was off and said with a mean snarl, "Damn that woman. I'll kill her."

"Later," I said. "For now we're going to get out of here."

"How the hell do you expect to get out? For God's sake, you're in Cuba, Morgan. Where will you go?"

"For now, out of this damn room. Now, where are my clothes?"

Before Jesse could say anything the door with the squeaky hinges slammed open against the wall. Alexandra was standing there, a big revolver held out in front of her, in both her hands.

"That's good, Alexandra," Jesse said. I could feel the tension leave his body. He was rescued, and I assumed he thought I was going to die. "Drop the knife, Morgan. Drop the knife, and you won't die. I promise."

I had no choice at all. One of the most important lessons I have ever learned was to never take a knife to a gun fight.

I had no idea what Alexandra was up to. She had given me the knife. She had to be the one who turned off the camera. Yet her damn big revolver was held in both her hands and was pointed right at my head. The hammer was cocked. So, I dropped the knife and let Jesse go. I stepped away from him. As he began to turn towards me Alexandra began pulling the trigger. She fired all six shots in the cylinder and kept pulling the trigger after all the bullets had been fired.

Jesse was hit in the chest with all six bullets. He fell hard against the wall behind him and collapsed to the floor, leaving a trail of blood down the wall to the floor. Alexandra stepped to him, slowly, one step at a time, as she went on dry firing the revolver. Tears were flowing from her eyes as she gazed down at the dead Jesse Wilson. I went to her and slowly, gently took the revolver from her hands. She was crying freely, her hands covering her face as she wept.

I sat her on the edge of the bed and put my arms around her. I held her and let her cry it out on my shoulder. After a minute or two she pulled away from me and looked over my shoulder at Jesse.

"That son of a bitch," she said softly in her middle European accent. "I hate him."

I knew the obvious thing for me to do right then was to run for the door. But I couldn't help feeling sorry for the woman. I put my hands on her shoulders and asked in a soft voice, "Why? What did he do to you?"

She sniffled, wiped her nose with the back of her hand, and said, "I loved him. Once I loved him . . . And he said he loves me, too. He is lying bastard. He wants only to use me. I am servant . . . Nothing more."

"Well, he's dead now . . . And all that is over for you. I can help you, Alexandra. I can bring you to safety."

"You are good man, Mr. Morgan. Please, you call me Alex . . . Like my family, yes?"

"Sure, Alex," I said. I touched her cheek to wipe away a few tears and tried to smile. Alex was staring down at the dead Jesse Wilson. Her tears and crying had stopped, but she seemed to be in a dreamlike state. I had to say something to her; I had to get her help.

I am terrible when it comes to comforting people who are ill or crying over something. I never know the right words to say, and what I often say is the wrong thing. But I had to think of getting us out of there. I asked, "My clothes, Alex. Where are my clothes?"

SEVENTEEN - Trees In The Desert

Sandy reached for the big bottle of water that was in the cup holder of the rental car as she drove down the dusty, bumpy road to San Pedro Escobar. It was hot that day in the South Texas desert. She had prepared herself for the drive by dressing in tan shorts, a light weight, short sleeved cotton blouse and tough hiking boots. She had a broad brimmed hat on the seat next to her.

As she was packing her suitcase back in Houston she had given some thought to bringing a gun with her. She would go to Mexico after leaving San Pedro, but she was aware of the Mexican laws concerning bringing guns into that Country. It would have made her feel more comfortable and secure, but spending years in a Mexican prison wouldn't help anyone. So she didn't buy a gun to take with her.

A long eared skinny rabbit darted from behind a tall cactus and ran across the road as she approached the little town of San Pedro Escobar. At first she thought it was a ghost town, a forsaken collection of mud brick buildings that had not seen people for years. On either side of the thin road into town all she saw was sand, brush, and some cactus.

But as she slowly drove into town, three old men appeared from the doorway of one of the buildings. They stood and watched the strange sight of yet another gringo in their town. Two gringos in new automobiles in such a short time. That was something they could talk about for many days.

She stopped the car in the middle of the dusty road, rolled down the window, smiled at the men, and called out, "Hello! . . . Buenos dias! . . . Puedo hablar con usted?"

"Sí, chiquita. I speak English," one of them said. He tossed the stub of his cigar onto the ground and crushed it with his scuffed boot. He said something to his two friends and walked to Sandy's car. She left the engine running, the transmission in 'drive,' and her left foot on the brake, while her right foot hovered over the gas pedal. She would floor the gas if she had to get out of there.

The man was old; his skin was wrinkled and like dry leather from years in the hot sun. His hair was thick, curly and ash grey. He wore dirty and faded blue jeans, a blue plaid shirt and kicked about boots. He smiled kindly as he walked to the car.

"This, she ain't no place for a lady," he said, standing a few feet away from the car.

"I'm looking for my husband," Sandy said. "I think he was here some time ago. Has an American been here?"

"Sí, a Yankee gringo, he was here."

"A tall man . . . I guess you could say he's a little fat . . . Morgan Crew . . . That's his name."

"Nobody comes here, chiquita. It was very strange when he come. He was here. I talk to him."

"You did? Did he say where he was going? Who he was looking for?"

"Oh, sí. He say he want señor Omar."

"Omar?" Sandy questioned. "Did you tell him how to find Omar?"

"Sí, I tell him. You look for Omar, too?"

"Yes. How do I find him? Does he live around here?"

The old man told Sandy what he had told me. She thanked him and gave him a twenty dollar bill. He broke out in a big toothy grin, turned towards his two friends and waived the bill over his head happily as Sandy drove away.

It took some time, but she found the old trailer and searched around it and inside it. The snake that had greeted me had long since wandered off. There had to be something, she told herself, less sure of that than hoping there was something. Inside the dust covered trailer she ripped open every drawer and tore open all the doors inside the trailer. It was filthy and full of spider webs and little bugs that scampered away from her. But there was nothing to help her.

She went outside and sat on the steps at the door. It had finally hit her; she was at a loss. What could she do? It was a dead end. She put her hands to her face and started to cry. She would have to go further into Mexico. But Sandy was determined, and if she had to search the entirety of Mexico to find me, she would.

The sound of an old pick-up with a bad muffler stopped her tears. She looked to her left. A 1970's something pick-up, more rust than blue paint holding it together, was bouncing down the dirt road toward her. She stood and wished she had brought a gun regardless of having to cross into Mexico.

The truck came to a slow stop next to her. It was the old man she had spoken with back in the town.

"Señorita," he said speaking across the truck, out of the passenger side window. "I think maybe you need my help, no?" Sandy is quite good at Spanish, if not fluent. She knew that this man was flattering her by calling her señorita which means 'miss' or a young lady and not señora which means 'misses' or an older lady.

"Help? Help with what? What do you want?"

"Señor Omar . . . He is a bad man, no? You and your man, you no should go to him."

"You know Omar?" Sandy asked. "How do you know him?"

"He comes to San Pedro, and he buy food sometimes. He does not like us. He swears at us, and sometimes he does not pay for what he takes. He has hit me and my amigos. The women, they hide when he comes. You should stay away, señorita."

"But he's not here," Sandy said. "It's filthy inside. He hasn't been here in a long time, right?"

"It has been many days . . . Weeks I think. Maybe more."

"Was he alone when he was here? Did he have a car? Is there anything that might help me find him?"

"Sí, señorita. He was with a little chica . . . a little girl . . . a young girl. She maybe a little loco, you know?"

"Where did they go from here?"

"South I think . . . Across the border, sí?"

"And you don't know where in Mexico?" she asked.

"That I do not know . . . But maybe there is someone who does know. But first, why do you want to find this Omar?"

"I don't know your name, señor," she said.

"I am Felipe, señorita. May I get out of this hot car?

We can speak maybe in the shade somewhere?"

"OK, Felipe. Let's talk . . . And if you can help me there's more money in it for you. If you try anything stupid . . . I can take care of myself, got it?"

"Oh, sí, señorita. I need the money, not the woman." He laughed as he pulled his old body from the cab of the truck. They found some shade at the front of the trailer. Felipe pulled two rickety chairs from inside, set them in the dirt, and they sat.

"Felipe," Sandy started. "That man you spoke to who wanted to find Omar is my husband. I think he's in trouble. I think he may have been kidnapped. He's been missing for a long time. I need to find him."

"And this Omar," Felipe asked. "He is bad as I think he is?"

"He could be worse. Now, who is it who might know where Omar is?"

Felipe pulled a thin cigar from his shirt pocket. He lit it with a wooden match he lit with a flick of his thumbnail and blew the acrid smoke towards the sky. Ordinarily, Sandy would object to anyone smoking near her, but she needed this man's help, so she said nothing.

"A few months ago," Felipe said. "This Omar he was here. There is a young girl from San Pedro. She is just a child, maybe catorce . . . How you say? Fourteen years, that is all. This Omar, he take her here to this place, and he keep her for many days. Then he leaves her, and he drives south, into Mexico. She think she love this man. She walked for many days through the desert to find him. She follows the tracks of the tires, you know? She no find this man, but she come home. We all think she is dead. She almost is. We care for her, and she does not die, but she is not the same. She is sick in the head, you know?"

"Do you know where she went?"

"She say across many miles of desert. She say she find a big building with nothing else there but lots of trees. The building, it is all gray . . . Like cement, she say. She say men with guns outside. I think she either loco, or she sees how you say, drug men?"

"How about Omar? Did she say he was there?"

"Sí, she say she sees him, but he beat her and make her go away."

"Can I talk to her, Felipe?"

EIGHTEEN – To Deal With The Devil

My new friend, Alex, brought me my clothes. They were in a rough, coarse hemp bag, unwashed and wrinkled. My watch, my wallet, and my money clip were not there. I didn't really care. Being free and away from wherever I was had to be a lot more important than money.

I dressed as Alex looked down on the body of Jesse Wilson. The clothes were loose on me. Although I had no idea how long I was there, weeks maybe, I had lost weight while being held a prisoner. If nothing else, Sandy might find some good in that. When I was dressed I asked, "How do we get out of here?"

"You must wait here. I will make the arrangements and come back for you. It is dangerous."

Alex tucked the big revolver into her belt and stooped to take Jesse by the ankles. She struggled but managed to pull him from the room, refusing my help, and leaving a trail of thick blood behind. The door with the squeaky hinges closed. I picked the knife up off of the floor. I was alone, dressed but with only the knife blade as protection.

I paced around the room, my hands in my pockets, the shoes feeling strange after all that time without them. I looked at the can in the corner and promised myself I wouldn't pee in that thing again. My eyes went to the camera at the ceiling; the red light was back on. Something bad had happened.

I went to the door, but it was locked. I wanted to start pounding on the door and yelling but that might bring somebody really bad with a gun. So I went back to pacing.

Time was not relevant. There was no day, and there was no night. Without a clock, and with the room lit constantly, the passage of time didn't exist, as Jesse wanted it. My head began to throb, and my stomach was turning, partly from hunger and partly as a result of what I had been put through.

I tired myself out by pacing in the small room. I found by stepping over Jesse's blood the room was six paces by eight paces, about eighteen feet by twenty-four. The math filled my mind as I tried to get an accurate measurement. Finally, I sat on the bed and waited.

Something had happened to Alexandra, I felt certain of that. Killing Jesse over a love affair gone bad had to be a bad idea. Someone out there didn't like it. Jesse had to be important, and she had killed him. Maybe my only friend was dead, too.

And if she was gone, what would I do? I remembered the tortured body of Bubba. Whoever did that could do the same to me. I still had the knife blade without a handle; my hand went to it, and I grasped it tightly. But I was in no physical condition to do any fighting. And besides, if I could fight my way out of the room, I would still be in Cuba, and how the hell do I get back home?

I lay back on the bed and stared at the ceiling. It was made up of those squares with a million tiny holes in them. Hospitals had them; I'd seen offices with ceilings like that. I'm told they are for sound proofing, but there was no sound in my little concrete room. I tried counting the holes, but I couldn't. I would go crazy doing stuff like that.

My eyes were getting heavy, and I felt sleep folding its

arms around me. I closed my eyes; maybe sleep would be good for me. If I actually did sleep I didn't know it. I don't remember if I dreamed, but at least I didn't have any nightmares. I held onto the knife as my one and only hope. The squeaky door woke me suddenly. I quickly slid the knife under the mattress. I jumped out of the bed; my feet hit the floor hard.

It was Alexandra, and she had the pistol with her. I felt like running to her and hugging her. I didn't. "You had me scared," I said. "How do we get out of here?"

"Out of here?" she questioned. "You will stay and do what I tell you to do."

"But . . . But I thought you wanted me to help you?"

"I did," she said as she walked across the room. "I gave you the knife, but you didn't kill him. I had to kill him. I didn't want to do that. I wanted you to kill him."

"That's the help you wanted? You wanted me to kill Jesse?"

"Of course," she said as if I should have known that all along. "Now, you will do as I say."

I sat back on the bed and let my feet hang over the side. My hand went to the mattress. I felt the handle of the knife. Alexandra raised her hand and pointed the revolver at me.

"I will take the knife now. Please understand . . . I will kill you if I have to."

I drew the knife from under the thin mattress and dropped it on the floor. "Why?" I asked.

"Money. Jesse, he was paid money . . . I want that. My life is not over . . . I want better for me."

Alexandra's voice, with her distinctive middle

European accent, was quaking with emotion. Her hand was shaking, but the pistol was cocked. There was no way I could span the distance between her and me before she got a shot off. So, I was back to learning while gaining trust.

I said, "Jesse had been teaching me about Communism. Will you take up where he left off?"

"That is to laugh. I am not Communist. I hate the Communists. I am Hungarian . . . I was told of when Hungary became free. My mother and father told me. It was terrible time for my parents."

"OK, so what do we do then?"

"There will be people here soon who will tell us."

I was about to ask who, but I was interrupted when the squeaky door opened. I jumped onto the floor when Donna Evans walked in. My first thought was that I was saved. Homeland Security had arrived, probably with Navy Seals, a bunch of Marines, helicopter gunships, and a whole lot of guns. My heart started racing, and I wanted to jump up and yell. When Donna walked to Alex, took her into her arms, and kissed her passionately on the lips, I sank back against the bed. Alexandra's hand, holding the gun, fell to her side, but she didn't drop the pistol.

The kiss lasted a long time; I guessed the lovers hadn't seen each other for a long time. I pulled them apart when I said, "Should you two get a room? . . . Or should I just leave you alone?"

Donna held Alex in her arms when she turned to me, smiled broadly, a real smile rather than her forced, pasted on grin, as I had never seen her smile before, and said, "Oh, Morgan. I'm surprised you hadn't figured this out. Do you really believe Homeland Security would step aside and allow you to run your own private little investigation? You must think you're really something very special. I always thought you were smart. But you really aren't, are you?"

"I'm smart enough to know that you couldn't hide the theft at Hillsdale from the Government. Yeah, I had questions about what you were doing. I never fully believed you had the power to independently stop the whole damn Government from doing what they had to do. My guess is, Homeland Security, the FBI, the CIA, and a dozen other acronyms are out there running their own . . . 'Little investigations,' as you put it. I'd bet my last million that only you and I . . . And of course Alex . . . Know of the deal you and I made. But I was willing to play the game, if in fact you were playing a game. I'm smart enough to know that once the truth was known, Hillsdale Technologies would bite the dust. Jeremy would be ruined. And my greedy family would take it in the wallet. So, if you were playing a game, I would make the most of it and try to save what is mine. If you were serious, I would do the same thing. I had nothing to lose. Winding up here wasn't part of my plan, however."

Donna stepped away from Alex; a questioning frown crossed her face. "Is that why you have been so secretive, Morgan?"

"Of course," I said proudly. "I never trusted you totally. You took a big risk taking the road you did. I read somewhere that a person takes a big risk letting others see who they really are. You failed at the lie you told me, and I had a hunch you weren't who you really are. You wanted me to get caught . . . You wanted me to end up wherever I am now. You knew the path I was on would lead me here. You knew I would never survive after I did whatever it is you want me to do, so you had no fear your thin cover would be exposed. I'm here for a purpose . . . Not to take lessons in Communism. Of course, you and Alex . . . Well that's a surprise. But I wish the two of you the best, anyway. So why not try being honest for a change. Cut the shit and tell me what you want."

Alex looked at her lover, asking a silent question. Was it time to tell the truth, to reveal what they really wanted? Donna shook her head in answer. She said, "We should wait until they arrive."

"Suppose I don't want to wait?" I asked. "Suppose I make a try at escape? Suppose I jump on the two of you and at least try to kick the shit out of you?"

"That would be stupid, Morgan," Donna said. "Even if Alex could not shoot you before you jumped off that bed, there are people outside who would kill you on sight as soon as you walked through that doorway."

"I have an idea that you don't want me dead. I think you need me for something, and if I'm dead . . . You lose."

Donna didn't answer me. She and Alex held onto each other as the two women left the room, backing away from me. Donna closed the squeaky door behind them. I was alone again, wondering what the hell was going to happen.

****

Money . . . That's what Alex had said was her purpose. It has been my life long experience that the old saying 'Money is the root of all evil' isn't correct. The thirst for money is the root of evil. The thirst for money, the gluttony for money, corrupts absolutely. Evil exists for as long as mankind has walked the Earth with two ends as its purpose: The acquisition of wealth and the acquisition of power. The history books are filled with conquerors whose stories go back thousands of years. From then to today, the real purpose behind evil is personal acquisition of wealth and power.

These two women had it in mind to make a lot of money doing something illegal. They probably wanted to escape together, somewhere. They wanted a life together free of what they felt was binding them. They needed money to do that. And I was needed for them to get their grubby little hands on that money. I went to the door thinking I was locked in, and I was right. I would have to wait on the lovers to find out what they wanted me to do.

****

My only clock during my imprisonment had been the three meager meals brought to me. A man I had not seen before continued to bring me these meals, on what seemed like a regular basis, after it looked like Alex had disappeared. Of course, I had no way of knowing that it was morning when a clay bowl of corn meal mush, a distinct change from the watery soups, and a clay cup of warm water were brought to me. What I thought might be the lunch meal had changed to a couple thick slices of hard brown bread and a clay cup of warm water. Nor did I have any way of knowing it was evening when a clay bowl of the usual watery soup and a clay cup of warm water were brought to me.

But my clock said three days had passed since the lovers, Donna and Alex, had kissed. I had nothing to do except wonder and worry. I was lying on the bed, the only furniture in the room, after an hour or two of pacing the room, checking on my measurements of its size. Doing that had become my diversion from cracking up and falling into insanity. I had no one to talk to; even the dark skinned man said nothing to me when he brought my meals to me. The loneliness, what it must be like to live abandoned on a desolate island, was devastating.

I had to concentrate on something to keep my mind from collapsing. I tried mathematics, but I am far from a mathematician. But that didn't matter. I tried counting the little holes in one ceiling tile and then counted the tiles. I multiplied the number of holes by the number of tiles. I really didn't care if the answer was correct. Then I counted the holes in another tile and did the same math. I took brakes from counting tiles to walk the room and use math to determine its size. The concentration kept me from thinking of my imprisonment. Over and over I did this as I lay on the bed and then walked around the room. Occasionally I found myself talking to myself out loud. That both angered me and worried me. Was it someone's intent to drive me crazy? Was insanity what they were after?

The lights in the room remained on, never turned off, but I was able to get used to sleeping with them on. I slept whenever I felt sleep near me, not knowing if it was night or day. The big light over the bed had not been turned on again, and no torture other than loneliness was inflicted on me.

The squeaky door opened, and the man who had been bringing my meals entered the room with the bowl of bread and cup of water, indicating it was time for lunch.

It was the same man every time. He was big, taller than me, and loaded with muscles that threatened to tear at the seams of the dark green fatigues he wore. He wore a beard of jet black, and his hair was cropped very short, very military in style. His skin was dark, very Latin; his eyes were dark. Jesse had told me I was in Cuba. The man looked Cuban. He might have been trying to imitate a young Fidel.

He said nothing when he brought my meals. He merely handed me the bowl and cup, turned and walked away. He was just too damn big for me to try to jump, especially in my weakened condition.

That day there were three people following him into the room. Donna Evans led two others, one a young black woman and the other looked to be an Arab. I took the bowl and cup and laid them on the bed next to me. The man who had brought my food left the room quickly, leaving the squeaking door open behind him.

"Well," I said as brightly as I could. "Visitors! It's so good of you to visit. I just wish you could have let me know you were coming. I would have had a nice lunch prepared for you. Can I offer you a drink? Some wine perhaps?"

My joke seemed to float over their heads. Donna took a step forward and said, "These are the people we were waiting for."

"Well, now," I said trying to sound like a wise cracking guy who wasn't afraid. "How about an introduction?"

Donna stood silent for a minute and then said, "This is Omar and Tamara. Last names aren't important right now. You will help them in their task."

"I will, will I? I kind of have doubts about that."

"I'm afraid you have no options, Morgan."

"Sure I do. You can kill me. That's an option."

"No, I won't do that," Donna said. "You're much too valuable. But your wife isn't important . . . And your daughter isn't important."

That scared the hell out of me, but I wasn't about to let them know that. I said, "I'd like to see you try to kill Sandy. She'll see you dead before that can happen. You have no idea who she is and what she's capable of."

"But your sweet little daughter . . . How about her? Will the little child be difficult to kill? Will she fight back?"

"I have a hunch that since I disappeared, Sandy has taken measures to protect our daughter. She's somewhere outside of society right now. She's with people, underground somewhere, who will protect her. And I also have a hunch that Sandy is out there looking for me. Like I said, you have no idea who she is and what she is capable of."

Donna's face told me she already knew what I had told her. She wasn't happy; I'd love to play poker with her sometime. Her face would reveal the cards she held. She said, "In fact I have been with your wife very recently. She is off on a wild goose chase, I'm afraid. I imagine she is searching all over Mexico for you."

"As I said, you have no idea who she is."

"Morgan," Donna said, taking a step towards me. "You saw what happened to Bubba. I can do the same to you."

"Yes, you can. But Bubba wound up dead. Will I wind up dead, too? I doubt it. You can cut me up and beat the crap out of me. But you won't do that. I've been tortured before. I've been shot before. When you start that I will die before I do what you want. Tell me what you want and maybe . . . Just maybe . . . We can negotiate. As I said, you need me alive."

The Arab man standing behind Donna and to her right said, "I can make you feel pain . . . Great pain. You had a taste of that pain from Jesse. I can do worse."

"Let's stop all this silly, childish back and forth," I said. I slipped off the edge of the bed and walked across the room to stand in front of them. "Just tell me what you want, and I'll tell you if I will give you what you want. If I say no . . . Just kill me. But remember, if we make a deal, will *I* be making a deal with the devil . . . Or will *you*?"

NINETEEN - Lost

Sandy followed Felipe back to San Pedro. Felipe's old pickup truck not only kicked up a lot of sand and dust, it also left a cloud of exhaust behind it. Sandy dropped back a hundred yards. It seemed fifteen miles an hour was about as fast as Felipe's old truck could bounce along the rutted, unpaved, rocky trail.

In the center of the town Felipe turned right onto another unpaved, thin road, and stopped in front of an adobe house. What was once a white picket fence surrounded the front and sides of the house. The fence now hung at an angle on old, weather rotted posts, and a dozen or more of the pickets were missing. A few flowers and several small cacti tried to make a garden inside the fence. There was no lawn; neatly raked sand took the place of greenery. No trash or garbage of any kind could be seen inside the fence, although on the other side paper and trash blew everywhere.

At the front of the old house, a woman was sitting in a rocker on a wooden porch, shaded by a roof above. She held a well-used bible in her hands. When Felipe pulled to a stop at her gate, she put the bible aside on a small table and stood, trying to see who was visiting through her old, cloudy eyes.

The woman walked from the porch, stepping slowly with her age, as she recognized Felipe. He got out of his truck and waited for Sandy to walk to him. He spoke in Spanish to the old woman; Sandy understood much of what they said. Felipe explained that the gringo woman wanted to speak with the woman's daughter, Camellia. The woman looked at Sandy who was standing at the open gate, outside the fenced yard. She walked to Sandy.

She spoke in slow, broken English, "Why do you speak with Camellia?"

"I want to find a man she knows . . . Omar."

The woman's face went ashen; she took a tentative step away from Sandy. "I am Camellia's madre . . . mother. Camellia, she has suffered much. She should no suffer more."

"I am very sorry your daughter has suffered so. But if I can find this Omar, I can bring him to justice. Justice for Camellia and for everyone else Omar has hurt."

The woman took a moment to think and then said, "Come inside. And por favor, be kind."

Sandy followed Camellia's mother into the little adobe house. A young girl sat in an old, sagging, upholstered chair, softly singing a tune in Spanish. Felipe touched Sandy's shoulder and whispered, "The girl, she is blind. She had spent too many days in the desert. The sun, it blinded her. She maybe is still out there . . . In her head . . . You know?"

Sandy went to her and knelt on one knee in front of her. She took the girl's hand and asked, "Puedo hablar contigo? Can I speak with you?"

"Oh yes," The girl said brightly, a pretty, young girl's smile breaking out on her face. "I do speak English," she said without a trace of accent. "I learned in school, you know."

"That's fine," Sandy said.

"Please sit down," Camellia said brightly, happy to have someone to practice her English on. "Mama, podemos tener una bebida fría?" she asked and said to Sandy, "I asked my mother for something cool to drink."

"Thank you," Sandy said. "I could use something cold."

She sat on a hard wooden chair near Camellia. Felipe stood near her. The girl stared straight ahead. She wore dark glasses that rested on a thin, fine nose. She had a good smile, and her face was pretty and soft as every young girl's face should be. Her black hair was parted in the middle and hung long, thick, shiny, and silky across her shoulders. Sandy wondered what this girl's life would be and what it could have been if she had not met Omar.

"I had heard you came to town," Camellia said. "No one knows your name or who you are."

"My name is Sandy . . . Mrs. Morgan Crew. My husband was here some weeks ago. He's missing now. I want to find him."

"And Omar must have something to do with that," she said as more a statement than a question.

"I'm sorry," Sandy said. "But I have to ask . . ."

"It's alright," Camellia said. She tried to keep her smile, but Sandy saw her eyes, behind the dark glasses, filling with tears. "I know what he does . . . I know he's a bad man . . . I do love him . . . But I know he is a bad man."

Her mother brought a tray with a plastic pitcher of something sweet and fruity. Sandy hadn't realized just how thirsty she was until she drank from the blue glass she was given. The drink was cold and amazingly refreshing. Sandy drained the glass and asked for more. The woman was happy at that. A proud smile filled her dark, weathered face that had been aged beyond her years.

When she had finished half of the second glass, Sandy asked, "When Omar was here . . . Out at the trailer . . . Was he alone?"

"Oh yes. Omar was alone," Camellia answered. Her smile drifted away, and she spoke in soft words, as if in a dream. "He will come back soon, you know. I am waiting for him, you know. If you wait, he will be here for me. You can speak with him when he comes back for me."

Felipe looked at Camellia's mother. A sad cloud crossed both the faces. Sandy turned and looked at both of them. She nodded, understanding.

"Camellia," she said. "I understand you went out to find Omar when he left."

"Yes, of course," she answered, once again bright and young. "We are deeply in love with each other, and I have to be with him. Oh, I know he is not a good man . . . But when he and I are together I can make him into a good man."

"Where did you go? . . . To find Omar, I mean?"

"Omar must have had important business. That is why he had to leave so suddenly. That girl who went with him . . . She had some business with him. I know that was it. Just important business."

"There was a girl with him?" Sandy asked.

"Oh, yes. A very strange girl. I think she might have some trouble in her head, you know what I mean?"

"Yes, I know," Sandy said. "Where did they go, Camellia?"

The young girl had a dreamy look on her face. She was remembering the man. Sandy didn't want to delve into their relationship. Whether it was sexual or not was none of her business. But she had to press the issue of where Omar had gone.

Camellia removed her dark glasses and wiped her tearing eyes with a small lace hanky. She put her glasses back on and said, "He went south. I saw him drive away. Across the border."

"And you followed?"

"Yes, of course. I knew he had important business. I wanted to go with him. But he said I couldn't. Oh, he wanted me to go with him . . . I know that. But he had important business."

"Where did you follow him to?"

"Into the desert . . . I followed the car's tracks . . . It was many days . . . But I followed him . . . To be with him."

"And where did the tracks take you?" Sandy pressed. She looked up at Camellia's mother and Felipe. They were whispering to each other. Sandy knew she had only a few more minutes with Camellia before she would be asked to leave.

"Camellia," Sandy said softly. She touched Camellia's arm. "This is very important because my own man is missing. I know how you feel . . . The loss . . . The pain. I have to find my man, too. Please, where did Omar go?"

"The angels helped me, you see. The angels guided me because they knew Omar loves me. It was the angels who guided me to a rancho . . . Far away . . . Many days . . . In the hills . . . An old rancho . . . Far away. There were old horses that looked funny. There was cool water coming from the hills. It was good water . . . I drank there. The angels took me to the water. And there were trees and green grass and a funny looking building under the trees. It was all gray, like cement, you know? I knew Omar had to be in a good place because the angels had to have taken him there, too."

Camellia's mother spoke softly in Spanish, "Please, no more."

Sandy rose to her feet and thanked Camellia. The girl said, "Tell Omar I'm waiting for him. Please?" She was crying freely, her tears running down her child's rosy cheeks.

"I will," Sandy answered. "I will."

Felipe led Sandy outside; Camellia's mother knelt at her daughter's side, brushing her hair out of her eyes and trying to comfort her. Outside, Sandy asked Felipe, "Do you know the road Omar took?"

"Sí, señorita. I know. But please, do not go. You will be like Camellia."

"I have to go, Felipe. Please, what road did he take?"

Felipe was deep in thought as he lit a short, bent, black cigar. He paced a few steps away and then back again as he considered what to do. He said, "Some of the men, we went after little Camellia. It took many days, but we found her wandering in the desert . . . Across the border, sí? There is no road, an old cattle trail only maybe. We did not see the rancho. Maybe there is no rancho? Maybe the girl, she just imagines a rancho, sí?"

"How do I find it?" she asked.

"I ask you to no go there . . . If you do I can no stop you, sí?" Felipe paused, stared at Sandy with old, tired eyes squinting sharply. He blew some smoke from his cigar into the air and said, "Go to the trailer. She is in Mexico. South from there is a creek. Cross it, and you will find the trail. From there, I cannot say."

Sandy took his hand in both of hers. "Thank you Felipe. Is there anything I can do for you?"

"I only wish a doctor for Camellia. There is no doctor here."

"When this is done, there will be a doctor," Sandy promised.

She stopped at the little store in the center of San Pedro on her way to the trailer. She bought four big plastic bottles of water and filled the car's gas tank at a pump behind the shop. She thought about food, but her worry wiped out any hunger she might have felt.

She drove quickly out of the little town and crossed the border into Mexico. Turning the car to the south at the trailer, she had no trouble finding what was once the little creek Felipe had told her would be there. Very little water flowed through the rocks, but it was certainly a creek. She turned the engine off and got out of the car. She looked to the south, beyond the little rocky creek. It was nothing but sand, cactus, and brush. The land was flat for what looked like a hundred miles, but in the dim distance, to the southwest, there was a mountain, brown and very dry looking.

She looked at the rental car. It was a small Toyota. "I could kick myself," she said out loud, wishing she had rented a big four wheel drive. But she was determined, and the car would have to do. She drank some water from one of the bottles she had bought. It was warm already but, as with the car, it would have to do.

She got back in the car and drove across the creek. There had been no border, no sign saying 'Welcome to Mexico' behind her. But there was a trail as Felipe had told her there would be. It was little more than two rutted indentations in the sand, but it was a trail that had once been a trail to drive cattle north to market in the States.

The drive was difficult; the ruts that passed for a road were full of potholes and rocks. It didn't take many miles for Sandy to realize that the Toyota wasn't going to take her all the way to the mountains.

It was late in the day; dusk was racing in, and the sky was darkening. A million stars made their appearance in the sky, and a full moon shown down on Sandy. She pulled the car to a stop, turned off the engine, made sure the doors were locked, reclined the seat back as far as it would go, and she slept.

On the second day, the desert, the heat, and the rutted cattle trail, were too much for the Toyota. It gave up its last breath mid-afternoon. Sandy raised the hood, but she is no better a mechanic than I am. She left the hood up and kicked the car out of revenge for leaving her stranded.

She put the broad brimmed, straw hat on her head, she took the three bottles of water that were left from the four she had bought, and she started walking. She spoke out loud, "Damn, I wish I had a better car." Her legs were bare under the shorts, and her blouse was short sleeved. "Damn," she said again.

She walked back to the car and began tearing at the leather seat covers. Her first thought was that it was impossible, but she overcame the impossible and with a lot of work, tore enough of the leather to wear as a shoulder cover, pulling it down to cover her arms as much as she could.

For the better part of three days, Sandy walked along the little cattle trail towards the mountains. The water was gone, the bottles dropped onto the sand. Lack of water and food began to take its toll; her head was spinning, and her eyes began to play games on her. She saw lakes of cool, clear water. She saw forests of shade trees. But all she walked across was hot desert sand.

The sun, in her dazed condition, was huge and burned down on her, wrapping her in arms of flame. She stumbled and thought of her goal, got to her feet, walked and stumbled once again. Black unconsciousness fell around her like a thick, heavy blanket. Death, robed in a black shroud with his sickle in hand, gazed down upon her and laughed a maniacal cackle.

TWENTY – Just An Object Lesson

I was left alone, locked in the room for six meals. The meals were my clock, and they told me two days had passed. The meals had reverted back to the first few meals I had suffered; more water than food. But I left nothing in the clay bowls, and I drank all the warm water I was given.

With my 'breakfast' on the third day, Omar and Donna Evans returned. They stood against a far wall silently watching me drink the meal. When I was done I intentionally dropped the clay bowl and the small clay cup onto the cold gray concrete floor. They crashed and broke into pieces. I smiled at the two of them. It was my only means of revolution for the moment.

"Tsk-tsk, Morgan," Donna said. "Such waste. But no matter. It's time to discuss what you will do for us."

"You make assumptions," I said.

Donna took a step or two towards me. She folded her hands in front of her letting her arms hang long. She looked at the floor and then back at me. She said, "You are in a weakened condition, Morgan. You've lost a great deal of weight while you were here. You won't last long when Omar here gets his hands on you."

"Donna," I said and paused. "May I still call you Donna . . . Or should I call you Commissar Evans?"

"Oh, my dear," she laughed. "I am not a Communist. Jesse . . . Poor Jesse . . . He was, but that was all silliness.

278

Communism has been a proven failure. No, I am a pure Capitalist. I love money, and I want wealth."

She turned to the side and started walking back and forth in front of me in the small room. "You've heard the story, of course, of Willy Sutton? He was a famous bank robber back in the 30's. When they finally caught up with him, someone asked him why he robbed banks. His answer was 'because that's where the money is.' That's my answer, also."

She stopped pacing and looked hard at me. She folded her arms in front of her and spat the words out, "They say I am old. They want to retire me. They want me to take a pittance as what they call retirement benefits. I've spent my life . . . My youth . . . Everything I've ever had . . . Defending our Country. I have no family and very few people who even like me. And for their thanks they expect me to live on a few thousand a year. So I went to where the money is . . . The Arabs and their oil and their wealth. When this is all over . . . When you've done what you will do . . . Alexandra and I can go away somewhere. Somewhere where the beaches are soft, the sand white, the sky blue, and the weather warm. We will spend . . . Our latter years, I guess you could say, unfortunately . . . Comfortably. I hope you understand."

"I understand," I said. "It probably feels good to be able to tell the truth finally. I've heard it said that truth and loyalty are equal when we speak of morality. I guess that's not exactly correct. Your truth unveils your disloyalty to your Country. What moral plane is treason on?"

"On the contrary, Morgan. My Country has been somewhat disloyal to me. As I said, I never married, I have no family. My whole life has been devoted to my Country, and now my Country thinks it can toss me aside. That is the truth, Morgan. Who is being disloyal to whom?"

I leaned back on the edge of the bed. There it was again. Money is what has driven so many people to do wrong. I knew from experience that money drives people to commit crimes, to murder, to treachery, to treason. Donna Evans was no different from a hundred other people I've run into in my life. People who, otherwise, could have been good, could have done good things, but are driven 'to the dark side' as they said in those cosmic-space movies. For money and nothing more.

"So, Morgan," she said. "Now we will discuss what you will do for us."

I relaxed and listened. Donna did all the talking while Omar stood to the side, leaning back against the white wall, arms folded tightly in front of him and a mean look clouding his dark face. There was no doubt that man was dangerous. I could see it in his shadowy eyes. His personal fanaticism, be it religious or simply hatred of America, made him capable of losing all feelings for the people he would hurt and kill. There was no human empathy inside the man. I felt certain that Omar, or certainly someone quite like him, had been the one to inflict the torture on Bubba and had finally killed him. I was equally sure I did not want to give him the opportunity to do the same to me.

I would feign cooperation flavored with just enough negatives to make them believe I was relenting unwillingly. I did the same with Jesse, and it had worked until he was murdered. Then, when I was able to free myself from the room, I would take my revenge on them. At that point, after being so long locked in the room, starved and tortured, it made little difference if I lived or died. I would make sure they died before I did.

I knew there was no chance to leave Cuba even if I could leave this room; to think differently was stupid. I would be dead, and I would not see Sandy or Caroline again. But they would be safe, and their lives would be good . . . Even though I wasn't with them.

So, I listened. Donna explained that what had been stolen from Hillsdale Technologies was a new guidance system for unmanned drones and the bombs they carried; the drones would be used in Afghanistan, Iraq, any place the U.S. thought it wise to kill people silently and without warning.

"You see," Donna explained. "Omar was an agent for Al Qaeda . . . But Omar, over the past year or two, has come to enjoy the life styles of the west. He sells information to anyone who will pay for it. And that job, which he does very well by the way, keeps him in the west and the life he enjoys so much."

Omar interrupted, "Allah . . . All praise be to him . . . Seeks the destruction of the devil America. Anyone who will fight for that is worthy of praise and an honored place in heaven."

"The enemy of my enemy is my friend?" I asked.

"Yes, exactly," Omar said smiling satisfyingly.

"Especially where money is concerned," I added.

The smile fell quickly away from Omar's face, and the red hot look of hate returned.

I looked at Donna as she took a cigarette from her purse and lit it. She said, "Oh, I forgot, you don't like smoking, right, Morgan?"

"I used to smoke. I still enjoy an occasional premium cigar with a good bourbon or a cognac. But I imagine you don't have anything like that lying around do you? But you go ahead. Maybe it will speed up the lung cancer that will kill you."

"I like that," she said. "You're not trying to throw a con job at me. It's good to know you aren't faking anything. Anyway, I've been around long enough to know that as soon as Washington knew that the specs for Firebird Guidance had been stolen, they would require a change to the specs. I read the reports, and Washington . . . In all their superior intelligence . . . Thought it best to let the people at Hillsdale make the changes since they knew the system so well. I want the new specs. I don't want anyone to know I have them. I want to be able to sell them for a great deal of money. And I want you to get those new specs for me."

"You're kidding right?"

"No, I'm perfectly serious, Morgan," Donna said as she paced back and forth, drawing deeply on her cigarette. "I know I can't bribe you. My God, you've got all the money in the world. You wouldn't like to give me a couple hundred million would you?" she laughed. "But I can throw you into Omar's hands, and I assure you your death will be very long and very painful. I would require that if you don't help me."

Not being either stupid or a hero, I agreed to help, sounding reluctant to make it sound believable, but I still had it inside of me that I would try to escape at the first opportunity, and then I would kill these two. Maybe I would kill Alexandra, too. I would go along with them, reluctantly agreeing to whatever they said.

I pushed myself off the edge of the bed and stood on the concrete floor. It was cold on my bare feet, but the cold felt good and stirred my brain a little. My legs were weak; my knees wanted to buckle. I held onto the bed to keep from falling. I forced myself upright and said, as proudly as I could manage, "I'll listen and maybe do what you want. But I want something in return."

"I will not let you go, Morgan, if that's what you want.

If you do exactly as we ask, you might just live afterwards. But you will never return to your previous life. I cannot let you go and tell everyone about me. You will live a comfortable life, but a restricted life somewhere far away."

"That's not what I want . . . Although not being dead would be nice," I said. "I want a couple of things immediately. One, if you're going to keep me in this room, I want clean sheets on this bed. For God's sake, these damn sheets haven't been changed since I woke up here. They stink."

"That can be arranged," Donna said.

"Next, I want food. Real food, not the hot water you've been giving me. I won't be any good to you if I'm starving and my brain stops working."

"If you cooperate," Donna said, "then the food will get better . . . Little by little . . . As a reward."

"And I want a chair to sit on. My back is killing me from sitting on this damn bed."

"Done."

"Finally, I want to shower and shave," my hand went to the rough beard on my face. Time meant nothing to me, but the same didn't apply to the growth of beard. "I want to be clean for a change. And I want clean clothes, too. My clothes smell like they haven't been cleaned in weeks."

"That's not impossible," she said. "We'll see if that can be arranged. Is there anything else?"

I thought a bit of revolt might be good about then, so I said, "Yeah, a gun to blow your friggin' brains out."

"Now, now, Morgan," she said, laughing a little. "Be nice. Later today I'm going to come back with Omar and the young woman, you remember? Tamara. We will then start to make plans on getting the revised specifications for Firebird Guidance. Until then, I suggest you rest a bit. You look awful, you know."

When they had closed and locked the squeaky door, I did lie down on the bed. My head was spinning, and I felt weaker than I can ever remember. I closed my eyes and managed a little sleep. I was awakened by the squeaky door. Two men in green fatigues and long dark beards were in the room. I remembered seeing pictures of Fidel Castro from years ago. They looked a lot like him, as the man who had been bringing me my meals. I laughed at that. They seemed not to notice.

They swept up the broken clay dishes I had dropped on the floor. When that was done one of them carried in a chair, old and worn, but clean, soft and upholstered. It wasn't much of a chair, but it was a chair I could sit in.

A small wooden table was brought in and placed next to the chair. A cracked ceramic dish, not deep but wide, was placed on it. A small bar of rough yellow soap was in the dish. A plastic pitcher filled with water was put next to it. A rough cloth was laid in the dish.

As they left the room one of them said, "Wash." I heard the squeaky door lock when it was closed. Pushing myself off the bed I glanced up at the camera on the ceiling. The red light was on; I was not alone. A good show might be appropriate, I thought. So I gathered what little strength I had and proceeded to perform a slow striptease as I pulled the dirty clothes off of me. When I was naked I bent over and mooned whoever was watching. I turned facing the camera and shook my stuff for them. I hoped it was a woman who might like what she saw. It was fun, but it also tired me. Ignoring that, I did a slow walk around the room, showing off my nakedness to the camera. "I hope you enjoy this!" I said, looking at the camera.

I sat in the chair, regaining my breath before washing as best I could and getting dressed once again. Being somewhat clean was refreshing, but my clothes were still filthy.

It felt good to sit in a chair rather than on the edge of the bed. I felt my eyes getting heavy, but sleep was interrupted once again. Alexandra returned to the room. Behind her were the two goons who had brought the chair and table.

"I will shave you," she said. "But first . . ."

The two men came to me and pulled me from the chair. They dragged my arms behind me and handcuffed me. They then threw me back onto the chair.

Alex said, "Please excuse. I don't trust you, no?"

While the two uniformed men stood at the open door, Alex first cut my beard with scissors, and then she shaved me, using an aerosol shave cream with words on it I had never seen before. They weren't Spanish and certainly not English. I guessed the can had been imported from Eastern Europe or maybe Russia. But she worked very efficiently with a polished straight razor and did not cut me even once.

While she was doing that a woman, short and very heavy, dark skinned and dressed in a flowery, Caribbean native-type, long dress, changed the sheets on the bed. I was surprised at how quickly everything I asked for was being given to me.

Alexandra poured some fresh water into the dish, dipped a white cloth she had brought with her in the water, and wrung it out. She wiped the shave cream from my face, took the razor and both the bowl and plastic pitcher with her, and walked out of the room. One of the goons removed my handcuffs and they, too, left the room, locking the door behind them.

It felt good to be clean and shaved, even though my clothes reeked. It felt better to just sit in the chair. I needed sleep before Donna returned with what she wanted me to do; I needed my brain to operate as well as I could expect. Sleep came quickly but didn't last long.

The squeaky door slammed open. The two goons who brought the chair in raced into the room, grabbed me by my arms and pulled me from the chair. They held me tightly by my arms, stretching them out and twisting them behind me. I thought they might rip my arms from my shoulders.

Omar walked slowly into the room. He stopped in front of me and smiled viciously. He was wearing black gloves that fit his hands like a second skin. The first punch was to my jaw, followed by two more left and right to my face. My stomach was next; I lost count of the punches.

Omar was good at his job. His punches were slowly aimed, even, well timed, and well placed; very professional. They inflicted pain but broke no bones. I tasted blood in my mouth. His punches to the sides of my face closed my eyes. Unconsciousness stopped the pain and the beatings.

I awoke when a bucket of water was thrown on me. I was on the floor, my hands cuffed behind my back. Omar was standing over me. He kicked me hard in the stomach and then kicked me again. I retched, losing my last meal, and tried to roll away from him. With my back turned he kicked me in my kidneys and at the back of my head.

I heard a voice, "That's enough." Omar stopped. I heard the footsteps of heavy boots. The squeaky door closed, and I was left alone. I tried to roll away, but the slightest movement sent lightning strikes of pain through my body. So I relaxed and let my body go as limp as I could manage. The pain eased enough for me to breathe.

I have no idea how long I lay there, half awake and half completely out of it. Then I heard the door open. I could barely see through blood soaked and almost closed eyes; I wish I could have wiped the blood from them.

It was Donna Evans . . . At least I think it was her. Whoever it was stood over me. I heard a fog filled voice say, "It's just a lesson, Morgan. Just a lesson."

I thought I was alone again, as the door closed. I hadn't seen the person leave. But I wasn't alone. Hands were on me, pulling me to my feet. I groaned at the pain, but I didn't resist. I was on the bed; my hands were freed of the handcuffs. Someone was softly, gently, washing the blood from my face. A cool wet cloth gently touching my bruised body was easing some pain. I worked hard to open my eyes. Focusing was difficult, but I think it was Alexandra.

"Lie still." I heard the words, although they were wrapped in a mist of fog. A soft clean white sheet was pulled up to my shoulders. A hand, tender and compassionate, brushed the hair from my face. "Sleep," she whispered. I did.

I woke, rested but stiff and sore. I turned my head, and there was Donna Evans, sitting in my chair. She had that forced, false grin on her face and a lit cigarette in her hand.

"Good morning, Morgan," she said.

"Morning? Is it morning?" I mumbled. I raised my hand to my face. I could feel the cuts and swollen bruises. I looked back at her and asked, "Is it a *good* morning?"

"Believe it or not, Morgan," she said as she stood and walked to me. Her hand touched my arm as she said, "Believe it or not, I *am* sorry. But it was just an object lesson. Remember Jesse's little box of chemicals? The pain and the pleasure?   Those would affect your brain. Omar only affects your body . . . temporarily. Soon all the pain will be gone, and you'll be as good as new."

"OK," I said. The words were hard to speak. My lips were cut and swollen. "I learned . . . What do you want?"

Before Donna could answer, Alex walked to my bedside. She had a tall glass with something cloudy in it; a glass straw sat in whatever it was. She held it to my mouth. "Drink," she said. I did the best I could, and in fact found whatever I was sucking through the straw tasted pretty good.

"This will be good for you," Alex said.

I drank some more of it and then pushed the glass away. I could take no more. Alex and Donna walked away, and the squeaky door told me I was alone again.   Sleep overcame me quickly once again.

I had lost my clock of soup being brought to me. Alex brought a glass of the creamy liquid that I took through the glass straw seemingly on a regular basis. In what seemed like a short time, I was able to sit up once again, and soon after I was able to sit in the chair. I was sore all over, but I knew I had no broken bones. My eyes opened gradually, and I tried to speak with Alex when she brought me my glass of liquid food. She would say nothing to me, eventually handing the glass to me when I could hold it myself, and walking away.

When I could I walked, first only a few steps due to the pain in my back, low around my kidneys. Then a few more steps, and eventually I could pace the borders of the room once again. The biggest problem, one that seemed most serious to me, was that I was pissing blood. Little by little the blood turned pink, and then it was gone.

On the day Alex brought me the first solid food I had

had in a long time, Donna and Omar were with her.

I ate the soft, white bread and creamy cheese voraciously. A glass of cold milk accompanied the food. When I had finished, Alex took the plate and glass and left the room. The squeaky door was left open leaving Donna and Omar in the room with me.

"So now down to work, Morgan," Donna said. "As I've told you, we need to get the revised specs on Firebird Guidance. How do we do that?"

TWENTY-ONE - Mirage

Sandy woke up in bed. It was dark wherever she was. Her hand went to her face. The sun had burnt her; there were painful blisters on her forehead and nose. There was some kind of cream on her face and hands, a soothing, cooling cream that took some of the pain of the blisters away.

She was covered with a clean, soft, white sheet; her head lay on a thin but soft pillow. She tried to focus her eyes to become accustomed to the dark all around her. She strained to look around the room. It was a hospital room; that much was obvious. She closed her eyes, and sleep folded itself around her.

When she opened her eyes, the room was bright with daylight. A sweet odor of flowers filled the clean air. She looked up, and she said to the person standing over her, "You're an angel! Camellia was right. You're an angel. Am I dead?"

Whoever . . . Whatever . . . She was all in white, a flowing white gown that covered the person from head to toe. A face came into focus. It was a woman's face, tanned, wearing wire rimmed glasses that were bent on the left stem. She smiled down at Sandy. "No, dear. I'm not an angel, and you are not dead. I am Sister Mary Margaret."

"Sister? Where am I?"

"Jose Martinez found you in the desert, my dear. You

would be dead if he hadn't come across you. What in the world were you doing out in the desert?"

"My husband . . . Where am I?"

"Is your husband out there somewhere, my dear?"

"No . . . Where am I?"

"You are in our convent hospital, my dear," the woman said. Her voice was soft and full of compassion as she smiled down at Sandy.

"What . . . Convent? I don't understand."

"Ours is the Convent of Santa Alicia Maria, my dear. We are Alician Sisters. We are nurses to the poor." Sister Mary Margaret spoke softly, kindly, gently. Her accent was from the Northeast of the United States; that was plain to recognize. 'Probably Boston,' Sandy thought. Her eyes smiled down at Sandy. Her hand touched Sandy's shoulder lightly.

"Where . . .?"

"Why you are in Mexico, my dear. Near San Remo. We are very remote here. This is the Chihuahua desert, my dear. A few people live here and raise goats. They try to farm, but it is a difficult life for them. The poor come here when they are very sick. They come here to die very often."

"I need to leave . . . My husband . . ." Sandy said as she tried to push herself up.

Sister Mary Margaret's kind hand touched Sandy's shoulder softly, and she smiled a compassionate smile. "You need to rest, my dear. Sleep, and you will feel better. You've been in the desert for many days."

The Sister took a clay cup from a small bedside table and held it to Sandy's lips. "Drink some water, my dear. Then sleep."

"Phone . . . Please . . . A telephone . . . Do you have one?" she pleaded, her voice straining to say the words clearly. She sipped at the cool water. The water eased her parched throat. She smiled her thanks.

"Yes, my dear," Sister Mary Margaret answered as she pulled the clean white sheet up around Sandy. "We have a telephone . . . But you must rest first. In the morning you may phone your husband."

"Not . . . my husband . . ." Sandy managed before sleep engulfed her once again.

The next morning, when she awoke after twelve hours of sleep, two Sisters brought an old black dial telephone on a long black cord to Sandy, and she did make the phone call she had to make.

****

Sandy stayed at The Convent for three days. The Sisters nursed her, treated her burns, and brought her strength back. She was strong enough on the third day to meet the Mother Superior of the Convent. A very young Nun, thin and tall, walked Sandy through the cool halls of the thick walled adobe convent and to the office of the head of the convent.

Sister Mary Thomas was a gentle and sympathetic woman of elder years. Anger was something that did not know Sister Mary Thomas. She was kind to everyone, she was compassionate, and she was sympathetic as well as empathetic to people who suffered. She honestly felt the pain of the people who came to her. Several times over the years robbers came to the convent to steal. They left having been given freely whatever the Sisters had and with food and water, too. Sister Mary Thomas actually thanked them for coming to her and wished them well on their travels.

She was loved by all the Mexicans who lived in the rural desert surrounding her little convent and hospital. These people eked out a meager living herding their goats and sheep, and struggling to grow their corn. Sister Mary Thomas was thin under her white Habit. Her face was tanned like soft leather from the desert sun. She wore eyeglasses on a thin brown plastic frame. They sat on the end of her long, thin nose, threatening to fall off but never daring to do such a thing.

Sister Mary Thomas sat behind her small, old, scarred and battered wooden desk in her office, a drab little room decorated with only a framed print of The Virgin Mary and a large Crucifix. The cross had been carefully and lovingly hand carved by an old man as payment for saving the life of his granddaughter who had been bitten by a rattlesnake.

As Sandy was shown into Sister Mary Thomas' office, the old nun struggled to stand, pushing herself from her chair with great effort. "Good morning, my dear," she said brightly. Her voice was soft with an ever so slight Irish lilt behind the words. "I'm so glad that you are feeling better. Please come in and sit. May I offer you some tea? What we have is very simple. Just Lipton tea bags I'm afraid, but it is very refreshing."

"Thank you, Sister. That would be nice."

The Sister nodded to the young Nun standing behind Sandy and sank carefully back onto the thin cushion on her wooden chair. The Nun turned and quickly went to the kitchen, happy to be of service.

"So, my dear," Mary Thomas said, "We do have an auto. A very old station wagon, I'm afraid, but we can take you home."

"Thank you . . . Do I call you Sister . . . Or is there . . ."

Sister Mary Thomas smiled and said, "My dear, I would not be offended at anything you say. But most people just call me Sister."

"Thank you, Sister. But going home just isn't an option for me right now."

"And why is that?"

"I have to find my husband. He's been missing for many weeks now. I have to find him."

The Sister nodded, understanding. She asked, "Your husband is in Mexico?"

"I don't know, Sister. There's a man who might know. Someone called Omar. I have to find him."

Sandy studied the Nun's face for any sign that she might know, or know of, Omar. There was clear evidence there that Sister Mary Thomas knew the man, and Sandy couldn't imagine that the woman ever felt as she obviously did about anyone else. Her face could not hide a lie. She knew Omar, that was clear, but she wouldn't admit to it.

"Well, my dear. Is there something we can do to help you?" Sister Mary Thomas asked.

"I guess it would help if I knew where I am right now. I mean, where in Mexico? I'm looking for a small rancho near the mountains. I'm told there are old horses there and a creek of cool water running through the rancho."

"Yes," the Mother Superior said. "I do know the place. It is very far away. But I'm afraid no one lives there, my dear. It has been abandoned for many years now. The local farmers believe it is haunted, and they go near it only when they have to. For the water, you know, in the dry times when water holes dry up."

"But I'm told there are old horses corralled there," Sandy said.

"Yes, some of the farmers, the brave ones who do not believe in ghosts, use the corral to hold their donkeys and horses while their goats and sheep drink. Many bring their animals there for the water, but they stay only long enough to let their animals drink. They do not stay there long for fear of what they do not understand. These are very poor people, my dear. You must understand this. We try to help them as we can. We help the sick and injured. We try to teach the children, and a priest comes once a month to say Mass. But the farmers have fears built from a lack of education. It is a difficult life here. They utilize whatever they can to scratch a living from the desert."

"There was a young girl . . . Camellia . . . From across the border."

"Ah, yes," the Nun said. "I do remember her. The poor child was badly injured by the sun. She was blinded you know."

"I spoke with her," Sandy said. "She was trying to find Omar. She told me of the ranch and the stream running from the hills. That's how I know it is there. I think you brought the young girl there," Sandy said sitting forward in the chair. "Some time ago. She was trying to find Omar."

"Oh, no, my dear," the Sister said. "I would not have had anyone here take her there."

"She said the angels guided her," Sandy said. "I guess I just assumed your people here were the Angels."

"No, my dear. She was found after going to that place. She was brought here after going to that place. If she found Omar there it was without my doing."

"But Camellia did find that place with the water?"

"When she was found wandering in the desert and taken here, she told us she had been there. Her mind was gone by that time, the poor child. We pray for her every day now. Is she well?"

"As well as can be. I intend to send a doctor to her after I find my husband. Did she tell you why she went there?" Sandy asked. "She was looking for Omar; she told me that. Did she say how she figured Omar would be there?"

"Before Camellia arrived here, while she must have been wandering in the desert, one of the farmers had brought his goats to the stream. He was shot at and chased away. It was only a guess on my part, you understand. I asked the child if it was Omar. Camellia seemed to think it was this man. In speaking with Camellia she told me what a bad man Omar is. Please my dear, do not go there."

Sister Mary Thomas leaned back in her chair. Her hands went to the long rosary beads looped around the course cord that was a belt. She fingered the beads and stared at Sandy who stared down at the floor. The Sister took a deep breath and said, "My dear, if Omar has your husband I'm afraid no good will come of that. He is a very bad man. I am very afraid his soul is black beyond redemption."

"Thank you, Sister. But I do need to go there. It's the only lead I have to where my husband might be."

"This . . . Lead as you say . . . Can you tell me more?"

The young Nun who had gone to make the tea returned with a wooden tray holding a rose patterned ceramic tea pot and two china cups, only one of them with a saucer. "I must apologize my dear," Sister Mary Thomas said. "Things break, and we have no way of replacing them. There is only one pretty saucer left."

The Nun placed the tray on Sister Mary Thomas' desk and filled the two cups with steaming tea. She turned to Sandy and asked a little proudly, "Would you like milk . . . Or perhaps lemon? We have both."

"Thank you, neither," Sandy said. "I like mine straight." Both Nuns laughed, understanding the meaning behind the word.

The young Nun handed Sandy the cup with the saucer and left the room. Sister Mary Thomas took the other by its delicate handle.

Sandy and Sister Mary Thomas were left alone once again. Sandy explained, holding back on most of the things that happened to make the story seem real. Who would, after all, believe what really happened?

"Something was stolen from my husband," she began. "The police want to blame the theft on him. He went off trying to find the real thief. I think Omar had something to do with the theft and my husband's disappearance. I don't know if my husband is alive or dead. But I need to find him, and I think finding Omar is the best bet I have of doing that. I think the place in the hills that Camellia saw may be where Omar is."

Sister Mary Thomas leaned back in her old chair and thought for a moment. She smiled once again and said, "That place is many miles away. Wait another day, my dear. Rest, and then we will give you food and water to take with you. I'm afraid our old auto could not make the trip. The desert is just too difficult for the poor old thing, and there are no real roads there. And I will not send any of my Sisters there. But we will help you as we can."

Sandy did wait that day. The nuns were kind, funny, and friendly and spent good-natured time with her. They played checkers with Sandy, who let them win and laugh and have some fun, and they shared their simple food with her. It was cool inside the adobe convent, and the shade of two big desert trees in the garden offered some comfort from the hot Mexican sun outside, if not from the heat.

The Sisters had tried to make a garden of cactus and desert flowers, but it wasn't much of a garden. They grew some vegetables with great difficulty, but there was enough for them, and the farmers brought them corn and chickens and eggs. There was a well, dug decades ago, that provided water, although it was bitter. But the Sisters never complained. Big copper pots were on the old wood burning stove constantly, boiling the water to make it fit to drink and cook with.

Early the next morning, after a breakfast of weak coffee and dark bread, seven of the white robed Sisters and Sister Mary Thomas said goodbye to Sandy as she left the convent. Sandy's clothes had been washed and carefully ironed. They had given her a colorfully handwoven bag with long shoulder straps. In it were three clay jugs of water and a few sandwiches of cheese, the cheese made by the goat herders of the desert. They found an old green and red serape to cover her shoulders and arms to protect her from the sun. Sandy hugged each Nun and waved goodbye as she started out.

The walk across the desert was hard; the far off brown and gray mountains were her only compass. The mid-day sun was brutal; Sandy decided to stop walking when the sun was directly overhead. She lay on the sand, using the serape and her broad brimmed hat for as much protection from the sun as they would provide. Hours later, when the sun was setting, she drank some water and started walking again.

It was the evening of the fifth day when Sandy stood on a hill of rocks and sand, a tall Saguaro cactus standing next to her, and looked down on the rancho that Camellia had said would be there. It was still a mile away, but Sandy could see it was what she was looking for.

The ranch house was a dilapidated adobe building with a roof that had collapsed some years before. Sun dried wood rails were the corral she had been told would hold old horses. None were there the day Sandy came upon the place. And to the right, cascading down the dry mountainside and past the old corral she could see the small creek Camellia said she had drunk from.

Sandy thought as she laughed that no one but ghosts could possibly live there, yet Camellia said she had found Omar there. She looked beyond the old ranch house to the foothills, several hundred yards further away. There was a stand of trees there, green pine trees that could not possibly exist in the desert but seemed to thrive hidden in the foothills of the brown, dry mountains. In the failing light of day and from the far distance she was away, Sandy thought there might be something amongst the trees, but whatever it was, it was too far away to be sure. She would wait; she had to be cautious. Omar might be as dangerous as she thought he would be. It would neither be safe nor smart to confront him or anyone else in the dark. She had to laugh again when she thought it would probably be as dangerous to meet anyone out there in broad daylight, too.

She lay down on the rocks of the little hill and tried to find a place that was not too uncomfortable. She ate the last of the sandwiches and finished the water in the second jug. She decided to fill the empty jugs at the stream in the morning. Water, she knew, was the most precious and necessary thing in the desert.

Draping the serape over her back and across her shoulders, she lay on her stomach and watched for anything to move down at the rancho.

Her eyes were heavy by the time night was fully around her. She rolled onto her back and gazed at the sky that was filled with millions of stars she had never seen before. The moon was a mere fingernail in the black sky. She shifted around and moved a few rocks away, finding a place between two big boulders where she might get a few hours of sleep. A bright flood light amongst the far away trees flashed on, and she flinched, waking suddenly. The deep black of the desert night was broken by the light that cut like a sharp knife though the dark. She lay flat, pulling the serape over her head, and watched.

Something was moving among the far away trees in the light. A person, a man, she thought. He walked through the trees and around what the light revealed was a building. It was gray, perhaps adobe, perhaps concrete, as Camellia had said.

The man walked out of Sandy's sight behind the building and reappeared. He stopped under a tree to light a cigarette. The flame of the lighter carried a long distance in the night. Sandy strained to see what the man did. He was only a dark shadow in the light, so far away. Leaning against the tree, he smoked slowly, crushed the cigarette out under foot and disappeared, seemingly to the side of the building facing the mountain. The flood light went out, leaving the trees in the night's dark.

Sandy's heart was racing; her breathing was fast. She knew what she had to do, and she had to calm herself to do it. She took deep, slow breaths and felt her heart slow from its racing beat. After a minute or two she threw the serape to the side, left the bag the Sisters had given her, and started to move slowly down the rocky hillside, bending over to make herself what she hoped would be a smaller target.

She tossed aside the idea of waiting for daylight. The

dark, she thought, might be a good cover. She had to know what was down there, among the trees.

She moved slowly, taking each step carefully, knowing that the desert night held many dangers: snakes and Gila monsters sleeping under rocks she might disturb, as well as men with guns. There were people down there, she knew, who might be more dangerous than the reptiles of the desert. But that might be where I was, she hoped silently.

She took the mile slowly, keeping her eyes focused ahead as well as shifting to the sides and stopping often to look behind her. She reached the rancho after more than an hour of slow approach, climbed easily over the rails of the corral, and went to the porch of the adobe house. The door was hanging from broken hinges. She took one step inside the house. The broken roof allowed some starlight light in, enough for Sandy to see no one was living there. The few pieces of wooden furniture were covered in dust and cobwebs. Something small ran across the floor at the far side of the house. Sandy stepped outside and, stepping easily over the thin, rock lined creek, she started for the trees.

She counted her slow steps as she walked and figured the trees were over four hundred yards away. It took some time for her to get there walking as slowly as she did, trying to make no sound at all as her feet touched the ground. She stopped at the edge of the little forest. The trees had been planted in good order, not as if they were wild growing. They were thick and green; the ground underneath was thick grass, framed all around in desert rocks, and it was well maintained, cut and free of weeds of any kind.

As she stood there wondering what the hell was going on, an irrigation system came on, watering the lawn and trees. She watched as the sprinklers moved back and forth; the swishing of the water was the only sound breaking the stillness of the night. In the middle of a desert there was an irrigation system keeping a grove of trees and grass green! Sandy thought the heat had finally gotten to her, and she was seeing a mirage. She stepped closer to the trees and grass and put her hand out. It was real water. She cupped her hands and filled them with the cool water to splash onto her face. Still, she had a hard time believing what she was seeing and feeling.

Sandy looked at her watch; for ten minutes the grove was watered, and then the irrigation shut off. Almost immediately, a flood light hanging from a tree above her came on. She turned and started to run back toward the rancho's adobe house. The light lit everything around her. She jumped behind a boulder twenty feet from the trees and hid in the deep shadows.

A man appeared suddenly from the far side of the building. Sandy lay in the dark, motionless, watching. The man walked slowly around circumference of the building and back to the trees, where he stopped to smoke a cigarette as he had at his last patrol. He was tall and heavily built, and he wore a full, long beard. He was wearing military fatigues, dark green in color, his pants bloused into tall, highly polished, black leather combat boots. And he had a webbed belt with a polished holster hanging from it.

When he had smoked the cigarette down to a short stub, he crushed it on the grass under his boot and disappeared around the corner of the building, as he had done the last time when Sandy had watched from the hills. She rose from behind the boulder and moved slowly, quietly, back to the grove of trees. She walked across the wet grass to the building. She touched it; it was concrete, not adobe.

"What the hell?" she whispered to herself. She

started around the corner where the man had disappeared. The building was less than two stories tall, solid concrete and without windows. It looked to be more than four hundred feet long on each side. Around the corner on the mountain side of the building, Sandy found a steel door. It was tall and appeared to be thick. There was a wheel on it, like the wheel on a bank's vault. The door was meant to be hard to penetrate. Circling the entire building, she found no other way in or out of the building.

Studying the building, Sandy had not seen the CCTV cameras hidden in the trees above her. When she turned the corner where she had started, two men were waiting for her. Both were big, both were dressed in green fatigues, and both wore sidearms. Sandy stopped, raised her arms above her head and said in an attempt to sound as nonthreatening as possible, "I'm lost. Where am I?"

TWENTY-TWO - Serendipity!

Old but clean clothes had been brought to me. Baggy and faded jeans and a plaid shirt that had seen better days. But they were clean, if too big for me. My own clothes had been taken away.

I was trying to explain to Omar and Donna, without getting Omar's fist in my face again, that I had no idea how they would get the new specifications for Firebird Guidance. "Please, understand . . . I own Hillsdale, yes . . . But I have no special access to that place. And the best I can do with a computer is turn it on and type . . . Very slowly."

"I think you can order people around, Morgan," Donna said. "I think people understand that you own Hillsdale Technologies. They will bow to your wishes."

"So, you're saying I should just walk in there and steal the plans . . . If they even exist, which we don't know . . . Then walk out with them and hand them over to you? Is that what you want me to do?"

"Oh, the new specs do exist, Morgan," she said. "You forget I'm still with Homeland Security. I'm still in the information loop. They don't know I'm working for myself now. I know the Hillsdale engineers have been changing the system specs. I know that what we had stolen is trash now."

She was right of course. There was no way the military would accept a guidance system known to the people they wanted to kill. Knowing how the guidance system operated, a fairly good computer person could override the system or even redirect the armed drone back to where it came from and kill Americans. Apparently that is just what had been happening. That was why Donna Evans had convinced the Government to leave Hillsdale open, to leave the contracts with Hillsdale. If the contracts had been moved to another company and Hillsdale had been shut down, Donna . . . And whoever was paying her . . . Would have to start from scratch in order to get their hands on the new guidance system. With me, they had a way in immediately.

****

Sandy was brought into a room in the windowless, concrete building that sat hidden in the middle of the pine tree grove. The two men pushed her into a room and slammed the heavy oak door closed, leaving her alone. The room must have been for meetings for whoever lived or worked there, Sandy assumed. A long table stood in the center of the room, surrounded by six expensive looking high back leather chairs. The room was lit by recessed fluorescent lights in the ceiling, six of them. There was no telephone, but a side table held pads of paper and a box of yellow pencils.

She sat on one of the chairs, spun it around over and over again, and nervously waited for something to happen. There were no windows in the room; the concrete walls were painted a soothing shade of very pale blue. It was cool inside; air conditioned air blew down from vents at the tops of two walls.

Sandy sat forward when the door opened suddenly. A man with Arab features and a young, very attractive black woman walked into the room; a green fatigued guard followed them and closed the door behind them. The guard had a holstered pistol on his hip and carried a Kalashnikov AK-47. Sandy wondered if they considered her really dangerous.

"Who are you?" the woman asked.

"Mary Smith," Sandy answered.

"So, if I search you and find some I.D. with a different name . . . What do you think will happen?"

Sandy leaned back and thought that she was probably in a lot of trouble. It was no time to play games with them. Maybe they would know the name. So she said, "My name is Mrs. Morgan Crew . . . Sandy Crew."

The woman looked at the Arab man, both not able to hide their surprise.

"You are Morgan Crew's wife?" the woman asked.

"Yes. Do you know the name?"

"Oh, yes," the woman said, smiling, almost laughing, and showing off big, very white teeth. "We are *very* familiar with the name."

She and her friend turned their backs on Sandy and whispered. The woman laughed and slapped the Arab man on his back. He laughed, and they whispered some more.

He went to the guard at the door and whispered close to the guard's ear, and the guard left the room. When the door was closed the Arab man leaned against the wall, he crossed his arms in front of him, and a wise-ass smirk fell across his face. He knew something, and Sandy didn't know what he knew.

The young girl looked back at Sandy. She had this wondering look on her face, as if she had just discovered stars in the heavens.

"Why the hell are you here?" she asked.

Sandy knew something was wrong. They were playing her; they were happy about something. She had come looking for someone called Omar, and here was an Arab looking man. Omar? She didn't know what she had walked into, but she knew she was in it now, up to her neck.

'No sense lying,' she thought. If this was Omar, maybe Morgan was close, she thought again. She said, "OK, I'm looking for my husband. He's been missing for weeks. That's all. Whatever you've got going here . . . Some kind of drug operation is my guess . . . Is none of my business. Just let me go, and I'll keep looking for my husband."

They both laughed at the joke Sandy didn't understand.

****

I was in the room that had been my prison for . . . How long had it been? I had no idea. It could have been a few days or months. Time meant nothing. Donna was with me that day and still trying to convince me to do what she wanted me to do. The squeaky door opened slowly, and one of the green fatigue uniformed men walked into the room. Donna and he walked to a far corner, and he whispered in her ear. She whispered to him, and he left the room, closing the door behind him.

"Dare I ask what's happening?" I asked.

"Serendipity, Morgan . . . Just plain old serendipity," Donna said, obviously very happy. There was a genuine smile crossing her thin lips for a change. She was so excited that she came close to actually dancing a jig as she stiffly, uncomfortably, turned in a circle, an almost forced chuckle emanating from her. She stopped suddenly, turned back to me, and said, "But let's get back on the subject. You're going to see once again a young lady very soon. She has been trained to do the kind of work necessary to get what we want. We want you to take her into Hillsdale . . . Preferably when no one else is there . . . At night or perhaps on a weekend . . . And help her find what we want."

"I'm gonna' make a broad assumption here," I said, taking the risk of asking. I had to know but I also didn't want to anger this woman who could order pain to be inflected upon me. "This young girl . . . She's the same one who broke into Hillsdale in the first place. She's the one who killed the security guard, right?"

"That's very perceptive of you, Morgan. Yes, the girl is very, very talented. She not only steals very quietly, she also kills very quietly. It is unfortunate that the guard had to see her that night. If he hadn't, you could be home in San Marcos right now, drinking your bourbon and playing with your child. No one would have known she had been there, and we would have what we want."

"And now you want me to walk into Hillsdale with her on my arm and steal what you want?"

"Who else can do that, Morgan?" Donna asked. "I know the security at Hillsdale has been changed. You ordered new security, and they spent close to three million dollars on a new electronic security system. I get regular updates, you see. From the FBI and Homeland Security. They have no idea what I'm doing, as I said. The new system is not completed yet, but enough of it is there to make a surreptitious entry more difficult . . . Not impossible . . . But more difficult certainly. And more risky than we are willing to undertake."

"Bill Trangent made sure your girl could get in?" I suggested. I had to know the truth.

"Yes, but he's no longer with us. Jeremy Hillsdale is being watched very closely by the F.B.I. That leaves only you," she said as she took a cigarette from a pack and lit it. The small windowless room was filling with acrid smoke that had no way out.

"That's very true," I said. I pushed a little harder to get at the truth. "I assume it was this young girl who I met who killed the family?"

"No, no, Morgan. You know, of course, so there is no sense in trying to hide the truth. Omar had an easy in when approaching the Trangent family. Their slightly off balance daughter, as you know, had been using Omar for sex for a long time. Once inside the Trangent house, he made sure that any investigation would reach a brick wall with them."

OK, so I had more information. But what could I do with it? I was too weak to fight off a bunch of really big and mean looking guys with guns. I had to get out of there somehow and tell the FBI what I knew. This group holding me was dangerous, and they had to be stopped. But I had to do it smart. If I went along too easily these people would be suspicious.

"Look," I said. "The minute I set foot anywhere near Hillsdale the Feds are going to start asking questions. I've been missing for . . . How long? It's stupid. They'll never let me near the campus. You must know that they'll arrest me immediately. What you want will never work. So, I guess I'm never going to leave Cuba, right?"

"Cuba?" Donna said and laughed. "Is that what Jesse told you? You're not in Cuba, Morgan . . . You're in Mexico.

Those damn people in Cuba would throw my old ass in prison forever if I ever set foot there. Those damn Fidel types are completely paranoid. I was there once, doing a job, before I moved to Homeland, and I just barely made it out without getting killed. I can't believe Jesse told you that. What an ass he was."

I wanted to say that in the spy game all the paranoids are out to get the other side's paranoids. But why piss her off. Instead I said, "Mexico? I'm . . . We're in Mexico? Where?"

"Of course you're in Mexico . . . Never mind where for the time being. Now do you do what we want or not?"

I had to think of something. There was a chance, if they let me go back to The States in order to help them do whatever they wanted me to do, that maybe I could somehow get away. But I was sure I would be telling my story from behind the bars of some Federal prison somewhere. I had been missing for too long a time. The Feds might not believe me. I didn't like the idea of spending even more time locked up.

Then an idea occurred to me. It might look like I was trying to help and not be too anxious to get away. I suggested, "Look, it's stupid for me to try to walk into Hillsdale with somebody. I wouldn't make it past three miles down the road to the campus. The Feds have to be out looking for me. But Jeremy Hillsdale . . . He could take someone in, and no one would question him. Even if the F.B.I were watching him, he is still the CEO there, and they wouldn't question him going to his office."

"So you're saying he's important, and you're not? If you're not important, then I might as well kill you here and now."

"You will need me if you want Jeremy to work for

you."

"He's not here, and you are," Donna said.

"Let me go to him. I can get to him and avoid the FBI. He'll do what I tell him to do."

"Actually," Donna said, thinking about what I had said as she paced in a tight circle around the small room. She faced a wall as she crushed the stub of her cigarette out against the concrete. "That's really not a bad idea. He's frightened of you. He will do what you tell him to do. It might be easier for him to get inside. I think we may do just that."

Something was wrong; something was obviously wrong. She was just going to let me go and expect me to talk Jeremy into helping them steal from his company? I watched Donna pace back and forth in front of me; for once an honest smile was on her face. I stopped her when I asked, "OK, what do you know that I don't know?"

"Serendipity," she repeated. "I'll be right back."

I was alone for only a minute or two when Donna returned. With her were Omar, the two khaki clad guards . . . And Sandy. The two guards roughly pushed her ahead of them into the room. She stumbled at first, regained her feet and turned to glare at them. They reached out and took her by the arms. Then she turned to see me.

When Sandy saw me, sitting on the edge of the bed, she shook off the two guards holding her and ran to me. I slid off the bed and we held onto each other. We kissed, long and hard. Holding her tightly to me was the first pleasure I had felt in the long time I had been a prisoner. I didn't want to let her go.

She pulled away from me and looked me up and down, "Christ! You look awful! What have they done to you?"

"We've been playing fun and games," I said. "Not to worry. I think that may be all over."

Tears filled Sandy's eyes as she touched my bruised and cut face. "Well . . . At least you've lost some of that weight I wanted you to drop. Have they been starving you?"

"Close, but not quite. But, what the hell are you doing here? Did they go get you? Where's Caroline?"

"Caroline's fine. She's with Betsy. I guess I just stumbled onto this place trying to find you. What the hell's going on here?"

Donna stepped forward and said, "Enough of that. You two can have some time together later . . . If I find we can work together."

The two guards started to pull Sandy away from me, but she put her face close to mine, kissed me on the side of my face, and whispered in my ear for only me to hear, "I'm not alone."

They sat Sandy in the lone chair that had been brought to the room for me, which was across the room, far from me. Donna and Omar left the room, leaving the two guards to stand between Sandy and me, one facing her and one facing me.

I waited a moment and then said, "Don't say anything . . ."

The guard facing me interrupted me, "Shut up."

I finished my thought, "Let's see where this is going."

"I said, shut up!" the guard said again, this time with more threat in his voice. He wasn't Mexican despite his full beard. His voice was deep and hard, but it was American with a Southern twang to it. His face had been tanned dark by the Mexican sun, but there was no doubt where he had come from. His bearing was military. My guess was he had been trained in some Special Forces group and was now selling his very specialized services to the highest bidder.

And so we waited, in silence, gazing at each other from across the room, both of us wishing we could be close, holding each other, feeling our kisses. That would come, I assured myself. Now that I knew I wasn't in some far away land . . . Cuba, as Jesse had told me . . . I had hope. Getting out of the room in Cuba would have been useless. But in Mexico, well, we might just make it home again. She had found this place, so she would know the way to the border and a semblance of safety.

Plus, she had said she was not alone. What the hell that meant I didn't know, but if there were others coming for us, I wouldn't be surprised. Sandy, I know, always knows what she is doing.

Our eyes were locked on each other. Sandy was obviously upset at what weeks locked up there had done to me. She was wiping a few tears away, and she tried to smile. She knew that being together, we had a better chance of getting free than we would have being separated. Patience was the thing; we shared that unspoken reality.

The two guards were big, brutish looking soldiers, but we had seen only the two. Omar was big but not too big. And there were Donna and Alexandra. If we could somehow overcome the two guards, the others might be only small problems. But in the uncounted weeks or more I had been held there I had lost not only weight but a lot of strength, too. It would not be easy. I had come to the conclusion that I had to use intelligence to overcome their strength; I had to con them.

We waited until the squeaky door opened again. I said, "Man, I wish you folks could put some WD-40 on those damn hinges."

Omar and Donna walked into the room. This time they were followed by the very attractive young black lady whom Jesse had introduced me to. They stood in the center of the room as the two guards moved away to stand next to each other against a wall.

"This is Tamara Jackson," Donna said. "Morgan, we are going to get you back into some condition that won't be a surprise to anyone back home. We want you to look healthy. You can tell people that you and your wife were on a vacation, getting away from all this for a while. During the time you will be brought back to some health, you are going to work with Tamara for a week or two. You two are going to get to know each other and build a background on Tamara that will stand up to short term scrutiny. We don't want any mistakes as you return to New York with her. You will then convince Jeremy Hillsdale to take Tamara into Hillsdale Technologies where she will do what she needs to do. I hope that is all clear to you?"

"And what about my wife?"

"You and she will be together during the time it takes to get you back into some condition. She will stay locked in this room with you. She will help you and Tamara. But she will remain here when you return to New York. Sort of a security deposit," she laughed a little uncomfortably-restrained laugh without cracking a smile of even the smallest kind. I made a promise to myself that when this was all over, I was going to have her face examined to find out why the hell she had such a problem smiling . . . If she was still alive when all this was over, that is.

Over the next two weeks Sandy and I ate fairly well, mainly rice, beans and some tough, chewy beef in hot Mexican spices. We had eggs and some good chorizo sausage for breakfast. The coffee was bitter and weak, but it was hot. Corn tortillas accompanied each meal, and I even got seconds on anything I wanted. It felt good to eat real food for a change, and I could feel some strength return to me.

Sandy and I were never apart, sleeping together, holding each other, in the small hospital bed. We were aware that the camera on the wall was watching, so holding each other tightly as we slept was all we could do.

I wanted to ask what she meant when she had whispered that she was not alone, but the risk was too great. I knew the camera was watching, and I guessed there were microphones to pick up what we talked about. Overt talk, inconsequential talk, would be seen as normal; whispers would be seen as conspiracy and secrets. I would wait and trust in Sandy who had never let me down yet.

We were taken to a bathroom as we needed one, the guards standing outside. The bucket I had used had disappeared, thank God, and the small room smelled better for it. And we used the shower every day. The guards had a good time standing on the outside of the wooden door to the shower. We made a lot of noise as we showered together to keep them happy. We weren't doing anything because we didn't know if cameras were watching, but we made it sound like we were doing incredible things for their enjoyment. The guards seemed to enjoy it. As the hot water ran, we held onto each other and whispered under the noise of the shower.

"You're not alone?" I asked.

"People will be coming for us soon," she whispered.

I was given fresh clothes, jeans again and a light cotton shirt, neither of which were new, but they were clean anyway, and they fit me better, too. Sandy was given a bright red robe to wear as her clothes were washed. Alexandra treated Sandy's sun blistered skin with a cooling ointment, and she slowly began to return to normal, which for Sandy is beautiful. Amongst all our captors, Alexandra seemed to be the only one who felt any compassion for us. If it weren't for her relationship with Donna, I believe she would have helped us to escape, even if it meant losing the money Donna wanted.

We met with Donna, Omar, and Tamara on a regular basis, at first in the conference room Sandy had been in. We sat at the table and listened as Donna repeated over and over again what we were to do, salting her lectures with threats. The two guards stood nearby. The table always had a bowl of fresh fruits, bananas mainly, but the fruit was welcomed by Sandy and me.

Six meals later or two days by my clock of food, we were taken outside to sit in the shade of the grove of trees, at a wooden picnic table that rested on the thick green lawn. It was the first I had seen the sky and outdoors in too many weeks. My eyes hurt at the bright light, even in the shade of the tall evergreen trees. Donna told one of the guards to get me a pair of sunglasses, which he did at a quick run.

Tamara turned out to be a bright young woman, pretty and well mannered. Her voice had no accent at all, just pure, educated English without a trace of regional dialect. Donna led the conversations among the four of us, always with the aim of creating a story that would be believed by everyone. Tamara's background had to be believed, so she had to be able to speak that background. Not knowing details would be pulling the veil off. That could not happen.

The young lady was very bright and quick to learn. Three days into our talks it was decided she would have a computer background of some sort. Tamara was good at computers and picked up extensive knowledge as fast as it could be taught. Omar brought in a man, obviously Arab, who spent two hours a day for three days with Tamara, teaching her basic programming and engineering, enough to make her sound real. I was to have her hired by one of my companies as a computer engineer, under a false name, of course. Jeremy and I were to bring her into Hillsdale to assist with the security upgrades. She would work late hours on a regular basis, and on one of those evenings she would get what Donna needed. That was what Donna decided and told us without giving us a chance to object.

In the days we spent preparing I wasn't going to regain the weight I had lost, but I was stronger and clean shaven, and Alexandra even gave me a haircut. But it was time to go.

We were in the conference room, Donna and Alexandra and Omar and Tamara, with Sandy sitting at my side. "I want it to be understood," I said. "There's nothing I can do to stop you from keeping my wife here. But understand this, if Sandy is harmed in any way . . . I will bring the wrath of all the gods . . . And Satan himself from the very deepest dungeons of Hell . . . Down upon you. I will hire armies and murderers if I have to. I will kill you all . . . I will kill your families and all your friends. Nothing will exist to remember you by. And that is not a threat . . . I do not make threats . . . Only promises. Do I make myself clear?"

Omar laughed at that and said, "Allahu Akbar."

I knew the meaning of the phrase. "Try me," I said. "And we'll see if your god will protect you from me."

TWENTY-THREE – The Grieving Time

The clothes I had arrived there wearing, tan cotton slacks and a blue polo shirt, had been cleaned and pressed. I changed quickly and found them a size too big thanks to my weight loss. I said a long goodbye to Sandy; we held onto each other until Donna told us I had to go. One last embrace and I whispered in Sandy's ear, "I hope you really aren't alone." She smiled a sly smile and nodded.

Sandy and Donna stood in the shade of the grove of trees as Omar drove Tamara and me away in a new and clean Humvee that could handle the rough desert roads. I was surprised at the new car arriving at such a desolate spot. It, and the teacher who arrived to instruct Tamara on computer science, did answer one question for me. Omar and Donna were not alone in their project.

I was told to sit in the rear seat while Omar and Tamara sat up front. Sandy waived; I looked out the rear window, hoping that would not be my last look at her. Even after days in the desert, with sun blistered skin, she was still beautiful. Just glancing at her as we drove away caused me to want to feel her in my arms.

We bounced along for a couple of hours, sometimes on wagon wheel rutted dirt paths that were filled with rocks and pot holes, sometimes on hard packed desert. It felt good to be outdoors, and I sat on the side of the car where the sun could wash over me. The car's air conditioner kept it fairly cool inside, but I wanted the warmth of the sun on me. I knew the desert sun was baking everything outside the car.

I had been given my wallet with all my credit cards and my money clip with all my cash, but my Rolex seemed to have disappeared. Somebody wanted that more than I did. So time was difficult to measure as we drove on. I glanced out the side window and saw the sun in the Eastern sky not yet directly above us, which meant it wasn't noon yet.

After what had to be a couple of hours with Omar trying to avoid most of the bigger rocks, we stopped in the middle of nowhere. There was nothing anywhere that I could see but sand, rocks, bush, and cactus. The brown, arid mountains near where I had been held were in the far distance, behind us.

Omar climbed out of the big car to relieve himself against a tall, spiny cactus, apparently not caring if Tamara was watching or not. I took the opportunity to get out, also. There was nowhere to run to, so they ignored me as I walked in circles around the car. I stretched my stiff and aching muscles and smiled up at the deep blue sky I hadn't seen in too long a time. Walking on something other than gray concrete in that little room back there felt really good. It was burning hot that day; the sun was huge in the sky above. I was very pale from my time in confinement. The sun was burning on my white skin, but I didn't mind. My semblance of freedom felt good, even in the oven of the desert.

I was standing still after walking slowly for a few minutes, facing the sun, my head up, with my eyes closed; the heat felt good and loosened up my sore muscles. I heard Omar's feet stepping lightly across the sand as he walked to me. When he spoke I didn't open my eyes.

"Now is a good time," he started. His English was very good, but there remained a trace of Arabic behind the words he spoke. "You will think you are safe and on your own when you return to Hillsdale with Tamara. You will not be. Tamara has been trained to kill quickly. And if you do not do what I want, your wife will die, also. It is as simple as that. You have no choice if you wish her and you to live."

There was no sense arguing with the man out there in the Mexican desert. I simply said, without opening my eyes, "I fully understood back there what you want. There's no need for more threats. I'm going to do what you want." But I had other plans. I opened my eyes and turned to look at Omar. "You should not forget what I said about killing you if you hurt my wife." Omar started to laugh at that, but the lethal look in my eyes made him stop. I think he knew I was deadly serious.

As we drove on into the afternoon heat I slouched back on the seat and slept a restless sleep. I awoke when Omar pulled the Humvee to a slow stop. Rubbing the sleep from my eyes I looked out the side window. We were at what looked like a dirt runway with nothing around it but sand and scrub. A small, single engine plane was there; a not-too-nice-looking fat and dirty Mexican fella was leaning against it, smoking a black and twisted cigar. He was dressed in dirty and faded old blue jeans and a bright red plaid shirt not any cleaner than his jeans. His fat stomach hung over his worn brown leather belt. He wore a pistol tucked into the belt, and a big knife in a sheath hung at his left waist.

Omar and Tamara got out of the car and opened the rear door. "Get out," Omar commanded.

I followed them to the airplane and waited as they spoke to the man who, I assumed, was the pilot. Money was exchanged and counted. The rough looking man climbed onboard, into the pilot's seat. Omar motioned for me to climb in behind the pilot, and Tamara climbed in after me.

As the pilot started the engine, Omar, standing outside with the door open, told me, "This plane will take you across the border. It will be a short ride. There will be a car waiting for you. Tamara will drive. You will go to Houston and buy tickets for you and her on the first available flight. Use your credit cards. You will fly to New York City. There, you will make arrangements for Tamara to get what I want. Do you understand?"

I looked at Omar, smiled and said, "Perfectly."

The plane's engine sputtered roughly to life, spitting out smoke and the rough odor of burnt oil and gasoline fumes. Omar slammed the door closed and stepped backward, away from the airplane. The pilot pointed the small plane to the east and started it down the dirt runway. I held on and closed my eyes because I was sure the damn thing would never take off and would crash and burn with me locked inside. But we swayed back and forth as the little plane rose into the sky, slowly climbing towards the few cotton clouds that drifted across the deep, blue sky.

As we approached what I assumed was the border, we flew close to the ground, very close. If there had been trees there, we would be at tree top level or maybe even half way up a tall tree. The pilot seemed to know what he was doing. I guessed he had made this flight many times before; his passengers in the past were probably drugs.

The engine noise was hard to speak over, but I tried. I turned to Tamara and said loudly, leaning close to her, "Drugs, right? This guy flies drugs into the U.S.?"

She was looking out the window; she didn't turn her head when she said, "Shut up."

"I was just asking," I said. "Just curious, you know?"

"Shut up," she repeated.

I checked the position of the sun to try to make sure we were actually flying north. It had to be noon or close to it because the sun was almost directly overhead. Without a wristwatch I couldn't keep track of time accurately, but it seemed we flew for over an hour before landing at a desolate little place with some cracked concrete that probably passed for a landing strip. The surroundings were pretty much desert that mirrored the desert we had left from.

The little airplane came to a bouncing stop and turned ninety degrees. The engine was shut off, and the pilot climbed out. I waited until Tamara said, "Get the hell out."

Standing at the side of the plane, I looked around. Scrub brush, some cactus, rocks and sand were all I saw. The pilot lit another black, twisted cigar; Tamara stood in the shade of the wing, her eyes down. It was hot standing in the sun; I started for the other side of the plane to take advantage of the shade under the other wing. Tamara said, without looking up, "Get back here." So I didn't go.

A cloud of dust on the horizon drew everyone's attention. The three of us watched as two cars came to us across the sand. The first was a new Toyota pick-up truck, the second a bland tan Ford sedan.

I had slowly and carefully eased my way into the shade of the wing Tamara stood under as her attention was drawn to the two cars, and waited. When the two cars stopped near the plane she said, without looking at me, "Stay here."

She and the pilot walked to the two cars and spoke with the drivers. I couldn't hear what was being said. The pilot and the driver of the pick-up truck walked to the airplane, opened a door to a storage compartment, and began carrying out plastic wrapped, brick size packets of what clearly had to be drugs, heroin or maybe cocaine. I stood aside and watched. My thought was to report this to . . . Whomever . . . But what was there to report? I had no idea where we were, who the pilot was, who owned the drugs . . . If in fact the brick like packages were drugs . . . And who was picking them up.

My only clue was the numbers that were on the side of every airplane. I looked but found none on that plane. That shouldn't have surprised me. Why would drug smugglers have a registered airplane?

When the pickup truck had been fully loaded, the driver and the driver of the Ford sedan drove away together, leaving the Ford behind. The pilot returned to his airplane, started the engine, and took off, leaving Tamara and me alone with the car and a cloud of dust and smoke left by the airplane.

She walked around the car to the driver's side and said without turning to look at me, "Get in."

I went to the rear door, but she stopped me by saying, "Not there. Get in front. I don't want you behind me."

She drove northwest, slowly, across an old, rutted, paved road to Laredo, Texas where we picked up Highway 59. The signs along the highway told me where we were. At least I knew we were back in the good ol' U.S.A. We made a stop at a gas station. She pulled next to a pump and told me, "Fill it up. Don't use your credit cards. I will follow you into the station so you can pay cash. Do something stupid, and you and a lot of other people will die."

I didn't argue; I knew what I was going to do, and the time when I would do it had not arrived yet. The gas tank was filled; I bought a couple of wrapped beef and cheese sandwiches, a couple bags of chips, a half dozen candy bars, and four big bottles of water. It felt good to do something on my own, without asking permission and without having to wait for a bowl of watery soup.

We continued northeast on Highway 59 in silence. I ate some of the food; Tamara drank some water and ate nothing. I got really bored just watching Texas go by.

I had no doubt that once Omar, Donna and Tamara had what they wanted, they would have no use for Sandy and me. We were dead when they had what they wanted. Tamara wasn't going to kill me until she had what she wanted, and she couldn't allow me to walk into Hillsdale Technologies beaten and bloody. So I took a risk.

"Look," I said. "It's going to be a long drive and a long plane flight. Why can't we talk like ordinary human beings?"

She had both hands so tightly wound around the steering wheel that her knuckles were pale under her dark skin. I looked at the speedometer. She was carefully keeping the speed just under the posted limited. She turned to look at me. The look was piercing and lasted a long time. She was thinking; I knew that. She was weighing the options and deciding if she should speak with me . . . Or maybe just kill me there and then, and get the new specs any way she could.

She relented and said, "What do you want to talk about?" Her eyes returned to the road.

"Nothing special," I said. I hoped the deep breath I took wasn't audible. If I could talk with her, I could gradually learn what I needed to know, and eventually I could gain some control. "I just thought we could talk like two ordinary human beings."

"So talk."

"OK," I started. "You know who I am . . . But I know nothing about you. Tell me." I know that people's favorite subject is always themselves. I've never met anyone who didn't like to talk about themselves and all they thought they knew. I wanted her to start talking about herself. When people do that, slowly they feel comfortable enough to say things they wouldn't ordinarily say. They might feel comfortable enough to reveal things held in confidence.

"So you want to know why I'm doing what I do. Is that what you want to know?"

"No, not really," I said. Take it slow . . . Don't press . . . slow and easy. "Where are you from?" I asked.

"Originally . . . From the mid-west . . . Chicago."

"Believe it or not, I really like Chicago. Great steak houses there."

"Yeah," she said in a sneering voice. "Not where I grew up."

"Oh, really? I've heard about the south side. Is that where you grew up? I'm sorry you had to grow up there."

"You ain't . . . I mean you've never been to that part of town, have you? All you ever did was *hear* about it, right?"

"No, I guess I haven't," I said. I did not miss the fall back to what I assumed was the real Tamara's method of speech. I learned with that, that she used to be a street girl from a tough neighborhood. But she had been educated, I guessed in more than proper English. I had no intention of finding out how well she had been educated in fast killing.

"Typical. People like you keep people like me in cages . . . Keep us far enough away so you can read about it in the newspapers, and see the news reports on your ninety inch televisions hanging on the wall of your thirty thousand square foot homes. But you would never think of living in the places we live in."

"I don't mean this as a defense," I said. I had to get her talking, keep the conversation moving to that area where she felt some empathy with me. It would be hard, but I had to try. "My wife and child and I live in a nice place but not a mansion.   Sure I was born in what people would call a mansion. We had servants, cooks, the whole ten yards. But I knew at an early age it wasn't for me. I got out of it as soon as I could."

"Yeah, I know all about you," she said, nodding and smiling. "I read your file. You got out by going to Yale University. Hardly an escape from white privilege."

"All that's true, Tamara . . . May I call you Tamara? Anyway, I admit I went to Yale, but I played more than I studied. I did military service after that, and now I try to live a simple life. Fishing and golf take up a lot of my time. My wife and daughter always come first."

"How about the San Marcos Country Club? You play a good round of golf."

"All that's true," I said. "I assume you know about the charities my family funds?"

"Oh, of course. You white folks hand out crumbs of bread and expect thanks for it. I read the file about all the money you folks have. And I'm pretty good at math, too. You give away just enough to make a sizeable deduction on your income tax every year."

We were sinking into an argument which would do me no good. I had to change the subject. I paused for a moment and then said, "Your folks . . . Do you see them often? My parents are both dead. I miss them."

"Well, good for you," she said. "I don't know who my father was . . . My mother is a crack cocaine, coke, and heroin addict. She's a five dollar street hooker."

"I'm sorry . . . But you're here and not there. It must have been difficult to get out of that environment." I had to get her back to talking about herself. Only doing that would loosen her up.

"I was lucky," she said simply. Out of the corner of my eye I could see the expression on her face, an almost sad look that hinted at a possibility that she wasn't happy in her present life.

"I guess so," I said. Keep her going, but slowly, easily. "Can you tell me how you got away?"

She smiled again; good thoughts were running through her head. "Jesse saved me. He took me away. I don't know where I'd be today if it weren't for Jesse."

"I'm sorry," I said. "You must feel terrible about him."

"Why?" she demanded. She turned away from the highway in front of her to look at me.

"I mean . . . You must miss him . . . His death must be hard on you."

Her foot slammed on the car's brakes as she turned the wheel to the right in front of a line of cars in the right hand lane. The car came to a screeching halt on the highway's shoulder. She threw the gear shift into park before the car stopped completely. She shifted in the seat, turning to me.

"What the hell you mean? Jesse's dead?"

"I'm sorry . . . I thought you knew . . . Alexandra killed him . . . She shot him." That might be a key, something to unlock the chains that held her to what Omar and Donna demanded.

"You're lying, you sick son of a bitch. You're lying,"

she whispered.

"I'm not lying, Tamara. I was there. I saw it . . . In that room where I was locked up. I'm sorry. I didn't know you and Jesse . . ."

"Shut up!" she screamed as she pounded her fists on the steering wheel. "Just shut up!"

Her eyes overflowed with tears that flooded down her cheeks. Her eyes were closed, her mouth open as she sobbed. I unbuckled my seat belt and slowly opened my arms to her. I moved closer, and she leaned into my shoulder as she cried. I put my arms around her shoulders and held her gently. "I'm so sorry," I whispered into her ear. "I'm so sorry."

I held her for a minute or two until she had cried out all she could cry. She pulled away from me, wiped her eyes with the backs of her hands, left and right, and then looked at me. She asked in a weak, quavering voice, "How do you know? Why is he dead?"

"I promise you I'm telling you the truth. I was there when he was murdered. The why is hard to explain. I have no idea what you folks are doing. But I do know a few of your friends need psychiatric help really bad."

"Tell me," she said.

"Alexandra and Donna are lovers . . ."

"What? They're damn dykes?"

"Yes . . . I guess so. At least they are way too friendly. Alexandra shot Jesse. I think she may have been jealous of his relationship with you; I'm not sure of that. But I was there . . . In that room . . . I saw her shoot and kill Jesse. She dragged him from the room by his heels."

This, I thought, might be a way in, a way to get

Tamara onto my side in all this. Love and hate are mutually side by side in human nature. One gives birth to the other. Love all too often sinks to dislike and often hate. When anger slips away, hate often disappears and may generate love. Slow, I told myself. Don't press, don't rush. Let it work out naturally.

"Alex killed Jesse?" she said bewildered at the thought. "You're lying . . . I don't believe you."

"I assume you have a cell phone? Phone him . . . Phone anyone back there. Ask for Jesse. If I'm lying . . . Kill me now."

She hesitated for a moment, and then reached into the leather shoulder bag that was in the rear seat. She pulled a cell phone from it, punched in a number that did not have an international prefix and waited. When there was no answer, she tried another number and waited. Then a third. Omar answered.

"Omar," she said. "I want to speak with Jesse."

He said nothing; Tamara waited and then repeated, "Did you hear me? I want to talk to Jesse."

Again Omar said nothing. She asked, "Is he dead? I want to know."

"Listen, Tamara," Omar began. "These things happen in this work. You have to know . . ."

She pushed the disconnect button and threw the phone into the rear seat. She stared out the front window as car after car sped by. With the engine off, it was getting very hot inside the car. I tried the auto window control, but it wouldn't work without power from the engine.

I put on a very soft and comforting voice and said, "I'm very sorry, Tamara. I'm surprised you didn't know. I wish I had known that. I wouldn't have said anything. I honestly don't want to hurt you. I just didn't know."

She surprised me when she said, "That's alright . . . You didn't know."

I waited and counted ten breaths before asking, "Do we go back now?"

Her voice was soft and sounded far away. She spoke as if she were in a dreamlike trance. "No, I have to finish this job . . . Then I'll go back and kill Alex."

She started the engine, put the car in drive and floored the gas pedal as she pulled into traffic. I quickly fastened my seat belt and held on. I watched the little needle on the speedometer keep going up until it passed 100, and then she slowed the car.

I waited, patiently, before saying, "This work you do . . . How did you get into it? Was it Jesse?"

"Yes," she said and wiped another tear from her eye. "He saved me . . . He took me away from who I was . . . He saved me."

"You loved him, right?"

"I still do," she said. "I always will."

I waited again. Slow and deliberate, I told myself. Direct our conversation to what I needed to know. I asked, "Did Jesse teach you all . . . All the things you know?"

"No, not really," she answered. Her voice told me she was loosening up towards me. "I mean, he taught me how to be what I am now. He taught me how to speak and how to dress. All that. Jesse is a real gentleman. I mean . . . He was a real gentlemen, damn it."

"Who taught you the rest?" I asked. "I mean, who taught you how to break into Hillsdale?"

"I went to school . . . In Cuba . . . Two years . . . I guess it feels good to finally talk about it to someone . . . Even you. There's been a lot built up inside me that I need to let out. They taught me all the tools needed to break into buildings without leaving any clue that I was there. They taught me a lot of things."

That was the first sign of trust. She was beginning to break down the barrier between us. I had to grip my thigh tightly, so tight it hurt, to keep from pressing the issue too fast.

"That's interesting," I said. I had to be careful here. I could not sink into a useless debate on the flaws of Cuba and Communism. "Look, I know all about the crappy security that was at Hillsdale. It had to be fairly easy to get in, right?"

"Easy? It was too easy, but there's always a risk."

Careful now, go easy. I took a deep breath and asked, "That security guard . . . I forgot his name . . ." I hadn't forgotten his name; Danny O'Keefe. I could not risk showing Tamara how important he was. He was dead because of these people. To me, he was more valuable than the bunch of them. I went on, "I guess that was something that couldn't be planned for."

Tamara was thinking deeply as she drove. I'm not sure she even realized she and I were talking. My guess is she was thinking of her lover, Jesse. She said, "No, you plan for everything. No contingency can be overlooked."

I waited again, digging my finger nails into my palm to keep from saying something wrong. I counted my breaths . . . . Ten slow breaths . . . And then I said, "I'm curious . . . And you don't have to tell me if you don't want to . . . How the hell do you open those doors with the electronic keypad locks?"

She smiled as she wiped her eyes dry again. "There's a reader," she said. "It reads codes inside the lock."

"Amazing," I said, trying to sound authentically amazed. "I'm not much on technology. My God, there must be some stuff out there right out of a James Bond movie."

She smiled again and nodded.

"Do you think I can see that thing?" I asked.

"I don't have it with me," she answered.

That made sense; after all, I was expected to get her into Hillsdale. She wouldn't need any of the burglar tools of her trade. I leaned back in the seat, counting breaths again. Then I asked, "Are you feeling OK? Do you want me to drive for a while?"

She smirked and said, "No . . . But thank you for caring."

I was getting there. If I didn't make any mistakes she would be easier on me and easier to be controlled by me.

We passed the first road sign for Houston. I would be quiet for a while, until we reached the airport. Let her think about Jesse's death for a while. Let my gentleness with her sink in.

We arrived at the airport where Tamara parked the car in the long term lot. She locked the doors as we got out of the car. As we walked towards the bus stop that would take us to the terminal, she dropped the car keys in a trash can. The bus brought us to the terminal. I walked at her side. At the Delta desk I asked her, "Coach or first?"

It was as if she hadn't heard me; she was staring off into nowhere, thinking of Jesse. So I bought two first class tickets on the next non-stop flight to New York, which wasn't going to leave until the following morning. Tamara wasn't paying attention, so I used my black American Express card, knowing that the record of the credit card use would be good evidence if I ever needed it.

Tamara followed me as I walked away from the counter. "We have to find a hotel," I told her. "The plane leaves in the morning."

She nodded but said nothing. We rented a car at the Hertz counter and found a nice airport hotel. I asked for two rooms; Tamara said, "One room . . . Two beds."

In the room Tamara sat on the edge of one of the beds still looking at something only she could see, in a faraway grey fog. I had to be careful; things were going well so far, and I didn't want to screw up. I went to the room's honor bar and found two bottles of Jack Daniels.

"Would a drink help?" I asked.

She slowly looked up at me, a wondering gaze in her eyes. She said, "What?"

"Would you like a drink? You look like you need one."

She thought for a moment, trying to understand what the words she only half heard meant. She nodded and then looked away from me again. There wasn't any ice, and I assumed Tamara wasn't going to let me go down the hall to get some from the machine. I opened one of the bottles and poured the whiskey into a glass. I gave some thought to it and then poured the second bottle into the same glass. It would do me more good if she drank it than if I drank it. I brought it to her; she took the glass and drank the glass dry quickly.

"Thank you," she said in a whispered voice.

I took the glass from her and sat on the bed opposite her. Tears were filling her eyes once again as she thought of Jesse. She wiped her hand across her nose. I handed her my handkerchief.

"It might help if you could talk about it, Tamara," I said. "I know you're hurting. Tell me . . . I'll listen."

She began to cry again, sniffling, and wiping her eyes with the handkerchief. I spent the evening and into the night listening to Tamara tell me her ever so short life's story. It was as if she were talking to herself, speaking out loud all the thoughts and memories she carried with her about her teen years: the gangs, the drugs, the sex, and the abortions. And then a man came into her troubled life.

Jesse Wilson, she told me, took her away from all the horrors and showed her a brand new world. She told me of how gentle he was and how he demanded nothing from her. She told me how much she longed to be in bed with him for so long a time and how he wanted to teach her first.

The night . . . That wonderfully warm night, she said with a sad smile on her lips, under the Cuban sky that was filled with stars she had never seen before . . . The night Jesse came to her as she lay on the blanket on the soft sand of the beach, naked after swimming in the ocean, and he finally made love to her. She told me how it was so different from what she had experienced in Chicago. He was gentle, soft, more giving than taking. He caressed every part of her, and they made love over and over again. It was, she said, something she never imagined could exist.

I listened, and I knew that because she was telling me all her secrets, our positions had changed. From that point on, from that night on, I would be in control.

We stayed at the motel for two days. Tamara didn't argue when I said we would not leave on the morning's flight I had booked. She had mourning to get through, and I let her mourn for those two days with soft pressure from me to do so.

During that time I was as kind with her as I could be, while knowing I was causing her to look upon me as a friend rather than a captive. That is what I had to do, to act as if I were her friend so that I could manipulate her in the direction I wanted to go. She ate little during that time and drank the booze in the honor bar just enough to keep her relaxed. But she cried often and slept a little and talked freely about Jesse. I listened, and I was comforting, so she would continue.

All the while I tried to imagine what she was feeling. I tried to imagine what I would be feeling if I had lost Sandy. That thought was an anathema; I chased it from my mind. But I would use Tamara's grief. I would bend her to what I wanted. And if I were successful, all the people who had kept me prisoner, who had tortured and starved me, would wind up either dead or in jail. My preference was that they all die, but jail was almost as good.

TWENTY-FOUR – We Need To Find Him

Sandy sat in the chair in the room I had been held captive in. No one came to her, except to bring her three meals a day. One or the other of the uniformed guards brought her meals to her. Her meals were better than I had been given; she had chicken and rice and beans and corn tortillas for lunch and dinner. Her breakfast was yellow grits and more corn tortillas. She was allowed to drink bitter coffee and bottles of cold water. She was taken to a bathroom when she needed a toilet, and she was allowed to shower once a day. But no one spoke to her, and she was alone most of each day. She didn't complain because she knew she would not be there much longer.

When sitting became boring, she paced around the small, grey, concrete room. She didn't see Donna or Alexandra or Omar during that time. The one difference she experienced while there was that in the evening, after her meal, the lights in the room were turned off.

Once each day, in mid-afternoon, both guards took her outside to walk in the shade, on the green lawn, and then in the sun. Neither of the men would talk to her. That didn't matter; soon she would leave there, she knew. That was the plan.

On the evening of the third day after I had left, the noise outside the concrete room was so loud that even the thick walls of the room could not keep the racket from her. She jumped from the bed, went to the door and tried the knob. The door was locked, but she knew what was happening. She waited.

The door was flung open and crashed against the wall. A man dressed in black combat gear stood in the doorway. He was holding an HK MP5 submachine gun.

"Mrs. Crew?" he asked.

"That's me," Sandy answered. "What took you so long?"

****

FBI Special Agent Adam Carter was waiting in one of the rooms of the concrete building. Sandy walked down the hallway, stepping over the bodies of the two guards and two other people, Mexicans in civilian clothes, one male, one female, she had not seen before. Inside the room Donna Evans sat in a hard wooden chair, her hands cuffed behind her back. Alexandra was sitting on the floor, leaning against the wall, her hands cuffed behind her back, a faraway gaze on her face.

The room had been a break room of sorts, for the people working at the concrete building in the grove of trees, at the mountain's foothills. A couch and a couple of chairs lined one wall; a big screen TV hung from the opposite wall. A soft drink machine and a candy machine sat in a corner, and a rack of books and magazines and DVD movies stood nearby. To anyone not knowing what the building was used for, that room would seem a pleasant place for anyone working there to relax.

Donna looked across the room at Sandy. There was a quizzical look on her face, almost a childish expression of having completely lost the meaning of what had happened in front of her.

"How . . . ?" she began, stammering.

Sandy sat on the edge of the couch and took off her right hiking boot. She fiddled with the thick heal until the hinge allowed it to slide sideways. She took out the small tracking device, the size of a quarter, and tossed it on the floor at Donna's feet.

"It seems you weren't trusted, Donna," Sandy said. "You were too eager to keep the investigators out of the Hillsdale theft and murder. It didn't ring true to a lot of people. I guess you thought Morgan and I would screw around and give you time to make good on the failed theft. Agent Carter and I made a deal. He gave me some leeway to find you and Morgan if I wore that tracking thing. When I stopped moving, he would move in. We agreed that three days without movement from me meant I was either dead or captured by you. I had spent some time at a convent far from here. I had to phone Agent Carter to tell him to wait, not to come then."

She turned to look at Carter and asked, "So what the hell happened to the three days? I've been here a couple of friggin' weeks! You had me worried."

"It takes time to put together an operation like this," he said, almost apologetically. "We had to get Mexico's permission . . . I had to get a team together . . . DC demanded financing . . . There's a lot of hoops to jump through . . . It isn't easy . . . But I'm here now."

"Gee thanks," Sandy said. "If you could have gotten here earlier, Morgan would still be here. Now I have to go find him."

She turned to Donna, paused, smiled a toothy smile and said, "I got you Donna."

It took an hour to clean up the bodies Carter's team had killed and take them out to the two Chinook helicopters waiting in the desert outside the grove. Carter and his men tore every room in the building apart. Sandy was feeling very good at having Donna Evans in handcuffs. But she was still worried at what was happening to me. She was looking around, watching, making stupid jokes until something occurred to her.

She walked fast to Carter, pulled his arm to stop him in his tracks, and asked, "What about Omar? Where is he?"

"Omar? You mean Omar Maalouf was here?"

"Yes, of course. You mean you didn't get him?"

All Carter said as he spun around and threw a pile of papers he had collected onto the floor was, "Shit!"

****

The two days we spent at the airport motel in Houston gave Tamara time to grieve. It also gave me time to keep the little refrigerator in the room re-stocked with whiskey, vodka, and gin. The booze probably didn't help her, but it loosened up her words even more than her grief did.

I learned even more of her training in Cuba, where the school was located, the people who did the training, what she had been taught, and most important, I learned about the future operations she had been trained for. I did not take notes; I would remember because it was important. All the various Government acronyms involved in intelligence and law enforcement would be very interested.

On the morning of the third day Tamara, for the first time, refused more from the honor bar. She was able to eat, and I saw her trying to restrain a smile at one of my stupid jokes. She was able to talk with me for the two days in the motel room, almost like two normal people would converse. It was time to leave, she told me. She said she had a job to do and would do it. Then, after the job was done, she said resolutely, she would kill Alexandra. I had no doubt she would, given the chance.

We sat up in first class on the non-stop flight to New York. She refused the free drinks but drank coffee like it was going out of style.

"I've never been up in first class before," she said to me. She was relaxing luxuriously in the wide leather seat, sitting next to the window and wondering at the spectacle of the clouds below like a child seeing all the toys under the tree on Christmas morning. "This is wonderful."

"Yes," I said and took a risk by adding, "But they don't have first class in Communist Countries."

"That's right," she said and turned to look at me. "And that's wonderful, too. I keep thinking of the hundred people sitting back there, jammed in like sardines in a can. Too bad we all can't be the same."

I rented a car at JFK after we stopped for a hamburger and a couple of beers for lunch in one of the awful airport terminal restaurants.

"I have an apartment at my lawyer's building. We can stay there," I said as we drove away from the airport.

"I can't stay long," she said. "I need to finish my mission and get back to Mexico."

"You're still going to kill Alexandra?" I asked her.

"Of course," she said as if it were a silly question that I

should know the answer to.

"What will that accomplish?"

"She'll be dead . . . She deserves to be dead."

I knew that she would never have the opportunity to kill Alex. What I had planned would stop her from doing that. But she didn't know that. So I let her go on thinking she would be able to kill Alexandra.

I parked the car at the red curb in front of Peter Jascro's building. Maureen would have it moved, and I really didn't give a damn if I got a parking ticket. Tamara followed me to the elevator and stood in the rear corner, behind me, as we went up. The doors slid open at the apartment where I had Jeremy Hillsdale holed up.

Before I stepped out of the elevator I could hear the music. Jeremy must be throwing a good party judging by the laughter and loud voices. That was not in the plan and would certainly put Jeremy at risk. I would have to talk with Peter about that.

And then it occurred to me that the police guards weren't there. Something had happened.

We stepped into the apartment, and we were both stopped at the sight of a half dozen women, all naked, dancing, drinking, singing and being X-rated as they surrounded a short, fat, old, Japanese man with thick grey hair who was also naked.

I pushed Tamara back, out of the apartment and into the elevator. I pushed the button for Peter's floor.

"What the hell was that?" she asked. "Some kind of joke?"

"I'm not sure what's going on," I told her. "Jeremy Hillsdale was supposed to be there."

Maureen, Peter's private secretary, met us as the elevator doors opened.

"OK," I said to her. "What's happened?"

"You'd better come with me. Who's the young lady?"

"She's with me," I said as we followed Maureen.

Peter was at his big desk in front of the big windows in his big office. Tamara looked at everything, the very expensive furniture, the every expensive works of art, everything, with a look of disgust. I could imagine that her education in Communism made her believe that once Capitalism was defeated, there would not be offices like that one. Too bad she was not educated in the fact that the bosses of Communism, the Inteligencia, the dictators, would have these offices, while the common folk struggled to survive on short food rations.

Peter stood, shook my hand and looked at Tamara. I introduced her. "Tamara and I have some work to do. Where the hell is Jeremy?"

"Morgan, you've been gone for nearly two months. Where have you been? You look like you've lost some weight."

"Forget that, Peter. Now, where is Jeremy?"

"He got tired of being locked up in the apartment. I couldn't keep him here."

I had known Peter since I was a very young child. I had never been angry with him . . . Until then.

"Where is he?" I asked. "Are the guards with him?"

Peter stood and walked around the desk to me. He took me by the shoulders and looked deeply into my eyes. He said, "Morgan, you've been gone too long. I don't know what you've been doing, but Sandy was here looking for you.

Where have you been?"

I shrugged away from my old friend, took two steps back, and said, "That's not important. I need to speak with Jeremy now. Where is he?"

"I don't know, Morgan . . . At home I suppose."

"Get on the phone, Peter. Call his house!" I spoke in a tone Peter had never heard from me before, that of an employer, demanding, ordering, giving instructions to an employee.

Peter hesitated for a moment and then walked back to his chair. He sat and called on the intercom for Maureen to phone Jeremy's home. We waited. Tamara and I stood while Peter sat behind his big desk and stared up at us, wondering just what the hell was going on.

A half minute later Maureen's voice came over the intercom. "Mr. Hillsdale is in his office, Peter."

I nodded and took Tamara by her arm. The elevator was slow, devastatingly slow, as we rode down to the street. Outside a cop was at the car, still parked at the red curb, writing a ticket. I ignored his warnings as she and I got into the car and sped off into traffic, leaving the officer with his ticket book in hand. Ordinarily, I would have a good laugh whenever I had the opportunity to flaunt authority, but right then I couldn't care less. I had to get to Jeremy.

I cut back and forth through the mid-day New York City traffic, missing collisions by inches.

Tamara was holding on to whatever she could inside the car, leaning back and forth, left and right, as I drove like a crazy man. Neither of us had taken the time to buckle our seat belts.

"What's wrong?" she said, her voice trembling.

"I'm not sure," I said as I twisted the wheel to the left in front of a cab and then back to the right to pass a truck. "Something's wrong. Jeremy wouldn't have left so easily. He's very smart in business, but he's a coward. He would need the guards . . . He can't take care of himself. Something happened to get him to leave."

"So you're going up to Hillsdale Technologies?"

"Yes. You're going to do what you have to do as fast as you can . . . Sandy is going to be released . . . And I'm going to talk to Jeremy."

We made it onto I-80 without getting ourselves killed. It was, I knew, an eight hour drive to Buffalo. I kept the gas pedal floored, and we made it in six. I glanced in the rearview mirror regularly. In the six hours it took, I saw a police car coming up behind us with lights flashing ten times. Ten times they turned off the lights and dropped away from us. It was working. Peter had done what I assumed he would do, phone the FBI and have them give us leeway.

It was after sunset when we arrived at the Hillsdale Technologies campus.   There were lights on in the Administration Building; the other buildings were dark. I parked near the main gate, and Tamara and I walked to it.

The guard on duty that night came out of his little guard shack and walked towards us, a look of suspicion on his face. He walked slowly; his right hand was on the pistol that hung from his belt.

"What can I do for you?" he asked. He stood back, away from the chain link gate, out of any possible reach anyone might have.

I looked around and saw that there were three times the flood lights at the campus as the last time I was there. It would look as bright as noon in the middle of the night. And the parking lot and the trees nearby were also lit up. Changes had been made; that was good. And the guard this time, as with the last two times I was there, was not a rent-a-cop. He was armed and looked like he knew what he was doing.

"We're here to see Mr. Jeremy Hillsdale." I smiled as I said that; I did not want to put on any face or posture that might be intimidating.

"IDs, please," he said.

"Please, just go and phone Mr. Hillsdale's office. I know he's there. Tell him Morgan Crew is here."

"Morgan Crew?" the guard said. "We were told about you. Show me some ID."

I took my California driver's license from my wallet as he stepped close to the gate. I handed it to him through the chain link. Rather than come too close to the gate, he reached out and grabbed it from my hand quickly.

"Wait here," he said and backed away, his hand on the pistol, not turning his back to us.

Inside his gate house he picked up the phone. I could see him talking to someone as he looked at my driver's license. It almost seemed as if he were arguing with whomever he was speaking with.

While he was on the phone I looked at the gate. The thin metal poles at the gate had been replaced with thicker, heavier poles as was the chain link itself. The chain and padlock that had held it closed were long gone. The new lock, obviously electronic, buzzed loudly, and the gate slid open to the side. Tamara followed me inside. We stopped, turned and watched the gate close and loudly lock us inside the barrier.

The guard waited at his little guard shack for us to go

to him. His hand was steady on the pistol, his suspicious glare still there.

"Mr. Hillsdale said to meet him at the front entrance."

I got my license back, and with Tamara at my side we walked to the front doors. The big double glass doors hadn't changed, and there was a keypad on the right hand side. I asked Tamara, "Can you open that? I mean you did it once before."

"As I said, there's a tool," she said. "A little computer that reads the codes and opens the lock. I told you I don't have it with me. I don't need it now, do I? I thought you were supposed to get me inside."

"That's the plan," I said as Jeremy walked from the elevator.

He slid his company ID through a slot inside, at the side of the doors, and pushed the right hand door open.

"Morgan!" he said, surprised to see me. "What are you doing here? Where the hell have you been? We were all worried about you."

"I need to talk to you. Can we come in? Maybe get some coffee?"

"Sure," he said. He held the door open, and Tamara and I walked past him. As we rode the elevator up to his fourth floor office he said, "Jeeze, Morgan. You look terrible. You've lost a lot of weight. Are you OK?"

I didn't answer him. We stepped off the elevator and went to his office. There was a Mr. Coffee there with a half full pot on it. I poured a cup, but it was stale and barely warm.

Jeremy sat at his desk and forced an uncomfortable smile. "So what did you want to talk about, Morgan?"

I pulled a chair from against the wall to his desk and sat. Tamara stood with her back to the door.

"I need to get inside your computer systems, Jeremy. I need the revised specs on Firebird Guidance. The young lady with me will download what she needs, and we'll be gone, OK?"

"That's crazy, Morgan," Jeremy said, trying to smile like it might all be just a bad joke. "You know I can't do that."

"Yes you can, Jeremy," I said. "You see, if you give me any trouble, we will wait here in your office until everyone has gone home. Then this young lady will kill you, won't you Tamara?"

She answered simply, "Of course," as if it were a foregone conclusion.

"But . . . But . . . Morgan . . ." Jeremy stuttered.

"Jeremy," I said, "You don't have a choice here. Do what I tell you to do, or you *will* die . . . Here . . . Tonight."

We took the stairs down to the third floor, where Tamara had been before. Jeremy went to the caged filing cabinets. I stopped him and asked Tamara, "I need to know that we're at the right place to get what you want. Is this where you were before?"

"Yes," she answered.

"Can you open the cage door?"

"I told you, I don't have the tools with me. You're supposed to get me inside."

I told Jeremy to punch in the code that would open the cage door and stood aside. Tamara walked in and went to the same filing cabinet she had taken the flash drive from before.

"I need you to unlock the cabinet," she said to Jeremy.

Jeremy walked into the cage, took a set of keys from his pocket and unlocked the padlock. While he was doing that, I slammed the cage door closed, locking both inside.

Tamara jumped; Jeremy started to scream like a little girl and almost fainted. Both were glaring at me as I stood smiling at them from outside the cage.

"What the hell, Morgan!" Jeremy said.

Tamara said nothing. A deep sigh left her, and she leaned against the filing cabinet. She knew what had happened; she was caught. She thought about what had gone wrong and quickly came to the conclusion that she had trusted me too much. My feigned sympathy at the loss of her lover had gotten to her. It was over.

Jeremy finally understood what had happened. He was slow at the realization. Jeremy, being the man he was, started to cry again.

"Please Morgan," he sobbed. "Please."

"Forget it, Jeremy. You see, I knew from the very beginning that you were dirty in all of this. You are a very good businessman, the best I've ever met . . . And you are a micro-manager. There's no way you would have let Bill Trangent set up that laughable security system all by himself. You approve of everything before anything is done. Christ, you even OK the damn menus at the Christmas parties. You knew all about it and why he was doing it. You and he were in on this together. Money, right? They must have paid you what you thought was a lot of money."

He tried to get his fingers through the cage to reach the keypad, but his fingers were bigger than the spaces in the steel cage, and the keypad was too far away.

"For God's sake, Morgan . . . We're family . . . For God's sake."

"God isn't going to help you, Jeremy. No one is going to help you now. I wouldn't be surprised if you wind up in some super-max prison somewhere."

I went to the nearest desk and picked up the telephone there. It took me a minute or two to figure out how to get an outside line, but I finally did. I dialed the FBI office in Manhattan and asked for Agent Adam Carter.

"He's not in," the woman on the other end of the line said.

"This is Morgan Crew . . ." I started but she interrupted me.

"Oh, yes. We've been expecting your call. There is a team waiting. Shall I have them move in?"

"Yes, that's a really super idea. But no guns, please. I've got them locked up."

"You what? Did you say they're locked up?"

"Yeah, sure, why?"

"But . . . You weren't supposed to do that," she said. "That wasn't what we planned for. This was all planned with your wife."

That's what she had meant by not being alone. Sandy had planned everything knowing I would lead Tamara into a trap. I knew she would be free by that time and on her way to me.

"Gosh, I'm sorry," I said. "Should I let them out so they can run, and you guys can chase them?" I slammed the phone down.

I pulled up a chair and sat, looking at the two of them

locked inside the cage. Tamara had slid down the file cabinet and was sitting on the floor, her knees pulled up to her chin. She was thinking, wondering, how could she have been so stupid? I had done a good job spreading it so thick that she hadn't seen the truth, that I had been leading her into a trap.

Jeremy was pacing back and forth in front of the locked cage door. Every now and then he would stop and try to squeeze his fingers through the steel wire to get at the key pad. He was mumbling to himself, crazy mumbling. His forehead was wet with sweat; his lip was bleeding as he bit into it.

He stopped; his head lowered, he turned and said to me, "Morgan, you've got it all wrong. I didn't do anything. Please . . . I didn't do anything. You've got it all wrong."

"Don't insult my intelligence, Jeremy. You're a greedy little bastard who sold out his Country for a few bucks."

He started pacing again, mumbling and swearing. A dark stain spread across his pants as he wet himself without knowing it. He was going over the edge mentally. I had seen it before. I knew what was happening to him. It was all over for him; he would never return to this world. I would take care of his family, and if I could ever find Tangent's daughter Ashley, I would take care of her, too.

Tamara was a different story. I honestly felt sorry for her. What chance had she in life? If Jesse hadn't found her, she would have lived a short, unhappy life in the slums with drugs and gangs all around her. What other choice did she have when she was taken away by Jesse? I knew she wouldn't walk away free, but I would try to help her as best as I could.

Less than an hour later the door behind me slammed open, and eight men dressed in black combat gear flooded into the room. They carried nasty looking machine guns at the ready to kill someone. I sat and watched as they went through their paces; I would have laughed except that if I did, they might just shoot me.

When they had surrounded me, I said, "Hi ya' fellas'. Glad you could make it."

An FBI Agent walked into the room; I could tell he was an FBI agent because he wore a dark suit, white shirt and muted blue tie. His wing tip shoes were highly polished, and his hair was cut short and neat. The FBI uniform of the day . . . Every day.

I had my feet up on the desk I was at; I was leaning back in the chair, my hands cupped behind my head. The Agent came up to me. "Who are you?" he demanded.

"I'm Morgan Crew. Who are you? Hey! That rhymes, doesn't it?"

He pulled his ID case from his inside suit jacket pocket and flashed it in front of me. "I'm FBI Special Agent Jason Mason."

"Jason Mason! Is that a joke or something?"

"No, it's real. I get that all the time. My folks were comedians . . . On the stage I mean. They wanted to be famous, but Burns and Allen were better in their day, and nobody wanted a husband and wife comedy team anymore."

"OK, Agent Jason Mason," I said. "Your prisoners are in the cage. I don't know the code to open the door. You can either bust it open, or maybe Jeremy there will give you the code."

****

Agent Jason Mason took Jeremy and Tamara away in handcuffs. Agent Carter and Sandy brought Donna and Alexandra from Mexico on a midnight helicopter without waiting for all that extradition nonsense. They were charged with various crimes of treason, theft of Government secrets, murder, etc. etc. etc. Hillsdale Technologies did eventually lose all of the Government contracts and a year later would file for bankruptcy. I didn't particularly care, but the family did and blamed me for the loss of millions of dollars. I didn't care about what they said, either. The family would survive; they always did.

Two days after trapping Tamara and Jeremy, I waited in Peter's office for Sandy to arrive. She had been taken down to Washington, DC to complete a statement and what the FBI called an "After Action Report." They had wanted me to do the same in their offices, but I had had enough of confinement. I went to the local New York City FBI office and spent an hour or two telling my story to a stenographer.

I was impatient as I waited; I had been told Sandy would be there that day but not when that day. Peter smiled as he watched me fiddle with things on his desk, with magazines, with anything I could find to touch nervously.

"Hey, Peter," I said as I walked to the big windows that were the entire side wall of his office. "I sure am glad you picked up on what was happening with that young woman. Did I ever say thanks? I mean for contacting the FBI. I guess if the cops had stopped me for speeding on the way up to Hillsdale there would have been a shoot-out."

"Yes, Morgan. You've told me that a couple of times already. Calm down already. She'll be here soon."

His secretary, Maureen, brought in a tray of sandwiches and a big pot of coffee. Peter called to her as she turned to leave, "Maureen, please sit with us. Have a sandwich." I think Peter felt a little more comfortable with a third person there. Maybe a witness?

The three of us ate and talked and laughed a little at stories Peter told about when I was a rambunctious child, always playing tricks on people and getting in trouble. And I waited.

It was sunset when the tall double doors of Peter's office opened, and Sandy was standing there. I ran to her and swept her up in my arms. She was sunburnt still but as beautiful as always.

Peter welcomed her with a hug and a kiss on her cheek. "It's good to see the two of you together again," he said fatherly. "Now, you two need to go home and rest up. Put all this behind you."

Sandy saw the small bar of crystal decanters. She went to it and poured vodka over ice. She took a sip with her back turned to us, holding the glass tightly in both hands.

"I'm afraid we can't do that," she said without turning to us.

I went to her, turned her to me, and asked, "What does that mean? Why can't we go home?"

"Omar wasn't there when Carter raided that place."

"Omar? But I thought . . . He didn't go back there when he dropped me off?"

"He's out there somewhere, Morgan."

"But there's nothing to get at Hillsdale," I argued. "The Feds aren't exactly stupid. They're in the process of shutting everything down. Firebird Guidance isn't there anymore. He'll just go home. He failed, and there's nothing more he can do."

"I'm afraid, Morgan. I'm afraid he won't just go home.

A man like that . . . The hatred he has in his soul . . . I'm afraid he'll come after us for revenge . . . Caroline . . . We have to think of her."

"So what are you proposing?" I asked. I went to the bar and poured a stiff bourbon over ice for myself. Peter didn't keep any club soda in his office, so I drank the bourbon straight. I knew, of course, what Sandy was thinking. More trouble. And I knew I wouldn't be saying 'no.' She was right. We had to protect ourselves, and we had to protect our daughter. But how?

I said, "I've got to think of a safe place. Some place to hide until the Feds find him."

"And how long will that take, Morgan?" she asked. "You and I know that people like Omar live in shadows, in greys, in half lights, in the back of alleys. It might take years for the FBI to find him. Do we just hide in a cave until then? We need to find him ourselves Morgan . . . And stop him."

TWENTY-FIVE – You Want To Kill Her?

Our house in the San Marcos hills above the harbor seemed different somehow. Everything was still as we had left it almost two months ago, yet there was something out of the ordinary. It was stale, of course, after having been shut up for so long. It was dusty, something easily remedied in short order. But it seemed different to us.

Caroline and Betsy weren't there. We had spent several days with them, in a nice hotel down in San Diego. We played on the beach and ate good Mexican food. Sandy and I tried to explain why we had to go away again. Caroline cried, and said she wanted to go with us, but in the end she waved goodbye, as Sandy and I drove away.

Betsy took our daughter to safety once again in San Francisco where they would stay with Betsy's friends, a motorcycle gang well suited to hide them and protect them. I gave her $5000 in cash as payment for their services. The house was quiet without them; perhaps that was what was different.

Sandy and I settled into as normal a life as we could. We stocked up on food and wine; we watched some TV; we waited for Omar. When he came to us, we would use the guns we had in every room of the house to kill him. The FBI refused to give us guns. Bob Sommers, our friend and the San Marcos Police Department's only detective, supplied us with five guns. And he had a patrol car stationed in the street outside our house 24 / 7.

Once a week, on Friday afternoon, we received a telephone call from FBI Agent Carter.   Every U.S. Intelligence agency and every law enforcement agency was looking for Omar. A nationwide 'All Points Bulletin' had been put out on him. In the three weeks we had been home, there was nothing on him.

I kept my little .38 Special with me everywhere. Bob had given us a Berretta M9 9mm among other pistols and suggested I carry it, but it was big and heavy. I kept it in the bedroom lying on top of the night stand where I could reach it if anything woke me. There was a small Sig Sauer .380 in the kitchen. A pump 12 gauge shotgun stood against the wall at the front door. Sandy carried a 9MM Smith and Wesson. We left the 10 MM Ruger on a side table in the living room. We hoped we were ready.

We were on the deck trying to eat something, but neither of us had much of an appetite. Carter had phoned an hour before with nothing new to report.

"Maybe," I said to Sandy, "Maybe he just went home? Like we did. Maybe he's back in Afghanistan or someplace like that."

"That would be good, Morgan. Do you really believe that? You've met the man. Is he normal . . . Or is he insane?"

"He's a religious fanatic, Sandy. He believes in death. He's waiting for his . . . What is it? A bunch of virgins, right? I think he's OK with his own death . . . But is he fanatic enough to want us dead?"

"Aren't religious fanatics a little bit insane?"

"I suppose so."

"And do we assume an insane person who would like to see us dead just went home and is now living in some mud hut somewhere?"

She was right, of course. We could go on for months, even years, looking over our shoulders. Caroline could spend the rest of her life hiding out with bikers; Betsy could drop out of college. Our life could never be the same again.

I relented and told her, "OK, but I don't think we should just sit here forever waiting for Omar."

"So what are you suggesting?" she asked. "I think I know, but tell me anyway."

"I want to go find him."

Sandy sat back in her chair, a quizzical look on her face. She was staring at me with a complete lack of understanding. She said, "You want to go out and find an Islamic terrorist who is somewhere in the world . . . Anywhere? You want to do what the whole damn Federal Government can't do? And then what? Are you going to kill him?"

"If I have to," I said. "I mean, I'd rather turn him over to the FBI. But if it means my family can sleep safely at night . . . I will kill the bastard."

We contacted Betsy at the home of her biker gang friends. Sandy would go there and stay safely with her and Caroline. She would be safe there, I thought; a couple dozen crazy gun wielding bikers would be good enough guards. And they wanted the thousands of dollars coming their way to protect my ladies.

Sandy objected at first, but I reasoned that alone, all I had to do was protect me. Even if Sandy thought she would not need me to protect her, I knew I would feel the need to do just that. Protecting her while trying to kill Omar would make the job harder. She would wait with the biker gang for a phone call from me when it was time for her to come home with Caroline and Betsy and be safe.

****

The biker gang, The West Coast Royals, dealt in guns and hijackings. They financed much of their illegal operations by importing Mexican heroin and selling it in bulk to dealers in Northern California. They ran the streets in South San Francisco and paid off the local police to keep them off their backs.

Sandy arrived at their headquarters, a long abandoned store front with a gas station next door, in the warehouse district in the late afternoon. Fourteen motorcycles were lined up along the curb in front. She had one small suitcase with her, and an envelope filled with hundred dollars bills.

Caroline ran to her and jumped into her arms. "Mommy! Mommy!" she cried out.

Sandy hugged her and kissed her and held her out at arm's length. "You've grown," she said. "How could you grow so much in so short a time?"

Caroline shrugged her way out of Sandy's arms and stood on the cracked concrete sidewalk looking up at her. She was dressed in white and pink cotton shorts and a white and blue sailor's middy blouse. The outfit was brand new. Sandy felt bad that she had left our daughter for so long a time that someone had bought her new clothes. Sandy wanted to do that. But she held it back, inside her. She smiled.

With a very stern face, Caroline said, "Mommy, I missed you. You can't go away again."

"I'll try not to dear . . . But I'm here now." Sandy looked up to see she was surrounded by The West Coast Royals and Betsy Concanon standing with them. She spoke to them, "And if it's alright with you, I need to stay here for a while."

She handed Betsy the envelope of cash, and she gave it to Spanish Jake. Spanish Jake was a giant of a man, 6' 6" tall and something over 300 pounds of intimidating muscle. His head and face were shaved clean exposing a nasty looking scar that ran from the center of his forehead down the right side of his face to his neck. He opened the envelope, flipped through the hundred dollar bills, and smiled. "Yeah, lady. You got a place to stay."

Betsy smiled, and she and Sandy hugged. "Caroline has been very good," she told Sandy. "We've been keeping up on her reading, and she knows her addition and subtraction. We've been getting help from Hammer's woman. She's a school teacher and a very good one, too."

"Hammer's woman?" Sandy asked. "Who's Hammer?"

"That's me," a biker said as he stepped forward. He wasn't as tall as Spanish Jake, and he wasn't as big. But he wore a sleeveless leather jacket that showed off big biceps and arms covered in tattoos. And his hair and beard were long with traces of gray showing. "She a good woman," he said maybe a little defensively.

"I'm sure she is . . . And I want to thank her for teaching my daughter."

Betsy picked up Caroline, and Sandy followed them into the store front. The windows had been painted black, so no sunlight lit the inside. A row of globed lights hung from the ceiling. A couple of ratty couches and a half dozen stained chairs filled the room. A big, but old refrigerator stood at the back of the room.

Sandy looked the place over and whispered to Betsy, "This is where you've been staying?"

"Oh no, only sometimes during the day. C needs to get out now and then, and she likes playing trucks with the guys." Betsy had been calling our daughter C ever since we took her into our home to care for Caroline.

"These guys play trucks with Caroline?" Sandy asked, not believing what she had heard.

"Don't let them fool you, Sandy. They may do a rough business, but they're really nice guys. They care . . . And they won't let anything happen to us, either."

Betsy introduced Sandy to the rest of the bikers and then led Sandy and Caroline up a back staircase. On the second floor was a very nice, very clean and very comfortable apartment. The furniture was clean and well maintained. There was a good carpet on the floor, and nicely framed pictures hung on the walls, pictures of landscapes and flower gardens. Sandy thought that she might actually hang similar pictures in her own home.

Sandy was astonished. Betsy saw the look on her face. She said, "Some of the money you and Morgan have been sending them went into furnishing this place. There's a nice kitchen and a big tub in the bathroom. There are two bedrooms and a big TV hooked up to cable. But we limit C's time in front of it. A couple of the girls go food shopping for us . . . They make sure C has a good diet, too. No junk food and no sugary drinks. Lots of fresh fruits and vegetables. They really are good people, Sandy; no matter what they look like."

****

I drove home slowly after taking Sandy to the airport. The reality that I was alone hit me, not fear so much as actual loneliness. I had no one to talk with. And as I drove my mind became centered on just what the hell I would do to stop Omar. Where could I start? In what part of the world would I find him? What could I do? I had to do something or leave my family, my wife and child, to live in hiding with a biker gang for the rest of their lives.

It was evening as I drove into San Marcos. I stopped at Downtown and realized I was hungry. I could turn right and go to the Country Club or turn left and go home. Too much was running through my head to bother with the Country Club crowd, so I turned left and drove up the hills to home.

The police patrol car that Bob Sommers had assigned to the street in front of my house was there. I parked my beloved MGB in the driveway and started for the front door when I thought it would be nice to invite the cop in to share a meal with me.

I waived to him as I walked to the patrol car. Then I saw the driver's side window, smashed and broken. Inside, the young officer slumped back in the car's seat, his throat cut deeply, and blood covered the front of his uniform. I froze and pulled the .38 from my belt. There was a slight breeze coming in from the Pacific, but the early night was otherwise still and hot. A bird sang, and a brown squirrel scurried across the road and up a tree in my front yard. Everything else was still.

I was standing between the patrol car and my house. Do I take cover outside? Do I run for the house? Do I run for the MGB and get the hell out of there? I had my cell phone. Do I call Bob Sommers and get his cops here?

It was Omar, I knew that. It had to be. And Omar was the professional; I wasn't. He had to know what I would do; experience and training would tell him that. But standing tall and looking around was not the smartest thing I could do, so I ducked down, ran for the police car, and hugged against it.

The evening's silence was broken by a laugh, a loud laugh, followed by Omar calling out to me, "Stand up Morgan! I will kill you quickly if you stand up!"

That meant I wasn't a clear target. But how long could I stay there before Omar simply came to me? I had a gun . . . Did Omar? I moved quickly to the front tire using it as a shield so that I was not exposed to gun fire under the car.

"Morgan! Don't be stupid Morgan! You can die slowly, or you can die quickly. But you will die."

His voice was coming from the trees across the street, on the hillside. That meant he would have a clear shot at me from above me. I could spray the trees with the six bullets I had in the .38, but what would I do then?

I moved back to the passenger side door and lifted my head enough to look into the patrol car. The dead cop had a semi-auto pistol in his holster, and there was a shotgun in a rack attached to the dashboard. I needed those; with them I might make it to my house and the guns inside.

I was at eye level when the glass in the door shattered. I heard the shot first, but I wasn't quick enough to pull myself away. The glass shards flew all around me and over my head. I felt a piece of glass cut across the top of my head.

I tried the car's door, but it was locked. Omar might have done me a favor by shooting out the glass. If I could reach in without getting killed, I could open the door, and I might be able to get the guns I needed.

I pointed my .38 over the door and through both broken windows. Quickly, I fired all six shots, spraying them wildly into the trees on the hillside. After the sixth shot I reached through the window and managed to open the door. Crouching down and crawling into the patrol car, I took the semi-auto pistol from the dead cop's holster, and I tried to remove the shotgun, but I couldn't quickly unlock it from the rack.

Then I saw the radio and the microphone. Keeping low inside the car, I grabbed the microphone and yelled into it, loud enough for Omar to hear. I called for help, and I called again. "This is Morgan Crew! I'm being shot at! I need help! I'm at home! I need help!" I screamed more for Omar to hear than for the police. I hoped he would run if he thought help was coming to me.

A hail of bullets rained down on me, hitting the car and smashing the windshield, but missing me. I slid backwards out of the car and crouched low at the curb. Omar kept firing, wildly I think, hoping to get me before help could arrive.

Once when the shooting stopped, I assumed for Omar to put new clips in his guns, I rose up and fired off six quick shots with the dead police officer's gun into the trees on the hill. Then I heard the sirens, far off at first, but getting louder. Omar fired off a series of quick shots, hitting the car already torn apart by all the bullets hitting it, and then it ended.

Three police cars came racing up the hill, lights flashing and sirens screaming. They came to a quick stop.

Three uniformed officers and Bob Sommers jumped from the cars, pistols in hand. I stood and called to them, "He's gone by now! He was up in the trees," I said pointing up the hill across the street.

Bob told the cops to go there and look as he went to his dead patrolman. He used the car's radio to call in for an ambulance. He was mad, as angry as I've ever seen him. He threw the microphone down and walked around the car to me. He followed me into the house and told me to wait by the open door as he looked through the house. He came back to me, putting his pistol back in his shoulder holster.

"What the hell happened?" he demanded. "That boy had his damn throat cut!"

I told him I had come home after bringing Sandy to the airport and found the officer dead. "Omar must have been waiting for me," I explained. "He was too quick. He should have waited for me to start for the front door. If he had, I'd be dead, too."

"Well," Bob said, "You aren't going to stay here. I've lost one good, very young cop. I'm not going to lose my best friend, too."

"And I don't want you to lose your best friend, either. I have some planning to do, and then I'll be gone."

"Where to?" he asked.

"I think it's best I keep that to myself, Bob. No offense, but the more I keep to myself the better I feel."

"Then I'm staying here with you," Bob said as he took off his jacket.

"Actually," I said, feeling pretty good at the idea, "That's not a bad idea. Can you afford another car out front?"

"No . . . I don't want to lose another officer. These are young guys, Morgan. I'll stay with you."

****

My three ladies spent two pleasant days with The West Coast Royals. As they were enjoying burgers grilled outside, behind the store, Spanish Jake interrupted the good times.

"You have to move," he said.

Sandy put her big burger down and asked, "Why? I mean, you're getting paid, right?"

"Not that lady," he said. "There's word out on the street that there's someone lookin' for you. There's a ten grand reward for whoever finds you. People all over are askin' questions."

"Who is looking for me?" It had to be Omar, of course. Sandy knew that.

"Don't know, lady," he said. "But you got my protection so you gotta' move. We got a place you can stay. Out in Oakland. Lousy neighborhood but a safe place to stay."

Sandy thought about that, looked at our daughter and Betsy, and thought about me, out there alone. She had no idea of the encounter I had with Omar. She stood and looked up at Spanish Jake. "Take Betsy and Caroline. Keep them safe. Give me a gun. I'm going to stay where he can find me."

"That's crazy, lady. You gonna' get yourself killed. I'm supposed t'be protectin' you. I can't let some suck'a get at you."

"Look, Jake," Sandy said. "My husband is out there somewhere. I don't know where. And there's a man . . . Omar Maalouf . . . Out there looking for him and me. That's who put the reward out for me. He wants to kill us both. Now, we can stay running and hiding forever. You can make a lot of money hiding us. But what kind of life is that? I want this man to be dead. I want to get back home and back to a normal life with my child and husband. I want to wait here . . . Let Omar find me . . . And then I'll kill him."

Spanish Jake stared down at this woman who was talking like no other woman he had ever known or heard of. And he believed Sandy was telling the truth. Her face revealed that fact. She really wanted to face down a man who wanted to kill her. He relented and said, "You can't stay here, lady. I ain't gonna get my place shot up. But I got a place you can stay near here. If you don't mind shackin' up with a bunch'a hookers, that is."

Spanish Jake gave Sandy a Colt .45 and three magazines of bullets. She said goodbye once again to our daughter and Betsy, promising that everyone would be home soon. Caroline cried and wanted to stay with her mother. Sandy promised, once again, that we would all be together again soon.

Spanish Jake took Sandy five blocks away to a gaudy and cheap bordello. Sandy gave $500 to a skinny and dirty man with a pock marked face who showed her to a room at the back of the place. It was a small room, with only a sway back bed and some red bulb lamps. The walls were covered with Playboy centerfolds that had been taped to the walls a couple years ago.

"You can stay here," the skinny man said. "Ain't nobody gonna' bother you here." He paused and grinned, exposing black teeth. He leered at her, his eyes working over her body and said, "I got this spare room up front. You wann'a make some money while you're here? You can use it if you want."

Spanish Jake moved between Sandy the guy and looked down at him. He growled, "This lady's got my protection, unner'stand? She tells me you ain't treatin' her right, and I'll break both your damn legs."

Sandy stayed in the room for the next three days, leaving only to walk a few steps to a small kitchen where she ate some food, mainly canned things and a few Chinese take outs, with the prostitutes who worked there. Save for a couple of hardcore women who had been in the business for too many years, they were nice young women, even if they weren't college professor types.

It was a little after two in the morning of the fourth day that the shouting and yelling woke Sandy. She jumped out of the bed and grabbed the Colt pistol. It took a moment or two for the sleep to slip away. She sat on the edge of the bed, the pistol held tightly in both her hands, and cocked the hammer.

There were a lot of screams and yelling and swearing, but no gunshots. She was tempted to go to the door and look outside, but good sense wiped away that idea. She would let Omar come to her.

She looked down at her hands and the big Colt. Her hands were shaking, and for the first time she realized she was scared. But she knew it was something she had to do. Either Omar would be dead, or she would; she set her mind to that.

The door crashed open, and Sandy's finger went to the pistol's trigger. But she pulled the gun to the side when a uniformed policeman stood in the doorway.

"You Sandy Crew?" he asked.

Sandy answered, "Yes."

"Stay here," the cop said and closed the door.

An hour later Spanish Jake opened the door and stepped into the room.

"You OK?" he asked.

Sandy stood and said, "Yes . . . But what the hell happened?"

"The cops raid this place every now and then. Good for the newspapers I guess. But I told them 'bout you, and they left you alone. I own this place. I let the cops have some fun now and then, and they leave me alone most of the time. This place will open again in a couple days. Stay here anyway. I'll have some of the girls bring you food and stuff."

TWENTY-SIX – To Find Omar

I tried to get some sleep on the jet to Colorado Springs. It had been a tough ten days getting to that flight. Bob had insisted I fill out forms and sign reports about the murder of his officer. That took almost three whole days with him at my side all that time. He collected all the guns he had left with me, even asking that I turn over my own .38 which I refused to do . . . Politely. But I finally made it to the airport and onto the Delta 757 to New York which was my first stop. Bob had notified the TSA and had pulled some strings. I was led through a door avoiding the security lines and out onto the tarmac. I climbed the stairs at the side of the plane and sat in first class with my pistol in my small carry-on bag.

My mind was on Sandy and Caroline, and how I could ever repay Betsy for all she was doing. She was supposed to be in school, but she had chosen to help us and make sure little Caroline was safe.

In New York I went to the Federal Building and waited thirty-five minutes before Agent Carter would see me. He at first laughed at my proposal and told me to get out of his office, but when he saw the look on my face he knew I was serious. I think he also knew I could bring some very heavy weight from Washington down on him whenever I felt that necessary.

"You want what!" he said, astonished at what I had asked for.

"As I said, I want to talk to Tamara Jackson."

"You're kidding, right? You want to talk to the woman who you caught for us?"

"Yes . . . What's the problem?" I asked.

"The problem is she's in a super-max prison. If it were up to me, she'd be rotting away in Gitmo, but our ever so enlightened Government isn't taking any more folks there. That's a mistake, but it isn't my mistake."

"OK, so make the arrangements for me to go to where she is. Is that so difficult?"

"Difficult? My God! I don't know where to begin! People are going to think I've gone flippin' crazy!"

"Well, figure it out, Agent Carter. If I have to, I'll go over your head. Don't forget that my family supports a couple dozen people in Congress. They want that money to keep flowing into their pockets. You won't look very good if they have to get angry with you."

I sat patiently while Carter started phoning people and filling out stacks of forms. It was strange, but for the first time in years I wanted a cigarette. I think the idea of having a cigarette in my hand might have calmed me. I was scared and nervous, and listening to that little voice in the back of my head yelling at me to "Run Away! Run Away!" was getting to me. But I waited.

In fact, Carter's superiors did think he had gone 'flippin' crazy, but once he told them who I am he started making progress. If I live to be a hundred I'll never stop being amazed at what money can buy. People give me what I want, people show respect, but I know that respect is not for me but for the money I control.

Ten days after leaving San Marcos, I was trying to sleep up in the front cabin of a commercial 777, having bypassed the TSA once again, heading for Colorado and the ADX in Florence where Tamara Jackson was being locked up. ADX is this Country's toughest super-max prison. It is for this Nation's most violent and dangerous men . . . And one woman – Tamara Jackson. Any other woman who is considered extremely dangerous is housed in Fort Worth, Texas at a Federal 'medical' facility. But Tamara was different. She was classified as someone beyond 'very dangerous.'

Tamara was being questioned daily by teams of Government people and cops. She had refused a lawyer and said nothing – not one word – to any of the people questioning her.

I parked my rental car in the lot in front of the imposing and fearful looking prison. Inside the prison they were expecting me; in fact three FBI Agents were in the main office at the front gate, waiting for me. They were big men dressed in combat gear: bullet proof vests, helmets with black visors, and very big guns, everything common to members of the FBI's Strike Force.

One of them stepped forward. He took his helmet off so I could see his face. He was older than I had expected, with short cropped grey hair and a tough history of combat on his scarred and wrinkled face.

"Mr. Crew," he said. I took his hand and felt the too-tight grip of it; he was trying to send a message to me that he was in charge. I just smiled and let him squeeze. I wasn't going to let him know he was intimidating me, even though he was doing a damn good job at it.

"We are going to escort you to the woman," he said in a gravelly voice. "She will be in our custody while you speak with her. You will have fifteen minutes, and then she will be returned to her cell. But first, you need to leave your weapon here at the desk."

Leaving my .38 at the front desk, rather than walking it into a prison where the worst of the worst were housed seemed logical, so I handed it to a guard with sergeant stripes on his sleeve at the desk.

"Thank you very much for coming all the way out here," I said to the Agent with the powerful grip. "I assume you aren't stationed here fulltime. Unfortunately, what is going to happen is not what you planned for. You will escort me to a room where I can talk with Tamara, and you will escort Tamara from her cell to that room where I will speak with her in private. You will wait outside, and I will spend as much time with her as I wish. And there will be neither cameras nor recordings of what we talk about."

"That's not what has been arranged."

"Sorry about that," I said. The two men standing behind their leader raised their visors and looked at each other. They shrugged their shoulders. "It's my way or the highway, gentlemen. If I leave here without getting what I want, I'm going to bring heavy weight down on you and the FBI. You'll be testifying before Congress, and I have serious questions as to what will happen to next year's budget. Now, shall we go to where I will speak with Tamara?"

I was shown, in bitter silence from the three of them, to a small room with a gray steel door and concrete block walls that were painted a sickly pale green. The air inside was old and musty. I looked around and saw only one very small vent for fresh air to be pumped into the room. A metal table and two wooden chairs were the only furnishings. One of the chairs, on the far side of the table from the door was securely bolted to the floor. I looked down at the table legs and found them sunk firmly into the concrete floor. On the table top was a steel bar. It looked strange at first before I realized that the bar was meant to hold prisoner's chains, securing the chains to the table.

I sat on the chair across the table, with my back to the door, waiting. I kept checking my wristwatch, waiting there for over ten minutes. At my back a panel of thick glass encasing wire was the only view outside the room. I repeatedly got up and looked out the window. The door was locked, keeping me inside the small room. I wondered, after a few minutes of tapping my foot nervously on the concrete floor, if this was to be my own cell after arguing with the FBI.

I jumped to my feet when the door behind me suddenly opened and slammed against the wall. The FBI guard who I had spoken with stood in the open doorway and said, "You have to sit, Mr. Crew. You may not stand while the woman is here."

I gave them that much and sat, folding my hands together on top of the table. The guard stepped aside, and his two companions brought Tamara in, each holding tightly to her arms. She was dressed in a bright orange jump suit of heavy, rough material, faded with age and frayed at the cuffs. She wore rubber flip-flops on her feet. A heavy leather belt was fastened tightly around her waist. Her arms were bound to the belt by thick chains at her wrists. Another chain hung from the belt in front of her to her feet and was attached to shackles at her ankles.

Tamara had been a very attractive young woman the last time I had seen her. I almost thought they had made a mistake and had brought someone else to me. Her hair was uncombed, shaggy and in need of a good shampooing. She had no makeup on; her face was grey, drawn, and sad. Her dark eyes were sad, and heavy rings of forgone hope hung under them. She was thin; she kept her head and eyes down, not looking up at anyone.

They sat her on the chair across the table from me. One of the men fastened her ankles to the bolted down chair and used handcuffs to fasten the leather belt to the sides of the chair. The other unlocked the chain that held her wrists to the belt and locked the chains to the bar on the table top. Either they weren't taking any chances, or they just liked to be tough with this little girl who was half their size.

The two FBI guards stood on her left and right, waiting. I said nothing for a moment, looking at them, back and forth. Then I said, "Thank you. You can go now."

They looked at their boss who was standing behind me in the open doorway. I didn't turn to look, but he must have nodded or something because the two guards walked around the table, slowly, dramatically, and left, glaring down at me all the while. I heard the door close behind me, and a lock snapped closed.

Tamara looked up at me. I held a finger to my lips, telling her not to say anything. I bent and looked under the table. I found a small transmitter fastened there. I ripped it off the table, dropped it on the floor and smashed my heel down on it.

"I'll reimburse them for that later," I said.

I walked around the room looking for some sort of camera. I found it unusual that there was nothing that could be called a hidden camera. In fact there was nothing at all in the room save for the table and chairs. I looked out the glass on the door and saw, across the hall, a camera hanging on the wall, pointed at the window. I decided to stand, leaning against the glass with my back to the glass, blocking the camera's view.

"Tamara," I said. "I wish I could say it's good to see you again."

"Cut the crap," she said. Her voice was weak, hoarse, and angry. "Why are you here?"

"I have a deal I want to talk with you about."

"Deal? You plan on getting me out of here?"

"I'm afraid you will spend a long time in prison, Tamara. The kind of prison could just maybe be your choice, however."

"I don't understand," she said. But a bright light suddenly was turned on in her eyes. She tried to sit up but found the chains would not allow her to move.

"I need help, Tamara," I said. "I need your help."

"Doing what?"

"I want to find Omar Maalouf."

"You're joking, right!" she said and laughed, probably for the first time in months.

"No, I'm perfectly serious, Tamara. I need to find him. I know who he is. I know all about his religious fanaticism. I know he is pretty pissed off right now that his big plan was stopped. His bosses are probably pretty angry, too. I know he blames me . . . Rightly so . . . For screwing things up. I know because of that he wants my wife and me dead. I know he wants revenge. I want to find him before he finds us."

"And just what do you think you'll do when you come face to face with him?" she asked. I am pretty good at reading faces. Her face told me there was a spark of hope there.

"If I can, I'll see him spend the rest of his life right here. If not that . . . I will kill him. He tried to kill me a few days ago. He ambushed me in front of my home. He had no way of knowing my wife and daughter were not there. He failed, but he got away. I want to find him."

"You're crazy, you know that?"

"You're probably right . . . You're not the first person to tell me that. But that's what I want to do."

She tried again to shift in the metal chair she was chained to. She leaned back as best as she could and asked, "And just what do you want from me?"

"You know Omar . . . You know the system . . . You know how he thinks . . . You know where to look for him."

"Christ Morgan! I met him in Cuba . . . At that training school! How do you plan to get into Cuba and kill him and then get out again?"

"Is he really there?" I asked. "Think about it. Somebody put up a lot of money for Omar's operation to steal the Firebird Guidance specs. All that money was flushed down the toilet. Are the people who financed the operation going to welcome Omar with open arms? I don't think he ran off to Cuba after trying to kill me. No, I think there's a good chance his first worry will be hiding from the people who paid for the operation and the FBI. And then he'll want to take revenge on me."

"And what can I do for you from this damn place?" she asked. I could hear a tinge of hope in her voice. There was a 'maybe' there; maybe she could do something for herself.

"One thing at a time," I said. "First, give me a few places I can look for him. Give me some leads. After that . . . Well, we'll see."

"No good," Tamara said. "All my life I've been lied to and harassed by you damn white folks. I need more than a promise."

"What more do you want?"

"You said that I could maybe get out of here. This place is hell. I'm gonna' go crazy sitting here. I don't talk to nobody . . . Sorry, I mean they don't allow me to speak with anyone. I sit in that damn box day after day with nothing to do but go crazy. All they do is pull me out day and night to ask me questions that I don't answer. I'm all alone. You have the power to get me transferred, right? You have the influence . . . The power, right?"

"If you help me, I can have an army of attorneys representing you. At trial, with the right attorneys, you may not wind up with a life sentence. I have the influence to get you transferred to a less restrictive prison somewhere. But understand, if I do that for you, and you try to escape from whatever prison you're in . . . You're on your own from that point on."

Tamara smiled for the first time in the weeks she had been locked up at ADX. She had been spending 23 hours a day locked in a windowless cell. She had nothing to read, no TV, no radio, and no one to talk to. Three meager and basic meals a day were brought to her and slid through an opening in the door, enough to keep her alive but little more than that. One hour each day, in the late afternoon, she was led out in chains to a courtyard of tall concrete walls and a concrete floor, open to the sky, where she could walk in the thirty foot by twenty foot rectangle. If it was raining or snowing she would be kept in her cell that day.

She was the only woman in the super-max prison, so she was not allowed near the 'commons,' a bigger area where men who earned the privilege gathered. The guards who watched her as she walked were men, and they would not talk with her. It was, to Tamara and the men who lived in isolation in super-max, a living hell.

I was giving her a chance, a possibility. I could see the excitement on her face. She said, "Alright. I'll try. But Omar is special. He's not an amateur. You might wind up dead . . . And then what happens to me?"

"Dead or alive, the deal is the same. I'll have my attorneys here to speak with you in a couple of days. They will start the process of having you transferred."

She nodded vigorously; I think if she could have – without the chains – she would have jumped up and yelled her happiness. I took the small spiral note pad and pen I had brought with me from my jacket pocket. Tamara gave me a half dozen addresses in a half dozen different cities. She said they were safe houses she had been told about, places to run to, places to hide.

"It's a start," she said. "If you don't find him in any of them, I'll try to think of something else."

I left her smiling and almost giddy. There was hope for a future in her head. Her eyes were once again alive with hope. She even thanked the guards who took her back to her cell and locked her inside.

I booked a private jet to get back to New York and to Peter's office and to avoid the TSA. We had dinner that night, just the two of us, at Le Cirque, and I ate everything that Sandy would not have let me eat if she had been with us. It took two bottles of expensive wine for me to convince Peter to represent Tamara. He thought it would be bad publicity for his firm to represent a terrorist. To me, that made little difference.

Peter agreed, and he started the legal process I knew he would be successful at.

TWENTY-SEVEN – Tamara's Help

Tamara had given me six addresses in six different cities. I hired Private Detectives in each city to watch each address twenty-four hours a day, seven days a week. Each address was in a less than reputable part of town, a place where people could disappear and be unseen. Sitting in a parked car in front of these places would not be the smartest move, so I told each Detective to rent a room or apartment or a house as near as possible to each.

A week later none of the Detectives had anything to report. I stayed in my home in San Marcos all that time, waiting. Bob Sommers moved in with me. I had pizza delivered, I had burgers and French fries delivered, and I had beer delivered. And I spent a lot of time out on the deck, looking down onto the harbor, with Bob Sommers and one of his guns very near at hand. Bob brought all the guns he had taken back to the house. Each room had one gun in it, and I kept my .38 by my side.

I wanted to get out and go fishing or play some golf, but I had to stay by the phone, and I had to stay by my .38. If Omar came for me, I felt more comfortable on my own territory and not exposed out on the ocean or swinging a golf club. And I had Bob watching my back.

Every time a car drove by the house, I reached for my .38 and looked out the front window. I slept every night fitfully, tossing and turning and reaching for the 9MM Berretta on the night stand at every slight sound.

On the morning of the eighth day I finished the last of the coffee. There were no eggs in the refrigerator; in fact there was little food at all except for three slices of two day old pizza. Bob has a ferocious appetite and ate the food that would have lasted me at least two weeks. I had had enough.

I showered, shaved, and packed a small suitcase. I said goodbye to Bob, and thanked him, but I didn't tell him where I was going or what I was going to do. I took both the .38 and the Berretta and drove my beloved little MGB down the hills to the San Marcos airport. The airport was a small one, for small, private planes. There was a leasing company there that had three Lear Jets for overpaid company CEOs who lived in San Marcos to fly down to San Francisco and Los Angeles. I rented one big enough to fly across the Country. The big jet with a full crew would take me to Colorado and Tamara in her prison.

They weren't expecting me at the prison. Visitors normally applied weeks or sometimes months in advance to do a rarely allowed visit of an inmate. Visitors often travelled many miles to the prison, filled out pages of papers, and were often denied visitation anyway. But as so often in the past, I used my family name to bypass all the things 'normal' people have to do. One of these days I'm going to give away all the damn money and just live like anybody else, maybe even fulfill that longtime dream of mine of owning a commercial fishing boat. But at that time I was glad of the power and influence the Crew name carried.

It took an hour and a half for phone calls to the prison warden from a couple of Representatives in Congress and one very powerful Senator for me to be sitting in that same little room I was in last time, waiting for Tamara once again. I checked for microphones – there weren't any that time. I guess they weren't going to waste another 'hidden' microphone on me. I looked across the hall through the door's window for a camera – there wasn't one that time. They were learning.

I sat and waited patiently. Finally, Tamara was brought in and shackled to the chair and table as she was last time. She was happy to see me this time; she was smiling and bright and almost laughing. I wasn't as happy as she was. She saw I wasn't happy and asked, "What's wrong, Morgan?"

"None of those addresses worked out, Tamara. I had detectives watching them. He never showed up at any of them."

"Well, the world's a big place. Omar is a professional. He could be anywhere."

I sat forward, leaned my elbows on the table and said, "My wife said that you people exist in the shadows, the greys, the half lights and the dark alleys. Is she right?"

"She's one smart woman," Tamara said. "She's right. That's why it's going to be hard to find Omar."

"So where do I go to find him?"

"Omar's not a coward," Tamara said as she thought. "He might go to some Arab Country. But I doubt he'd stay. He likes the western world and all the sins here. I don't think he wants to wait until he's dead to get his 27 virgins. I think he likes to get them right here at strip clubs and with expensive hookers. He likes his liquor, too."

"If he were somewhere far away . . . I wouldn't care," I said. "But I believe he's near, and he *will* try to kill me again . . . And try to kill my family, too. I need to find him."

"Having rent-a-cops stake out houses won't work, Morgan. There are hundreds of those places . . . On every continent. I only know of a few. You need to talk to people.

People who can lead you to other people who will lead you to other people. I can give you some names."

I was discouraged. I wanted to find Omar and get my family back . . . Safely. What Tamara was telling me would take weeks, months . . . Longer maybe. And what do I ask these people? Will they just open up and talk to me? I doubted all that.

I asked her, "Are these people going to talk to me?"

"I doubt it . . . Look Morgan. People like Omar . . . And me . . . We live in a small world. When I was in school in Cuba I was given names and places. I was amazed that I could remember everything I was told. I never thought I had it inside of me to remember everything. I never thought I was smart, you see. But I do remember everything."

"Why did you have to remember names and places?"

She laughed and said, "Morgan, you've got a lot to learn. On any operation, I might run into trouble. I would need safe places and safe people. I'm not going to carry a list of people and places around with me."

"And these people would just help you? They would trust you? You'd be a stranger to them."

"I know how to talk to them . . . I know what to say."

"And Omar knows the same places? He knows the same people? He knows what to say?"

"Of course," Tamara said. "He taught me."

"So you could talk to those people and find out where Omar is?"

"Yeah . . . Sure . . . One problem. I'm here, and they aren't. They won't even let me near a phone."

****

I left Tamara chained to the chair and table and raced back to the airport and the waiting Lear Jet. It took one refueling stop, but we made it to Manhattan safely. A taxi with a dirty back seat got me to Peter Jascro's building by mid-evening. I got off the elevator and found Peter waiting for an elevator to take him down to his waiting car.

"Morgan!" he said. "What are you doing here? I wasn't expecting you."

"I have some work for you, Peter. Can we talk?"

"Of course," he said as he patted me very fatherly on my shoulder. "Let's go to my office."

"I'm hungry, Peter. I haven't eaten all day. Can we get some dinner?"

Harper, Harper, Jascro and Nettles has standing reservations at several top flight restaurants in the City. Important clients from every corner of the world were in the offices almost daily, and they needed to be wined and dined. Peter and I ate an early dinner at one of those restaurants, Peter Luger's Steak House. It took another two bottles of wine, a very good California Merlot, and a huge cut of very rare beef for Peter to agree to help me.

"Let me make sure I understand just what the hell you want, Morgan," he said. "You want a person who committed a murder, who is a spy, who stole classified information, who is a trained terrorist and killer, who hates America and wants to destroy us . . . You want Tamara Jackson released into your custody so you can find Omar Maalouf . . . The man who trained her to kill? Are you out of your mind?"

"I'm not out of my mind, Peter. I want you to arrange

it and do it quickly."

"OK, Morgan," Peter said, sitting back in the tall chair at our table. "Tell me why. I have to know that what I'm doing is the right thing." He grasped his glass of Merlot in both hands and glared at me, his pale blue eyes staring like knives trying to cut into the truth behind the curtain of what I asked of him.

"Omar is a professional. He can hide anywhere in the world. I can't think like these people think. My mind doesn't work like Omar's mind works. Tamara was trained by him, and she knows him. She knows where he will hide . . . She knows how he will come after Sandy and Caroline. I want to stop him, and I don't have a lot of time to do that. I need Tamara's help."

"And you think this . . . This murderer is just going to step up and help you find her mentor? Why do you think she'll do that?"

"Because I'm going to offer her a deal," I said, and I had to stop myself from laughing in the middle of the restaurant at my brilliance . . . Well, not brilliance I guess. More simplicity than anything else.

★★★★★★★★★★★★★★★

I spent the next three days and nights in one of the apartments kept above Peter's office, not the one the Japanese client preferred. I couldn't stand to be in that place for very long. The other apartment was a reflection of Louis XVI grandeur. I didn't care that the furnishings were royally expensive and yet very uncomfortable; in fact I didn't even take notice of the surroundings. I tried watching TV but couldn't keep my mind on it. I tried reading a book, but the words jelled and meant nothing to me. I wanted to talk with Sandy, to have her near me, but I knew that was not possible while Omar was out there somewhere. Omar had to be perfectly capable of tracing cell phone calls. It's easy if you know how. I tried to cook some food now and then, but I had no appetite.

The phone rang as I was finishing my fourth cup of lousy coffee on the morning of the fourth day.

"Mr. Crew," FBI Agent Carter said. "I need to speak with you. Can you come to my office?"

"Better idea . . . You come here," I said. "I feel safer here than walking the streets of New York."

He slammed the phone down without saying anything. I waited for him, because I knew I had given him no choice. He showed up, but he wasn't happy.

"I should cuff you and run you in," he said by way of greeting me at the apartment's door.

I tried to say, "For what?" but he pushed his way past me and walked into the living room ignoring my words. He sat hard on the couch and slammed his fist down on the couch's arm.

"I'm very close to putting a bullet in your damn head," he said, spitting out the words. "Do you have any idea what the hell you're doing?"

I sat in a chair not too near to Carter, crossed my legs, forced a calm and reasoning façade, and said, "I have no idea what you're talking about. Why are you so angry? You'd better slow your breathing, or you might have a heart attack. Would you like a nice cup of coffee? Perhaps some nice hot tea?"

"You know damn well that Senator Brandon and Representative Collingsworth have been putting pressure on the FBI. I was in a meeting with two of their top aides the other day. They threatened to cut our budget, God damn it! You did this! Just who the hell do you think you are?"

"I am the man who is trying to protect my family," I said calmly as if he should have known that already. "I am also the man who caught Tamara and Donna and Alexandra and shut down their operation when you folks were running around in circles." Carter's face was scarlet with anger. I had to project composure even though I was going crazy waiting for something to happen. I moved from the stiff arm chair and sat in an even less comfortable chair a few steps closer to Carter, crossing my legs. I asked, "So why are you here?"

Carter took a deep breath trying to slow his rapid heart. His fists were clenched so tightly that his knuckles were white. He said, his voice stammering, "I have been ordered to go with you to Colorado and see to it that Tamara Jackson is released into your custody."

"Yeah? So? Why are you angry at that?"

"Because she's a killer, you God damned idiot!" he screamed.

"Watch your language, Carter," I said. I pointed a threatening finger at him. "She hasn't had a trial yet, and even Tamara Jackson is to be presumed innocent until proven guilty."

"So now you're telling me she's innocent?" he growled. His level of anger told me I was in control. People who let their anger run wild don't think or act rationally. They lose whatever control they may have had over a situation.

"I didn't say that, Agent Carter," I said softly. "All I want is to have her help me find Omar Maalouf."

Peter had done what I asked him to do. I said, my

voice calm still, "If you've gotten orders from somewhere up above, you should understand that this is something I am going to do, no matter what you think. Face the facts, Agent Carter. I can arrange anything I want. That being the case, watch your language and let's get going to Colorado."

Carter leaned back, discouraged at losing his argument. "And if she turns on you and kills you . . .?"

"That's why you're going to be with us," I said. "You're going to be my body guard and Tamara's jailer . . . so to speak."

"I'm going to be with you?" he asked. "They didn't tell me that."

"You should assume that you will be with us. If I have to . . . And you don't want me to do this . . . I can arrange it quite easily. Your bosses won't like me pulling weight on them again. They'll hold it against you. I'll tell them it was your idea. All it will take is a couple of phone calls."

I packed my suitcase, and Carter and I left for JFK and a waiting private jet, this time a Boeing 737 outfitted for the very, very rich. I slept most of the way to Colorado, stretched out on a comfortable couch; Carter just sat and fumed. Shortly after take-off, before I fell asleep, I offered Carter some bourbon, a mediocre brand but bourbon all the same. Carter's face told me he didn't want any. His anger was not yet under control. He turned his head away and stared out the plane's window. I had two bourbons over ice with just a splash of club soda anyway and slept peacefully for the first time in many days.

****

There were a fleet of uniformed guards and civilian authorities in cheap suits waiting at the ADX Super-max prison in Florence, Colorado. A stack of forms and papers were waiting for me in the administration office. I signed anything that was put in front of me; a dumpy, middle-aged woman with a very unhappy expression on her face explained what each paper was, but I really didn't care. All I wanted was to get on with it.

When I was done, Carter stood across the room with a bunch of people who had not been introduced to me. None were any happier than everyone else involved in this. They kept looking at me with scowls on their faces, their arms folded in front of them. Finally, Tamara was led out of a thin hallway and into the office.

She was dressed in baggy blue jeans, two sizes too big for her and unbelted. She was handcuffed behind her back. She tried to hold the jeans up from behind. They had given her a wrinkled, extra-large, light blue work shirt that some man had worn so many times and laundered so many times it was faded and frayed. She wore the same rubber flip-flops she had on the last time I had seen her. Her hair had been combed, and her face had been washed but was without makeup. My guess was that the clothes they had given her were the only "gottcha" they could throw at her and me.

She smiled when she saw me. "Hello, Tamara," I said from the other side of the room. "Did they tell you what's going on?"

"No," she said. She tried to take a step towards me, but a guard at her side grabbed her arm to stop her.

I looked at the guard and said, "Let her go . . . And lose the handcuffs."

He looked at the group of men standing with Carter.

One of them, a grey haired man with a prominent beer-belly in a cheap brown tweed suit, nodded. Tamara's hands were freed. She tugged at the jeans, pulling them up, and walked, slowly, cautiously, to me. She turned to face the guards and stood very close to me, our arms touching; I think she was feeling protected somehow.

"You're going to come with me, Tamara," I said. "I have you for two weeks, no more. If we find Omar in that time, you will not be coming back here. If we find Omar, you will go to a less restrictive prison while you await trial. You're not going free, but your prison life will be a little bit better. It's your choice. Tell me if you will cooperate or not."

Tamara stood about 5'7" against my 6'2". She looked up at me and smiled again. "OK," she said. "But I'll need better clothes than these. I don't think you want me dropping my drawers in public." We both laughed at that.

We walked out of the prison under the gaze of the befuddled guards. Agent Carter trailed three paces behind us. Our first stop was in Colorado Springs, where Carter and I spent the afternoon following Tamara from shop to shop as she bought clothes, a lot of clothes. I didn't remind her that when she returned to prison, everything she bought would be taken from her. I figured she needed an afternoon of fun before the work started.

We stopped at a fast food hamburger place that she insisted on and watched her down two really big double cheeseburgers, fries and a strawberry shake. When she had finished all that, she slouched back in the booth and said, "Man, I wish I had a cigarette."

Carter produced a pack of Marlboros from his jacket pocket, and he and Tamara lit up. A waitress came over and told us there was no smoking inside. Carter flashed his gold badge at her. She walked away.

After they had finished their smokes in the restaurant, using the dirty paper wrappers on the table for an ash tray, ignoring the scowling waitress, we walked out, also ignoring the customers' angry words. In the parking lot I said, "The fun's over now. It's time to get to work. Where do we go, Tamara?"

The cheerful look on her face faded away quickly. It had been a good day for her after too many weeks in solitary confinement. She said, "The people who trained me were two types. Jesse, he was a Communist. Omar, he's an Islamist. They both want to overthrow the United States, but for different reasons. They work together for the same purpose. You know, the enemy of my enemy is my friend? Omar, he's really smart. He knows he's on the run from you people. He knows he can hide inside a couple of Mosques with a couple of Al Qaeda and ISIS Imams who will take care of him. I know where those places are. But I think Omar is smarter than that. I think he knows those are the first places the FBI will look for him. There's a couple of Mosques we can check quickly if you want, but I'd bet we'd find he ran to some of Jesse's people."

"Why?" Carter asked.

She smiled up at him and started, "Because you damn white folks are friggin' stupid and . . ."

"OK, Tamara," I said, stopping her. "Either we work together, or you go back to solitary."

"Alright," she said, still grinning. "I am so very sorry, Agent Carter," she said with an exaggerated bow and a sly grin. "What I mean is that Omar is very smart. He probably will avoid his own contacts and go to Jesse's contacts because . . . Well, because he probably believes you won't figure that out. I think he will understand that you will look for him in obvious places, and he will not be obvious. And I think he's right on that . . . Meaning no disrespect, of course."

Carter asked her, "And you know where Jesse's friends can be found?"

"A few of them. I was told by Jesse where a few safe places to run would be. People . . . Families mainly . . . Who believe in Communism but live a normal American lifestyle. You call a few of them 'sleepers.' A very few are left over from the old Soviet Union. Some are their children. Some of them are very overt and political, but Omar will avoid them. Others are just believers in Communism. They help when they can, and they wait for Capitalism to crumble."

"Alright," Carter said. "Let's start there. Tell me where the sleepers are first. I'll check them out to start with."

I stepped into the conversation. "Carter, we aren't here to break up a spy ring. I have only one interest, and that is finding Omar. I won't be diverted into helping you break up a bunch of Communists gangs. If you feel you need to do that, do it after we find and stop Omar."

"I guess I have to do what you say," Carter said grudgingly. "But when you get what you want, I will go back and bust up what I can bust up."

Tamara laughed and looked up at the Agent. "Do you really think these people are that stupid? Once they see you, they won't be in the same place the next day."

"Let me worry about that," he said.

She laughed again and shook her head. Tamara had been trained in covert operations and knew that a couple thousand people had been living covertly in the United States for many years, often generations, without the FBI able to find them or even know they exist.

"I want to talk with Morgan for a minute," she said. "In

private."

Carter, slowly and not too happily, lit another cigarette and walked a few paces away. Tamara said, "Look, you promised I could go to a less restrictive prison. I've been thinking. I know I'll be in prison for the rest of my life. I can handle that. But I want one more thing from you. I want the prison where Alexandra is. I don't care where it is, I want to go there."

"You're telling me you want to kill her?"

"Yes. Does that surprise you?"

TWENTY-EIGHT – The Communists

Tamara told us that there were Communist 'sleeper agents' all over the United States. These were, for the most part, second or sometimes third generation people whose parents or grandparents came from Russia and the old Eastern Europe. Many of the original sleepers had passed away years ago. Their children and sometimes even grandchildren inherited the sleeper status. A few of them were the children of Russian Communist NKVD agent/sleepers who were carrying on after their parents and after the fall of the Soviet Union. These descendants had been raised in the Communist philosophy, often having been secreted to Moscow as children for Communist education and espionage tactics. Others were just believers in Communism who waited for the fall of Capitalism.

"So Jesse wasn't alone in is beliefs?" I asked.

"Oh, my God, no. There are many hundreds who are very active and communicate with each other . . . Quietly, underground, secretly. There are probably hundreds, maybe more than a thousand who are not active but will pick up a gun when the time comes. They are what you white folks call 'leftists.' People like me call them patriots who want to change America. Many of these people are known to the true Communists and are called upon to do the good work when needed."

"So how do we contact these hundreds of people?" Carter asked. "You don't have that much time, you know."

"There is a small cell that Jesse is . . . I mean was, damn it . . . Attached to. He told me who they are and where they are. He said it is a perfect place to hide if I ever needed a place to hide. Very isolated, and the people in the cell are deeply Communist. There are two people who live at the site; about a half dozen others work with them."

"You know their names?" Carter asked.

"Of course I do," Tamara said.

"And you remember all that? Names and address of . . . How many places?" Carter asked. "Or are you just scamming me to get out of jail?"

"Please stop thinking I'm stupid. I was given excellent training. One day, when you white folks are a minority and not in charge, you'll find out how intelligent we really are. I remember everything I was taught, Agent Carter," Tamara said angrily. "I'm not stupid. My memory is very good . . . For what I deem important. I'm here because of what Morgan promised . . . Not because of you, not because I love the society you white racist bigot types run. I know that I have to find Omar, or Morgan doesn't have to keep his promise. Don't push me, OK?"

I stepped between Carter and the girl before fists were used. I was fairly certain if that happened I would put my money on Tamara to beat the crap out of Carter.

"OK," I said, "Enough of that. Where do we go from here?"

Tamara turned her back on Carter and spoke to me. "There's a little town south of Chicago. Orion it's called. Farm country, really. There's a man there who is . . . I mean was . . . Jesse's direct contact and control. He gets his orders from higher up in the organization. We start there."

****

I had given up the leased jet, and we were relying on a Federal jet, one from the FBI. I was tired of spending my own money, and I thought I could scam a few of my tax dollars back from Carter by flying at the Government's expense. I was amazed at the luxury inside the Gulfstream G200. I turned to Carter as we climbed onboard and said, "My tax dollars at work, I see."

It was raining when we landed at O'Hare. I refused Carter's offer of a Federal car, a very obvious black Ford without hubcaps that shouted, *"LOOK OUT! IT'S THE COPS!"* and rented a cream colored Cadillac Escalade. We drove south out of Chicago and found the little hamlet of Orion after getting lost only twice.

It was, to be sure, a small town. A Post Office with a flag pole flying a frayed American flag out front centered the town. A pair of gas stations were at either end of the only street there. A small grocery store, one ratty looking tavern, and a few vacant buildings made up the rest of the town.

We drove past Orion and 40 minutes later arrived at the farm. It wasn't much of a farm; the wood sided house needed painting a few years ago. The roof was peeling, and the front yard, if you could call it that, was crowded with rusted out farm implements, old tires, a pickup truck left over from the fifties that stood on concrete blocks, and a weather beaten old refrigerator with its door hanging open. Knee high weeds grew everywhere, and most of those were brown and dead. An old barn in even worse condition than the house lay fifty yards behind the house.

As we pulled to a stop, a man walked from the barn. He was carrying a shovel, his head and shoulders bent from too many years working a failing farm. He walked towards us, holding the long handled shovel like a weapon.

Tamara looked at the man, and without turning to Carter and me, she said, "I'd better talk to him by myself. You two stay here."

"No way," Carter said. "I have to stay with you. Any funny stuff and . . . Well you know what will happen."

"Look, Agent Carter," she said turning to him. "These people have been living a lie for a generation. They are diehard Communists. They have been waiting for the revolution all their lives. They can see a cop from a hundred yards away. They've lasted this long because they are very cautious, and they trust no one. I know how to talk to them. I know the words to use to make them trust me. Let me do this the right way, OK?"

I put my hand on Carter's shoulder and nodded. There was no place for Tamara to run to. If she tried, we had a car, and she was on foot. I could feel his shoulders relax, and he, too, nodded. Tamara opened the car door and walked towards the man with the shovel.

She waived and called out to him. He stopped, looked suspiciously at the young girl, raised the shovel to his shoulder, ready to swing, and waited. He looked beyond Tamara at the car she had come from and then back at her. He was thinking that she didn't look like a cop, but what the hell do cops look like in this damn putrid world?

I watched her as she reached the man and held out her hand. He took it slowly, and they talked. I couldn't hear what was being said, but the man seemed more at ease. He stuck the shovel into the ground at his feet and leaned on it as they talked. He nodded several times and pointed to the north. He shrugged his shoulders, and I think he said, "I don't know," several times.

Tamara shook his hand again, and she walked back to the car. The man watched her and didn't move until we had driven away.

"So what did he have to say?" I asked.

"I didn't tell him about Jesse being dead. I didn't think bad news would be a way to go. He was Jesse's contact and his handler, like I said. He said he hadn't seen Omar in over a month. He said he didn't like Omar. He didn't trust people who were religious. 'Religion is a curse,' he said. He said the last time he saw Omar, Omar had gone north after spending the night at the farm. He didn't know where Omar was going."

"Tell me about the man," I said. "What's his name?"

"Jack Higgins . . . Although that's probably not his real name. His father and mother were from Russia. He was born here, but they probably gave him a Russian name when they registered his birth in Moscow. That was when the Soviet Union was still there. There are a lot of people like Jack. They just hang on . . . Waiting for what will probably never happen. When he was very young he was probably sent to Russia for basic political education. That's all I know about him. Jesse used to talk about him and his wife a lot. Jesse liked them a lot."

I was driving; Carter and Tamara were in the back seat. Carter was writing down everything she was saying, I guess hoping for a bunch of arrests when this was all over. He said, "Let's go back to Chicago so I can make a report."

"No," I said. "There's a little motel I saw out by the highway, on the other side of Orion. Let's stay there tonight."

"Why?" Carter asked.

"I have things to do. You take care of Tamara. I'll be

gone for an hour or two."

****

I left Carter and Tamara at the motel and drove away. I pulled the car to a stop in front of the drab old farm south of Orion. There were lights on inside the house; dusk had passed, and it was dark outside. The moon was full, and the air was cool.

Tamara had told me that the farmer was a devout Communist, working now for the remnants of the KGB, an active control of active agents. That meant the man was dangerous, and I didn't have the right words, words that Tamara had, that would put him at ease and make him want to talk to me. But I had to try because I had a gut feeling there was more there than Tamara had learned. And Tamara said he was married. That meant there might well be a dangerous woman to deal with, also.

The ragged house was surrounded by a dilapidated picket fence that once had been white but was now weather aged with bare wood under flecks of left over peeling paint. The gate was closed but hung loose on one hinge. I pushed on it, and the loud squeak reminded me of the door back at the concrete bunker I had been held in. A dog barked, and I heard and then saw this big, black brute of a dog run around from the side of the house. It was chained, letting it reach the open gate but no further. I stepped back as the dog growled, barked and jumped, mouth frothing with anger, trying to get at me.

At the house the door opened, and the man Tamara had spoken with stepped out onto the porch. "What'ya want?" he called out over the barking. He was tall and thin, wearing faded bib-type overalls. His greying hair hung over his ears, and his wrinkled face needed a shave.

"I just want to talk with you for a minute," I yelled.

"'Bout what?"

"Can you call off your dog? Do we have to stand here yelling at each other?"

He walked off the porch and grabbed the thick chain holding the dog. He pulled on it and called the dog back. He held the dog close to him, scratching him behind his ear, and said, "Come on in."

I stepped slowly and carefully across the broken flagstones that passed for a walkway. The dog was sitting at the man's side, growling and threatening, showing his big teeth. It would have been easy for the man to simply let go of the chain. The dog would have ripped me apart.

I stood a safe distance away and said, "My friend, Tamara, was here earlier. You spoke with her."

"Yeah . . . So what?"

"She and I . . . We're trying to find Omar."

"Yeah . . . So what?" he said again.

"I think you know where he is," I said.

"Yeah . . . So what?"

This was getting old and wasn't getting me anywhere. I tried a different tack. I looked around at the junk in the yard and the old house that looked as if it would fall down any day now. He saw me looking and said, "You don't like it here, get the hell outta' here."

I asked, "Do *you* like it here?"

"It's where I live," he said. Behind him, the door

opened again, and a woman walked out onto the porch. Three children hugged onto her old, flowered dress. The children were dirty and in scruffy clothes. The woman looked haggard and worn out from her life of hard work on the farm.

"Would you sell your farm?" I asked.

"What?"

"I said, would you sell your farm?"

The woman standing on the porch said, "Jack!"

Jack turned and looked at his wife. He turned back to me and asked, "You wanna' buy this place?"

"I'll buy you out," I said. "I'll buy you out of this life. I'll give you enough money to get a fresh start somewhere, Jack. Face the facts; look at the life you're giving your family. For what? Do you really believe the U.S. is going to collapse? For God's sake, the Soviet Union doesn't even exist anymore. The KGB people you work for are all probably with the Russian Mafia now, dealing in drugs and guns. Do you really believe world Communism will take over? And if it does, what does that do for you and your family? You'll spend the rest of your life right here . . . But the State will own the land, and you'll slave away for the state. Your kids will slave away for the state after you're dead. You've got a chance now . . . Right now . . . To get enough money to get your family away from this. You'll be able to start a new life . . . For you and your kids."

Jack's wife said, "Let's listen to him, Jack. Let's at least listen to him," she pleaded.

Jack pulled the big dog around to the side of the house and wrapped the chain around a post enough to keep the dog from the front of the house. He walked back and waived at me to follow him into the house.

Inside, I immediately wanted to get the children out of the environment they were in. The house was a garbage pit; piles of trash and old newspapers were everywhere. The few pieces of furniture they owned were torn and dirty. The house smelled of old garbage and food gone bad.

Jack stood next to his wife and children, and said, "This is my wife, Mathilda." He told his kids to go to their room and pointed at a chair for me to sit. I pulled a few rags off of the chair, dropped them to the floor, and sat. They sat close to each other on a couch as far away from me as they could.

"Now, what d'hell you talkin' 'bout?" Jack said.

"I will buy your farm . . . And some information."

"What information?" Mathilda asked.

"I want to find Omar Maalouf."

They looked at each other, silently looking for answers. She asked me, "Why? What do you want with Omar?"

"I'm not going to lie to you," I said. "Omar wants to kill me and my family. I want to get to him before he can do that."

"So you want to kill him?" she asked.

"If I have to . . . But I'll turn him over to the FBI if I can."

They were wrapped in each other's arms, holding onto each other tightly, and looked at each other again. They were frightened; I could sense that. Omar was a dangerous man, a fanatic who thought little of human life. I decided to go with that.

"Correct me here if I'm wrong. You don't like Omar any more than I do. You wouldn't spend any time crying over his demise."

"Demise?" Jack said. "What's that?"

Mathilda said, "He means dead, Jack."

She told me, "Me and Jack, we don't like Omar. He's not our kind. We don't like religious types. Omar wants people in religious chains . . . We want people to be free."

I wasn't about to argue with them about what chains Communism keeps people in. It would do no good, and it would only anger them. So I asked, "Why do you help him?"

She answered, "Somebody said, 'The enemy of my enemy is my friend'."

I'd heard Tamara say the same thing. That must be part of their basic training; hang close to people who hate the same people you hate, even if you hate them. "I get it," I said. "So tell me where I can find him, and I'll buy your farm. Name your price."

They looked at each other; she turned back to me and asked, "If we tell you, who are you going to tell?"

"This will stay between you and me. You'll have enough money to move away and be safe."

Jack said, "This place ain't worth 'nuff."

"It's worth a great deal to me, Jack. I'll give you five hundred thousand dollars for the farm and where I can find Omar."

Mathilda took her husband's hand and squeezed it hard. She said, "He's not worth it, Jack. Omar is a pig. You know it. We got us a chance to get away, Jack. Tell him, and we can give the kids a life."

Mathilda found a piece of paper and a Bic pen. I wrote out the offer to buy the farm for $500,000.00. I signed the paper, and both Jack and Mathilda signed under my name. I wrote below our signatures, Peter's name and address and phone number in New York. I explained that the lawyers would honor the deal whether or not I survived my hunt for Omar.

"When do we get the money?" Jack asked.

"You tell me where I can find Omar, and if you're telling me the truth you'll get the cash. My attorneys will complete the deal."

"Even if Omar kills you?" Jack asked.

"Dead or alive, you'll get the money if you tell me where I can find Omar."

Jack hesitated for a moment and then said, "He's in San Francisco."

A chill of fear ran up my spine. San Francisco . . . That's where I had sent Sandy, Caroline and Betsy. Could Omar have somehow learned where they were? Or was it just a coincidence? I've never believed in coincidences; nothing happens just because it happens. Omar had to know.

"We got him a ride on a truck going there," Mathilda said. "He says he wants to kill you. He told us who you are, one of the Capitalist pigs . . . Sorry 'bout that . . . Anyway, he told us all 'bout you and all the money you got."

"Tell me where I can find him."

They gave me an address, a warehouse south of the airport in San Francisco. My god! That's the same area the motorcycle gang was hiding my family.

It was a little past ten at night when I arrived back at the motel. We had two rooms, connecting, a single and a double. Carter insisted he and Tamara would take the double that had two beds in it. I found them there, watching a fuzzy picture on an old TV.

Carter did not get up off of the bed when I walked in. "So what did you find out?" he asked.

I pulled my .38 from my belt and said, "I'm leaving you here, Agent Carter. Don't argue with me. Tamara, walk around me, behind me, and get Carter's gun and handcuffs. Don't walk between Carter and me."

She didn't hesitate to do as I told her.

"Now, Carter, get off the bed and lie on the floor."

"You can't do this, Crew!" he snapped. "I'm an FBI Agent! You can't do this!"

"On the floor . . . Please." I said. "I'd hate to have to shoot you in the leg, but I will if I have to."

He finally slid off the bed and lay on the floor on his back, between the two beds.

"Tamara, handcuff him," I said. "Wrap the cuffs around the bed frame."

She quickly bent, and Carter was locked down. She stood and walked to my side.

"What now?" she asked.

"You and I are leaving. Carter, in about an hour or so I will phone your office in Chicago and tell them where to find you. Tamara, get his cell phone and any keys he has on him. Take his gun and spare ammo clips and give them to me."

"Shouldn't I keep the gun?" she asked. "You're going to need help when we find Omar."

I looked at her with as stern a look as I could muster and said, "Two reasons. First . . . Because I said to give me his gun. You'll do what I tell you to do. Second, because I don't fully trust you yet. I don't know if Jack told you what he told me."

"What did he say?" Carter asked.

I ignored the question and watched as Tamara took his gun and spare clips from a bureau. She searched through his jacket and found a key ring with several keys on it. When she had brought these things to me I told her, "Pat him down. Make sure there aren't keys anywhere . . . And take his cell phone."

Tamara said nothing but did as I told her. She stood aside, unhappy, but she was willing to do what I told her to do. I had guessed that the chance she saw to get her hands on Alex was enough to make her do what I told her to do.

TWENTY-NINE – Inside The Warehouse

In the car Tamara said, "I hope you know what the hell you're doing."

"I hope so, too," I said. I wanted to laugh, but fear was filling me. It was too late to worry about that now. It was also too late to give up and go home. If Omar was near Sandy and Caroline and Betsy, I had to kill him.

"Where are we going?" she asked.

"San Francisco," I said. I had no intention of telling Tamara that Sandy and Caroline and Betsy were hiding in San Francisco. How could Omar know? At the time I had no idea he had put a $10,000 bounty on them. All I had was hope that Omar didn't know. But if he didn't . . . Why San Francisco? And I didn't fully trust Tamara. If she knew and was able to tell Omar . . . Well, what the hell. I had to stop Omar.

"That's where Omar is?"

"That's what Jack and Mathilda told me."

"How the hell did you get that out of them? They never told me that."

"I bought their farm for three times what it's worth."

She laughed, throwing her head back and slapping her thigh. "Real friggin' Communists! God! I hate you damn white folks!"

"I think you'll find that very, very few Communists are really what they say they are, Tamara. Inside, they love money and comfort as much as anyone else. It's human nature."

"They're damn liars, then," she said.

"I would bet most of them, the real ones who are what you'd call sleepers, have been in the United States long enough to like what they see. They like the freedom, the schools, the money and what money can buy. You said Omar likes it in the West. I doubt he would ever go back to wherever he came from. Jack and Mathilda see what can be if they have a way out. They want what America can offer their children. But they're frightened. It would be a big risk for them to let their Comrades see who they really are. So they play the game until they can get out. I gave Jack and his family a way out. They can escape and live a good life. In a matter of days my lawyers will go to them with a whole lot of cash. Communists . . . True believers . . . Wouldn't take it."

We drove all night, west towards San Francisco. Tamara curled up in the rear seat and slept soundly, breathing softly. I had time to think about just what the hell I was doing. Jack and Mathilda had confirmed my suspicion that Omar wanted to kill me . . . And Sandy. He had told them that. And he may have somehow learned where my family was hiding. I hoped the motorcycle gang could protect them from him. I knew I had to stop him or spend the rest of our lives running and hiding from him.

Maybe, someday, if I couldn't find him, the police or the FBI would catch him. Omar was smart and a well trained professional who was perfectly able to hide in plain sight. He had contacts and safe houses. It might take years for the

FBI to catch him. I couldn't wait for that to happen. I had to protect my family; I couldn't leave them in the protection of a motorcycle gang forever.

If I could, I told myself, I would surprise him somehow, catch him off-guard somehow, and turn him over to the FBI. I would prefer that, but, I kept telling myself, maybe to convince myself, that if I had to, I would kill him.

It was still night when we reached Des Moines, Iowa. I pulled into the rear lot of an all-night diner on the outskirts of the city. Tamara stirred, almost awake. I stretched out in the front seat, lowering the seat back as far as it would go. I slept and woke when the sun was above the horizon.

I smelt food and coffee. I raised the seat back and found Tamara in the passenger seat next to me, grinning at me.

"I stole your wallet and got us some food," she said. She handed me a bag with an egg sandwich in it. There was a big cup of coffee in the cup holder next to me.

I reached for the cup and drank some of the pitifully bad coffee. "I don't get it," I said. "You could have run. Why didn't you?"

"I guess I like you, Morgan Crew. You ain't . . . I mean, you aren't like the other white folks I've met. You're OK. I guess I like you. You've got guts, and I think you're honest. Not like most of you folks."

"And I'm the only chance you've got to get near Alexandra, right?"

She laughed and said, "Yeah, there's that too."

I left Tamara in the car while I stepped into the diner and went to the restroom. When I came out she was standing outside the car, leaning on the fender, smiling because she had surprised me once again. I had not thought to take the car keys with me, leaving them in the ignition. She stood there waving the keys at me. I had to laugh even though I felt stupid.

I walked to her, taking the keys from her, and started to use my cell phone to call the Chicago FBI office.

"Better not do that," she said. "They can trace you on that. Turn it off, and use the pay phone inside. Those cell phones are traceable even if you leave them on and don't make calls on them."

I wished I had thought of that. After phoning and telling them where they could find their Agent Carter, I found a regional airport that had a private jet service. It took less than five hours to fly to San Fran.

I rented a car at the airport, and we found a quiet little Mexican restaurant where we had lunch and talked about what we would do.

"Do you know anything about the warehouse Jack told me about?" I asked Tamara.

"There are several places to hide out for short periods in this area. No long term places however. If he's there, he's not planning on staying for long." She ran her fingers through her hair, thinking, and then said, "You know, if I were hiding out I might do what everybody thought I wouldn't do. I might just plan on a stay there for more than a day or two. You know, to plan my next move. To make the arrangements. To contact people. To rest up. You live up north somewhere, don't you? I'll bet he's here planning on how he's going to go there and kill you."

I decided to tell Tamara of my encounter with Omar at my home. "He's tried that already. I walked into an ambush. The police got there in time, but he got away."

"And he didn't get you?" she asked.

"Just a small cut on my scalp. I was very lucky."

"Then he's here planning a way to get you."

I hoped she was right. I hoped Omar was planning on killing me and not in San Francisco to kill Sandy. I'd put myself into a deep swamp leaving Carter as I did. I had gators snapping at my ass and nowhere to run. I hoped Tamara was right, that Omar had retreated to San Fran and was figuring out a way to kill me. If Omar wasn't there, I didn't know what to do.

"These warehouses," I asked. "Are they well protected?"

"Not really. They are stocked with some food and things like that. Just places to rest up. No real long term things."

"And you know where they are? How many there are?"

"Sure. There is only one with food and a place to sleep in this area. All the others are just places to hide for a day or two. We can go to each one, but I'd bet Omar is where the food and bed is."

"OK," I said. "So we go to each one. At each one I go in, and you wait outside. If he's there, I'll do what I can. If I get killed, you call the FBI. My lawyers know about our deal, and they will carry it out. You'll be OK and sent to a better prison . . . Except, if you ever want to get out of prison, don't kill Alexandra."

"Yeah, well, we'll see about that. Just one change to your plan," she said. "I'm going in with you."

"No you're not . . ."

"I can talk to Omar. He knows me. You can't talk to him. If you want him alive, that's your best chance. If you want Omar to kill you . . . Go in alone."

I looked at the very young girl and thought of Sandy. They were so much alike; I couldn't win an argument with either of them.

"Tamara," I said. "I don't think there's going to be time for talking. I will shoot him only if he doesn't immediately put his hands in the air."

"You know he's going to kill you, don't you?" she whispered.

"People have tried to do that before. I'm still here, and they aren't. Besides, I have to protect my family if I can. If he kills me, maybe that will satisfy him. Maybe he will leave my family alone. Maybe . . . Maybe you might think about killing him for me."

"OK," she relented. "Then just one thing. Wait until the morning. Omar likes to sleep late, and then he spends time praying. He'll be involved, and maybe you'll have a minute or two advantage."

"That sounds sensible," I said. "I like advantage. Let's find a motel for the night and get some food."

I was tempted to find Sandy and tell her Omar was in San Francisco, but I couldn't risk Tamara finding out. So I spent a sleepless night of worry. All I had was hope and my willingness to kill Omar.

****

The neighborhood south of SFX isn't the kind of place to find a five star resort. It is filled with warehouses, marginal businesses, and low rent housing. We managed to find a crappy looking 'no-tell motel' and checked in for the night. There was a ratty and dirty brothel next door; I had no way of knowing Sandy was there, only a few feet away from me.

The scruffy looking desk clerk at the motel grinned at me and winked, thinking I had a young black prostitute for the night or maybe just an hour or two. He asked how long I wanted the room for, I said for the night. He laughed and said, "You gonna' keep it up that long?" I said nothing; I just took the room key and parked the car under the only light in the potholed parking lot.

There was a dingy beer bar across the street where I bought a couple of cheeseburgers that I hoped wouldn't make us sick. Four bottles of Budweiser completed our meal. The room had only one bed with a thin mattress that was sunk in the middle. I turned on the small TV and found a baseball game on. I stretched out on the right side of the bed leaving my clothes on and laying the .38 and Carter's 9 MM Berretta on the little table next to the bed. Tamara pulled the musty cover back and lay down on the other side, her back to me. She said, "Don't try nothin' white boy. I'll rip your balls off if I have to."

I finally managed to fall asleep for an hour or two with the TV on. It was bright daylight when I woke up, alone in the room. Tamara was gone. I jumped out of bed and checked my pockets. My wallet and keys were there, the two pistols were still there. She had taken nothing. But why? Where did she go? Had she run off to warn Omar? He and she could hide anywhere. The world was a big place, and their combined assets – Communist and Islamist – were a deep cave that they could be lost in forever.

"Shit!" I yelled and slammed my fist down on the table causing the .38 to fall to the floor. How stupid could I be? I actually had thought I was better and smarter than two very professional spies and killers. And what to do now? I gave some thought to bursting into all the warehouses and shooting at anything that moved. I imagined both Omar and Tamara lying in a pool of blood.

Then reality started to creep into my brain. Tamara would have gone to Omar, and they would be far away by this time. Far away to where? I had failed. All I had left was to go home and somehow protect Sandy and Caroline and Betsy. For the rest of my life we would be living behind locked doors, with guards all around, with guns everywhere, unable to travel or even go shopping safely. "Shit!" I said again, and then there was a knock on the door.

I grabbed the little .38 from the floor and pointed it at the locked door. She had told Omar where I was! He was there to kill me!

I took a step closer to the door and yelled as loud as I could, "OMAR! I've got a gun! I'm going to kill you!"

"What the hell you talkin' about?" Tamara said. "And stop that damn yelling. People are going to hear you. Open the damn door."

I hesitated but finally unlocked the door and opened it an inch or two. Tamara was standing there, alone as far as I could see. She had a paper bag in her hands. "Are you going to let me in?" she asked. "You still dreamin' or something?"

I opened the door to let her in. I was holding the little .38, cocked and ready to shoot, expecting Omar to push his way in, but Tamara was alone.

She put the paper bag on a small, round table that had one cracked wooden chair next to it. "I got some breakfast," she said. "Coffee and some sweet rolls from a gas station down the street."

I closed and locked the door and asked, "Is that where you've been? Why didn't you wake me? And where did you get the money to buy that stuff?"

"I took it from your money clip, of course," she said. "You were asleep. I didn't want to wake you."

"You got into my pocket without waking me?"

"Of course," she said and laughed as she pulled the two cups of coffee from the bag. "I was a very good student. They taught me well."

"But the door?" I asked. "It was locked, and you didn't take the key?"

"Cheap locks," she said. "Easy to open and close with just a hairpin."

"So you just walked off to get breakfast?"

"Well, not exactly," Tamara said. She sat on the one chair in the room and pulled the lid from a cup of steaming coffee. "I waited for you to go to sleep. Man, you were tossing and turning all night. I went out about four o'clock. I wanted to scope out the neighborhood and the warehouse."

"You what!"

"Look, Morgan. You would have been like a damn white snowflake in a tar pit out there. This is not your country club neighborhood. I can walk around like I belong; you can't. So I walked the streets for a couple of hours. I found the warehouse, and I made sure Omar would be there."

"You went inside the warehouse?"

"Of course I did," she said. "What the hell did you expect? If I had let you barge into that place at night, in the dark, like you wanted to do, a couple dozen gang bangers would have jumped you before you got within a block of that place. Daylight around here, that's your time. Night time is my time of day. And I had to be sure we weren't wasting my time. I had to be sure Omar was there."

"And is he there?" I asked.

"Certainly," she said with a satisfied grin on her face. "He was sleeping on a mattress on the second floor of the place. There was a young girl asleep with him."

"You managed to get that close?"

"Morgan, please stop underestimating me. I spent two years learning everything I need to know."

I finished the cup of coffee and ate some of the stale cinnamon bun. My heart was pounding, and I was breathing fast. Tamara saw this, and she said, "Look, you better calm down, or you're going to get yourself killed."

I took the Berretta from the table. I tucked it at my belt behind my back. I put the .38 inside my belt at my right side. I had slept in my clothes, but my sports jacket hung from the back of the chair. I threw it on, and we left the room. We left the car in the parking lot after Tamara said, "We'll walk."

It was a six block walk to the warehouse. The streets were empty that morning. The sky was grey with clouds. The air smelt of rain soon to come. I shivered, but it was not from cold. The warehouse Tamara had said Omar would be in was in a district of small workshops and warehouses that seemed as deserted as the streets when we got there.

"What day is it?" I asked Tamara.

"I'm not sure . . . Maybe Sunday."

"That's why no one is here."

"You know," Tamara said, "You're actually right for a change. I guess you damn white folks can't be wrong all the time." She laughed at that.

We stood a block away and looked at the warehouse she had brought me to. It was a big, three story building, roofed in rusty corrugated steel. The walls were concrete block on the ground floor and metal on the top two floors. A tall, rusted metal, double sliding door fronted the building; a wooden door with a broken glass window was at the side of the building at a parking lot.

Looking at the place, I got the idea that it had been deserted and abandoned some time ago. The asphalt parking lot was cracked, and foot tall weeds were growing in the cracks. The concrete driveway from the street at the double doors was filled with trash and papers blown around by the wind; the concrete was broken and crumbling.

Tamara must have read my mind. She said, "It wouldn't be safe if it were in use. It's been abandoned for a couple of years. Food, some clothing, and maybe some weapons are stored inside. Enough to keep a person for a week or two."

"So," I said. "You're the expert here. How do we get in without being seen?"

"Not possible if he's awake," she said. "If you really want to do this, we go in through that side door like I did last night. He knows both of us. He may want to know why I'm there. But don't count on it. He may just start shooting and ignore the questions he might have."

"You're not going, Tamara," I said. "I told you that."

"Morgan, do you actually think you can stop me? You'll be unconscious in a matter of seconds if you try."

There was no use arguing with her; she was right. I was no match for her. "But the girl . . .?" I started. "And you said he'd be praying. Maybe he won't see us coming."

"I was just saying that to get you away from the idea of going in after dark. Omar may be a Muslim, but he believes in war and terror more than Allah. He gave up praying a long time ago. The girl was probably a hooker, and she would have left already. It's just possible Omar is eating breakfast if he's awake. If he is, he won't see us. If he isn't, expect to get shot at before we get to the warehouse."

My .38 was at my waist, at my right side. I pulled the big Berretta from my back and slid it under my belt on my left side, hoping my sports jacket would conceal both of them.

The second floor had grimy windows lined from front to back of the building. If Omar was there, there was a very good chance he would be looking out and would see us. The ground floor and top floor were windowless.

I figured that walking across the open ground of the parking lot was the most dangerous part of what we were doing. We were clear targets from the second floor with no place to run to for shelter. If he had a rifle, we both would be dead.

But we made it to the door safely. I wanted to run, but Tamara said that would just draw attention. "Walk slowly," she said. "Like you belong here." I had kept my eyes moving along the windows as we walked and saw no movement from inside. Maybe, I thought, he was busy sleeping, screwing or eating.

I tried the knob on the door; the door was locked.

"Well," I said to Tamara, "You're the expert. Pick the lock."

She smiled and pointed to the broken glass on the door. She reached in to unlock the door. "I did that last night," she said as she pulled the door open.

"I tried the big receiving bay doors. They were locked. So I came around here. Omar can't see down to this door."

She started to go inside, but I stopped her. "Inside I want you in front of me," I said. I pulled the Berretta from my belt and pushed the safety off. She understood that I didn't fully trust her yet.

In my mind I knew there was a possibility that Tamara had gone to Omar before getting our breakfast and warned him. I didn't want her at my back. If she was in front of me, and Omar was there waiting for me and started shooting wildly, she would be the first one hit.

Inside was dark and smelled like an overused toilet that needed flushing. Trash lay everywhere; a dozen rusting and dented fifty-five gallon drums were lined up to the left, a few lying on their sides, and a ten foot tall pile of pallets lay to the right, covered in dirt and cobwebs. The ceiling was fifteen feet above us; big lights hung from it, but none were lit. The air was still, hot, humid, and stale.

The first floor must have been some kind of receiving area because it was wide open and now empty. On the far side from us was an office with grime covered glass walls. Next to it was a wooden staircase leading up.

I pointed to the stairs, and Tamara nodded. She walked in front of me across the empty space. I held the pistol out in front of me, waiting and I hoped ready. I had Tamara go first as we climbed the stairs slowly and quietly. The second floor must have been for storage. Metal shelves were everywhere, most empty, but a few were holding dust and dirt covered cardboard boxes. Yellow daylight came in through the grime covered windows on both sides of us. The only thing to do was to walk across the room and try to find where Omar was waiting.

I could have gone left or right, but I chose to walk straight ahead. 'What the hell,' I said silently, to myself. The aisles between the shelves were just wide enough for Tamara to walk in front of me; she stayed slightly to my left, knowing instinctively that I was right handed and would need a clear right side to shoot.

We walked slowly. When we got halfway down the aisle, a shadow moved at the end of the shelves. "Omar!" Tamara called out. She put her hand on my arm, and I stopped. "It's me . . . Tamara."

The shadow moved again.

Tamara took a step forward; I grabbed her shoulder and pulled her back. I called out, "Omar! Look I just want to talk to you! I think we can work out our differences!"

"Our differences will be settled when I kill you, Morgan Crew!"

"What will that gain you? Sooner or later the FBI will catch you. They'll follow the same trail I did. Why not let me help you?"

"Is that why you brought him here, Tamara? To help me . . . Or to help you?"

"Let's just sit down and talk, Omar," I said. I took a few steps forward; Tamara stayed at my side.

"I will kill you, Morgan Crew . . . I will kill your wife and your child. Allah has willed it, Morgan Crew."

"Then let it be my God against yours, Omar! I can help you stay alive. I have attorneys who will represent you. Believe me, prison is better than death. No matter what you've been told, there's not a bunch of virgins waiting for you. Let's just talk and make a deal."

The shadow stepped from between some shelves and

stood in front of us, thirty feet away. Omar had a gun in his hand; he was grinning like a crazy person, his eyes ablaze and wide enough to pop his eyeballs from their sockets. He hadn't shaved in days; his hair was a long rumpled mass. He was dressed in tan pants and a white dress shirt, unbuttoned halfway down, both having been slept in.

He raised the gun slowly, and I pushed Tamara to the left between shelves that were crowded with boxes as I raised the Berretta. I jumped to my right and got behind bare metal shelves that provided little cover. Omar stood his ground, not looking for something to hide behind. He let himself be a clear target. He and I started shooting at the same time. I had fifteen rounds in the clip, and I was intent on firing every one of them. I had Carter's two spare clips. I would use every bullet I had to kill the man.

From the shadows at Omar's left a young girl, Ashley Trangent, ran to Omar's side. There was a pale white look of insanity on her thin face. She held a gun and pointed it at me and started firing. She was screaming something, but the sounds of the guns firing kept me from hearing.

I felt one of Omar's bullets hit my left shoulder. It spun me against the shelves behind me but it didn't stop me from firing. I pointed the gun through the shelves and kept pulling the trigger. Another bullet grazed my left side, and the next cut through my left thigh. The pain was intense, but I managed to ignore it.

Tamara called to me, "Throw me the revolver, Morgan! Throw the revolver to me!"

I was on one knee and pulled the little .38 from my belt. Would she use it to kill me or to help me? "What the hell," I thought, and I tossed it, but it went high; Tamara reached up and caught it deftly. She smiled, pointed the gun at me and laughed. I could not hear her, but her lips mouthed "I hate you stupid white folks." With that she quickly turned and started firing, not at me but at Omar.

When the shooting was done, there was a thick cloud of cordite smoke hanging between Omar and me. I dropped the empty Berretta onto the floor and pulled myself to my feet. Silence filled the smoke clouded room.

Holding onto the metal shelves, I limped toward Omar. My leg was bleeding badly; I grabbed the wound on my side with my left hand and squeezed as hard as I could, making my wounded shoulder hurt as bad as my leg. I bit my lip rather than cry out in pain. When I could see through the cloud, I saw Omar lying on the floor in a pool of blood that was pouring from his chest and head. He had been hit six times. Ashley lay face down across Omar, blood pouring from her head.

I struggled to pull Ashley off of Omar. Her face had disappeared from a hail of bullets. I bent and put my fingers to Omar's neck to feel for a pulse. Omar was dead.

I pushed myself to my feet again and smiled. It was over; I could get my family back. I turned and smiled. Tamara would get the prison she wanted, and she could kill Alexandra. I really didn't care. Alexandra and Donna meant nothing to me, but somehow, Tamara did. I had come to like the young girl. I felt sorry for her. She never had a chance in the life she had been born into. I had to at least try to talk her out of murdering Alexandra. She deserved some life, some truth, and some freedom. All she had ever known were lies and violence. I would put Peter and all his lawyers on the task of getting her out of prison someday, no matter how long that took. All that was true if . . . If she hadn't run away during the shooting. I really didn't care if she had. She was no danger to me or mine.

Holding onto the shelves to keep from falling, I limped

back to her. I saw Tamara on her back on the floor. I ran to her, my left leg and shoulder aflame with pain. Holding onto the metal shelves I bent to kneel over her, ignoring the pain of my bleeding leg. Her chest was covered in blood that was pouring from the hole near her heart. I put both my hands over the wound to try to stop the bleeding. She was groaning almost in a whisper.

"Look at me, Tamara . . . Look at me . . . Open your eyes, Tamara . . . You're going to make it . . . I'll get you to a hospital . . . Tamara . . . Tamara . . . Don't close your eyes."

Her lips began to move; I put my ear close to her. She whispered, "It's better this way, Morgan." I felt her lips brush across my cheek in a cold kiss. She smiled, blood trickling from her lips, and she tried to laugh but only coughed up blood. She whispered into my ear, "I love you Morgan Crew . . . But I hate you damn white folks." The light went out from her eyes, and the breath left her body. Tamara died in my arms.

THE END

www.ingramcontent.com/pod-product-compliance
Lightning Source LLC
Chambersburg PA
CBHW030759260626
47169CB00001B/115